Emily McIntire is a #1 *New York Times* and #1 *Sunday Times* bestselling author whose stories serve steam, slow burns, and seriously questionable morals. Her books have been translated into over a dozen languages and span across several subgenres within romance.

A stage IV breast cancer thriver, you can find Emily enjoying free time with her family, getting lost in a good book, or redecorating her house depending on her mood.

ALSO BY EMILY MCINTIRE

Be Still My Heart: A Romantic Suspense
(co-written with Sav R. Miller)

THE SUGARLAKE SERIES
Beneath the Stars
Beneath the Stands
Beneath the Hood
Beneath the Surface

THE NEVER AFTER SERIES
Hooked
Scarred
Wretched
Twisted
Crossed
Hexed

Burning Daylight

EMILY MCINTIRE

PIATKUS

PIATKUS

First published in the US in 2025 by Bloom Books,
An imprint of Sourcebooks
Published in Great Britain in 2025 by Piatkus

1 3 5 7 9 10 8 6 4 2

Copyright © 2025 by Emily McIntire

The moral right of the author has been asserted.

*All characters and events in this publication, other than those
clearly in the public domain, are fictitious and any resemblance
to real persons, living or dead, is purely coincidental.*

All rights reserved.
No part of this publication may be reproduced, stored in a
retrieval system, or transmitted in any form or by any means, without
the prior permission in writing of the publisher, nor be otherwise circulated
in any form of binding or cover other than that in which it is published
and without a similar condition including this condition
being imposed on the subsequent purchaser.

A CIP catalogue record for this book
is available from the British Library.

ISBN 978-0-349-44615-8

Printed and bound in Great Britain by Clays Ltd, Elcograf S.p.A.

Papers used by Piatkus are from well-managed forests
and other responsible sources.

MIX
Paper | Supporting
responsible forestry
FSC® C104740

Piatkus
An imprint of
Little, Brown Book Group
Carmelite House
50 Victoria Embankment
London EC4Y 0DZ

The authorised representative
in the EEA is
Hachette Ireland
8 Castlecourt Centre,
Dublin 15, D15 XTP3, Ireland
(email: info@hbgi.ie)

An Hachette UK Company
www.hachette.co.uk

www.littlebrown.co.uk

To the ones who loved anyway.

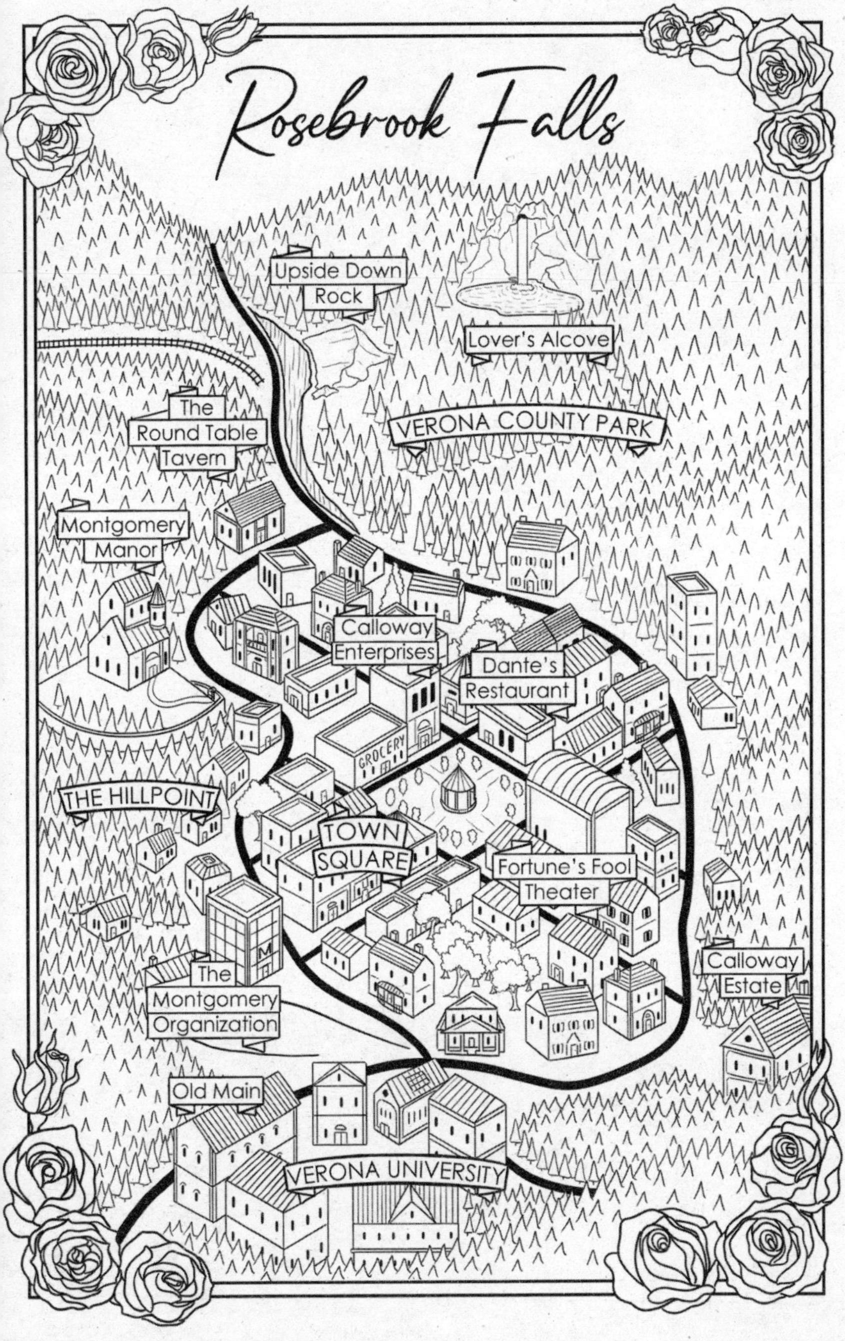
Rosebrook Falls
Upside Down Rock
Lover's Alcove
VERONA COUNTY PARK
The Round Table Tavern
Montgomery Manor
Calloway Enterprises
Dante's Restaurant
GROCERY
THE HILLPOINT
TOWN SQUARE
Fortune's Fool Theater
Calloway Estate
The Montgomery Organization
M
Old Main
VERONA UNIVERSITY

AUTHOR'S NOTE

Burning Daylight is a contemporary romance and the first book in an interconnected standalone series.

The main couple will get their happy ending in this book; however, there are plot points and storylines that will not be resolved in book one and will continue through the series.

While not necessary, it is strongly recommended to read this series in order for a full reading experience.

Burning Daylight features strong language, explicit sexual scenes, drug use, terminal illness (cancer), violence, and mature situations that may be triggering for some. A detailed list of trigger warnings can be found on EmilyMcIntire.com or by scanning the QR Code at the end of this note.

This story is told through a first-person limited point of view. It is shaped by trauma and past hurt and may not reflect the full scope of a complex situation.

It is not meant to define addiction or the people who experience it. If you or a loved one are struggling, you are not alone. You are not less than. You are worthy.

You can find resources at the end of the book.
Reader discretion is advised.

PLAYLIST

Teenage Dirtbag—Wheatus
Love Story (Taylor's Version)—Taylor Swift
Save Tonight—Eagle-Eye Cherry
As I Lay Me Down—Sophie B. Hawkins
Lovefool—The Cardigans
we can't be friends (wait for your love)—Ariana Grande
I Don't Want to Miss a Thing—Sonny Tennet
I Love You, I'm Sorry—Gracie Abrams
The Night We Met—Lord Huron
Someone You Loved—Lewis Capaldi
Paris—The Chainsmokers
You Are the Reason (Duet Version)—Calum Scott & Leona Lewis
I Get to Love You—Ruelle

My only love sprung from my only hate,
Too early seen unknown, and known too late!
Prodigious birth of love is it to me
That I must love a loathed enemy.

—William Shakespeare, *Romeo & Juliet*

THE WAYMONT COMPACT AGREEMENT

ROSEBROOK FALLS, CONNECTICUT

This Agreement entered into on this 13th day of August 1930, by and between the undersigned founding companies (collectively referred to as the "Founders").

WHEREAS the Founders wish to collaborate in the establishment of a new town within Verona County, to be named Rosebrook Falls, with the goal of creating a thriving and sustainable community.

The Founders recognize the importance of ensuring fair representation, equitable development, and avoiding any monopolization of resources, leadership, or decision-making within the town.

IN WITNESS WHEREOF, the Founders have executed this Agreement on the date first written above.

COMPANY A:
    Calloway Enterprises
    Name: Alabaster Calloway
    Signature: *Alabaster Calloway*

COMPANY B:
    The Montgomery Organization
    Name: Theodore Montgomery
    Signature: *Theodore Montgomery*

Prologue

Juliette

Thirteen Years Old

I'M NOT SUPPOSED TO BE HERE.

I crouch in place while my nanny Beverly and our chef Aaron carry in groceries and gossip like they're reporters for *The Rosebrook Rag*.

Beverly would kill me if she knew I was eavesdropping.

Especially since today is my fitting for the annual Founders' Gala that happens every year at Verona University.

"Do you think Marcus Montgomery knows his wife is fucking Craig?" Aaron asks her.

"Please. Worst kept secret in Rosebrook Falls."

"You don't think that's why Marcus killed—"

Beverly smacks his arm. "Hush. Don't speak about the dead. It's uncouth."

Chef Aaron throws his hands up, palms out. "I'm just asking. It's weird Marcus is *here*, right?"

Beverly shrugs. "I don't have time to care about that, and neither do you. Help me find that little rascal Juliette."

I press myself deeper into the shadows beneath the stairs. It's a lot of nothing under here, just a dark corner with a lamp that flickers and staged books with blank pages.

But it's the only spot in this entire mansion that feels like home. The only place I can go where I'm not choreographed to perfection.

School. Piano lesson. Etiquette class. French lesson. Rinse. Wash. Repeat.

That's my life.

But today is Sunday, and it's the only day I get to hide away and write.

That's what I *was* doing until the two gossips across the hall started yammering like they are.

My brows scrunch. I've seen Marcus Montgomery over the years at the Founders' Gala or any other event that requires I dress nicely and play the part of a perfect Calloway kid, but the loathing of the Montgomery name is bred into my entire family's veins from the moment we are born.

Even *hate* seems like too nice a word.

So, Marcus being at our estate? It's…odd.

Beverly and Aaron disappear around the corner, and I snap my notebook of stories shut, darting from my hiding spot and sneaking to the wing where my dad's home office sits.

When I get there, I peek through a tiny slat between the door and frame to the room, adrenaline flooding through me when I see him and Marcus.

I shift my weight, and the hardwood creaks, echoing off the tall ceilings. My pulse pounds like a drum as I ease open the door just enough to see better.

When neither of them notice, I let out a shaky exhale.

My father is all starched suits and perfectly placed smiles so sharp they can cut you like a knife, and tonight is no exception. Even in his own home, he looks battle ready, just waiting for the right time to bend your will to his.

His black hair, the same color as mine, is combed back and styled, and his thick eyebrows bunch together until it looks like a caterpillar is on his face. He's frowning as he stands rigid, his pale knuckles turning white where they press against the top of his big desk.

Marcus looks similar, but somehow totally different.

Where Dad is stiff and polished, Marcus Montgomery is… fluid.

They both radiate power, though.

Marcus is wearing dark jeans and a navy-blue sports jacket that's open to a white T-shirt underneath, and his blond hair is the antithesis of my dad's. Light and mussed on top like he's been running his hands through it. I can't see his eyes, but I know from his pictures in our local tabloid *The Rosebrook Rag* that they're so icy, they'll chill you to the bone.

Marcus leans against the bookshelf on the left side of the room, his ankles crossed like he doesn't have a care in the world.

"No," he says, glancing at his nails.

"Don't force my hand," my dad replies, his voice tight.

It's the same tone he uses when my brother Lance gets in trouble…which is almost always.

Marcus straightens. "Nah, fuck you, Craig. I won't break the WayMont agreement just so you can bully people out of their homes in the HillPoint and build with *him*."

My heart thumps faster. The HillPoint is on the west side

of Rosebrook Falls, and it's Montgomery territory through and through. I'm forbidden to even go there.

Dad shrugs. "People aren't forced to do anything because of me. I simply make suggestions."

"Yeah, well, when your suggestions aren't followed, people end up hurt. Funny how that happens."

"The innocent act is cute, Marcus, but it's just us here. Nobody's watching; there's no need for dramatics."

"Then don't be a cunt."

My father chuckles. "You know what they say—you are what you eat. How *is* your wife, by the way?"

A sick feeling swirls through my belly. *Is he cheating on my mom?*

Marcus stiffens. "Is that what this is about? You're doing Eleanor's bidding?"

My dad shrugs. "And what if I am?"

"You're welcome to her pussy, Craig, but you're testing me, trying to take everything else that's mine."

"And you're putting way too much faith in a century-old contract signed by two dead men," my father replies cooly. "Especially after my wife's brother just died. I'd hate for tragedy to strike *your* side of the line."

Marcus stalks over until he's about two inches from my dad's face. "Stay away from my family, Craig, or I swear to God, you'll regret it. That *is* a threat."

My chest tightens with worry, but my dad only grins and says, "I would never hurt Eleanor."

"That's not who I mean, and you know it." Marcus's voice drops to a dangerous whisper.

"Sign the papers and you'll have nothing to worry about."

Marcus smirks. "Are you really that threatened by me that you'll go to these lengths? He's a kid, he's not even in my life. He won't cause any problems."

"He has your last name, so forgive me for not finding your claims reassuring," my father replies.

"You're delusional, and I'm not signing shit."

My father smiles so wide it sends a chill down my spine. "Tell your guests I said hi, then."

Marcus scoffs and spins toward the door.

My heart shoots to my throat as I stumble away, hightailing it down the hall, past the dining room, into the foyer, and up the stairs to my room. Slamming the door behind me, I flatten my back against the wood, sucking in giant helpings of air.

Once I can breathe again, I grab my notebook, flipping past the story where my mom turns into an ogre, and scribble down everything I just saw.

It didn't make any sense, but still, I don't ever want to forget.

When I'm done, I check that the French doors to my balcony are locked, and then I slip under the covers, throwing my comforter over my head until it feels like I might suffocate in the dark.

Eventually, I fall asleep.

Two days later, my father's sitting at our oversized circular table in the breakfast nook, sipping his coffee and ignoring everything around him.

I stare at him, confused. *Why is he home again?*

That's twice in one week. More than I've seen him in months.

I lean against the white marble island and take a sip of my orange juice, my eyes snagging on the TV playing the local news.

The screen's split. One side showing a *Rosebrook Rag* social media post, the other the anchor's tense expression.

A photo flashes of a mangled car wrapped around a tree, flames licking through the shattered windows and twisted metal, before the screen goes back to the tabloid's post.

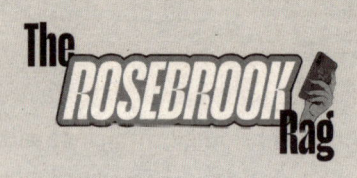

The ROSEBROOK Rag

DEADLY CRASH IN HILLPOINT: ACCIDENT OR SUICIDE?

An up-and-coming artist Heather Argent and her two children are dead after a late-night crash in Montgomery territory. Cops say brake failure. Some whisper suicide.

Sources say hours before she was seen screaming at Marcus Montgomery.

Was she spiraling…or was this simply a tragic twist of fate?

Either way, Rosebrook Falls is buzzing—and we're not done digging.

#RosebrookRag #TownWhispers
#MontgomeryMess #WasItSuicide

My heart sinks.

When I look up at my father, he's smiling.

The Rosebrook Rag

PAXTON CALLOWAY ENGAGED?!
LOVE OR LEVERAGE?

Rosebrook Falls's most elusive bachelor, Paxton Calloway, is officially off the market, and the town is spinning.

The lucky lady? *Tiffany Heartinger*. Oil heiress, diamond lover, and professional enigma. Sources say the proposal was private, perfect, and suspiciously well timed.

Is it love? Or just a high-stakes merger dressed up like a fairy tale?

Word on the street: The Heartinger name has been circling Calloway boardrooms for *months*.

Whatever it is, this wedding (if it actually happens) will be pure Rosebrook spectacle. And you know we'll be watching.

#PaxtonPutARingOnIt #CallowayPowerPlay
#HeartingerHustle #LoveOrLeverage
#RosebrookRag #CallowayWatch

Chapter 1

Juliette

Seventeen Years Old

ROSEBROOK FALLS IS CURSED.

At least, that's what the legends say.

Beverly has always told my three brothers and me stories of the town's lore.

She'd whisper about how the actual buildings were poured on top of broken hearts and buried secrets. How two people fell in love despite being promised to others, and how it ended in despair.

I hadn't believed her tales. Not really, anyway. Until she told me one of them was a Calloway, and the other a Montgomery.

That part I believed.

Loyalty means everything in this family, so it makes sense the generations before felt the same.

She's never said it specifically, but I imagine she's talking about the actual founders of the town: Theodore Montgomery and *my* great-great-grandfather Alabaster Calloway.

A construction juggernaut and a real-estate tycoon.

They had a deal. They'd build Rosebrook Falls together, sign the WayMont Compact Agreement to make sure everything was split fifty-fifty, and then they'd keep the power and influence in the family by marrying off their kids to each other.

So, when Theodore's son Kenneth went and found himself a *Voltaire* girl to fall in love with instead? Alabaster took it personal.

The Voltaire girl wound up dead, and accusations were tossed out like candy on Halloween.

I don't know if there's any truth to it, but I *do* know that Marcus's wife Eleanor was a Voltaire before she wound up dead, too.

My brother Alex loved to tell Beverly's tales anytime we'd go camping. He'd jump up on his soapbox, creating visions of death and destruction where civil hands were stained with civil blood and fierce love went to die.

I loved watching him in his element, acting out scenes and capturing his audience. Sometimes I'd even fantasize about writing novels with him starring in their adaptations.

To this day, Alex swears they're all true stories, but considering they were told with a flashlight under his chin and his voice wavering like the spirit of our great-great-grandfather was about to jump out and snatch us, I don't really trust his claims.

My eldest brother Paxton says Beverly was creating tragic fairy tales to explain why our parents are constantly at each other's throats.

It makes sense, I guess.

To be honest, it's been years since I've given much thought to the Rosebrook Falls wives' tale at all.

Today, though, it's stuck in my brain.

Maybe because Paxton just announced his engagement to Tiffany Heartinger, the oil heiress from Pennsylvania, and while everyone else is gazing at them with heart eyes, I can tell Paxton doesn't give a damn one way or another.

For him, it's just another business deal. Strengthening the family ties and all that.

But seeing him so resigned to his fate has me thinking maybe Beverly is right, after all.

Maybe the town *is* cursed.

Either way, I'm thankful to get away from the celebration, even if it is because Mother sent me on a wild goose chase.

Freaking Lance.

I'm going to punch him in the throat when I find him.

It's just like his dumb ass to disappear, and somehow, whenever he goes missing, it's always me who has to track him down.

I've checked all the usual spots, everywhere from Verona University's small college campus to Fortune's Fool, the local theater in the town square.

But my troublemaker of a brother is nowhere to be found.

So now I'm at my last resort, hiking up to the tallest spot in Rosebrook Falls: Upside Down Rock, a secluded area hidden off the overgrown trails in Verona County Park.

My phone rings as I'm trekking the steep hill, but I already know it's either Paxton or Mother, so I don't answer.

As I walk the weed-filled and dusty path, nostalgia hits me in the center of my gut.

For my thirteenth birthday, Lance taught me how to sneak out and come here. Said it was "a rite of passage for a teenaged Calloway."

He claims the area calms him.

I think it's his getaway spot for whenever our dad pisses him off.

There's a large boulder perched on the cliff's edge, its surface the size of a small SUV. We'd always carefully climb on top of it, lying with our feet toward the sky until the blood rushed to our heads and we thought we'd either faint or fall.

It was exhilarating…and dangerous.

I can't remember the last time Lance had that carefree look in his eyes; the way he did back then.

Nostalgia hits even harder when I stop in front of the rock, and I place my hands on my hips and glance around.

Rosebrook Falls itself sits in a valley, and this is the best lookout. Everything is visible, from VU in the east to the train tracks that skirt along the edges of the HillPoint in the west, closest to the cliff.

It's quiet. Peaceful. Serene.

And Lance is definitely not here.

I soak in the gorgeous orangey reds and pinks of the sunset sky and my phone vibrates again, pulling me out of my reverie. Sighing, I grab it from my back pocket and open the group chat with my brothers.

THE CALLOWAY KINGS (AND QUEEN)

ALEX:

> It's actually impressive how pissed Mom looks.

> **ME:**
>
> That's just called resting bitch face.

> **ALEX:**
>
> Well, it's EXTRA today. She's staring at the front door like she can summon Lance from the underworld. It's fucking eerie. 😵‍💫 👻

> **PAXTON:**
>
> She'll live. Jules, any luck?

And cue the guilt. It's not like *I* lost Lance, but not being able to find him makes me feel responsible.

> **ME:**
>
> Nope. Lance if you're reading this just know you're dead to me.

> **ALEX:**
>
> Samesies.

I snort.

> **ALEX:**
>
> Did you check the theater? He's been banging the lead in A Midsummer Night's Dream.

My nose scrunches up in distaste.

ME:

Ew, isn't Heidi the lead?

ALEX:

Yep.

ME:

Gross.

ALEX:

I KNOW! I SAID THE SAME THING.

ME:

Idk, I've checked everywhere. I'm tired, sweaty, and Mom's gonna murder me when she sees what I did to this dress.

I actually changed out of it before leaving, but they don't need to know that.

ALEX:

Like everywhere, everywhere? 👀

I know what he's asking. He wants to know if my "everywhere" includes the HillPoint.

ME:

Negative. I'm not trying to get shot.

ALEX:

> Please. They don't shoot people over there, they shank em.

PAXTON:

> Where are you now, Jules?

ME:

> Being your resident park ranger. 🎒

PAXTON:

> You're at Verona Park? Don't hang out there after dark.

ME:

> Okay, DAD.

I roll my eyes at Paxton's overprotective streak, but I won't lie, it warms my chest a little.

Technically, Verona Park is neutral ground, but the park's director owes his job—and his annual bonus—to my dad, so the odds skew in our favor.

ALEX:

> Hate to see you mauled by a bear and land on the cover of The Rosebrook Rag.

PAXTON:

> There are worse things than bears and tabloids. Get home before dark.

ALEX:

> Yeah…like getting shanked by a Montgomery goon.

I spin so my back faces the cliff and Rosebrook Falls sprawls behind me, then snap a picture of me flipping them off with a sarcastic grin.

After I pocket my phone, I stroll to the rock, climbing on and twisting until I'm lying with my legs above my head, my spine pressed to the stone. My heart flutters as I lean back, my hair blowing in the breeze at the cliff's edge. Adrenaline kicks in, just enough to feel that soaring, reckless rush, and I close my eyes, breathing in the scent of red birch trees that are so Connecticut-coded, it makes my chest ache.

A twig snaps from somewhere behind me, and my stomach jumps into my throat. I squeeze my eyes tighter, hoping it isn't a coyote or a bear.

I swear, if I die up here and prove Paxton right, I'll come back and haunt this place forever.

"Lance?" I call out hopefully.

There's no reply.

A few seconds, and then there's another noise.

Footsteps, I realize.

I jerk too fast, trying to scramble off the rock, but instead of sitting upright, I slip entirely.

Air punches out of my mouth as my body slides, and my fingers claw at the smooth boulder, but there's nothing to grip onto. A scream tears from my mouth as my legs flip over my head, nails breaking against stone as I try to find something—*anything*—to grab ahold of.

Suddenly, something clutches my arm, yanking me back.

I crash onto the ground hard, breath knocked forcefully from my lungs.

My eyes are squeezed shut, and my heart pounds in my ears, so it takes a second to realize the earth isn't as solid as it should be.

And that it's *breathing*.

It's warm, and malleable, and—my lids fly open—definitely a person.

Our eyes meet, my chestnut browns locked on icy blues.

Chapter 2

Juliette

IT'S A GUY.

His body is all hard lines; lithe, lean muscles that are taut beneath me, and thick fingers that dig into my waist, making it impossible to tell if he's about to pull me closer or push me away.

I shift without thinking, and he grunts. It's a low, raspy noise that sends a flare of heat through me. I jolt back, my hands scraping the gravel as I scramble to my feet. My heart slams against my chest, and I blink down at him.

He's sprawled on the ground, and where I'm sure I look like a deer in headlights, he looks suave.

Relaxed.

Like nothing in the world could bother him.

A lock of brown hair—so dark it almost looks black—falls across his forehead, and he brushes it out of his eyes. A tattoo winds from his veiny hand up over his wrist, disappearing beneath the sleeve of his blue hoodie, the black ink stark against his pale skin.

Heat slams into me, flaring through every nerve ending like I've been electrocuted.

He's hot.

Of course he is.

I nearly die, and the universe rewards me with a jawline sharp enough to finish the job. *Typical.*

The remnants of adrenaline makes my hands shake. There's no doubt that he just saved my life, so that must be why I can't. Stop. Staring.

I expect him to stand up. To say something, or—I don't know—do *anything*, but he doesn't.

Instead, he grins. Dimples indent his angular cheeks as he blinds me with his smile, and his jawline somehow sharpens further.

Ugh, of course even *that* looks good.

When his gaze drags over me, my skin flushes.

I roll my shoulder back and wince when a pulsing ache stabs at the joint, but I ignore the pain, flattening my expression, like he doesn't faze me at all.

He stretches out, ankles crossed, leaning back on his elbows. His hoodie falls open just enough to flash a white tee and a silver chain, and his hair is so artfully messy, there's no way he doesn't spend as much time as me getting ready in the morning.

His grin turns into a full-blown smile as I catalogue his features.

Like there's nothing he'd rather be doing than getting picked apart by my gaze.

"Who are you?" I ask, lifting my chin in that practiced Calloway fashion.

He quirks a brow, his tongue swiping across his lower lip. "I'm the guy who just saved your life. Who are *you*?"

I frown. I can't tell if he's being sarcastic or genuinely clueless. "You don't know?"

Regret hits the second the words leave my mouth. I sound cocky, but I'm not trying to. It's just unusual for someone in Rosebrook to not know Craig and Martha's only daughter.

He stands, brushing off his jeans, that grin of his lifting higher like I'm the most amusing thing in the world. "Wow. Gorgeous *and* humble."

"No, that's…" I shake my head, color flushing up my neck. "I didn't mean it like that."

He slips his hand through his obnoxiously perfect hair, mussing it up even further, and maybe I was wrong about how much time he spends on it.

Does it just naturally fall like that? God, where is the justice?

He steps closer. Too close, actually—the toes of his boots brushing against my Adidas.

My neck cranes as I look up at him, and my stomach tightens.

He's tall. I'm five-nine, and yet he towers over me.

If I were to write him as a character in my stories, there's not a single physical attribute I would change.

The only logical conclusion is that he's a complete douchebag. The world wouldn't be biased enough to give him a good personality *and* make him one of the hottest guys on the planet. That defies the laws of physics or something.

He leans in, and my stupid heart skips.

"I think the words you're looking for are 'thank you,'" he murmurs.

For some reason I can't force the words out. Maybe because I don't like strangers telling me what to do. *I get enough of that at home.*

"You're not from here," I deflect.

He sighs, spinning a ring on his finger with his thumb. "That obvious?"

Something about the way his voice dips in defeat makes me feel bad, so I flash him a tiny grin. "A little."

"At least you're honest."

My gaze drops to his tattoos and then runs back up. He's unpolished in a way that seems so effortless, it looks manufactured. Rough around the edges, like he could try harder if he wanted but doesn't care to.

He's the kind of guy my parents would hate.

Unfortunately, that makes him infinitely more attractive.

"I appreciate it," I force out.

He cocks his head. "Appreciate what?"

I throw my hands up. "Did you want a thank-you or not?"

"Are you always so combative?"

"Are you always this insufferable?"

His smirk spreads, dimples and all. "This is fun, getting to know each other like this."

I scoff. "I do not want to *know* you."

"Ouch, Princess." He grips his chest and staggers like I've wounded him. "Straight to the heart. Ever heard of etiquette?"

Color blooms on my cheeks. I've been in etiquette classes since I was old enough to hold a fork, but I am *not* going to give him the satisfaction of knowing that.

Who the hell does he think he is, anyway, judging *me*?

There's just something about this guy. His energy rubs across my skin like sandpaper, leaving me raw and exposed.

"Don't call me princess," I snap.

"Whatever you want…Princess." He says it slowly, like he's tasting the word.

I flush deeper.

"Do you always blush so easily?"

"It's not like I can control it." My hands fly up to cover my face. "You know, you ask a lot of questions."

The stranger tsks and steps closer.

And for whatever reason, I stand still as he does.

"Don't do that," he utters softly, peeling my fingers from my cheeks. "It'd be a shame to hide something so gorgeous."

My stomach flutters again, and I don't like the feeling.

"That sounds like something a serial killer would say," I tell him. "Are you a criminal?"

"Depends. Is it a crime to want to know a pretty girl?"

"Maybe," I reply. "You're attractive. And you're a guy. Statistically, I'm pretty sure that makes you a red flag."

His eyes spark with mischief. "So you *do* think I'm hot."

My mouth pops open, but words trip and stumble on my tongue until I finally settle on, "I have a boyfriend."

Awesome, Juliette. Real smooth.

Guilt hits me, because this is the first time I've thought of Preston since meeting this stranger.

"Lucky guy," he says, unfazed. "Do you yell at him for no reason, too, or am I special?"

"I'm not yelling."

"Right. My bad." He grins. "For the record, I think you're hot, too. Especially when you're mad."

His compliment hits me like a shot of dopamine.

I narrow my gaze, biting the inside of my lip. "Yeah, well... Don't let it give you a big head."

He leans in. "Too late. You already accused me of attempted murder, and that level of confidence does something to me."

Okay, now I'm trying *really* hard to keep the smile off my face. "It's called being aware of my surroundings."

"Oh, is that what it is?"

The grin breaks through. I can't help it. He's charming, and I don't remember the last time somebody talked to me without an ulterior motive.

"You really don't know who I am?" I check again.

He quirks a brow. "Has it crossed your mind that maybe *you* should know *me*?"

"Fine. What's your name?"

He stays silent.

"Seriously? You're not gonna tell me?"

He just smiles, slow and maddening, and rolls his lips together.

"Okay, see? That's exactly what a serial killer would do."

"If I planned to kill you, I'd give you an alias, not keep a name from you altogether."

"If you killed me, the name wouldn't matter."

He shrugs. "Yeah, but what if something went wrong and you got away? Can't have you name-dropping me to cops. Gotta protect the brand."

I laugh. "The brand of a serial killer?"

"It goes without saying, I'd be infamous by the end of my reign."

My eyes narrow, even as my lips twitch. "You're kind of irritating."

"I've been called worse." He smirks. "*Criminal*, for example."

I wave my hand in his direction like he's smoke I'm trying to swat away. "Well, if the jumpsuit fits…"

"What happened to 'innocent until proven guilty'?"

"You won't even tell me your name. You appear out of nowhere, in the middle of the woods, wearing baggy clothes and covered in tattoos." I give him another once-over. "You *definitely* look like you're hiding something."

He lifts his arms, palms up, the picture of surrender, and that wicked smile still on his face. "You're right. I *do* sound dangerous. Feel free to frisk me."

My stomach explodes with butterflies.

I cross my arms, trying to look unaffected. "That's probably how you lure all your victims in."

"Objection," he says playfully. "Leading the witness."

"We're not in court." I eye him. "And you'd be a terrible lawyer."

"Says who?"

"Says me."

He tilts his head, studying me like I'm a riddle.

"What?" I ask, wary.

"Nothing, you just don't *look* like a lawyer."

"And what exactly does a lawyer look like?"

His gaze flicks over me, slow and unapologetic. "Not like you."

"I feel like I should be offended. For all you know, I'm planning to be one."

His smile deepens. "Guess I should behave, then."

"Little late for that, Trouble."

He shakes his head in a *you're cute when you're mad* kind of way and then pins me with a stare.

I cross my arms again and tap my fingers on the inside of my elbow. "Fine, don't tell me. What's in a name, anyway?"

"Exactly," he says, like I've just made his case for him.

"But I don't talk to strangers."

"Aw, come on, Princess, don't be like that." He chuckles, and the sound is low and teasing.

It hits me right in the chest.

I make a face. "Don't call me *Princess*, Trouble."

Right on cue, my phone vibrates in my pocket, and I pull it out, flashing it at him with a grin.

"I'm leaving. Saved by the text."

He smirks. "Bold move, announcing your escape plan to your *alleged* murderer."

I roll my eyes.

He slips his hands into his pockets again, his tattooed forearms flexing just enough to be distracting. "Maybe I'll see you around? Like tomorrow, same time?"

My heart flutters. "Doubtful. I don't come up here often."

"I can wait."

"Great. I'll be sure to avoid the area, then."

He walks back a few spaces until he's perched on the edge of the rock he saved me from. "Nah. I think you're bluffing."

"And why would I do that?"

"How should I know? Maybe so you don't have to admit how wildly attracted you are to me, *despite* your boyfriend."

I laugh. "Okay, I'm *really* leaving now."

"Sure thing, Princess."

Something flashes in the distance, quick but undeniable. I spin toward it, squinting, but don't see anything.

Still, I've lived here long enough to know better than to

stick around. What if it was one of those idiot paparazzi for the *Rag*?

"You shouldn't get too comfortable out here, you know." I twist toward him.

"Too late," he says, settling back with ease, his eyes perusing me. "I already like the view."

I fidget, pretending like his words aren't setting my nerves on fire. "Whatever. Bye, Trouble."

He nods. "See you when you come back."

"You'll be waiting a while."

"Guess I've got a lot of daylight to burn, then."

"I don't even know what that means." I purse my lips. "But have fun with that."

And then I force myself to turn around and walk away. If I don't, I'm a little worried I'll spend the whole night fake arguing with the guy.

Was this flirting? It felt like flirting.

"I guess you can thank me later!" he calls out to my back.

A smile breaks across my face.

Damnit.

My heart pounds all the way to my car, adrenaline pumping through my veins.

Who the hell was that?

When I'm back home, my pulse still thrums at the mere thought of him, so I pull out my notebook of stories and start to write.

The forest had no name; at least, not one spoken aloud. Travelers said it whispered secrets if you listened long enough, but it had never told her tales. She wasn't expecting to find anyone there, least of all him. The rogue on the rock, inked in runes she couldn't read, with eyes like an ocean and a grin that could unravel kingdoms.

He called her Princess with a mocking bow, as if he already knew how the story of them would end.

She told herself he was cursed. Or maybe a thief. But regardless, she found herself wanting to know him.

I don't go back to Upside Down Rock the next day.

Or the next.

I *do*, however, spend way too much time looking for trouble in an ocean of familiar faces.

But I don't see him again.

Chapter 3

Juliette

Twenty-One Years Old

MY BEST FRIEND SINCE CHILDHOOD AND roommate for the past four years, Felicity, demands things; she doesn't ask. So, when she says, "You're coming out tonight," for the thirteenth time in the past two hours, I know arguing with her is a lost cause.

I've tried that method and failed many times.

Lately, she's been up in arms about me taking myself too seriously. She goes on and on about seizing the moment while I have a few days left to do so. Before college is over and I'm on my way back home to "Mommy and Daddy."

Her words. Not mine.

Her family runs the Second Circle Market chain of grocery stores, so while she knows what it's like to grow up with money, she's not one of the founding families.

She's close enough to understand the world I live in, but distant enough to resent it. Plus, she can't stand how tightly my parents hold the reins to my life, and she hates even more how easily I let them.

I guess it's hard to understand the level of passivity someone develops when it's all they've ever been taught.

"Did you hear me?" She smacks the back of my notebook, and my pen jerks mid-word, turning my "s" into a squiggle.

Sighing, I close the story I'm working on and glance up.

She looks beautiful, like she always does, her curvy silhouette highlighted by the sliding glass door that opens to the California ocean behind us, her long, straight blond hair and suntanned skin shining in the afternoon light.

"What?" I ask.

She snaps her fingers in my face. "I *knew* you weren't listening to me, jerk."

I bat her hand away. "I heard you, I was just hoping you'd let me hermit in peace."

Felicity laughs. "If I did that, you'd end up a cranky old woman with twenty cats and no friends."

"I'm allergic to cats."

"Oh, yeah." She pauses, frowning. "But I love cats."

"Guess that means we can't be friends anymore," I deadpan.

"Please, I forced my way into your life when we were four and haven't left since. I'm basically a permanent limb now," she replies.

"More like a tumor," I mutter.

"Semantics." She flicks her hair over her shoulder. "Which is why it's extra insulting you think you'll get out of coming with me tonight. Please, Jules. One night of fun. I'm dying here."

The guilt hits hard, and I let the fight drain out of me. "Fine. I'll go."

"Yes!" She fist-pumps, her thin blond eyebrows arching high. "Will you actually enjoy it, or will you be a moody bitch all night?"

I sigh, running a hand through my hair, the dark strands tickling the backs of my arms. "I learned a long time ago that when it comes to you, resistance is futile."

She gasps. "Was that a *Trek* reference?"

Felicity's been obsessed with *Star Trek* for years, after she watched a marathon with my brother Paxton one weekend at my house. I'll never forget it because it was the only time they've ever gotten along.

"I dabble."

She splays a hand across her chest. "I have truly *never* been prouder."

Stretching my arms above my head, I lean back until a satisfying crack punctures the air. "Where are we going, anyway?"

"It's this—"

"Wait," I interrupt, throwing my palm in the air. "More importantly, *who* are we going with?"

Don't say Keagan. Don't say Keagan. Don't say—

"Keagan and some of his friends."

Felicity clearly sees my look of disgust. She doesn't say anything though, because she's suddenly distracted by her phone, fingers flying way too fast to be a casual response.

"Who are you texting?" I narrow my eyes.

"No one."

"If you're telling Keagan about me going already, I'm never leaving this couch again."

"Dramatic much?"

"Felicity."

She sighs, tossing her phone to the side. "It's not Keagan. It's Alex."

My mouth drops open. "Alex as in my *brother* Alex?"

She shrugs, trying to hide her smile.

"Oh my God."

"You act like I haven't known him my whole life." Felicity laughs. "He's funny. And sweet. And he's got that little crinkle when he smiles…"

I stick a finger down my throat and fake gag and that only makes her laugh harder.

"Kidding," she finally tells me.

Throwing a couch pillow at her, I whine, "I hate you."

She shakes her head, still grinning. "Come on, girl. You know I don't have a crush on Alex, he's like *my* brother."

"Yeah, well," I mutter. "Maybe. But just be careful with him, okay?"

Her smile falters. "What's that supposed to mean?"

I give her a pointed look. "You know he's half in love with you."

She straightens. "He is *not*. And it doesn't matter anyway, I'm with Keagan."

My face scrunches up at Keagan's name.

"You've gotta get over whatever your deal is with him," she says.

"Do I, though?"

She flops down next to me on the couch and holds up her palms so they're facing each other.

"He's my boyfriend," she says, wiggling one hand. "You're my best friend," she adds, wiggling the other. Then she smashes them together. "Coexist."

"I've had plenty of boyfriends you didn't like."

"That's different."

"How so?"

"You never gave a shit about any of them, so why would I?"

She's not wrong. Not really, anyway. Ever since Preston dumped me over a text and left me gutted for a month straight, I stopped letting anyone get close enough to matter.

"Fair. That still doesn't mean Keagan's any less of a douchebag."

"Maybe," she agrees. "But he's *my* douchebag."

My mouth drops open again, but when Felicity's eyes turn into slits, I snap it shut.

"What?" I ask innocently.

"Your thoughts are loud," she complains.

"Okay, fine. God, you act like the world's gonna end if I'm a little grumpy."

She beams and leans forward, throwing her arms around my neck, her strawberry shampoo flooding my senses.

"It'll be fun tonight," she says against my shoulder. "You'll see."

"If you say so."

She pulls back and grabs my hand, a flicker of sincerity breaking through her sass. "When will you admit I always know what's best for you?"

"That's *incredibly* debatable." I laugh. "I can list off several times you've put me in bad spots."

She narrows her gaze. "I told you to forget about those."

"What do you want me to do, give myself a lobotomy?" I grin, tapping my temple. "My mind's a steel trap, baby."

She groans, sitting back. "Whatever. The point is, you've

only got a few days left here in the land of the free, and you've never once really let go of who you think you should be to just…"

"Just what?"

"You know…let loose. Just be Juliette."

I nod, but I swallow the words that rise in my throat. I'm not sure I even *know* who Juliette is. That little girl who used to sneak around corners with a notebook and a nose for gossip disappeared somewhere along the way. After years of saying yes to my parents and smiling pretty for the papers, I became exactly what they wanted. Just another cookie-cutter cutout.

It's only in college that I've started to find that little girl again.

Doesn't matter. Graduation is next week, and after that, it's back home to Rosebrook Falls. Back to being a polished, palatable version of myself.

"If you want my advice," Felicity cuts into my thoughts. "You should find someone to fuck before your archaic family rolls into town for graduation and ruins your chances."

I guffaw.

She frowns. "Why are you laughing? You could use a good dicking."

"Ew, don't say it like that."

She cackles. "What? I'm just saying. Ever since Keagan started giving me his, I've been in a much better mood."

My features screw up.

"Don't make that face," she says.

I wipe the look. "What face?"

"The one where it's clear you think Keagan's Satan. You wouldn't hate him if you saw how big his dick is, that's for sure."

"A big dick doesn't mean they know how to use it. And I still wouldn't be the one sleeping with him, so I doubt that."

"I'd let him fuck you." She eyes me. "I'd probably fuck you, too."

"You make it sound so romantic."

"Fucking *is* romantic."

"Is it?" I cock my head.

"It is when I do it." She grins.

"Tempting," I say flatly. "But I'll pass."

She watches me and then nods like she's made peace with my decision. "Smart move, honestly. I do this thing with my tongue that would ruin you, and then obviously you'd fall in love."

"*Obviously*," I echo.

"I'd try to let you down easy," she goes on, undeterred. "But you'd spiral, things would get weird, we'd stop hanging out, and you'd write some tragic novel and dedicate it to me with a passive-aggressive note. So really, it's better this way. I value our friendship too much."

I blink. "That was…a lot."

She shrugs. "Just trying to protect what we have."

"Right." I nod. "Wouldn't want *me* to make things weird."

She sighs, falling back against the couch. "Exactly."

"*Anyway*," I say, moving my notebook from my lap to the coffee table. "You said it's an art show? Who's the artist?"

Felicity must be able to sense the unease in my voice, because she doesn't miss a beat before saying, "Don't worry, I know better than to take you somewhere that could tarnish that fancy reputation of yours."

"I wasn't worried about that."

That's a lie.

Personally, I don't care, but my family does, and even this

far away from Connecticut, if I did something too scandalous, it would inevitably show up in *The Rosebrook Rag* back home. My family would have to contact their lawyer Frederick to bury the story, and I'd be cold shouldered until the next big scandal hit the news.

Felicity gives me a look, and I concede, "Okay, maybe I was, but you know how it is."

She pouts. "Being you is exhausting."

Tell me about it.

"It's actually for some street artist."

"Oh, really?" I don't particularly care about art, but it sounds interesting enough. "What's his name?"

She grins and wiggles her eyebrows. "That's the best part. Nobody knows."

"What do you mean, 'nobody knows'? Somebody has to know if he's got an art show."

Her lips purse. "Good point. But in general, he's anonymous. Tags everything with RMO and that's it. It's part of his mystique or whatever."

"How do you know it's a *he*?"

"I don't, I guess." She frowns like the thought has genuinely never crossed her mind. "But that doesn't matter."

"What does matter, then?"

"What *matters* is you getting out, breathing some fresh air, you know, living a little."

"I already said I'll go, what else do you want from me?"

Felicity beams. "Is it weird if I offer the threesome again?"

I throw another couch pillow at her, and she catches it, falling onto the floor and laughing.

Smiling, I pick my notebook back up and flip it open, but

the words don't flow the way they normally do. Instead, a hit of melancholy spreads through my chest when I realize I only have a few days left of this.

Felicity is coming back home, too, so we'll still be around each other, but…it will be different.

Silently, I promise myself that I really will try to have fun tonight.

Chapter 4

Roman

Twenty-Three Years Old

VISITING MY MOM IS NEVER EASY.

Not only because I don't know which version of her I'll get, but also because whenever I see her, the memories of who she used to be prick at me like a dull knife.

She *used* to be healthy.

She *used* to be a woman people looked up to.

She *used* to be someone who loved me.

Now, she's none of those things.

Still my mom, though, even if she'd rather forget that fact.

I trudge up the broken concrete pathway leading to the front door of her duplex. A few items of trash are scattered amongst the grass: a napkin here, a bright red chewed-up straw there. I nudge them aside with the toe of my boot before moving forward and remind myself one more time why I'm here.

Why I continue to show up.

For Brooklynn.

My gut tightens the same way it always does when I think of my sister.

Every day I try to find ways to help her but come up short because as much as I want to take care of her myself—get her out of this environment entirely—I don't have enough money.

There's never enough.

It's not even that I don't make a decent living. My art makes me enough to stay afloat. Or it would, if I didn't give my mom every spare cent.

The problem is, my mom has a drug abuse problem, so we're always one bad decision away from my sister not getting the care she needs.

Brooklynn's been chronically ill for the past four years. We don't know what's wrong with her, and no matter how many tests they run or hospital stays she has, nobody can seem to figure it the fuck out.

She has constant medical bills, frequent checkups, and a fear that any random ache and pain could spiral into something worse.

Most recently, she's been having seizures, and although her doctors can't find the root cause, they've gotten her stable with medication. But I live in a daily panic that they'll say she needs something like brain surgery, or that she's developed something we can't afford to fix.

Medical bills aren't cheap. And neither are her meds.

Fucking big pharma assholes.

I reach the front door, the aluminum screen corroded with spots of reddish-brown shining through the chipped white paint. I knock twice before it swings open, and I meet the doe eyes of my little sister.

She smiles when she sees me, her brown irises sparkling. She's the spitting image of our mom—or of how Mom used to look, at least—and every time I see her, it causes a phantom ache to rip open in my chest, reminding me again of how things used to be.

"Hey," Brooklynn says, bouncing on her toes.

It's a good day for her.

I grin back. "Shouldn't you be in class?"

She's seventeen and in her junior year, and like me, she tends to skip, although I have a sneaking suspicion it's because nothing in her classes challenges her. *Unlike* me, she's never met a textbook she doesn't like.

"School's boring." Brooklynn shrugs. "Besides, my last period is study hall, so I always come home instead."

She moves to the side and lets me in, and as soon as I hit the small living room, I hear my mom. "What are you doing here?"

The question is blank, monotonous even, but it punches me in the stomach anyway.

I spin around and see all five foot two of my mother standing in the doorway leading to the narrow kitchen. She has one pale hand wrapped around a chipped yellow mug and the other resting on her hip.

"Coming for the pleasure of your company like always, Ma."

She sniffs and pushes a stray piece of dark brown hair behind her ear. It's tiring, this back and forth between us, but like everything else, I shove it to the recesses of my brain and pretend like it doesn't affect me.

No, not pretend. It *doesn't* affect me.

It can't.

If I let it, then I won't be able to keep showing up, and

whether I like it or not, Brooklynn and I are all my mom has in the world.

For the longest time, my mom was all I had in mine.

Now, I don't even feel like I have that.

"I'm glad you're here," Ma says, her voice softening.

The subtle change makes me bristle, because I know what's coming next.

She moves closer, her grip tightening on her mug. "I've been meaning to call you."

I lift a brow but don't reply. From the corner of my eye, I see Brooklynn sigh and move to the couch, flipping open a philosophy book.

Probably tuning us out.

Good. I wish she didn't have to witness it at all.

"Things have been a little difficult lately," she continues. Her gaze flicks to Brooklynn and then back to me, a tight smile crossing her features. "I got laid off again, and—"

"You got laid off, *again*?" I cut in.

"It wasn't my fault," she snaps then draws in a breath, smoothing out her expression like she can will the irritation away. "It doesn't matter. But if I can't make rent in two days then…well…"

I grit my teeth until it feels like my molars might break. "There's an art show tonight. I'll see what I can do after that."

"Your art." She scoffs. "That won't be enough, and you know it."

My chest tightens, but I brush the feeling aside. It's not like she's ever been supportive. When I was little, I used to dream about the day I'd be able to make her proud. Now, resentment boils my blood whenever I think about that naive little kid.

"Fine, *fuck* the art," I say. "I'll cancel the show."

Something flickers in her expression. Panic, maybe.

"*No*," she snaps. "Don't be ridiculous. We need that money, and you need to show your face there. Do you know what I had to do to *get* you this show?"

She's right. She did pull strings; ones left over from her own art days, back when she used to care enough to create. If I try hard enough, I can almost pretend it was about me, and not about padding her pockets or fueling her next high.

"I don't know what you want me to do," I say. "There's nothing I *can* do."

She swallows, lifting her chipped coffee mug to her lips before mumbling into it, "You could talk to your father."

Sighing, I pinch the bridge of my nose. "Not this again."

"I'm just saying—"

"He doesn't give a fuck about us!" I snap, louder than I mean to.

Mom flinches like I've slapped her, but I don't take it back. It's ugly and rotted, but it's the truth. She just doesn't want to see it. She never has.

You'd think the guy has a magical dick with the way she's still clinging to the fantasy of him after everything he's done.

"Look, I'm sorry," I say, quieter. "It's just, what you're asking me is—" I shake my head. "I don't want to go to him. Not when he let us go—let *you* go so easily. You might not give a shit about yourself, but I still do."

Her eyes lift to mine, glossy and unreadable. "He had his reasons."

I let out a dry laugh, but she keeps going, her voice defiant. "And you're his only son. If you talk to him, he'll—"

"He'll *what*?" I interrupt. "Aren't you tired of this conversation? We've been having it for years and it never changes."

She doesn't understand. Or maybe she does, and she just doesn't care. Either way, she just looks at me with that pinched, too-tired expression. "He *owes* you."

"I have no interest in being part of his fucked-up legacy or anything that comes along with it." My voice slices through the air like a blade. "I haven't even seen him in four years, and you want me to what, call him up and demand money to help his bastard child, ex-mistress, and the daughter who isn't even his? The ones who are supposed to be *dead*?"

She frowns, her finger jabbing into my chest, the sharp edge of her nail dragging against my shirt. Her eyes narrow, and I brace for it, because I know whatever she's about to say will hurt.

It's the drugs, I remind myself. *It's not her.*

"I want you to be a man for once in your life and do something to take care of us."

My eyes sting, a flush of anger burning up my throat.

What does she think I've been doing this whole time?

Every scraped-together paycheck, every night I went without to make sure she and Brooklynn didn't, every stupid, *desperate* thing I've done just to keep the lights on, and the fridge full, and her from falling completely apart.

"What good *are* you, Roman?" she continues.

"Don't call me that," I spit, running a hand through my hair and gripping onto the roots.

She smiles sarcastically. "Well, that's your real name, whether you like to admit it or not."

"Not anymore." I lean in, my voice low and cold. "The man you seem to worship made sure of it."

Her pupils are blown out, wide and glassy. I stare into them, searching for any trace of the mom I used to know.

My heart thuds in an all too familiar rhythm. "You're high."

She sneers and jerks her face to the side. "My back hurts."

I let out a breath, heavy and bitter, like it's been trapped in my lungs for years.

"Every time you ask me to go to him," I say quietly, "another piece of me dies."

Somewhere deep inside me, I still want him to be something more. Something else.

A father.

I don't want his money. I don't want his power. I just want *him*, and I fucking hate myself for it. My hands curl into fists against my knees, nails biting into my palms until the sting grounds me.

I blink hard. Once. Twice.

Then I exhale through my nose, and shove that feeling back down where it belongs. Buried and forgotten, locked in a corner behind everything I've become despite him.

"He didn't want us, remember? We don't need him."

"He *does* want you. He wouldn't have given you his last name if he didn't. The problem is *her*."

I should point out the obvious: that it was my father who wiped our old identities from the face of the earth after my mom had us visit when I was fifteen. She wrapped our car around a tree, and he swooped in right after with his own personal brand of witness protection. A clean slate, and an easy way to keep the mistakes of his past from smudging his picture-perfect future.

I guess it wasn't enough that we never lived in his shitty

Connecticut town. He wanted to make sure we no longer existed at all.

The "her" my mother spits like a curse is my father's wife. His dead wife.

Eleanor Montgomery. Or Voltaire if we're going by maiden names.

And if she were really the issue—if she were who kept me out—then he would have let me in when I showed up after her funeral.

But he didn't.

Turns out everything I'd been told about Eleanor Montgomery was a lie.

But my mother loves to live in delusion.

My tongue pushes against the inside of my cheek. "Well, I don't want *him*, then."

She lifts her chin. "Even if it could save your sister?"

Guilt wraps around my chest and squeezes.

She sets her mug down and leans in, cupping my face like I'm still that child who's blind to everything but her love.

"You're still a *Montgomery*, Ry," she says softly. "Whether you like it or not. Maybe it's time you start to act like one."

Chapter 5
Juliette

THE GALLERY IS LOUDER THAN I EXPECTED, buzzing with voices, clinking glasses, and the moody hum of elevator music echoing from hidden speakers.

Felicity is already two steps ahead, scanning the room like she's searching for someone. That douchebag Keagan, probably.

I nudge her. "So, what exactly are we looking for here? Emotional growth? Mystery artist reveals himself and turns out to be a hot billionaire with a tortured past?"

She sticks out her bottom lip. "You promised not to be an asshole tonight."

"I promised to try and have fun," I correct. "I just don't know why *this* is the place you dragged me to for my 'let loose and live' moment."

She smiles now, almost guiltily. "Well, I'd tell you, but you'd get pissed, and I'm trying to keep you light and happy."

I raise a brow. "Name one time that's ever worked out for you."

Felicity loops her arm through mine, tugging me through the maze of art snobs and champagne trays.

"True." She sighs. "But you're like my sad little emo puppy, and it's my moral duty to drag you into the sun and pump dopamine into your cold, dead heart."

"I feel like I should be offended." I glance around. "But I see no flaw in your logic...other than picking an art show to do it."

"I didn't just randomly decide to drag you here, I actually talked to Bevie last week."

"Bevie." I falter. "Why are you talking to my childhood nanny?"

She shrugs. "She checks in on you from time to time."

Warmth spreads through me. I love Beverly. She's the closest thing I've ever had to a mom.

"She called me the other day and said your mother had that *look* in her eye."

"A look," I reply flatly.

"Yeah, and don't pretend like you don't know what I'm talking about. It's that twitchy, soul-snatching stare, like she's already picked out the earrings you'll wear at your funeral."

I cringe, because honestly, I could see my mother doing it. "That's morbid."

"Bevie was worried," she continues. "Especially once I told her how mopey you've been lately."

"Well, you shouldn't have told her that, then."

She shrugs. "Agree to disagree. Anyway, she's the one that hooked a girl up with these art show tickets."

"You want me to believe *Beverly* got tickets to this? An art show. In California."

Felicity knocks her shoulder into mine as we stop walking. "You can believe whatever you want, but I'm telling you the truth. I guess she used to visit here or something. She also told me about some coffee shop around the corner, The Em-Tee Cup."

I stare at her. Beverly never—not once—mentioned she knew the area when I talked about coming here for college.

"How'd she get the tickets?"

"Have you met Bevie? She's terrifying. Obviously, I didn't ask."

That's true. Beverly is not known for her soft edges.

"Why'd she pick an art show?" I muse, mostly to myself.

"She said you used to draw pictures with sidewalk chalk when you were little and then make up stories to go with them. Made Alex act them out with you. She probably thought you'd like it."

A reluctant smile tugs at my lips.

"I miss that girl," I admit, glancing at the wall beside us.

One of the pieces is all jagged lines and burnt orange chaos, signed RMO in the corner.

"Me too," Felicity says quietly.

It feels like a moment happening here. Like we've stepped into the past just enough to remember who we used to be, before we grew up and had to start thinking about things like our futures, and what we'd allow in them.

Or in my case, what my parents will allow.

Felicity perks up, body straightening as she spots Keagan.

"There he is, come on." She tries to tug me with her, but I let my arm slip from hers, grimacing.

"You go ahead. I'm gonna look around. Try to find some sidewalk chalk or something."

She smirks. "Yeah, fine, but don't get lost. And *remember*: stranger danger…unless he's volunteering that good dick we talked about."

I wave her off.

"I put condoms in your purse, FYI!" she calls out, *way* too loud.

A man in a suit looks at me appalled, like I'm about to choose someone to fuck in front of him.

I grin and roll my eyes. "Some people, right? Never met that woman in my life."

Then I keep walking until I hit the farthest wall and stop in front of the nearest painting.

My professor in an art history course I took sophomore year talked about the importance of different mediums. How he could go to a museum for hours and just stare at a singular piece hung up, losing himself to the way it made him feel. Back then, I never understood what he meant. Honestly, I figured it was him talking out of his ass, trying to give a deeper meaning to something that was just paint on a canvas.

But now... I marvel at the art, wondering how it's possible to create such intricate designs from a can of spray paint, and while I walk along to look at the different pieces, it feels like an itch being scratched in my brain.

It isn't until I physically bump into a girl from one of my college classes that I recognize I've been wandering in a daze.

"Shit, I'm sorry," I apologize. "Amanda, right?"

She tilts her head, her bleached-blond hair falling effortlessly over her left shoulder before she says in a clipped tone, "That's right."

Her cold demeanor throws me off, but I'm nothing if not adaptable. I was born and bred to shine and sparkle in uncomfortable situations.

"Juliette." I point to myself.

She looks me up and down and then scrunches her nose as if I don't quite measure up.

"I think we had poli-sci together." I try again. "Are you a fan of the artist or just art in general?"

She takes a sip of her champagne. "My summer art foundations course is offering extra credit if we attend shows around the city."

Her eyes float from me to the framed slab of concrete in the middle of the room.

I turn back to the piece. There's a small child on her knees at the base of concrete steps that lead to a large building with the word *Health* across its top. Money and pill bottles are falling from the sky, but as they float closer to the girl, they catch fire until there's nothing but ash and soot surrounding her on the ground.

The letters RMO are signed in the corner in all black, with sharp edges and overexaggerated lines. "What's RMO stand for?"

Amanda sighs. "It's obviously a signature."

"Ah, that's right. An anonymous painter." I wiggle my brows conspiratorially.

"People call him Romeo. Because of the 'passion in the work.'" She says it like it's the most ridiculous thing she's ever heard.

"You disagree?"

"I think people like to see romanticism in even the most... pedestrian pieces. This is his first official art show, anyway; normally, people just find his stuff on the sides of buildings randomly. I don't know that we should encourage that type of illegal activity by giving them platforms."

"Hmm." I nod along. "Even if they send a message?"

That's clearly what this mural is doing. It's intricate and hauntingly beautiful.

I've never experienced anything like what's depicted, so it's hard to relate to personally, but it still makes the center of my chest feel tight. I tilt my head as I look at the art again.

"I think it's poetic," I declare, bringing up my glass for another sip of bubbly.

"Some people can see poetry in anything, I guess."

My heart stutters, and I choke on the champagne, coughing until my eyes sting.

That is not Amanda's voice.

It's low and rough, and threaded with dark amusement.

I suck in a deep breath, but nearly forget how to breathe at all when my gaze catches on icy blue eyes.

Familiar icy blue eyes.

Trouble.

He's standing there, half shadowed beneath the gallery lights, dressed in a black button-up with the sleeves rolled to his elbows. A silver ring glints on his first finger, and ink coils along his forearms—more than he had four years ago. But it's *him*. The same messy brown hair, same lazy confidence, and that same damn smirk with those obnoxious dimples.

His stare finds mine and doesn't waver.

Amanda's voice barely cuts through the static in my brain. "Ry, this is—"

"Princess," he cuts her off.

I bite back a small grin. "Hi, Trouble."

His lips twitch, and Amanda scoots closer to his side. But he doesn't move. Doesn't even blink. His attention is locked on me.

And just like the first time we met, it tilts me off balance.

"You two know each other?" she asks sharply.

He doesn't answer. Just stares. And I stare back, even though I know I shouldn't. Even though it feels like the air between us is thinning with every second.

I don't know why, but this feels important.

"Hello?" Amanda snaps her fingers. "I said—"

"Yes," he answers.

"No," I reply at the same time.

There's a beat of silence and then my grin widens, impossible to hide.

"We met once," I say finally, dragging my eyes away from him to look at her. "A long time ago."

"It wasn't *that* long ago," he murmurs.

"The length of time doesn't matter," I argue. "Once is still a small thing."

"Sometimes the smallest things take up the most room in your heart."

I purse my lips, thrown by the response. "That's oddly profound."

He nods solemnly, his hand to his chest. "Winnie the Pooh said that."

"Of course he did." I laugh. "Leave it to a stuffed bear to make you sound enlightened."

"There it is." He grins. "That mean streak of yours. Still incredibly hot, by the way."

My cheeks flush, and Amanda stiffens next to him.

"I'm just saying it's irrelevant," I barb back. "That's not how I remember our first meeting going."

It's *exactly* how I remember it.

I haven't stopped thinking about him since that night, no matter how many stories I've written trying to erase him from my mind.

"I'd love to hear more about your version," he says, a slow smile curling up his lips. "*My* memory is that you thought I was the sexiest guy you'd ever seen, and it made you…unreasonably cranky."

I balk, tapping my nails against my glass. "I told you not to let that give you a big head."

He shrugs, slipping his hands into the pockets of his slacks. "Well, it has, unfortunately. It's huge now. I'm almost impossible to be around."

"So, you're the same as before, then."

Amanda's voice slices through the tension. "Okay, I'm confused. Do you two know each other or not?"

"Not," I say firmly. "It was so brief, I thought maybe I dreamed him up."

"Do you dream of me often?" he asks, eyes glinting.

"That's *not* what I meant."

"Ry," Amanda warns under her breath.

And it's only then I realize that maybe they're here together. Maybe he's *hers*.

"Like I said, we met once. It was nothing."

"I wouldn't say *that*," he says quietly.

Sighing, I face him again. "You know, you're even more irritating now than you were back then."

His grin turns magnetic, and I feel like I'm being sucked in by a vortex of gravity where *he* is the center.

It's weird, and I kind of think I hate it.

Amanda's glare yanks me back to Earth. Regardless of who he is to her, I'm clearly trespassing on her territory.

"Well," I begin, already stepping back. "This has been…a time." I point vaguely over my shoulder. "I'm just gonna…yeah."

And then I spin on my heel and walk away like my sanity depends on it. Because I'm pretty sure it does.

Chapter 6

Roman

HER CHEEKS FLUSH AS SHE WALKS AWAY, AND I can't help but watch her. Her spine is stiff, and her shoulders are tense, like she's trying to ignore something. *Or someone.*

I should let her go. Keep things simple. But my mind is still whirling with the realization that she's *here* of all places, and even though I've only met her one other time, she's been the only thing that's made me feel something other than the heaviness of my life in years.

She disappears into the crowd, and for a second, I lose her.

"Ryder," Amanda snips.

I look at her and frown. "You could have been a little nicer."

"And you could have acted like I was part of the conversation," she hits back.

I wince, knowing she's right, but it's not like I came here with her. She's not a date, she's just a friend who showed up for extra credit. She doesn't even know this is *my* art on the walls.

"Yeah," I say, but my eyes aren't on her. They're grazing over the crowd, searching. "Listen, I'll be right back."

And then I chase after my mystery girl.

I catch sight of her right before she pivots toward the glowing red exit sign at the back of the warehouse, and I'm after her without a second thought.

The moment I push through the door, the nighttime chill breaks over my skin like a fine mist, and the noise of the gallery fades behind me.

It's cooler out here, the air thick with smog and the faint rot of nearby dumpsters. A few stars blink dimly, buried like secrets the city doesn't want anyone to find.

She's already leaning against the brick wall in the alley, head tipped back toward the sky.

"Everything okay?" I ask, keeping my voice low.

Her shoulders stiffen and then relax like she already knew it was me. She cracks one eye open, just enough to look.

"God, you're like a lost puppy," she mutters.

My lips curve up, attraction flaring to life in my chest. *Damn*, she's fun to rile up. She's so wound tight and ready to snap.

"Does that mean you'll pet me if I'm a good boy?"

She doesn't answer, but her cheeks flush again, visible even under the alley light.

I pull out a hand-rolled joint, press it to my lips, and light it. Her eyes zero in immediately.

She raises an eyebrow. "I don't think that's legal here."

"It is," I reply, exhaling slowly, and hold it up between us. "Does it bother you?"

She leans back against the wall, arms crossed. "Not really. Just further proves my 'you're a degenerate' theory."

I chuckle, but there's a twinge in my chest that tightens at the word *degenerate*. That's probably what she'd think if she saw where I came from. Saw my mother strung out on the couch, a forgotten sketch in her lap.

"That's quite the privileged take, Princess…thinking everyone who lights up is a degenerate. Must be nice, seeing the world in black and white."

She doesn't reply, but there's a flicker of guilt in her eyes.

"How's the boyfriend?" I ask, trying to keep my tone light even though I feel anything but.

"What boyfriend?"

Satisfaction and a hint of hope curls through me and sparks like an ember. "Couldn't take the ice bitch persona or what?"

"I'm perfectly nice."

"Right." I smirk, taking another drag, letting the smoke twist between us.

"I don't see how it's your business, anyway," she snaps.

Her tone doesn't piss me off, but it *does* make me think of how badly I want to fuck the attitude right out of her. How easy it would be to press her up against the wall and give her mouth something to wrap around besides the cutting words she loves to throw.

I crush the joint against the brick, and then I'm moving across the alley.

She startles, and backs up until her spine hits the wall, like she needs the stability. I close the space between us until I can feel the heat of her body flaring against mine.

Her breath hitches.

"I could make it my business," I coax, letting my eyes drop to her mouth.

And *goddamn*, I want to taste her. Every single inch of her. I want to drag my hands down her sides, bury my face between her thighs, and let her claw at my hair while I fuck her with my tongue.

In fact, this chemistry between us is almost *too* intense. I've never felt anything like it, and part of me wants to run away while I still have my wits.

But I don't run. I don't kiss her, either.

Her eyes flare, and we're so close to touching that the warmth of her words blanket my lips.

"I hate you," she says.

I lean in and pinch her chin between my fingers, cataloguing every feature on her face and committing it to memory. "No, you don't."

Then I step back, settle against the opposite wall with my foot propped against the brick, and grin, hoping it comes across as casual and not like my heart's about to beat right out of my chest.

"She's not, for the record," I say.

"What?"

"Amanda. She's not my girlfriend."

Her eyes narrow. "Does she know that?"

"She does. We're just friends."

"Friends like... just friends, or friends like you save her from dying and then flirt until she starts naming your hypothetical children?"

Amusement curls in my chest, and I wonder if that's something *she's* been doing. The idea thrills me, to be honest. I like imagining that she's as obsessed with me as I seem to be with her.

I smirk and she flushes that perfect shade of pink.

"Friends," I repeat, slower this time. "Acquaintances, even."

She hums like she doesn't buy it, tearing her eyes away from me.

I follow her gaze, seeing some art tagged on the dented trash bin.

"You don't like graffiti," I guess.

"I don't feel any type of way about it, really."

"Then why are you here?"

She hesitates, her teeth sinking into that luscious bottom lip.

"I don't know," she admits. "That art inside? I've never seen anything like it. I mean, you've been to Rosebrook, you know how it is there. I never thought something that looks like that"—she points to the blocky letters on the garbage—"could be in the same class as what's hanging in there."

I glance toward the gallery, a hit of pride suffusing me because she likes my work. "How do you know they're not done by the same person?"

She laughs like I'm joking.

I'm not.

"You're serious."

"Art is art," I say. "Only difference is one gets framed. The other gets you arrested."

"And skill level," she shoots back.

I lick my lips to try and douse the fire she's making rage inside of me. "Didn't realize you were such a harsh critic."

She straightens, clearly bristling. "And what are you, then? Some tortured art savant?"

I spin the ring on my finger once. "I've been known to draw a thing or two."

Her breath catches. "Oh."

"Don't act so surprised." I tease.

"What do you like to draw?" she asks, softer now.

"All kinds of things." I pause, then add, "Right now? I'd like to draw you."

I'm not sure if I mean it. Mainly, I want to see what she'll say. If she'll react in that fiery, defensive way she does. The way that makes my cock hard and my heart flip.

She stares at me. "Excuse me?"

"You heard me," I say, moving across the alley again until my knuckles brush her cheek.

She shivers, and my jaw flexes from the feel of her skin. It's soft. Buttery. *Fucking perfect.*

"I don't... I don't know what to say to that."

"You could say yes."

She laughs, but it comes across a little too breathless and a little too loud. "I don't, um... no. That's... That feels personal. I don't even know your name. *And* I don't like you."

"Do you want to know my name?" I ask.

Right now, I think I would tell her anything.

"Sure, after you tell me what you were doing in Rosebrook Falls all those years ago."

And there it is.

The energy shifts, flashes of my deadbeat father surging to the forefront of my brain until the *heavy* sinks back in. No matter how much I try to outrun it, I am who I am. Even when I don't want to be.

If I let myself think too hard about it, I could probably guess exactly who *she* is, too.

I pull back, running a hand through my hair. "Pass."

"Why not?" she pushes. "You're the one who wants us to be friends, right?"

"I never said that."

Her smile goes flat. "Well, this has been just as frustrating as the first time I met you, so I'm gonna go."

Panic crashes over me. I don't want her to go yet. "Wait."

She ignores me, hurrying to the door.

"Hold up a minute," I beg, chasing after her.

I step in behind her, lowering my voice. "Don't go."

She turns, her spine pressed to the door, and my stomach catapults into my throat and then down to my feet. Every time I look at this girl, it feels like I'm on a rollercoaster. I wonder if she feels it, too. This pull.

She has to.

"I think you do like me," I say.

She lifts her chin. "Well, that just proves what a terrible judge of character you are."

My lips brush her ear. "I have excellent taste."

She swallows hard. "Tell me your name, *Ry*."

I hesitate. Then rock back on my heels. I want to tell her, I do, but her calling me *Ry* reminds me of all the reasons why I can't.

"Nah. I'm good."

"You're...good?"

"Yeah." I smirk, slipping my hands in my pockets so I don't do something stupid like reach out and touch her. "Feels like this is our thing now."

Her eyes squint. "We do *not* have a thing."

"Pretty sure we do."

She laughs, sharp and disbelieving. "Oh my God, you're so *annoying*."

And this type of flirtation with her is palatable. Easy. *This*, I can handle. "So I've heard."

The door bursts open, jostling my mystery girl. Her body hits mine and everything else disappears. Her hands land on my chest, her curves press into me, and the feel of her in my arms floods every rational thought.

I go still, my fingers twitching with the urge to pull her closer. Grip her tighter.

A woman comes out of the door, her eyes watery and makeup smeared, and the moment shatters.

"There you are," she chokes out.

My mystery girl straightens, pushing off me, instantly concerned. "What's wrong?"

Her friend sees me, falters, but tries to gather herself. "Nothing. I just want to go, can we go?"

I don't want her to go.

Her friend gives me a second glance before saying, "No rush."

"We were just talking," my girl replies. "Go tell Dimitri we're ready."

She nods, then disappears, leaving the door swinging shut behind her.

"Who's Dimitri?" I ask, a hit of unfounded jealousy surging through me.

"My driver." She doesn't look at me. "I've gotta go."

"Maybe I'll see you around?" I offer. Light. Hopeful.

"Doubtful."

So she does remember the first time we met the same as me.

A slow grin blooms on my face. "I can wait."

She grabs the door handle, glancing at me from over her shoulder. "You'll be waiting a while."

And then, just like the first time we met, she's gone.

The Rosebrook Rag

SPOTTED: Frederick Lawrence—Power Suit Edition

Making *yet another* appearance on behalf of Marcus Montgomery (interesting…), the ever-slick attorney was seen at the VU Foundation's brunch this morning, shaking hands, dodging cameras, and smiling a little too wide.

While we love seeing the enigmatic lawmaker, we do wonder where Marcus Montgomery is, and why he's suddenly so reclusive?

#RosebrookRag #MontgomeryWatch

#MontgomeryMoves #VUFoundation

Chapter 7

Roman

THE SHADING IS OFF.

Sighing, I stare down at my black book like it's personally offending me.

I've been lying around all morning in nothing but gray sweatpants and a nagging sensation, urging my fingers to pick up a pencil and sketch out a new design. But the design isn't *right*. And it has to be perfect before I turn it into an actual piece like the others from last night.

I run my fingers over the sketch, my brows furrowing.

It's a rose. Blood-red with thorns jutting like daggers from the stem. The petals drip like wet paint, melting and disintegrating.

It's a physical representation of what running into the girl from Rosebrook Falls feels like. Fragile in a way that isn't soft, and the kind of beauty that bruises if you get too close. She's attitude and defensiveness. Every word she throws at me laced with venom and thorns.

The color is *supposed* to be the shade of peach that blooms on her cheeks when I flirt with her. I've thought about that color so many goddamn times. Fisted my cock while I dreamed about wrapping my hand around her pretty little throat, watching that pink crawl down her neck and spill over her collarbone while she begs me to paint my cum on her skin.

Fuck.

I'm still recovering from running into her in the first place.

The last thing I expected was to ever see her again, especially in Cali. And I sure as hell didn't expect to have so much chemistry with her, or for her to be so affected by *me*. Which I think she is, unless I'm completely misreading the signals.

When I first met her four years ago in Verona County Park, she looked so familiar it made my stomach ache, and I fully intended to walk away. The only reason I was there in the first place was to look out from the cliff and find a spot to tag before I left. Something to leave my mark for my piece of shit father, a rebellion that would stain his precious town whether he wanted it to or not.

Maybe a glaring "I'm alive, bitches," or just: "Roman Montgomery was here." In the end, I didn't have the guts.

My mom has always said he faked our deaths to protect us, but that when I became an adult, as long as his wife was out of the picture, he'd want me back. So when I actually went back after her funeral and was still rejected? You could say that chip on my shoulder felt heavier than ever.

I went up to that cliff with one thing in my head: rage.

But then *she* opened that perfect little mouth and started hurling insults like me saving her life was a personal inconvenience, and *fuck*, if that didn't turn me on.

Suddenly, I wasn't thinking about my piece of shit father, or how badly I wanted to burn down everything he ever built—everything he kept me out of.

I was thinking about *her*.

About how easy it was to get under her skin. About how nice it was to experience something other than that gnawing rejection.

She made me forget how small he made me feel. How unloved.

Her irritation? That was something I could hold on to. A memory from Rosebrook Falls he couldn't taint.

The problem is, I think I know who she is.

My mother has always kept up on anything to do with my father, including the town he lives in, and that means I've seen my fair share of *The Rosebrook Rag* headlines and articles from various events and newspapers.

And even though I've been a bystander to his life, my mother made sure I knew everything there was to know about being a Montgomery, including the rivalry between him and the Calloways.

I'm ninety percent sure she's Juliette Calloway, but I've resisted the urge to look up her name. I don't want to have it confirmed, because right now, she's just a pretty girl who's fun to flirt with.

Potential is limitless when there aren't strings attached.

And recognizing that she's a Calloway would definitely attach some strings, even if I doubt she knows I exist.

It's not as if Marcus spent time parading me around like a trophy, and I've only ever been to Rosebrook Falls twice in my entire life.

My mind flashes back to when I first woke up after the car crash eight years ago: a dark room with wires taped to my chest, and the steady beeping of a heart monitor to my left.

"Nobody can know who you are to me, do you understand?"

My father's fingers grip my shoulder blades harshly, and I wince at the pressure, my body still too wrecked to pull away.

He shakes me slightly, and my head throbs from the motion.

"Answer me," he demands, low and sharp.

I blink away the fog, trying to focus on his face. "Ye-yes, I understand," I croak. "But why? Why can't they know?"

His eyes flick toward the door like someone might be listening. There's a manic energy around him, as though he's waiting for something terrible to happen, something that might walk through that door at any moment.

"Because if they find out you're alive..."

He stops. Cuts himself off, and the unspoken words buzz louder than the pounding in my head. The air grows quiet and tense, and then—

"Mr. Montgomery, sir," a voice interrupts, although my vision is so hazy, it's too difficult to see who.

"What?" he snaps, his blue eyes still staring at me like I might vanish.

"She's awake."

I snap out of the memory and swallow against the ache blossoming in my chest.

Not telling her my name was the right choice. The only

choice, really. After all, even if she didn't know of me, she could run home and mention me, and then who knows what would happen?

My entire body tightens when I think about my sperm donor and the way my mother still clings to the idea of him as some sort of twisted salvation. She wants me to crawl on my knees and beg for money. Thinks he'll welcome us back like some prodigal son story. Or maybe she just wishes he'd be her savior.

I know what's really waiting there.

Nothing but bitter disappointment.

Even when I had his last name, I didn't get the perks that came with it, so why the hell she thinks something would change now is beyond me.

My jaw clenches as I stare at the drawing in my black book.

Sighing, I run my fingers through the slight muss on the top of my head, gripping the roots and pulling until it stings. Physical pain is easier than the desolation that swirls when I focus on my family.

My phone rings, jolting me from my daze.

I glance at the clock. *Noon*.

I'm supposed to meet my mother at the coffee shop in ten minutes. *Shit*.

Rolling out of bed, I answer the call.

"Brooklynn?"

My sister sniffles on the other end.

"Brooke? You okay?"

"R...Ry-Ry?" she stutters into the phone.

My body freezes at her tone, panicking that she's had a seizure or is hurt somehow.

I'm dressed and at the front door grabbing my keys within seconds.

"What's wrong?" I ask.

"It's all g-gone." She gets out.

Relief that she's all right pours through me like a waterfall, but then her words register. My brows draw down. "What do you mean?"

"The m-money. The rainy-day fund you had me start? It's… Everything's missing."

I laugh, thinking she's joking, because there's no way. Between her working a part-time job and me funneling her every extra dollar from my art, she'd have saved up close to ten thousand dollars by now.

"What are you talking about?"

"The money… I kept it under my mattress, and I went to take some with me to pick up my Felbamate and… It—it's gone." She hiccups into the phone.

My stomach drops. "Wait, why the hell are you using the money I give you to pay for your seizure meds?"

Silence answers me, and I grind my teeth so tightly, I'm surprised my jaw doesn't crack. "Brooklynn. Has mom not been covering the cost of your meds?"

"Sometimes she does," she whispers.

Sighing, I pinch the bridge of my nose. I can't win here. "It's all gone?" I confirm.

Brooklynn hiccups again. "I should h-have had a better hiding spot, I just… I didn't…"

"It's okay," I soothe, trying to keep the anxiety from showing in my voice. "Just tell me what happened."

Glancing at my desk, I look at my wallet, already knowing

there's only a few hundred bucks in there. That's not nearly enough to cover a supply of her meds, even with the coupons we get her since we don't have any insurance.

"M-Mom said to call you. She...she said you'd be able to help."

Anger whips through me so violently, it burns my throat. "Did our mother do this?"

Brooklynn hesitates again. "She said she didn't."

I swallow hard, my tongue sticking to the top of my mouth like glue. "Listen, Brooke, I don't want you to worry, okay? I'll take care of it. How many pills do you have left?"

"I'm good for a couple days, but Ry, I'm sorry, I...I didn't mean to..."

I shake my head even though she can't see me, realization settling heavily into my gut about what my mother did. About what I know I have to do if I want to make sure Brooklynn stays healthy.

"Hey, it's all right," I say. "I've got you no matter what, okay?"

She sniffs. "Yeah."

"You trust me?"

"Always."

"I'll handle it." I grab my hoodie from the coat rack next to my door and put my phone on speaker while I slide it on. "And Brooke?"

"Yeah?"

"Quit trusting our fucking mother."

The Rosebrook Rag

Breaking! Mayor Penngrove Running It Back?!

Rosebrook Falls's favorite "man of the people" just launched his reelection bid, complete with shiny promises, big buzzwords, and a whole lot of Calloway cash.

Sources say the Calloway estate is hosting an invite-only fundraiser next week. But the real headline? Juliette Calloway, the golden girl turned college darling, may be finally flying home for the event.

Is she the next political pawn in Daddy's high-stakes game? Or is she finally stepping into the spotlight to play the queen herself?

#CallowayDrama #JulietteReturns #PowerPlay #RosebrookRag #CallowayWatch

Chapter 8

Juliette

"WHAT DO YOU MEAN YOU'RE NOT COMING?"

I throw a quick smile to the barista when she hands me my drink and then place the phone between my shoulder and ear as I make my way to the small table against the windows.

Normally, I don't come this far off campus, but after thanking Beverly for the art tickets, she basically demanded I stop in here and try their coffee, because it's the *"best in the world."*

Paxton sighs so heavily, it practically vibrates through the phone. "We'll have a celebration when you get back," he tries to placate. "It's already planned."

"Yeah." I scrunch my nose. "Who's planning it?"

"You know who."

My mother.

Which means it's not really a party for *me*. With Martha Calloway, it's never just a celebration to celebrate. There's always an ulterior motive, some type of positioning or posturing for the public.

"We both know that's as much for me as the VU Founders' Gala is."

There's a rustling of papers over the line, and then, "I'm sorry, Jules. It's out of my hands."

He says it monotonously, and if I didn't know my brother, I'd think he didn't actually care at all.

I bite the inside of my cheek.

Paxton is like my father in a lot of ways, including his belief that showing emotion in public is beneath him. He's the oldest child, and as a result, he's had to shoulder a level of responsibility the rest of us haven't had to endure.

As the VP of Calloway Enterprises, real estate development is all he seems to care about, and even before taking the position, he's always shadowed our dad in a way none of the rest of us can understand.

Felicity calls him "Golden Boy." Fitting nickname, I think.

A sudden thought hits me. "Wait a minute. When you say *you're* not coming, do you mean you as in *you*, or you as in *everyone*?"

Another hesitation and then, "Everyone."

"That's bullshit!" I snap loudly.

The lady next to me jolts from the volume of my shout, and some of her coffee sloshes onto her hand. I give her an apologetic look and then repeat in a whisper, "Pax, that's *bullshit*."

"Come on, Jules." Now he sounds annoyed, and that hurts, too. My feelings are valid.

"Things are tense, there are a ton of new projects we're waiting to have greenlit, and Montgomery's little soldiers are causing roadblocks at every *fucking* turn. Plus, you know Frank is about to start his campaign for reelection."

"Art's dad is running for mayor again?" I scrunch my nose, thinking about my brother Lance's best friend. "So, making sure the mayor's in our family's pocket is more important than my graduation."

He sighs like this conversation is tiring him. "That's not what I said."

"It's not fair. Everybody went to your graduation *and* Alex's."

Not Lance, though, but only because he dropped out.

"Hardly the same," he says. "VU is *in* Rosebrook."

I blink back the burning behind my eyes. "So, you'll make it when it doesn't inconvenience you too much."

"It's not like that."

Pain radiates through my sternum. "Feels like it."

"Hold on," he demands, and then he starts speaking again, only this time the sound is muffled, like he's talking to someone else.

Sighing, I pick at the cardboard protector on my to-go coffee and glance around the shop. My heart pitches forward and my breath stalls when my gaze locks on a familiar stranger standing at the front of the line.

Holy shit.

"Jules." Paxton's voice is soft now, like he's around people he doesn't want to hear his conversation. "Listen, I've—"

"Why are you whispering?" I interrupt.

"What?" he says a little louder. "I'm not."

"Don't gaslight me over your tone of voice, dude."

He sighs like talking to me is the most frustrating thing on the planet. "I'm not gaslighting."

"You're being weird. Is it because of me or because of the wife you hate?"

I shouldn't poke at him when he's obviously already on edge, but would I really be a little sister if I didn't?

"Don't talk about Tiffany," he says.

"Why not?" Anger spreads like a wildfire in my chest. "She's my sister-in-law after all. I should be able to talk about her as much as I want."

"We've got the jet ready to bring you home in two days." His tone is flat.

"What?" My eyes widen and I pull my phone away from my ear and look at it like he can see how crazy I think he sounds, before bringing it back and hissing, "Now *I* don't even get to go to my graduation?"

"You'll get your diploma in the mail. What do you need the ceremony for?"

"I can't believe you're saying that to me."

"Me neither," he mumbles.

I frown. "Fine, but *you* have to tell Felicity."

He grunts. "I don't have to tell that little brat anything. She has nothing to do with this family."

"That *brat* was a pseudo sister to you growing up, and you can pretend all you want that you don't know her, but it doesn't change the fact that she'll come home and kick your ass for not letting me experience graduation with her."

He's silent, and I can practically picture the way his jaw is clenching. "Fine."

My eyes narrow. "Who's making you do this? Is it Mom? Tell her to call me herself."

Unlikely.

"Of course it's Mother," Pax exhales sharply. "And of course it's not a party for you, Jules. Be realistic. It's a fundraiser. For Frank."

I blink. "You're kidding."

"I'm not. Are you happy now?"

"No, actually. I'm the opposite of happy. You're honestly telling me that I have to miss my own graduation just so I can play dress-up as Mother's political puppet?"

There's a pause, followed by a softer version of his voice. "This is how it is, Jules. It's how it's always been. Can you *please* just get on the plane? Come home."

A hit of guilt laces up my spine like a corset. I hate how he always feels like the world is on his shoulders. "You sound tired, Pax."

"Please," he adds, quieter now. "Don't make this harder than it already is."

Click.

I stare down at my phone, my mouth half open in disbelief.

Four years of freedom. Of space. Of breathing without the Calloway name coiled around my throat. And just like that, they've swooped in and slipped the leash back on. It shouldn't still sting, not after an entire life of it happening. But it does.

I run a hand down my face, fingers curling at my jaw, and I already know…I'm going.

Not because I want to, but because I never really had a choice.

Someone laughs loudly, and I look up just in time to see my stranger walking out the front door, shaking his head like he's disappointed by something.

My stomach flips. *He's still here.*

If anyone can take my mind off the way I feel right now, it would be him. He'll probably piss me off enough on his own to smother any other emotions I'm currently struggling with. And maybe that's exactly what I need.

I'm up and out the door right after he leaves, making sure to keep my distance. Just in case I chicken out.

We walk straight down the street for a few blocks and then finally make a right turn into what looks like a two-story motel but seems to be an apartment building with faded blue doors on the outside.

He disappears into one of them, so I assume he must live here.

I look around, debating what it is that I'm going to do.

This isn't like me. I don't follow people, and I definitely don't make rash decisions without analyzing every possible outcome and how it could affect me.

I should live a little while I've still got the chance, like Felicity implied last night. Maybe even get fucked.

The inner voice doesn't calm me down. In fact, the fire that started brewing while I was on the phone with Paxton rages like an inferno until my palms are clammy and my heart is pounding like a fist against my chest.

I'm leaving here in two days.

Gone.

Sucking in a deep breath, I race across the street before I lose my nerve and stop right in front of his door, my hand poised to knock.

My arms shake.

What the hell are you doing, Jules?

Squeezing my eyes tightly, I rap on the door.

Oh my God, I think I might throw up.

This is stupid. So, so stupid.

I'm about to run away, but before I can, the door swings open, and I come face to face with Trouble.

Chapter 9

Roman

SHOCK DOESN'T BEGIN TO DESCRIBE WHAT IT feels like to see my little rose, looking hot as fuck, standing on my front step like some sort of fever dream.

"What a coincidence," I murmur, leaning casually against the doorframe. "I was just thinking about you."

Her lips are parted, like she's surprised I answered the door, and when I speak, she snaps them closed and clears her throat. "You were?"

"I was." I cross my arms slowly. "Are you stalking me?"

She licks her bottom lip, her gaze lifting to mine from beneath those long, dark lashes, and my stomach tightens like a vise.

"I don't know what I'm doing here," she replies.

Something uneasy curls in my chest, because she's being oddly nice. But I'll take it, because if she leaves, then I'm left alone to face my problems—my family's problems—and she's a hell of a nice reprieve.

The perfect distraction.

Especially since my mom was a no-show.

Tilting my head, I let my eyes roam, dragging slowly down her frame before crawling back up again. When our gazes meet, she's blushing—because of course she is—flushed all the way to her ears.

It's the *exact* shade of pink I've been chasing in that damn drawing.

"Not that I'm complaining, but how do you know where I live?" I ask.

"I saw you at the coffee shop," she admits. "And... followed you."

A slow grin spreads across my face. "So, you *are* stalking me."

"I am *not* stalking you."

"It's okay, Princess. Really, I like it."

She squints. "You'd like to have a stalker?"

"Depends." I lean in, placing my arm above her head on the top of the doorframe, just close enough to feel the heat coming off her skin. "Does the stalker look like you?"

She scoffs. "So, it's only creepy if they're ugly? That's fucked up."

"I prefer the term *selectively unbothered*."

She groans, dragging a hand over her face. "Oh my *God*, why did I think coming here would be a good idea?"

"Anything involving you and me is a good idea."

Now she laughs, and it shoots straight through my chest.

"I like that," I blurt like an idiot.

She quiets, sending me a questioning look. "You like what?"

"Your laugh."

The air between us shifts, feeling thicker somehow. Charged. Like if I moved even half an inch closer, something would combust.

"I'm *not* stalking you," she says again. "I wanted to apologize, actually."

"Should I be worried? You're kind of giving… What did you call it? *Serial killer vibes.*"

Her blush expands, coloring down her neck. My fingers twitch with the urge to trace it. Or sketch it. Or lick it.

"Please, we are *not* the same," she protests.

"Oh, I agree." I smirk, letting my gaze drop to her mouth. "But you know what they say. Opposites attract."

She cracks a small grin. "Are you gonna invite me in so I can say I'm sorry or what?"

I gesture toward the open doorway, giving her space to step inside. But she doesn't move. She just looks at me, and *fuck*, she's so goddamn pretty it hurts.

Leaning in, I bring my mouth a hairsbreadth away from her ear, close enough to feel her breath stutter.

"That," I murmur, "was me inviting you in."

She smells like cinnamon and vanilla and something else. Something heady and warm and a little sultry. My mouth waters, wondering if that taste is artificial or if it's something I could have on my tongue if I buried my head between her thighs.

"Oh, right," she says. "Thanks."

I move to the side to give her room to pass, and she slips through, the front of her body squeezing by mine.

My breath hitches now, and a slow burn sparks in the pit of my stomach, unfurling through me like a flame licking up my veins.

I follow her in silence as she makes her way through the small, narrow kitchen off the front door, past the tiny bathroom to the right, and into the main area of my studio apartment.

There's a TV mounted a little crooked on the wall, a rectangular coffee table I found on the curb last year, and a small blue couch that probably predates both of us. Next to all of that is my bed in the corner, although really, it's just a mattress with a simple bedframe.

She stops in the middle of the room, taking everything in with a tilt of her head.

Like she's sizing it up.

And for some reason, that makes my stomach tangle and my chest squeeze.

If she really is Juliette Calloway, this apartment must look like a shoebox to her. The feeling of not being enough chokes me by the neck.

"It's not much," I mutter.

She turns, and then she smiles. *Really* smiles. The sight of it steals the breath straight from my lungs.

"It's perfect," she says.

"Okay, what's up with you?"

Her brows furrow. "What do you mean?"

"You're being weirdly nice." I squint. "Is this a setup? *Are* you here to kill me? Be honest. I deserve the chance to defend myself."

"I'm not, I swear." She chuckles. "This place just feels so *you*, it's painful."

"Coming from a girl who insists we don't know each other, that's either very creepy or very flattering."

She shrugs, smirking. "It feels, I don't know, homey. Like Sleepytime tea or something."

I stare at her.

"Did you just compare me to a drink that puts people to

sleep? Are you calling me boring?" I look around the space, attempting to see it from her eyes. "Am I boring?"

Her lips twitch. "I meant it as a compliment."

I take a slow step toward her, and then another. "Okay. But if you think I'm boring, I'm more than happy to prove you wrong."

Her smile fades, and the lightheartedness of our conversation evaporates like water, something heady taking its place.

"What are you doing here, Little Rose?" I ask, my voice a low murmur.

"I don't...I don't know," she stutters. And then, "What did you call me?"

Tilting my head, I lift my hand until the back of it ghosts across her jaw and then down the sleek line of her neck. Not touching...but *almost*.

"You don't like it? I can go back to *Princess* if you want."

She raises a brow. "I get to choose?"

"Always."

Her face changes then, heaviness flickering in her eyes. "I've had a really shitty day, and when I saw you at the coffee shop..."

She trails off.

I take another step in, until we're so close the air vibrates between us. I give into the urge, my hand dropping to the juncture between her neck and shoulder, my stomach flipping at the contact. "You *what*?"

Her tongue peeks out, wetting her lips. "I realized that every time we've talked, I've been mean to you. Even when you didn't deserve it."

I skim my fingers across her flesh until they rest lightly at the base of her throat. "I can handle you."

She sucks in a shaky breath, her eyes dropping to my mouth. "I don't need to be *handled*."

I slide my palm up until it's wrapped around the dip beneath her jaw. "Doesn't mean you wouldn't like to be."

Her breathing stutters, but then she snaps out of it and takes a step back. "You're awfully bold for someone who won't tell me his name."

I grin and cross my arms. She's flustered. Her chest is rising and falling rapidly, and a dusting of that perfect rose sweeps across her face. I bet if I pressed my fingers against her neck, I'd feel her pulse beating wildly.

Goddamn, she's sexy. I need to get her out of here, or else I need to think about something entirely *un*-sexy, like the Pythagorean Theorem or my eighty-year-old nurse from elementary school named Mrs. Tucker who hated me because I got the entire fifth grade to call her Mrs. Fucker instead.

Oh. Yep. There it is. Boner averted.

"I accept your apology," I say, raking a hand through my hair. "Is that all?"

She shifts, biting her lower lip. "I thought maybe I'd take you up on your offer."

My brows shoot up. "I've made several offers when it comes to you, so you'll need to be more specific."

"To draw me," she clarifies, her hands wringing together.

I won't lie and say I'm not interested in doing it. I originally offered that as a way to get under her skin because she's cute when she's feisty, but now that she's put it on the table, I want it. Badly.

But maybe that's exactly why I shouldn't. I'm having a hard enough time keeping her out of my head as it is. No need to willingly make it worse.

"I don't think that's a good idea," I admit reluctantly.

She blanches and then looks down at the ground like she's searching for her dignity, her toe rubbing a nervous half circle into the hardwood. "You're right. That was a stupid thing. Of course you weren't serious... I just thought it might be a good distraction, and I *need* a distraction right now."

Funny. I thought the same thing about her.

And to be honest, I don't like the way she suddenly looks so sad, like she's desperate for someone to *see* her and to make the bad go away. It tugs on that piece of me deep inside that I keep locked up tight, where I beg for the same thing.

"Lie down."

Her head jerks up. "Excuse me?"

I smirk. "I'm not asking you to get naked, Princess. I just want you to be comfortable when you pose. So, lie down."

She nods, her gaze flicking from the couch to the bed and then to me before doing it over again. She's nervous, and I tamp down the smile that wants to break free.

"The couch is fine."

"I prefer the other one, by the way, if you insist on calling me by a ridiculous nickname," she says as she moves to the sofa and positions herself against the cushions.

Heat shoots through me like a flare gun as I watch her get cozy on my furniture. She's on her back, fingers wringing together on her torso. Her hands fold, then unfold. Her legs shift. Once. Twice.

I walk over, lean down, and gently take her wrist. Her eyes fly to mine, and my heart thumps.

"Is this okay?" I ask.

"Yeah—yes."

She watches my face closely as I move her arm above her head, like I'm an equation she's trying to solve.

"I don't normally do this, you know?" she says.

The corner of my mouth lifts. "Good. I'm territorial."

"What's that mean?"

"It means you're *mine*."

Her lips part.

"To draw," I add, trying to save us both from wading into territory we aren't prepared for.

I tear my gaze from hers and focus on positioning her body the way I want it. I try like hell not to react to how good she feels under my hands. How I want to grip her tighter and position her in *other* ways.

Bent over the arm of the couch. On her back in my bed. Up against the wall with her legs wrapped around my waist.

I shift, willing my dick to behave.

"Do you want to know my name?" she breathes.

Fuck.

Yes. No. I don't know.

"It doesn't matter what your name is," I finally reply. "Fate seems to love putting you in my hands, regardless."

Reaching out, I smooth my palm along her jaw until I'm brushing behind her ear. My fingers twist in the silky strands of hair at her nape, pulling lightly until she angles herself appropriately.

"Perfect," I murmur.

She exhales, and I grit my teeth to keep myself from acting on this insane lust I feel for her. I've had plenty of one-night stands before and *never* has someone made me feel like this.

I clear my throat instead and move to the other side of the

room, grabbing my desk chair and positioning it a safe distance away. I pick up my sketchbook and pencils from the bed and then sit down across from her.

"Let me know if you get uncomfortable," I say.

"You don't make me uncomfortable."

My chest warms. "That's good. But I meant the pose."

"Oh. Right." She licks her lips and then stares up at the ceiling, studiously avoiding my gaze like it might light her on fire.

Probably smart.

"Try not to move."

"Okay," she whispers.

For a moment, I just look at her, my heart beating out a stilted rhythm as I soak in the curves and angles of her body. Every soft line, every tiny flicker of vulnerability she's pretending not to feel.

She's chaos and comfort. A contradiction I want to memorialize as the perfect piece of art.

I pick up my pencil, open to a blank page, and start to draw.

Chapter 10

Juliette

THIS FEELS DIFFERENT THAN ANYTHING I'VE EVER experienced.

It feels reckless, and hot, and...kind of perfect.

I've never been so vulnerable in front of anyone, and with every stroke of his pencil across the room, he strips away another piece of me, like I'm naked in front of him, showcasing my biggest insecurities all without saying a word.

I'm not sure how long it's been since there's no visible clock from this vantage point, and I'm afraid to move.

Instead, I just soak him in.

The way his brows dip in concentration, or how his jaw flexes when he tilts his head, his eyes ignited with the darkest kind of fire as he places them on different parts of me and then lowers them to the page.

His sketchbook rests on his leg, one ankle slung over his opposite knee, and the tattoos on his arms flex with every stroke of his pencil.

A lock of hair falls over his forehead, and he absentmindedly brushes it back, his tongue swiping against his bottom lip.

Fire scorches up my spine, arousal pouring through me until I'm drunk on it.

His dark gaze flicks up to mine. "You okay?"

The way he says it—low, rough, and raspy—sends a jolt between my legs. My thighs tense at his tone, heat curling low in my stomach, and the selfish part of me hopes he's just as affected by me as I am by him.

"Fine," I reply, but it comes out as a whisper.

"Try not to move," he instructs again.

"Sorry."

A small grin tilts his lips as he continues to sketch. "For a girl who doesn't like to apologize, you sure do it a lot."

"I never said I didn't like to."

"Call it an educated guess."

I swallow. "I don't mind apologizing to people who deserve it."

He stills for half a second, then his pencil moves again.

"Sorry," I say again. "Am I not supposed to talk?"

"I like your voice." He smiles. "It'd be a shame not to hear it."

My stomach flips, butterflies soaring back to life, and just like it always does, it puts me on edge.

"You flirt with me like this, but you don't even *know* me," I mutter. "Is this your thing? This blanket charm with every girl who stumbles through your door?"

"You didn't exactly stumble." He looks up, amused. "You stalked; let's not rewrite history."

I give him a look.

"Besides, I know about you," he continues, his tone more serious.

My eyes slide to his, locking onto his gaze. "Oh? And what could you possibly know?"

It's quiet for a few seconds, like he's trying to decide how much he wants to say, and then he's staring back down at the paper, his pencil moving again. "I think you're lonely."

His words slap my chest, and my muscles tense.

The pencil keeps floating from one area of the page to another, his eyes flickering to me and then back again, focused and calm. "When something's out of your comfort zone, you lash out with insults, cross your arms, and do that little squint with your eyes like you're trying to convince yourself you don't care."

Another stroke of the pencil. Another quiet moment.

"You chew on your bottom lip when you're overthinking, you twist your fingers together when you're nervous, and *every single* time you've smiled…like *actually* smiled in my presence, you look surprised, like you had forgotten what it felt like."

My throat tightens, an unsteady feeling growing inside me, and *damn* him for paying attention. For *seeing* me like that as if he has any right.

"Isn't everyone?" I ask. "Lonely, I mean."

"Fair enough." He nods. "Tell me about you, then, Little Rose."

My body shifts, but I try to keep as still as possible while he draws.

"I play the piano, although not very well, despite years of lessons. I can speak conversationally in four different languages, and I was the valedictorian of my high school."

"No doubt the prom queen, too." A small grin lights up his face. It's cocky and effortless, and I hate the way it fits his features perfectly.

I roll my lips together. He's right, but I'm not going to tell him that.

"I'm graduating this week," I continue, my voice growing softer. "And then I'll go back home to Rosebrook Falls. Well, I guess I'm going back before that, really."

His pencil slows. "You're not going to your own graduation?"

I try to smile, to…I don't know…laugh it off or something, but it feels brittle. A slow burn builds in my throat, crawling up until it pools hot behind my eyes. I blink hard and fast.

Don't cry. Don't cry. Don't fucking cry.

If I break in front of him, and he draws it into this sketch like it's just another part of me, I'll launch myself off the couch and out the nearest window.

From the corner of my eye, I see him zone in on my *nonexistent* tears. But he doesn't call it out. Doesn't make it worse.

He lets out a low hum and then drawls, "That's fascinating, but I asked about *you*. Not what you do, or don't do, as it were."

I frown. "I don't… I guess I'm not sure how to answer you, then. That *is* me. It's all I've ever known."

He stops drawing completely now, his eyes steady and dark and burning a hole through me. "That's a shame."

My face heats. I swallow heavily, my mouth suddenly dry. "I don't want to talk anymore."

His jaw clenches, and he nods, his pencil making broad strokes again.

The air shifts and changes, a different type of vulnerability laying in the space between us.

Minutes pass, and I spend the majority of them either watching him in a sick type of fascination or staring at the ceiling and trying not to regret that I asked him to do this in the first place.

"I love to write."

It's barely audible, but it feels like I screamed it into a silent room.

He pauses his ministrations, but then he continues drawing like he's afraid if he reacts to my words, I'll stop saying them.

"What do you write?" he asks.

"Anything. Everything. I don't know, it's like...these stories pop into my head, and the characters won't shut up until I get them down on paper."

"Is that what you went to school for?"

"Yeah, right." I laugh at the absurdity. My parents would never let me take up anything to do with writing as a degree. "Psychology."

"Ah." He clicks his tongue, tapping the pencil against his knee. "The degree you get when you don't know what to get."

"Some people love it," I argue.

"And do you?"

Do I?

"The only thing I've ever really wanted to do is tell stories," I admit.

He leans forward, watching me like I'm a puzzle he's trying to solve. His voice is low but firm. "So tell stories, Little Rose."

My stomach sinks.

He doesn't get it. Or maybe I'm just now realizing how pathetic I sound, pouring out this passion, only to follow it up with the confession that I've done absolutely nothing about it.

But what's the point?

My family will have my future laid out for me the second I go back home. It's *already* happening, quietly and strategically, just like it always does. That's why I'm missing graduation, after all, because when my mother says jump, I don't ask why. I ask, "How high?"

Fighting it would be pointless.

It's never worked out for anyone else in my family, and I have no delusions it would work out for me.

Especially not me.

"You don't get it," I mutter.

"Then explain it to me."

"With my family, it's…" I hesitate, because maybe I'm about to treat him like a therapist, and that's crazy considering I don't even know his name. But if I can't say it to a *stranger*, then I'll probably never say it at all.

So I take a deep breath in, and I let it all out.

"I'm the girl of the bunch. I'm expected to smile, stay quiet, marry well, and show up when I'm told. It's all about appearance, you know? Reputation. Optics…"

He hums, something flashing through his gaze. "And writing doesn't fit in that box."

I swallow around the knot tightening in my throat.

"Writing doesn't fit," I echo. "Is that how it is for you?" I ask, looking at his sketchbook. "You just want to draw, and so you do?"

He nods. "Pretty much."

I think about the freedom in his answer, and I can relate, I guess. These past four years, away from the suffocating proximity of my mother's voice and my father's absence, there's been…space.

Space to breathe. To think. To write.

And in those moments, when I've opened up my journal, or pulled up a blank page on my laptop and let myself fall headfirst into a story, I've felt something I hadn't even realized I was missing.

Freedom.

Not even just from my family, but from *me*. From the version of myself that's shaped around what everyone else needs. The agreeable daughter. The smiling Calloway girl. The one who nods when told, even when my vocal cords ache from holding back a scream.

But here in California, away at college? That version was allowed to disappear.

At least some of the time.

I think I'm mourning whoever *this* version is already. She's about to die—metaphorically speaking—once I go back home.

"Is it this *thing* inside of you just clawing its way to the surface, desperate to get out?" I ask. "When you draw, I mean."

He watches me for a long moment, and then he blows out a breath. "Yeah. It's exactly like that, actually."

"And is this what you do for a living? Your art?"

"I do what I have to do so I can take care of my family."

That wasn't really an answer to my question, but I don't push.

He sighs, setting his black sketchbook on the coffee table with a *thud*, and then rises to his feet. I track his movements, and in a few steps, he's looming over me like he's about to devour me whole.

"Done already?" I ask, my voice thinner than I want it to be.

He doesn't answer right away. He just stares at me with something wild behind his eyes.

"What is it about you?" he murmurs, his gaze dragging over me like he's starving.

My heart stutters. That same arousal from earlier rushes back, pinning me in place.

"You know...let loose. Just be Juliette." Felicity's voice whispers through my head, taunting me. And *God*, I want to.

But this feels like a line. One that my mother can probably sense me breaking from across the country.

Still, my body moves before my brain can protest, and I lift my arm from where it rests above my head, my fingers shaking slightly as I reach for him.

His jaw tightens, and his eyes are burning, but he doesn't pull away.

I curl my hand around his and guide it down, until it's resting against my collarbone, my pulse fluttering beneath his palm. "Touch me," I whisper.

He does.

His hand skims across my chest and up to my throat, his fingers lightly wrapping around it like a necklace.

I press my legs together to stem the ache blooming between them, but I don't move. I *can't*.

Every nerve lights up under his touch, like my skin has turned electric.

His other hand traces from my fingertips where they're still resting over my head, and along the length of my arm in one slow, reverent sweep, making me shiver.

He keeps going, down the curve of my shoulder, over the top of my chest, and then lower, until he's ghosting across my breast. My breath catches, and I arch toward him without even thinking, needing more.

"*Fuck*," he murmurs.

His grip around my throat tightens, not enough to hurt, just enough to remind me he's there, and his other hand cups me fully, palming me through the thin layer of my shirt, a low groan rumbling in his chest as he does, like he's barely holding himself together.

His palm slips from my neck and moves down my stomach, slow and possessive, until his fingers tease the edge of my waistband.

There's a pause. A moment of hesitation, of our eyes meeting; a question in his, and permission in mine.

"Say it," he demands, his voice low. "Tell me you want it."

"I want it," I practically beg.

And then he's *there*. His thick fingers beneath the fabric and cupping me where I'm begging for him the most.

I moan, and his eyes flash, his fingers exploring.

"Does that feel good?" he rasps.

"So good," I reply, biting my lip.

He presses harder, slow circles against my clit until I'm throbbing and swollen and aching for him to fill me.

"*Goddamn*, you're soaked." His tone is awed. "Is this all for me, Little Rose?"

"Yes," I whisper. "*God*, yes."

He dips his head, his lips brushing against my jaw as his fingers move slow and teasing, just enough to make me pant.

"You've been driving me crazy since the moment I saw you. Walking around like you don't know how fucking sexy you are."

I gasp, clutching the fabric of his shirt.

His mouth grazes my ear. "You're going to let me make you

come, right here on this couch, with my hand on your pussy like the filthy girl you are, aren't you?"

"Yes," I breathe out again, because apparently, it's the only thing I can say.

"Tell me what you need," he growls, his voice raspy.

"You, I need your fingers," I plead, heat spreading beneath my skin. "Put them in me."

He listens, sliding them from my clit down to my entrance and dipping them inside, and then before I can even *think*, his mouth crashes against mine, hot and demanding, his lips pulling a gasp from my throat. He takes full advantage, slipping his tongue in and tangling it with mine like he owns my breath now, too. He tastes like *trouble*, and temptation, and whatever this tension is that's been crackling between us since the second we met.

It's teeth, and tongue, and hunger, and I fist the front of his shirt like he's the only thing anchoring me on Earth.

He groans low in his chest when I bite down on his bottom lip, and the sound reverberates through me.

His free hand moves to frame my face, his thumb brushing over my jaw, and the contrast of his mouth being desperate and his touch being reverent is dizzying. I tilt my head and deepen the kiss, and when I suck his tongue, it's like a dam breaks.

Suddenly, we're not *just* kissing anymore, we're devouring.

He finally pulls away, his fingers curling deep inside me, and his palm pressing with the perfect amount of pressure against my clit and moving in slow circles.

"You feel so good," he says. "So soft. So wet."

I arch into him, every thought dissolving except how he's finger-fucking me within an inch of my life, and how is it *possible* that no other man has made me feel as good with their cock as he does with his hand?

"I've wanted this since the second you opened that smart little mouth on that cliff," he murmurs. "Thought about what you'd sound like. How you'd taste."

I whimper. "You're such a liar."

"I am." He smirks. "But not about this."

His thumb circles my clit in slow, devastating strokes. "Don't go quiet on me now, baby. Let me hear you."

"I can't—"

"You *can*."

My head falls back, eyes fluttering shut. "Don't stop."

His mouth finds my neck, his teeth dragging across the skin there, and the tension coils tight, heat spreading up my legs, wrapping around my back and squeezing into my chest.

My pussy pulses around his fingers.

"That's it. Just like that," he praises. "Give it to me."

I do. I let go, shuddering beneath him as waves of white-hot pleasure crash through my body and retreat only to surge back and drown me all over again.

He holds me through it, his fingers moving gently now, his lips soft as they brush my cheek, like he's keeping me steady in a violent storm.

I'm trembling as I come back down, aftershocks rippling like a current, and he has a dazed look on his face.

There's something visceral and desperate in his gaze, and he takes his fingers from inside me and brings them up, sucking them into his mouth and then groaning at my taste.

Jesus.

I shoot forward, reaching for him, my hands fumbling with

his waistband, a sudden desperation taking over me like I'm possessed. I *need* to return the favor. Want to feel his thick cock resting on my tongue, his grip in my hair, his moans in my ears.

He's hard as I slip beneath his gray sweatpants, palming him over his boxers, and his breath is ragged, his eyes locked on mine with a fierceness that makes my stomach clench.

"Little Rose," he starts, attempting to bat my hand away.

"I want to," I argue, rising on my knees until my lips brush his jaw. I stroke him through the fabric, and he pulses in my hand. "Let me make you feel good."

Another pull, and his dick jerks again. His features contort in pleasure, and he hisses through his teeth, muscles tightening.

"Wait," he says, his fingers catching mine.

I pause, blinking up at him, my heart hammering against my ribs.

A pained look crosses his face, like he hates himself for stopping me.

Honestly, I kind of hate him right now for it, too.

"There's something you should—" he starts.

This time, it isn't me that cuts him off.

It's a knock on the door.

Chapter 11

Roman

THE TIMING OF THAT FUCKING KNOCK IS THE most inconvenient thing that's ever happened to me.

Whoever is at the door knocks again.

"Just ignore it," I say, keeping my gaze on hers.

Her eyes glance toward the noise and then come back.

She hesitates, but then she nods.

Her taste is still on my tongue, hot and musky and a little bit sweet, and my dick jerks at the memory of how perfectly her cunt squeezed my fingers. The thought of feeling that same tight grip around my cock as I sink all the way into her?

Diabolical.

Another rap on the door, and this time, she sighs. "Maybe this is fate telling us we should stop."

"Ry, I know you're in there!" My mother's voice filters through from outside.

My hands fly from her body like they're on fire. I mutter a frustrated, "*Fuck*."

Her eyes widen, maybe from hearing my nickname—although

Amanda said it in front of her before—or maybe because she hears another woman's voice at the door and is making assumptions.

She shakes her head and pushes away from me, shooting to a stand, pulling her clothes back in place, and making her way to the door. I chase after her, because the only thing worse than her leaving would be her running into my mother face to face.

I grip her arm and move her softly to the side when we reach the door, opening it a crack so my frame fills the width and my mom can't see in fully. I stare down at her with a blank look.

Mom isn't actively crying, but there are black mascara tears drying on her cheeks, and she's wringing her hands together, a panicked look on her face.

"Ma," I say, anxiety prickling my skin. "Are you okay?"

"Yeah." She sniffs and then steps forward like she's trying to come inside.

I keep the door closed tightly, and it forces her back.

"You're not gonna let me in?" she questions.

"Now's not a good time."

It's possible Ma would know who the woman standing next to me is.

I don't know why it bothers me that my mom could be the reason I learn her name—or worse, how she could learn the truth about mine.

Ma scoffs, water bubbling up and lining her lower lids, and guilt breaks apart my resistance.

It's not like this thing between me and my mystery girl is going anywhere past today anyway, so what does it really matter in the end? I don't know her, and even though I have a complicated relationship with my mother, she's still my mom. I still love her and don't want to see her sad.

Sighing, I'm about to open the door a little wider to let her in and get this inevitable reveal over with. Suddenly, Ma shifts, her fingers scratching over her long sleeves, and I look at her closer.

Pinprick pupils.

Not just watery eyes, but a glossy gaze, and every couple of seconds, her head lolls the tiniest amount, like she's trying to appear more alert but keeps fading.

Sadness rips through my middle.

She's high. Because of course she is.

"I'm busy," I tell her, my walls firming back up.

She sniffs again and glances down the street. "You used to never be too busy for me."

Sighing again, I run a hand over my face. "Ma..."

"I'm here to pick up the money for Brooke's meds. You have time for *that*?"

My brows shoot to my hairline. *The fuck she is.*

"What are you doing anyway, are you—?" She stops suddenly, her eyes narrowing, a spark of something sharp cutting through her foggy gaze. "Do you have someone in there?"

She peers around the door like she's trying to get a good angle to see.

I block her view, even though my little rose shifts closer, like she wants to see my mother, too.

"Just go wait for me down the street at the coffee shop, okay? Where you were *supposed* to meet me earlier."

I give her a pointed look.

Little Rose is so close to my side now that the heat of her spreads across my shoulder blades.

"Oh my God, is it a girl?" my mom screeches.

My mouth ticks up, because that sounded like *Ma*, not the drugs. "Christ, you're nosy. Mind your business."

Her expression shifts, her eyes cutting to the door, then back to me, like she's happy at the possibility of me actually having a girl here.

There's a warm hand on my back, and electricity fires along my spine.

"It's fine, *Ry*."

Little Rose puts emphasis on my nickname, and I let go of my death grip on the handle, angling myself to face her.

It's not fine, for a multitude of reasons, but I can't tell her that. I can't even explain my tumultuous emotions about her right now, because they don't make any sense.

At least she doesn't look at me like she's three seconds away from killing me anymore.

She smiles and bites that lower lip, and then her hand covers the one of mine on the doorknob, and she swings it open the rest of the way, coming face to face with my mother.

The anxiety that was simmering explodes into panic, my stomach revolting until it feels like I might throw up, but I stand stoic.

I watch them both carefully, waiting for a spark of recognition to flare on either of their faces.

"Hi," Little Rose says with a grin, reaching out her hand. "I'm—"

"Honey, I really don't care."

My mom cuts her off without blinking.

Shit.

"Oh." Little Rose's palm drops. "Okay."

She turns to me and gives me a small smile that doesn't

reach her eyes, and I'm torn between stopping her from leaving and letting her get away while she can.

Instead, I do nothing. Because clearly, I'm an idiot.

She moves to slide past me, smiling softly again at my mother, who ignores her entirely, and pushes by her, knocking her shoulder. *Hard.*

That propels me into motion, and I glare. "Jesus, Ma, watch out."

She shrugs and moves into my apartment, making herself at home on my couch. And maybe it's my imagination—wishful thinking from that naive boy—but I could swear when her back is turned, I catch the faintest twitch of her mouth.

Like she's secretly happy for me.

Jerking forward, I step outside, shutting the door behind me.

"Are you all right?" I ask, squinting from the sun blazing directly into my eyes.

Slowly, she spins to face me. "Yeah. You know, this is all probably for the best anyway."

"It probably is," I agree slowly.

I'm not sure if I mean that.

She purses her lips and then nods before turning to walk away again, and this uncontrollable urge to stop her rushes through me.

"Hey, wait up a second." I jog after her.

She whirls back, her black hair whipping around her shoulder, defiance flashing across her gaze.

My chest pulls.

"Don't do that," I say.

Her brows jump high. "Do what?"

I point at her face. "Be mad at me. I didn't do anything wrong."

"I didn't say you did."

"This is for the best, you know? I'm fucked up."

She grins a little. "Nobody's arguing that fact."

I take a step closer.

She moves back, narrowing her eyes.

"You just said this was for the best."

"Yeah, well, you weren't supposed to *agree* with me," she snaps.

I throw my hands in the air. "Well, what the fuck do I look like, a mind reader?"

My outburst makes her pause, and her lips twitch before she starts to laugh; a giant, bent-over, arm-across-her-stomach, tears-streaming-down-her-face kind of laughter.

It's infectious enough that it makes me laugh, too.

"God, this was a terrible idea," she says, pressing her hand to her head. "We argue like a married couple."

I smirk, even though my chest is tight. "You say that like you don't start all the fights."

She groans. "You're *infuriating*."

"Don't regret this," I demand. "Don't regret us."

Her gaze softens. "How can I regret someone I don't know and something that never happened?"

She's right, and I know she's right, but it doesn't make the disappointment any smaller.

I kick at the gravel with the tip of my shoe. "Didn't *feel* like something that never happened when you were coming around my fingers and moaning."

Her breath falters and she lifts her chin.

"Maybe I'll see you around?" I ask, because it's what I always ask her.

She bites her lip. "Doubtful."

I don't know why the word feels heavier this time around, but it does. It feels like…a door closing. I press my lips together, feeling a little sick at the reminder of who she might be and where she's from.

Still, I can't stop myself.

"You never know," I say, trying to keep it light. "Might make a special trip, just for you."

She huffs. "Be serious."

"Okay." I slip my hands into my pockets. "So I guess we'll leave it to fate, then."

She grins softly. "What, like chance?"

"It's worked out for us so far."

She nods. "All right."

"And if it happens, I promise I won't try to fuck you again," I lie.

A smile breaks across her face, and my heart trips at the sight. "Pretty sure *I* was the one trying to fuck *you*."

"You're hot when you talk dirty."

She rolls her eyes like I'm being ridiculous, but I know we both feel it. This ache of whatever it is we're not saying right now.

Something that feels a hell of a lot like goodbye.

"Well," she says, resting her hands on her hips and rocking back on her heels. "See ya if I see ya, I guess."

My stomach tugs forward like it's attached to her by a string.

"Ryder," I whisper.

My heart slams against my chest, annoyed because I want to tell her my *real* name but I gave her this one instead.

"What's that?" Her head tilts.

"My name's Ryder."

A myriad of emotions crosses her face before it's wiped blank, and she smiles.

"Ryder," she repeats.

I hate how good it sounds rolling off her tongue, and I hate knowing that Roman would sound even better. She slips her hands in her back pockets, and I wait for her to return the favor. For her to confirm what I already know. That she's Juliette Calloway.

But she doesn't.

She just bites the corner of her lip and says, "Well…it would have been nice getting to know you, Ryder."

She turns around, and walks away.

Again.

Like she's always doing when it comes to me.

Chapter 12

Roman

"CONSORTING WITH THE ENEMY?" MY MOTHER snipes when I get back inside.

She's lounging on my couch, all the tears from earlier magically disappeared.

I shoot her a look and drop onto the other end, sighing as the cushions absorb my weight. "What are you talking about?"

Ma just got here, and already she's made me feel spread too thin.

"You know what I'm talking about." She waves toward the door with a flick of her wrist. "What's your plan there?"

"I don't want to talk about this," I bite out, irritation sticking to my insides like tacky glue.

She doesn't back down though, because of course she doesn't.

"Tell me," she says casually. "Does Juliette Calloway know who *you* are?"

My jaw tightens. "Ma, I just said…"

I freeze.

Juliette Calloway.

Realization settles in like a slap to my face. She *does* know who my little rose is, and she just proved my suspicions right. She *is* Juliette Calloway.

My mother's watching me like a cat with a caged mouse.

"Oh my God." She leans forward with a glint in her eye. "You didn't even know."

I swallow, not responding. But that's answer enough for her.

"You let her into your home and you didn't *even know*?" she repeats, her voice shocked.

"This is none of your business."

Ma hums. "Well, I sure hope that anonymity went both ways, because if she knows who you are, then believe me when I say she's about to run home to her daddy and tell him."

I scoff. "That's a little dramatic."

"She's your enemy."

"Not *my* enemy," I snap. "Just because Marcus hates the Calloways doesn't mean I have to. They've never done anything to me, and I have no loyalty to the man you used to fuck."

Her eyes narrow, but she doesn't react to my hurled insult. She just tilts her head and lowers her voice. "Call it whatever you want, but this is all the more reason to get in touch with your father."

I stare at her. "What the hell does Juliette Calloway have to do with me reaching out to Marcus?"

She shrugs. "Craig's been trying to get rid of Marcus for years." She scrunches her nose. "He's a nasty piece of work. If he finds out you're alive, you better believe he'll be here in a heartbeat making sure you don't stay that way."

My mouth drops open. "You're saying Craig Calloway would what…come here to *kill* me?"

"Don't be stupid," she spits, like she's at the end of her rope. "Why do you think we're here with different names and living a life we were never meant to live?"

I laugh, because she's so goddamn delusional. "You actually believe that? You think Craig Calloway orchestrated an assassination attempt on a kid?"

She doesn't blink. "The brakes failed, Ry. On a *rental* that his company owned. You think that's just bad luck?"

My head shakes slowly, but doubt starts to gnaw at my edges, her words sticking. "That's what accidents *are*, Ma. That's why they're called *accidents*."

"You're the last Montgomery," she says like it's the most obvious thing in the world. "All of Marcus's power and wealth… If you're gone? There's no legacy left. No heir. Get rid of you, then you get rid of *him*."

"This isn't some fucking mafia movie," I mutter.

She gives me a long look. "Sometimes truth is stranger than fiction."

I study her, searching for a crack. For something that tells me this is just another one of her drug-induced conspiracies, but the only thing humming is her certainty.

"Yeah, well, there's a flaw in your logic," I point out. "If I'm so necessary to his legacy, how come I'm a dead guy with a fake name who he turns away every time he sees me?"

"Because you weren't ready," she replies. "And neither was your father. So he buried you—buried *us*—to keep you safe until people forgot."

I roll my eyes, frustration bleeding into the moment. *Not this again.* She's had some version of this story for years—of my dad secretly wanting me but just needing to bide his time—only, this is the first time she's brought in things like murder and an over-the-top bad guy to sell the tale.

"Right, because Marcus Montgomery has always been such a thoughtful father."

She tilts her head. "You want to know what I think?"

"No."

She keeps going anyway. "I think that girl out there... Juliette." Her mouth curls around the name like smoke. "She makes you want things again. Things for yourself. Things you haven't even thought of because you've been so worried about me and Brooke."

I tense, not wanting to talk about this with her.

Ma leans forward, her voice silkier now. "Don't deny it, Ry. I *saw* it."

My jaw tics.

"Imagine how much easier it would be to have her if you went back and played the game."

My brows rise, incredulity racing through me. "Now you want me to go back to the town where you claim a man wants to kill me? You've really lost it if you think Marcus would let me come back. We've tried that before, remember?"

She looks at her nails like she doesn't care one way or the other if I go. "So maybe you don't give a choice. Force your father to pull some strings. Let *him* protect you properly."

"You make them sound like comic book villains."

"You play his game, so you can get *her*."

I scoff. "You want me to use her."

"No," she says quickly. "I want you to stop pretending that you don't already care. I want you to have something yourself, after all these years of living for me." Her eyes well up with tears and it digs into my chest and spreads outward in a toxic type of hope. "You don't think I realize all that you've given up?"

I stare at her, the air tense and silent.

"I'm not going back," I say, a finality to my tone. "Last time I listened when you told me to do that, it didn't end well for me."

Her face tightens and she sits back, nodding like it doesn't matter. "Whatever, I'm just trying to help."

Does she not even realize how wishy-washy she sounds? She wants me to get his money, now all of a sudden I'm supposed to go to Rosebrook Falls?

Delusional. Like always.

I drum my fingers on the back of the couch, my pulse ticking up. "Well, you're not. How do you even know all these things?"

"Believe it or not, your father loved me. He used to talk to me about things. I was a safe place for him, and he leaned on me."

Doubtful. I'm not convinced my father has the propensity to love anyone.

I must make a noise, because her eyes soften. "I wasn't always like this, you know?"

My jaw clenches. "Yeah, I know." *I remember.*

She scratches at her arm absentmindedly.

"She doesn't know who I am," I say, although at this point it sounds like I'm trying to convince myself more than her.

Ma tsks. "If you say so."

"I *know* so."

Her lips twitch like she's holding something back. "Then you'd better hope it stays that way, because if she finds out, and she's loyal to her father…" She doesn't finish, letting the implication hang in the air.

I shift, and she keeps going. "Of course, if you *do* want to keep seeing her, you might actually consider what I'm telling you to do. Call your father and maybe you can use what's rightfully yours to get the girl."

I throw my head back and groan. "Here we go."

There's no way in hell I'm having any more of this conversation with her. Not when I'm still reeling from the reality of who Juliette is, and the insinuation of how dangerous her family could be.

I had my hand around her throat, and my fingers in her cunt, and her sweet fucking ambrosia on my tongue, and ignorance really had been bliss.

Now the knowledge feels like a ticking bomb.

"Which is it, Ma? You want his money or you want me to go there and get the girl? Pick a lane."

She lifts a shoulder. "I'm just saying…you've got options."

It's surprising to see her so calm, considering what she just walked in on. But when her head lolls a bit to the side and she sighs, closing her eyes and reopening them slowly, I remember *why* she doesn't care.

Oxy does that to a person. And so does heroin.

"Tell me why you're here." I change the subject. "Or why you stood me up at the coffee shop."

Sighing, she leans back. "I already told you. I'm here to pick up the money for Brooke's seizure medicine."

My chest burns at the reminder of Brooklynn.

"And why was the original money gone, Ma?" I ask, my voice hardening. "Matter of fact, why the fuck is *Brooke* paying for her own meds in the first place? She's seventeen."

Mom straightens on the couch and blinks at me, but she

doesn't have an answer. Or maybe she does but stays silent because she knows I won't like whatever it is.

I smile tightly. "Nothing to say now?"

Her chin lifts, and for just a moment there's guilt floating through her gaze.

And there she is.

Heather Argent.

The mom I used to have.

The one who'd count my teeth while I brushed, and let me stay up late to watch her favorite Disney movies. The one who spun me around until we collapsed into piles of laughter, and who blew bubbles in the living room just to make Brooklynn and me smile, even though the soap soaked into the carpet and made the floor slick for days.

For just a split second, she's real. Like I could reach out and grab her.

And then...gone.

Snapped back into the woman in front of me, the one who got hooked on pain pills and never climbed back out of the hole they threw her in. The one whose eyes are half closed, whose words come a second too late, and who knows how to manipulate silence with the emotions that she caused me to feel.

Or maybe that flicker of guilt was never there at all, and it's just the homesick kid desperate to see a mother who no longer exists.

That seems more likely.

My gut cramps at the thought, and I push it down, down, down.

"You're not insinuating that *I*—"

I smack my hand on the coffee table, and it rattles the few odds and ends on the top.

Ma jumps.

"Don't bullshit me," I bite out. "I'm begging you to be honest. To dig down somewhere deep and show that you still have a shred of decency left. Brooke is your *daughter*, not some bartering tool. That money was for her to have a good life without depending on anyone other than herself. To be able to survive away from all this."

"Away from *me*, you mean."

I blow out an aggravated sigh.

"Yeah," I admit, the word scraping out of me. "Away from you."

The admission hangs there in the space between us. This ugly, heavy, true thing that neither of us wants to look at.

But it's real, and it's there. And at the end of the day, it is what it fucking is.

"If she leaves, then she'll have no one to take care of her."

That breaks the dam inside me, and I narrow my eyes, heat flooding my chest. "Because you're doing such a bang-up job of it now?"

My voice cracks, and I hate how it betrays what I'm feeling.

She's not wrong, though. Brooklynn doesn't know who her dad is. I don't think my mom even knows. The two of us are all she has in the world, and most of the time, she barely has that.

My mom's cloudy eyes meet mine. "That's not fair."

"Life's not fair." I shrug. "Haven't you figured that out yet?"

"Why are you being so mean?" she chokes out, big fat tears rolling down her face.

It hits me right in the fucking heart, but I let the resentment swell. Let it ice over the part of me that still wants to fix her.

"Ry, I'm sorry." She drops her head into her hands, her chipped pink nails clawing at her skin like she's trying to tear herself open. "You know that, don't you? I don't *want* to be like this."

"If you were sorry, you'd get some help." The words catch on my throat like splinters.

"They won't *help* me!" she shrieks, her eyes wild. "If I don't take something, I can't move. And if I go somewhere, they won't let me have what I need. Is that what you want? You want your mother in pain?" A sob escapes her, and she slaps her bony hand over her mouth, trying and failing to hold it in. "You think I want to be this way?"

I drop back against the couch cushions and pinch the bridge of my nose. It's always the same conversation. Her guilt-tripping me, then me begging her to get help, followed closely by her claiming injuries from the accident almost a decade ago make it impossible.

We're at an impasse, and I'm *sick to death* of being on this never-ending carousel. I give everything I make to her because of Brooklynn, but the byproduct of that is enabling this lifestyle. Enabling her to keep killing herself and destroying everything around her in the process. It's a ride I'm desperate to get off of but not sure how to stop.

"I can't do this anymore, Ma. I'm so tired. Aren't you tired?"

She sniffs, shaking her head. "Just give me the money for Brooke's meds and I'll get out of your hair, since I'm such a goddamn inconvenience."

I blink through the sting building behind my eyes. "I'm not

giving you any more money. I'll go with Brooke to get what she needs."

The tears evaporate from my mom's face like she turned off a faucet, a sneer pulling down her lips. "Good luck picking it up from the pharmacy without her legal guardian. I've already called and let them know to withhold it unless I'm there."

What she's saying slams into me like an uppercut to the jaw, and I rear back.

She's playing me.

Holding my little sister's health over my head.

I assumed my mother took the money to buy her next fix, but now I'm seeing this for what it is. This is deliberate. Premeditated. If there's one thing my mom knows about me, it's that I would do anything for my little sister.

My stomach sinks, and I let out a slow breath. "You did this on purpose."

She sniffs again and scratches at her arm, leaning her head back on the couch like she's about to pass out. "Like I said, I don't know what you're talking about."

Fury ripples up my spine, and for the first time in my life, I think I truly hate her.

I shoot to a stand and slam my foot into the coffee table, sending it skidding.

"*Don't* fucking lie to me, Ma."

She jumps, her head snapping up, but then it lolls again. She blinks slowly, and then she smiles. *Smiles.*

"Oh, Roman," she says, her voice syrupy sweet. "Calm down. It's not the end of the world. You could fix all this in a snap…if you'd just listen to your mother."

The name *Roman* grates across my skin, but I don't correct her. She's doing it to get a rise out of me.

"Did you spend it all?" I ask.

She lifts a shoulder and then looks down at her nails like we're talking about the weather.

Betrayal sinks its dagger through my chest, and I swallow the pain.

"I'll make you a deal," she continues, like we're negotiating a car and not my little sister's survival. "You call your father, and I'll make sure Brooklynn never goes without again."

I throw both my hands on my head as I stare at her. "Jesus Christ. Are you *blackmailing* me?"

She grins like it's the most reasonable thing in the world. Like she isn't breaking apart the very foundation of our relationship by forcing my hand.

"I'm protecting us," she corrects. "This family—your sister—deserves better. And he owes us at least that."

"And if I don't?"

She leans in, her eyes sparking. "Then you let him know we'll stop playing dead. And we both know how much your father values his spotless reputation."

Chapter 13

Roman

I GLARE DOWN AT MY PHONE.

It's been sitting in front of me for the past thirty minutes, next to the scrawled number my mom has had memorized for years and left at my apartment. But I haven't had the courage to make the call I need to make.

Talking to my father isn't as easy as just dialing a number and having a "catch-up" moment.

For me, at least.

I have no clue what it will be like for him, but I imagine it's akin to speaking to a ghost. For all intents and purposes, nobody knows I still exist, and I'm under no illusion that I'm anything more to him than a bad memory he'd rather forget.

My issues with him are so deeply rooted, it makes picking up the phone almost impossible.

But then I think about Brooklynn. How she has a mysterious condition that can shift in an instant without warning, and how we have no health insurance.

How even though I covered what she needs, a ninety-day supply of her seizure medication is almost a thousand dollars.

A thousand fucking dollars.

As much as I hate to admit it, my mom is right. Brooklynn isn't his daughter, but he might be the only one who can help her.

My throat tightens, and I shake my head to try and get it together.

Reaching out, I grab my phone, punch in the number from the piece of paper, and press send before I can talk myself out of it.

My leg bounces in time with my elevated heart rate, and it feels as if I'm running a marathon.

One ring.

Two.

I'm going to puke.

Three.

Four.

He's not going to answer.

Right before I hang up the phone, it stops ringing with an audible click.

"Ryder?"

My body reels in shock. I'm surprised he knew my phone number and more surprised at him answering.

His voice is warmer than I expected, but maybe I'm just misremembering it from the last time. We haven't talked since I was nineteen and standing on his doorstep after his wife Eleanor's funeral.

Looking back, I can almost see how my mom sending me then was a knife to the gut, but…still. I'm his *kid*.

"Roman, what are you doing here?"

His face is ghostly white, all of the color drained as he stares at me on his front doorstep.

"Isn't it obvious?"

Ma told me to come, so I did. I figured he'd be glad to see me, and I had hoped that maybe if I waited long enough to show up, he'd finally pull me into the fold. That he'd look at me as the man I became and decide I was worth claiming. Especially now that the woman who forced him to stay away is buried six feet deep.

My dad glances behind him like he's expecting someone, then steps forward, carefully pulling the front door halfway closed. He opens his mouth like he's about to speak when a voice cuts in.

"Marcus?"

A man appears in the doorway. He's older with a starched suit, pasty white skin, and narrowed eyes.

Marcus stiffens. "Go back inside, Freddy."

The man doesn't move, his eyes settling on me like a sniper. Then he pales. "Is that who I think it is?"

My chest clenches, realizing everyone really does assume I'm dead around here.

My father looks like he's about to kill the guy. "Frederick, go inside. Now."

He listens this time and then my dad is closing the front door entirely and rushing toward me.

He grips my arm tightly, and I stiffen my jaw, nostrils flaring at the aggressive hold.

"Let me go." My voice is flat.

He drops my arm like I burned him and runs a hand through his hair, glancing around again. "You can't be here, Roman. You need to leave."

My brows draw in. This isn't going at all like Ma said it would.

"Isn't that..." I swallow around the sudden nerves. "I mean, that's what Ma said. That we just had to stay away until Eleanor was gone and then you'd—"

Love me.

I cut myself off, not willing to say it out loud. Not wanting to admit that after all the years he spent not showing up, he still holds power over me.

His shoulders slump.

"Rom—Ryder, I..." *He runs a hand over his face, pausing on his mouth as he looks at me with pity.* "Go home. Grow up some more, get an education. Be everything I know you can be."

"I thought you'd want me here." *My teeth clench.*

It's pathetic how I almost choke on the words, and I shove the emotion down. The last thing I need is for him to see me as weak.

I can be a Montgomery again; he just has to give me the chance.

He blows out a heavy breath. "It's not the right time, son."

Anger burns in my veins, and my fists clench. "Then when is the right time, Dad?"

"I just lost my wife!" *he explodes.* "Put her still-warm body in the fucking ground, and your mother sent you here? Now?"

He lets out a hollow laugh.

"Go home and stay out of sight. Do not call me unless it's life or death, do you understand? And don't let anybody see you."

His rejection is a harsh punch into my chest, branding my bleeding heart.

"Yeah, Marcus. I understand."

I left him that day with more questions than answers, and I went to the county park with a backpack full of spray paint and a chip the size of Texas on my shoulder.

That's when I met Juliette for the first time.

When I came back to California with my tail tucked between my legs, my mom immediately blamed Eleanor. Said she'd been poisoning his mind against me for years, and if it weren't for her, this wouldn't even be an issue.

And I believed her, because it's easier to hate a villain than to accept the truth. Easier to imagine that someone twisted his love away from me than to admit that maybe he just didn't want me in the first place.

But with age comes wisdom, I guess.

I push the thought of Eleanor away because I can't stand that bitch, and that makes me a piece of shit, because who spends their energy despising someone who's dead?

"Ryder, are you there?" my father repeats.

"Dad," I force out. The word feels like grit on my tongue.

"Is something the matter?" He sounds genuinely concerned, and my guard goes up.

"Does something need to be the matter for me to call my father?" I spit the words like arrows, the deep resentment I normally keep locked up tight bleeding through every word. "Oh, that's right. Life or death only, huh?"

"No." He softens his tone. "You can call me, it's not—"

"I need a favor," I say through clenched teeth, hating myself more with every second.

"Of course, son. Anything."

The words raze over my skin like needles, and I will myself to get through this conversation.

How dare he call me *son*? How dare he even answer my phone call after years of silence? What was all this for if it's so easy for him to answer now?

"I, uh…" Leaning forward, I rest my elbows on my knees, my hand gripping the roots of my hair. I feel sick. "I need some money."

Well, there it is. I said it, and it didn't actually kill me.

My pride still stings like a bitch, though.

"You need money," he repeats.

"Yeah." I clear my throat. "Yes."

I brace myself for his refusal.

"How much do you need?"

My spine straightens. I hadn't expected him to agree so quickly.

I pull the phone away from my ear and look at it, making sure I'm talking to my actual father.

It can't be this easy.

"How much is it worth to you to keep a dead man dead?" I squeeze my eyes shut, my heart thrumming loudly.

This time, there is a slight hesitation before he responds. "Are you sure everything's all right?"

My tongue sticks to the roof of my mouth. *No. Nothing is all right.*

"Everything's fine," I say.

"So, tell me why you need the money."

My heart jolts. "It's Brooklynn."

Now the line goes completely silent, no noise except for the pounding in my ears.

He clears his throat, and then asks, "Is she okay?"

No.

"She's... I don't know how to help her," I say, letting a piece of the truth leak out. "She needs meds and doctors. Better doctors. And I can't—"

There're a few seconds of silence.

"She's sick," he deduces.

A heavy sensation settles in my gut. Some part of me always hoped he'd been keeping tabs all these years. I don't know if it makes me feel better or worse to realize he hasn't.

And yet...there's something in his voice. A flicker of care I didn't expect. Because why would he care about a girl who isn't even his when he can't be bothered to care about the son who is?

"And your mother?" he prompts.

I swallow, my throat thick. "She's...not in a place to help."

"God damnit, Heather," he mutters, more to himself than to me. "Did she put you up to this? You shouldn't let her manipulate you, Ryder. It's what she's always done; it's what she's good at."

Defensiveness thrums inside of me, even though the tang of betrayal from my mom sits on my tongue like sludge. She *is* manipulating me, and she has been for years. It doesn't change the fact, though, that I need money to help Brooklynn.

The thought of telling him that makes me want to throw up.

"Listen, I didn't call to play a catch-up game of twenty questions," I say. "You either *can* or you *can't*. I don't want to waste time if you're not going to help me."

A slight chuckle pours through the line. "You sound just like me at your age. Stubborn as shit."

His words hit me low, just beneath my heart.

I want to scream that I'm nothing like him. But I swallow it down, letting it scrape against my throat like knives instead.

"Then you let him know we'll stop playing dead." My mom's words float through my memory.

"Listen, if you don't help her, then I'll be forced to come visit with all my secrets, ones I'm sure you've spent a lot of time ensuring stay buried."

The words taste acidic as I spew them. But I guess the truth is always a hard pill to swallow.

"Are you threatening me?" His question skates across the air like ice.

I lean back against my couch cushions, staring up at the popcorn ceiling of my apartment. "Just stating the facts, *Dad*. Does it bother you that much to think of me there?"

He's silent for another minute or so, and I'm about to ask if he's even still on the line when he suddenly speaks.

"I'll help. Of course I will. If you had told me sooner, I would have helped then. There's really no need for dramatics."

I jerk upright, my brows shooting up. *What?*

"But you'll have to do something for *me*."

And there it is. The strings attached. Just like I knew there would be.

"What's that?" I ask.

"You need to come home. For good."

The Rosebrook Rag

She's Coming Back, But Not By Choice!

Juliette Calloway is heading home…but don't pop the champagne just yet.

Sources say the youngest Calloway is being dragged back early, skipping her own graduation to play the dutiful daughter at Mommy and Daddy's high-profile political fundraiser for Mayor Franklin Penngrove.

Word is, Juliette's not exactly thrilled about swapping Cali kegs for champagne flutes and fake smiles at her mother's side.

But here's the real tea: Preston Ascott is going to be there.

Looks like the prodigal princess's return might be less family and more setup.

Will we see them reunited in time for the VU Founders' Gala?

#JulietteReturns #CallowayDrama

#PrestonSpotted #RosebrookRag

#PoliticsOrPawns #CallowayWatch

Chapter 14

Juliette

I'M A MESS.

I couldn't sleep last night. No matter how many times I tried to tell myself that Ryder isn't important, that he's nobody to me, my brain wouldn't shut off.

Every time I closed my eyes, I felt his hands on me.

In me.

His mouth.

His voice.

Part of me is glad we were interrupted, even if it was by his mother who acted like I was a cockroach infesting his home.

I'm not a virgin by any stretch of the imagination. I lost it sophomore year in the back seat of Preston's Mercedes. It was awkward, painful, and over before it even really started. And over the years, I've had my share of flings full of random guys and forgettable nights, so I know how to stay detached.

But thinking about Ryder that way feels cheap. Hooking up with him didn't feel casual. It felt raw, like I left pieces of myself behind when it was over.

And that's probably why I'm back at this same coffee shop again, hoping he shows up.

Because apparently, I'm a sucker.

I glare at my to-go cup, fingers picking at the brown paper sleeve that has *The Em-Tee Cup* printed on the side, hating how vulnerable I feel waiting here like a sitting duck.

My phone pings.

FELICITY:

> Tell me you're on your way to get absolutely wrecked by Hot Artist Boy because if you're just getting coffee like a coward, I SWEAR TO GOD.

I tilt my phone like the angle might make her message less aggressive. It doesn't.

ME:

> Obviously I'm here for the ambiance.

My teeth sink into my lower lip, and I type out another one.

ME:

> And to tell him I want to be friends. Heavy emphasis on that last word.

FELICITY:

> BOO. You've been a buzzkill ever since your parents went full Romulan and sabotaged your graduation trajectory.

I roll my eyes at her calling my parents a fictional alien species. She's dubbed my mom a Romulan for years. Something about being manipulative, cold, and probably capable of war crimes.

ME:

Are you watching Star Trek right now? Quit using your weird obsession to psychoanalyze me.

FELICITY:

Let him rearrange your spine and restore balance to the galaxy. Live long and prosper. 🖖

ME:

Sometimes I genuinely wonder if you even like me.

FELICITY:

I love you. That's why I support your journey toward personal growth via orgasm.

ME:

Supportive is a word for it, definitely.

FELICITY:

Just remember that horny girls make bad decisions, but they also make great stories. Call it a character arc and write it into your next book. 🤓

I smirk at my phone and toss it on the table, picking up my coffee and taking a sip.

Someone slips into the seat across from me, and I jerk out of my thoughts, my eyes softening when I see Ryder, grinning at me, cocky as hell, like he knew I'd be here.

"Fate strikes again," he muses.

My heart jumps into my throat, and I clear it. "You're surprised?"

"Not really. Like every good creeper, you've got a pattern. I show up…you follow." He stirs his drink with a wooden stick, somehow making it feel like foreplay. "You're not glaring at me. Should I be concerned?"

A small smile tips up my mouth, and I hide it behind my cup. "You're right. I'll try harder."

He grins, but there's an edge to his expression that wasn't there yesterday. Tension in his shoulders. A question simmering in his gaze.

"I'm glad you came to see me," he says.

"Little full of yourself, Trouble. How do you know I'm not here all the time?"

He leans in, a lock of his hair falling across his brow. "Not likely."

"Why's that?"

"I've been coming here for years. If you had been around, I'd have noticed."

"Maybe you just didn't see me."

He takes a slow sip of his coffee without looking away. "Impossible."

"Is it?"

"There's no world that exists where I wouldn't see you."

Butterflies explode through my stomach and warning bells ring in my ears.

One arm is draped across the back of his chair; his legs are sprawled in front of him like he owns the floor. He seems relaxed, but there's something off about him today. Not that I'm going to ask him about it. That would involve *feelings*, and in my world, we pretend those don't exist.

"Has anyone ever told you that you're a terrible flirt?" I ask.

"Only the ones who end up liking me anyway."

"I think everyone probably likes you," I grumble.

He leans in slightly. "Well, I only care if *you* do."

Our eyes lock and my stomach flips.

"So why did you show up here again?" He reverts into that casual, leaned back pose. "And no lies this time."

I toy with the edge of my sleeve. "Because I wanted to see you again before I left."

He purses his lips. "I wanted to see you, too, so I'm glad you gave into that obsessive little habit of finding me wherever I go."

"You're not hard to find, Trouble. All I have to do is follow the stench of your ego."

He chuckles.

"Why did you want to see *me*?" I ask.

His gaze sweeps over me. "Purely artistic reasons, of course."

I swallow another mouthful of coffee to hide the effect he's having on me. "You didn't finish that sketch already?"

"Maybe I did, maybe I didn't." He shrugs. "I have something for you, actually."

I quirk a brow. "What are the odds?"

He gives me a half smile and reaches into his pocket, pulling out a folded piece of paper.

When he hands it over, our fingers brush. It's a light touch. Barely there, really, but it feels like a spark scorching up my arm and down the length of my spine.

I try not to show it.

"Don't open it," he orders. "Not yet. Wait until you're alone."

His eyes are on my mouth as he says it, and something thuds out of rhythm behind my ribs. The tension hums, thick enough I can reach out and grab it.

"Okay."

There's a pregnant pause and then I ask, "We're friends now, right? Even if we never see each other again?"

Something that looks like disappointment settles over him, but as quickly as it's there, it's gone.

"Yeah, Little Rose," he rasps. "We're friends."

"Okay. Good, that's…good."

"When do you leave?" he asks.

"Soon. Tomorrow."

I try not to dwell on how much it hurts now. How it's somehow worse than when I first found out.

Before it felt like a leash re-collared to a life I was trained to live. Now it's more jagged, like broken pieces ripping down my middle and digging into my sides.

It feels like…a door closing.

A missed opportunity.

Ryder hums, his eyes flashing.

"You done?" He nods to my now empty coffee.

I don't want to admit that I am, because I don't really want this to end, but I nod anyway.

"I'll walk you out."

"Okay."

The word barely leaves my mouth before he downs the last of his own coffee and stands, pushing his chair in with one hand and moving to my side.

From this angle, I'm directly facing his waist, and my eyes drop to his zipper, my stomach flipping when I notice the bulge behind it.

Memories of how it felt under my hand, twitching as I stroked its impressive length, make my mouth dry and my legs tense.

When I drag my stare away, he's giving me a filthy grin.

"You can touch it, if you want."

I blanch, half yelling, "*What?*"

He gives me a look like *I'm* the unhinged one, and then I realize he's holding out his hand, trying to help me up.

Mortified, I slip my fingers in his. "Oh, right. Yeah, let's go."

His head tilts as he pulls me upright. "What'd you think I meant?"

"Exactly what you said." I lift my chin. "Why? What did *you* think I thought you meant?"

His smile grows, eyes dancing. "You're blushing."

"It's *hot*," I snap, ripping my hand from his.

His gaze skims down my body, from my flushed cheeks to my shoes. "No argument there."

I burn even more.

Awesome. Love that for me.

"Where are you parked?"

It takes me a second to reply because his palm is hovering on the small of my back, and it feels like static crawling under my skin, zapping me in slow, torturous pulses until I might drop dead on the floor.

"I walked," I finally get out.

He nods, maneuvering us out of the café and onto the sidewalk. Cars zoom by so closely my hair whips around my face. He glances both ways, then shifts us without a word, putting himself between me and the street.

"Rude." I arch a brow. "What if I *want* to walk on your left?"

He doesn't look at me when he replies, "Then you'll have to be mad about it from the safe side."

A tiny smile tugs at my lips before I can stop it.

It's silly, really. Simple. Barely a thing at all.

But my heart does this ridiculous little flutter anyway, and I step a little closer, letting our arms brush as he threads our fingers together.

That feeling stays the entire way to my apartment, where we say goodbye and joke again about fate.

It's still there the next day as I pack up the rest of my boxes, Felicity crying fat tears and cussing out my entire bloodline, promising to have her minions key every Calloway car and write "Free Juliette" across the country club sign in glitter glue.

I almost dare her to do it, but nothing stops the inevitable.

And somewhere between the airport and the silence of my childhood bedroom, I finally open up the piece of paper Ryder gave me.

It's the sketch.

He *did* finish it.

It's gorgeous, and intricate, and looks nothing like how I see myself in the mirror. He drew me like I'm a story worth telling. A character worth remembering.

I slide it between the pages of my notebook, careful not to

bend the edges because I don't know if I'll ever see him again, but at least I can keep this.

I open to a blank page and begin to write.

Once upon a time, in a city too big for a small-town girl, she met a stranger who reeked of trouble. He drew her like he knew her secrets, and she let herself believe she was something more than just her name. For a moment, she was art.

Chapter 15

Roman

I CAN'T STOP STARING AT THE LAST TEXT FROM Brooklynn.

BROOKLYNN:

Don't talk to me.

ME:

You know I wouldn't leave unless I had to.

BROOKLYNN:

You don't HAVE to, Bear.

My eyes burn when she pulls out the nickname. She knows how to kick me when I'm down, that's for sure.

ME:

I'm doing this for you and Ma, kid.

BROOKLYNN:

> Doesn't feel like it. Feels like you got sick of being broke and went to where the money is.

Sighing, I darken the screen of my phone, slip it in my pocket, and stare out the window of my dad's private car.

The ceiling is stars, the upholstery is a buttery leather, and the driver—Bartholomew—keeps calling me *sir*.

I always knew my father was rich, but damn, had I underestimated what it would feel like to be part of it. It makes Brooklynn's implications burn a hole in my pocket.

A deep-seated hatred takes root, knowing how my sister has had to survive and how my father lives.

The trees blur together as we drive, and when they give way to Victorian-style houses with the Greek alphabet on the fronts, I know we're getting close. Verona University isn't a large school, but tradition holds true, and the various fraternity and sorority houses make up a large part of the campus edges.

Welcome to Rosebrook Falls.

A weird feeling hits me when we reach the actual town limits, like I'm entering an alternate life. Flashes of the *coulda, woulda, shoulda's* play like a movie, and I can't help but wonder what it would have been like if I grew up here instead of in California.

If my father hadn't been married to Eleanor, and had been able to love my mom freely.

My stomach cramps.

"How much longer?" I ask.

"About ten minutes until we're in the HillPoint, and then another five to make it to your father's manor."

"What's the HillPoint?"

Bartholomew's eyes meet mine in the rearview mirror. "The neighborhood your father lives in."

My brows furrow, because I'm not sure that I knew it was called that, but I guess it makes sense. My father's mansion sits on top of a hill, the largest one in the area, like he's looking down on peasants.

We pass by the entry to Verona County Park, and my breath hitches.

Juliette. This is where we first met.

A sick sensation whirls through my middle, because I know what will happen once she sees me again. Part of me is dreading it and the other part is anxious, scratching at my insides like a dog searching for a bone, desperately trying to get to her.

I assume she'll hate me just on principle alone, but I can't help the voice in the back of my head filling me with a sliver of hope.

Maybe if we're in the same town, there's a chance for... *something*.

I should've told her at the coffee shop. I had every chance. She was right there, sipping her drink and letting me flirt with her while I acted like I wasn't the biggest liar she's ever let into her life.

And I didn't say a damn thing. *Coward.*

The car rolls past the county park, and then before long, we're in the town square, historical buildings lining the streets, a grassy area in the center surrounding a large white gazebo.

If I had a nickel for every time the name *Calloway* showed up on a building or plot of land here, I'd be a rich man, but I guess I am anyway, now.

It's obvious when we hit the HillPoint.

Besides there being an actual sign signifying the area, the branding changes from the Calloway name to an intricate *M* with a rose behind it and a sword through the middle, filigree surrounding the image.

There's a white colonial-style building that sits right on the edge of the neighborhood with a faded red sign that says *The Round Table Tavern*.

The sidewalks are smaller. Streetlights flicker, and every few blocks, the lights don't work at all.

This is my father's area—the *Montgomery* area—and it pisses me off to see it not being tended to in the same way as the rest of the town. It isn't like Rosebrook is giant; there's no reason for so much disparity. Apparently, my father's habit of not taking care of the things in his life extends beyond an estranged child.

We creep up a large hill, and even from a distance, I can see my father's manor at the top of it, secluded from the rest of the neighborhood and behind a giant black gate so nobody can reach him.

The gate is a newer addition. When I was nineteen, I was able to make it all the way to the front door before I was turned away, and part of me wonders if maybe it was added *because* of that visit.

My knee bounces in place like a rhythmic clock as the car gets buzzed in through the gate and climbs up the gravel drive, the sound of pebbles crunching underneath the tires loud in my ears.

The driveway is shaped like a U, circling by the front of the mansion, and I stare at the place, frozen in my seat as the car rolls to a stop.

The house itself is nice, the upkeep far surpassing what we just drove through at the bottom of the hill, and another bit of resentment buzzes in my ear like a gnat.

It's Tudor-style architecture with so much green foliage, it's climbing up the walls. There's light-brown stucco on the front with darker brown wood pieces placed strategically to create a pattern of squares on the surface, and a wraparound deck that's half hidden behind meticulously trimmed bushes.

I'm frozen in place. *When I get out, everything will change.*

My phone buzzes in my pocket and I grab it, desperate for an excuse to put this off.

MA:

You there yet?

I grit my teeth and reply.

ME:

Yeah.

MA:

Remember what I said. Let him protect you. This is meant to be YOUR empire, Roman. Don't forget who put you there. And if you see Juliette Calloway, don't let a little thing like names get in your way.

Inhaling deeply, I reach out to open the car door and enter my new life, my heart in my throat, but before I can, Bartholomew is there swinging it open for me.

This is a different world.

I step into the crisp evening air, calm infusing itself into the moment.

It's quiet, other than the gravel crushing underneath my shoes. I crack my neck, the anxiety rolling off my shoulders. My thumb spins my ring on my forefinger, and I wish I had a joint to calm the nerves.

A flash goes off in the distance from the direction of the gate, and I turn toward the quick light but don't see anything.

"What was that?" I ask Bartholomew.

He turns to look in the direction I was. "What was what, Mr. Montgomery?"

I give him a sharp look.

"Roman," he corrects.

"You didn't see that flash?"

His bushy salt-and-pepper brows furrow, and he squints but then shakes his head. "Probably paparazzi from *The Rosebrook Rag*." He gives me a worn and tired look. "I'll have Frederick keep any photos from the press."

I don't know who Frederick is, but I don't ask questions. It's not surprising my father would have someone who knows how to control the media.

"Pop the trunk, Bartholomew. Guess I should get this over with."

He looks affronted. "I'll have your luggage taken inside, sir. You just go on in."

Oh. Right.

"Great," I say, acting like I know the first thing about having the type of money where people literally do everything for you.

It's a little off-putting, to be honest.

He tips his hat. "Have a good night, sir."

"Yeah, you, too," I reply. But my attention is already off him.

Is my father inside waiting?

Does he even care enough to be here?

I focus on the front doors, so large I have to crane my neck to stare at the top of them as I make my way up the porch.

One swings open and a young man walks out, his blond hair perfectly swooped, and a movie-worthy grin pasted on his suntanned face.

It's been years since I've seen him, but it doesn't matter. My mom rammed the idea of who my family is through my brain from a young age, showing me pictures and videos she collected from various news sources.

I'd recognize this guy from a mile away.

Benjamin Voltaire.

Eleanor's nephew and my dad's by marriage. Technically, my cousin, although we aren't blood related.

Last time I saw him, he was a kid, two years older than me, and I only ever interacted with him from a distance. I'm not sure if he even knew about my existence.

Still, the bitterness churns up like it's fresh. I remember being furious that Benjamin was treated like a son—that he got to experience my father in a way I never did.

Maybe because he's a Voltaire, so money was already in his blood.

The private schools, the summers on yachts, the nepotism that allowed him a life of advantage while others had to beg for scraps.

Privilege.

The kind you're born with, not the kind you work for.

"Roman fucking Montgomery."

It's a jolt to my system hearing my old name pouring from his lips, but I guess I should get used to it. Ryder Speare died the second I stepped on that private jet.

"Benjamin," I say coolly, tipping my chin. "I wondered if I'd see you here."

That's a lie. He hadn't even crossed my mind.

His brows rise high on his forehead, and his upper body leans back like my words surprise him.

"So, you *do* know who I am," he says. "I knew you, too, but hell, man, we thought you were dead." He laughs. "And it's *Benny*, by the way."

Before I can respond, a honey-slick voice cuts in from our right.

"Benny, don't be rude."

She's tall, with strawberry blond hair, and dressed like she walked out of a fashion magazine. She eyes me like she already knows everything there is to know about me, and she doesn't quite trust what she sees.

Benny throws an arm over her shoulder, and tugs her into his side harshly, whispering in her ear. "I thought I told you to stay in my room."

She shrugs, her eyes never leaving mine. "I got curious."

He grimaces and then looks at me. "Roman, this is Rosalie Bault."

She puts out a hand, and I take it. Her grip is firmer than expected. "You're his girlfriend?"

"His better half," she corrects.

"And I'm the prettier half," comes another voice, as a tall man with light-brown skin and short, wavy black hair walks into the room.

I watch him come closer, amused at how jovial he seems.

"*You* must be the Montgomery back from the dead," he says, giving me an exaggerated once-over. "God, I love a good family scandal."

Rosalie sighs. "Merrick, please."

"What?" he asks, eyes still on me. "I'm being welcoming."

"You're being dramatic," Benjamin pipes in.

Merrick slings an arm around my shoulder, mirroring Benjamin's hold on Rosalie.

"Welcome to Montgomery Manor." He winks. "And welcome to the family. *Officially*."

Benjamin grips Rosalie's hand in his and they both follow as Merrick walks me down a hall. I school my features as I take in the interior of my father's home, and another shot of something bitter hits me in the gut. All these years, and this is the first time I've ever stepped foot inside.

The foyer alone is the size of my entire apartment back in California, and it's sleek and stunning. Beige walls contrast beautifully against the shiny cedar floors, and a gorgeous stairwell is the focal point of the room. Just beyond it is an open archway with two long, thin steps showcasing a sprawling living area with floor-to-ceiling windows and dark wood banisters that line the vaulted ceiling.

It *feels* wealthy here. Like the floor itself is too expensive for me to walk on. I want to crawl out of my skin, discomfort raging through me.

"So," Merrick says, "how long before Roman figures out we're all fucked in the head?"

"I already figured that out," I mutter, smirking at him.

He grins. "Good. Then you'll fit right in."

Chapter 16

Roman

"UNCLE M, YOUR LONG-LOST SON'S ARRIVED."

I bristle at the words. *Lost* is a generous definition.

"Come in," my dad's gruff voice calls out.

Rosalie and Merrick have wandered off somewhere, and Benjamin swings open the door, waving his arm through the air as if he's giving me permission to walk inside.

When I do, I meet my father's gaze for the first time in four years, and just like his voice did on the phone, the warmth on his face catches me off guard.

He's dressed down, and his hands are poised over a keyboard, halted in midair like the sight of me has frozen him solid. Slowly, he thaws, a small smile tilting the edges of his mouth.

"Roman. You're here."

I move forward, not sure how to navigate the situation. I expected aloofness, and he's giving me the opposite. I take a seat in front of his desk, arching a brow. "Isn't this where you told me to be?"

He doesn't reply right away, just watches me as he leans

back in his chair, his hand rubbing at his chin. He looks the same as he did four years ago but older. His blond hair is tinged with white, and his frown lines are deeper. His face is a little more haunted, maybe. Gaunt, even.

"I wasn't sure you'd take me up on the offer," he admits.

"I wasn't sure if I would, either," I reply. "Considering it took you twenty-three years to make it."

Something flashes in his gaze, and his mouth tightens. "You're angry with me."

My chest squeezes. Leaning forward, I rest my elbows on my knees and stare at him unwaveringly. "I'm not sure there's a word in the English language that describes how I feel."

"That's fair." He nods like he understands. Like what he did wasn't the foundational experience that formed my life and how I live it. "But you're here anyway."

"I'm here anyway," I echo.

"And you're planning to stay?"

Tumultuous emotions run rampant through me, but I grit my teeth and nod. "Do I have a choice?"

"You always have a choice."

That's bullshit. The fact he's creating some illusion now is laughable.

You're doing this for Brooklynn, I remind myself.

"Can I ask you something?" I say.

He hums and bobs his head.

"Why do you even have me coming back here? What's your angle? It can't just be because you want to parade me around like a *long-lost* son, is it?"

I use the same words Benjamin did intentionally, gauging my father's reaction.

"You *are* my son," he retorts in a harsh tone. "That's not a parade, it's a fact."

"One you sent away with a fake name and a mom holding a bottle of oxy for the pain."

Stupid. I hadn't meant to word-vomit everything, but I don't see a point to keeping it all in. If I'm here, then I want to know why, and I deserve the gritty details, even if I'll hate hearing about them.

Shock coasts through his gaze. "I didn't have a choice about sending you away. It was the right decision, and I won't apologize for it."

I scoff, looking away from him, but my mother's words from the other day play in the back of my mind. Tales of attempted murder and tampered brakes.

His chair creaks as he leans forward. "Whether or not you believe me, I've always had your best interest at heart."

My heart stutters, but I grit my teeth.

"If your mother had warned me you were coming to visit all those years ago, I could have handled things more delicately."

"What, because you didn't want anyone to see us and find out about your mistakes?" I spit out, my gaze narrowed.

He frowns. "Because I could have protected you better."

"So, you're saying it wasn't a complete accident then?" I lift my chin, swallowing over the knot in my throat.

My father steeples his fingers and gives me a sad smile. "Men will do many things when they're blinded by greed and anger."

I snort. "That's a nice line, but it doesn't answer my question."

"For years, I convinced the Calloways the Montgomery line would end with me. Craig is in bed with some…less-than-savory people, and I had no interest in bringing you around when you weren't old enough to make the choice. When your mother brought you here on a whim, Craig realized you existed, and I did what I had to do to ensure that no other attempts on your life would be taken."

My world tilts on its axis. "So...what, this whole time you've been *protecting* me?"

"You're my flesh and blood. The only one capable of carrying on my legacy. I needed to keep you safe from him until you were old enough to hold your own. This town..." He shakes his head. "It isn't for the weak. We have to play our cards right or else everything will be stolen from us. It already *is* being stolen from us."

He uses *us* so easily, as though I've always been a part of him. And if I have, well then, that's news to me. My teeth clench so tightly, my jaw aches.

I'm not sure if I believe him.

I want to, though.

Badly.

Sniffing, I crack my neck. "And now I'm old enough to hold my own?"

He blinks. "Now...you're old enough to have the choice."

His words are arrows dipped in poison, spreading through my veins like branches on a tree. They smack against the old bruise he left when I tried to come here as a nineteen-year-old, begging for him to recognize that just because he wanted me to play dead didn't mean I actually *was*.

"I don't understand how things can change, how you go from one end of the spectrum to the other. You didn't want me here, and now you do? It doesn't track."

"Frederick's been on me for months," he admits. "Thinks you need to be here to make a statement."

My brows furrow, trying to place the name. "The man who saw me last time I was here?"

He nods. "My lawyer. He'll be thrilled you've returned just in time for the Founders' Gala."

I make a face. "I don't really have any interest in that."

"Tough shit. If you're here, you'll play the part. Representing the Montgomery name at the biggest annual event in the town is *the* part."

His tone leaves no room for argument, so even though the retort burns in my throat, I swallow it down.

For Brooke.

"I don't want to live here at the manor with you," I state.

"That's fine. I own plenty of property in the HillPoint. We'll set you up somewhere private."

"And I don't want to work at your shitty construction company," I add. "Or any of the others. I don't know the first thing about running a business."

"You won't need to. Not right now, anyway." He shrugs. "But one day you'll be expected to take it over, so get used to the idea."

"Great," I say, my tone flat.

"Good." My father grins. "I'll expect you to stay the night, at least. Freddy will be here in the morning with the papers."

"What papers?"

"The ones that will make you a Montgomery again. Officially."

Frederick Lawrence is an older man, mid-fifties maybe, with graying hair at his temples. He wears checkered argyle socks, shiny brown shoes that click when he walks, and a hat that reminds me of the 1940s gangsters in the movies.

Apparently, he's my father's most trusted confidant, despite him also being the attorney for the Calloways.

How the hell Frederick worked that out, I have no clue.

"So, what is it I'm looking at?" I peer at the papers in front of me.

"This is a trust agreement," Frederick says. "Yours, more specifically. It outlines your shares in the Montgomery Organization, as well as the assets your father has allocated to you. It also has a stipend you'll receive monthly, with the entirety of funds and shares in the Montgomery Organization being released to you on either your twenty-fifth birthday or should something happen to your father."

I swallow. There's about to be more wealth at my fingertips than I could even dream of, and the knowledge makes me feel sick to my stomach.

"Do I need to sign it?" I ask.

Frederick smiles and shakes his head. "Nope, it's always been in place. The only thing you need to sign is the petition to have your name changed back legally."

I furrow my brows. "How long does that take?"

Frederick glances at my father. "I've got some friends who owe me favors that will push it through."

Blowing out a breath, I lean forward and grab a pen, signing my name where he directs me.

"There is one more thing for you to sign, actually." He pushes another pile of papers toward me.

"What's this?" I ask.

"An agreement. If you leave Rosebrook Falls, or if you pass away, then you forfeit your inheritance."

"Why the hell would I sign that?"

Frederick chuckles. "It's just added insurance, really, to make sure you don't come here for a few weeks, get bored, and decide to head out again, taking everything with you."

I scoff. "So if I'm gone, and *he* dies..." I point to my father. "Who gets the money?"

My father clears his throat. "It would go into Freddy's name so he can disburse everything back into the town."

My brows rise. "I don't know why you think I'd want to sign that."

"Because the second you do, I'll put *this* trust in place," my father states, nodding toward his lawyer.

A new page slides across the desk, and this one has Brooklynn's name. Her real name.

Harper Argent.

"Your sister's trust."

My lungs collapse then expand, something deep inside me rattling loose.

Is it that easy?

"You'd give her this, even though she isn't yours?" I ask.

He shrugs. "If she's important to you, then she's important to me."

"Why haven't I had this trust the entire time again?" I ask, narrowing my eyes at my father.

"You did," he said. "I've had this in place for you since you were born. But your mother..."

He trails off, looking to the side.

"My mother *what*?"

"I couldn't allow a paper trail. You have to understand, all of this was to try and shield you. I shouldn't have even let her keep my phone number."

I rub my temples, leaning forward and resting my elbows on my knees. "And now you're using it as a bartering tool."

"Things are never in black and white, Roman," Frederick says, standing up straight and clapping me on the back. "Unless you're planning on dying or running off, you have nothing to worry about. And neither will your sister."

"Why now?" I ask. "Why did you agree so willingly? And don't give me the 'my choice' bullshit. There's something else here."

Sorrow passes through my father's gaze. "I'm sick."

His words hit me like a sledgehammer, but I mask the look on my face. "You look fine to me."

He grimaces. "Prostate cancer, unfortunately. Stage four. It's in my bones. My liver. My brain."

I sit with the words for a few moments, but I'm not sure what to say. What to do. I hadn't expected this. Should I feel sorrow? Grief? *Will I miss him?* I don't think so. How do you miss a person you've never really known?

I've mourned the loss of my father for years. This is nothing new.

My father leans forward, and I take in how pallid his skin is. How his frame is lean and frail beneath his outfit. How there are bags under his eyes that make him look like he's been running from something for years and is tired of the fight.

"I want to *give* you my legacy."

My back hits the chair, and I exhale heavily, running a

hand through my hair. "This is…this is a lot. How long do you have?"

He lifts a shoulder and shares a heavy look with Frederick. "We're not sure. Months, maybe?"

"Do people know?"

Another look with Frederick. "No."

I think about my mom, and I wonder if this will be the thing that sends her over the edge. I've seen her at what I thought was rock bottom, but there's a new fear brewing. If the man she's been obsessively in love with for my entire life is dead…there might be farther to fall.

"I want Brooke's trust to go to her immediately. None of this 'once she's twenty-five' bullshit. You give her the funds. You get her health insurance. You auto pay it every year. That's the deal, or I'll leave and never look back."

It's a risk to make demands from my situation, but if they want me here as badly as they say, then I have some bartering power.

"Done," my father agrees.

Frederick places a large hand on my shoulder and squeezes. "This is a good thing, I think."

Blowing out a breath, I resign myself to my fate, my eyes skimming over the trusts that will be put in place for both me and my little sister.

As long as I stay, that's the deal.

I sign the papers. And just like that, my fate is sealed.

The Rosebrook Rag

SPOTTED: A Midnight Mystery at Montgomery Manor

Is Marcus Montgomery making a comeback, or just cleaning house?

The former kingpin of Rosebrook Falls, silent and reclusive for the past few years, just opened his gates for a mystery man dressed in black.

Even juicier? He was personally escorted by Benjamin Voltaire, Marcus's very polished nephew.

So who's the guy bold enough to stroll into Montgomery Manor under the cover of night?

We're not sure. We didn't get the pictures.

But one thing's for sure: the house that built an empire doesn't open its doors for just anyone.

#MontgomeryWatch #WhoIsHe

#BenjaminVoltaire #RosebrookRag

#MontgomeryMoves

Chapter 17

Juliette

THE SHEETS IN MY BED ARE SO SOFT THEY FEEL like cashmere. I stretch slowly, muscles tensing and releasing as I luxuriate in the feel and listen to the birds chirp in the early morning air outside. It's dark in my room, but that's thanks to the blackout curtains that cover the private balcony.

I grab my phone from the end table and swipe it open. There's a text from Felicity, grinning like a fool, decked out in her cap and gown. She has a cardboard cutout of me propped proudly at her side, her arm slung over it.

It's possibly the worst picture of me in existence, and she swore that she deleted it. I'm mid-glare, wrapped in my fuzzy all-pink onesie, fresh off a forty-eight-hour NyQuil bender and looking like I've just clawed my way out of a crypt.

Even worse, she's added some fake lashes and drawn a giant margarita in my hand.

FELICITY:

Since you bailed, I brought your cardboard

> twin instead. She's stiff, but at least she didn't argue. Total doormat. Either way… WE DID IT! Happy Graduation Day, Jules! Wish you were here. 💌🎓🍸

I chuckle, but the ache in my chest creeps in fast, and I attempt to rub it away. I wish I could be there, and her text only reminds me that we didn't get to close this chapter of our lives together.

ME:

> If I'd known you had that cutout, I wouldn't have shown up to half the shit you dragged me to.

Sighing, I toss my phone down and yank the comforter over my head, sinking into the pillows, and resisting the urge to grab it so I can search Ryder's name again. I've been trying to find him ever since I opened that sketch, and I'm so mad at myself for not at least getting his number.

I give in, grabbing my cell and tapping it awake, opening a browser.

Just to check.

Burrowing my head beneath the covers again, I type: Ryder, brownish-black hair, artist

Nothing.

I chew on my lip, brows furrowed, and add: hot.

Rolling my eyes at myself, my stomach tightens as the results load.

Nothing.

I delete that and try: Ryder. Artist. Rosebrook Falls.

My teeth tear into my lip as I wait.

Still no Ryder, but one headline grabs my attention.

The ROSEBROOK Rag

Breaking: Preston Ascott Says He's Back...for Her?

Sources say Rosebrook's former golden boy Preston Ascott is telling close friends he's "ready to try again" with none other than his high school sweetheart Juliette Calloway, who just landed back in town.

Coincidence? We think not.

But will Juliette take the bait? Or is Prescott going to become the next most eligible bachelor of Rosebrook Falls?

#JulietteReturns #PrestonAscott

#SecondChanceSwoon #CallowayWatch

#RosebrookRag

I stare at the screen, pulse ticking in my throat.

Perfect. Just what I need.

Seconds later, my door opens, footsteps scurrying into the room followed by the squeaky wheels of a rolling tray.

I got in late last night, so I haven't seen anyone yet, but I'd know the sound of that gait anywhere.

Beverly.

She flutters about the room, and even though I can't see her, I can imagine exactly what she looks like. Long blond hair in a tight bun on the top of her head and a sharp jaw that makes her perma-frown more pronounced. Cool brown eyes that can communicate any emotion with a single look.

I can *feel* her glaring at me right now through the blankets.

Picturing it makes me grin. Growing up, she'd always stand at the foot of my bed with her hands on her wide hips and a practiced look of exasperation on her face as she'd try to get me up for school. She'd smack my feet and tell me to stop playing dead or I'd get stuck like that one day.

Morbid, but it always got the point across.

She's the closest thing to a real mother that I've ever had, and since I barely came home over the past four years, I've missed her something fierce.

There was never a day of my life growing up when Beverly wasn't taking care of me. She showed up in town asking for a job right before I was born, so I'm closer to her than any of my brothers, but we all love her.

"Rise and shine, you faker."

Her voice is sharp but melodic, and joy infuses my chest. Still, I don't move from under the covers.

I can't make it *that* easy on her after all this time.

"Enough." A slap on my foot jolts my body. "I can see the light from your phone, liar."

"Ouch," I whine as I toss the comforter off me. "Still violent as ever. You know, I think they have therapy for that."

She narrows her eyes. "Do they have therapy for how to get

the pain out of my ass, too? Or is that something that's a Juliette special, forced on me for the rest of my godforsaken life?"

I beam at her. "I missed you, too, Bevie."

Beverly gives me a soft look that contradicts the harshness of her words. "We don't have time for dramatics, child. Get up and act like you didn't forget all the manners I've taught you."

She throws a robe at me, and I grab it, standing and slipping it on, knotting the tie around my waist. "I could never forget you, Bevie. Your screeching voice is forever burned into my memory."

"Good."

She walks away from me and over to a pale-green rolling cart parked near the doors to my balcony, grabbing a mug and making me a cup of coffee. "Either get up now or risk the wrath of your mother when she sees you still in bed."

My grin drops, and I groan audibly, walking to the chaise next to her and falling down on it with a huff. I was hoping I wouldn't have to see my mom right away. "She's coming in *here*? Now?"

"Enough of that," Beverly chides softly as she hands me the cup.

"You *do* love me." I sit back up and grasp the coffee, inhaling the fresh aroma. I take a sip, relishing the heat as it scorches my tongue.

Beverly's already moving somewhere else, throwing open the door to my large walk-in closet that sits to the right of my en-suite bathroom.

"Say it," I demand. "Tell me you love me, or I'll think you don't."

She snorts from the other room, and then she's sticking her head around the doorframe. "Your constant need for verbal affirmation is exhausting."

Laughing, I move to the wall, hitting the keypad that opens the automated curtains, revealing the pool out back and the grassy area of the backyard just beyond it. My room is on the second floor, and if I step out onto the balcony, I can see beyond our personal tree line to the hills that surround the valley of Rosebrook Falls.

It's a gorgeous day, the sun shining brightly and reflecting off the water, creating prisms of sparkle that ricochet into the air. There are a few people milling about down there, and my stomach twists, knowing they're setting up for the Penngrove fundraiser.

I pout, sitting back down on my chaise and resting my chin in my hand. "How am I supposed to know about your love if you don't say the words?"

"You're an adult, Juliette. Act like it."

"You're right," I say. "I know you do, anyway. Don't forget that I know all about your secret phone calls and art tickets."

Beverly's in my closet, so she doesn't respond.

"I need to find my own place. Being here makes me feel like I'm twelve again," I say to myself as I sip my coffee.

My eyes float over to my phone that's still on my nightstand, wanting to continue searching for Ryder.

Now I'm annoying myself.

I will *not* be that girl.

Beverly walks out of my closet pulling a rack on wheels bursting with colorful garments.

"So, why exactly is Mother Dearest planning to come accost me today?" I ask.

Beverly gives me a disapproving look. "Your mother would like to help you prepare for today's festivities."

I make a face.

"Stop that," she admonishes. "She's going—"

Footsteps sound from outside the door, and my spine stiffens. Beverly's eyes hint at panic, her mouth forming a tight line as she turns fully to the dresses she's sifting through.

The bedroom doors swing open, and in walks my mother, her arms out at her sides and her chin lifted like nothing can touch her.

Cold and aloof. The same way she's always been.

"Juliette." She barely even glances at me as she says it.

"Hello, Mother." *Nice to see you, too.*

She looks every bit the proper socialite and queen of Rosebrook Falls that you would expect. Bespoke clothing that whispers its luxury like the passage of time hasn't come close to aging her. Brown hair slicked back into a classic French twist, so tight it pulls at her temples. Red lips and nails that contrast starkly against her fair skin. A perpetual frown that proves she is the pioneer of resting bitch face.

Her eyes soak me in—not with the gaze of a loving mother, but with the perusal of someone who's judging what they see.

She's *always* judging what she sees when it comes to me. You'd think after so many years, I'd have built up an impenetrable wall that makes me immune to her stare, but as much as I hate to admit it, her opinion still affects me.

It always has, and it always will.

"Hmm." She crosses her arms, and her fingers are so bony that the oval shapes of her nails make her look like she has claws. She taps one against her sleeve, and I imagine her digging those talons into my chest and ripping out my heart like a she-devil.

That would make a good fantasy story.

She tilts her head and then frowns before she spins around, her navy-blue pencil skirt clinging perfectly to her physique, one that she's honed with daily Pilates and a very regimented diet.

I know because she always expected the same of me.

She clicks her tongue as she walks toward the rack of clothing. "Beverly, these outfits are atrocious."

"I'm sorry, ma'am," Beverly replies, inclining her head. "They were sent by your personal stylist yesterday."

Mom makes a face of disappointment while she holds one of the dresses and slips her other palm down the side of it like she's inspecting it for imperfections.

If there's one thing that Martha Calloway is good at, it's finding the flaws in everything.

I should know.

"She has to look flawless," my mom continues, proving my point.

Then she turns toward me.

"You have to look flawless," she reiterates.

Swallowing another mouthful of coffee, I nod and beam at her. "Should be easy since I'm naturally perfect."

The joke falls flat.

My eyes fling from her to Beverly, who's now standing in the corner of the room with her head tilted down and her fingers clasped together like she's waiting on my mother's next command.

That's what's expected at the Calloway estate, but it still irritates me to see it.

"Juliette," my mother snaps, and my stare slingshots to hers. "Are you paying attention?"

"Yes, Mother. Unfortunately, you make it impossible to ignore you." Sighing, I place my coffee down on the tray table and walk toward her.

Her lips pinch tight, small vertical lines from years of smoking in secret becoming more pronounced around the shape of her mouth.

I stand straight and wait for her to pick me apart. There's no use fighting her; arguing with my mom is like banging my head against a reinforced concrete wall. One with spikes. It does nothing but fuel her, yet somehow, I always end up broken and bloodied.

A blue dress is in her hands, and she holds it up to me, frowning, stretching out the sides like she's trying to make it fit against my front. "You've gained weight."

My jaw tenses, and I stiffen my back, not responding.

This is the type of bullshit I did *not* miss.

She shakes her head, tossing the gown haphazardly into Beverly's hands.

"You'll come with me to Pilates tomorrow," she states.

Another dress. This time a light pastel pink. My favorite color. "Sure, Mom. Whatever you want."

We both know she won't make me actually go. I'm sure this is the only time this month we'll have one-on-one time. She's a virtual ghost in my life, only appearing when absolutely necessary.

Any extra energy she does have goes toward my brothers.

"I guess this is as good as it will get." She holds the pink gown to my front, her head tilting, lips pursing in distaste. "We'll need an entirely new wardrobe for the Founders' Gala. I had given measurements based off what you *should* be, not where you clearly are."

"I think it's pretty," I reply, ignoring her jabs about what I'll be wearing to the most obnoxious event of the town.

The dress for today is knee length and sleeveless, the pink fabric flowing like a waterfall.

My mother's eyes meet mine. "Preston will be here."

I frown, remembering that stupid tabloid post earlier. "Preston, as in my *ex*-boyfriend?"

"He's the governor's son."

"Yeah, I'm aware." My voice is flat. "Who invited him? I don't want to see him."

She looks at me as though I've lost my mind. "His father's up for reelection, and you know how important it is for whoever holds that seat to be someone your father backs. Preston is an upstanding gentleman, and he's eager to see you again."

I scrunch up my nose. "Is all that supposed to mean something to me?"

"Don't be ungrateful," she snaps. "You can hardly blame a man for wanting to go out into the world and make something of himself. It's knowing he always comes home that's important, and Preston is ready to come home, Juliette."

Her hand runs along the length of the dress, tilting her head to the side as she keeps it pressed to my front.

"Your father and I always liked the two of you together. He was a fine boy, and he's turned into a powerful man. You'd do well to be on his arm."

She gives me a severe look, and I get the message loud and clear.

Play your part.

Suddenly, the main reason for me being at this fundraiser instead of graduation makes perfect sense.

"Bevie," I say over my shoulder. "Can you open the window? It's feeling a little seventeenth century-ish in here."

My mother's frown deepens, and I grin at her, wide and obnoxious. "Just joking."

She sighs again, looking at the pink dress a final time before giving a sharp nod and handing it off to Beverly.

"Is anyone else home?" I ask her, hoping she says my brothers are here to see me.

I'm not naive enough to believe my father would be. Busy men don't have time to spend at home with their families; that's another life lesson my mother taught me at a young age, and it's one that's proven true.

"Don't be ridiculous. They're all living their lives. You'll see them later today at the party."

I suck on my lips to keep from saying something out of turn.

"Try not to cause any trouble in the meantime, hmm?" My mother watches me with an unreadable expression, her hand cupping my cheek.

My chest pinches, and I lean into the touch, surprise flowing through me.

"And don't eat that breakfast Beverly brought in." Her eyes trail up and down my form. "We're trying to make you *fit* in that dress, dear."

Chapter 18

Juliette

A modern-day cursed queen with ice in her veins, wearing a crown forged from the bones of those she's killed.

Death by Pilates: her favorite way to watch them go.

She smells of roses and arsenic, and when the princess disappoints her—which is often—she flashes those bright red talons. The princess often wonders if one day she'll dig them into her chest and rip out her heart, the same way she does to all the other people who annoy her.

Just another casualty bleeding in the name of perfection.

"WELCOME HOME, BABY CALLOWAY."

My cousin Tyler drops his arm across my shoulders, dragging me out of my head, where I was busy crafting the perfect villain origin story for my mother.

The smell of vodka is strong on his breath. So strong, in fact, that it makes my nose scrunch.

"Ugh," I complain, elbowing him in the side. "You reek, Ty."

Tyler grins cheekily at me, his strawberry-blond hair dropping across his forehead. "Just celebrating your homecoming."

"I don't know why. Nobody else is here for me."

Tyler's smile falters, and he squeezes me tighter to his side.

I've been poked and prodded until my hair is perfect, and my makeup is flawless, and the whole time, I've been trying my best not to stew in the fact that none of my brothers have even come by to say hi, and I have no real friends in the area until next week when Felicity comes home. Hopefully *sans* her boyfriend Keagan.

At least my dress is pretty. I run my hands over the soft pink fabric.

The late-afternoon sun casts a bright glow over the courtyard, and the light catches on deep, purplish-black shading underneath Tyler's eye.

I jerk forward, gripping his chin and yanking him closer. "What happened?"

Tyler flinches before covering it up with a smirk. He taps me on the head like I'm a pet and coos, "Don't worry your pretty little heart about it."

"I can't just *not* worry about it now that I've seen it."

"Sure you can," he replies, gesturing toward the groups of dressed-up people scattered around the pool in the middle of the courtyard. "Just pretend you're like every other member of your family."

I frown. "*Our* family, you mean. And that's not fair."

"Things usually aren't."

Scoffing, I cross my arms. "Have you been fighting with Lance again?"

It's not out of the ordinary—at least, it didn't used to be. It's possible that things have changed in my absence. Back when I was growing up, though, he and Lance were always attached at the hip, for better or for worse. They used to spend weekends practicing everything they learned in their Jeet Kune Do class, then trudging through the place with goose eggs on their foreheads and deep bruises on their ribs.

Tyler snorts. "Lance *wishes* he could land a punch like this."

I smirk at him, because Lance could beat the shit out of him. I don't know anyone Lance *couldn't* fight and win. He's been trained since he was five years old, and although Tyler's got repressed anger issues that could put down an elephant, fighting is Lance's outlet; it always has been.

"So, it's not from him?" I push.

Tyler's grin drops. "I don't want to talk about it."

"And I want to wake up with a mother who loves me," I reply sarcastically. "Tough shit."

He sighs. "I may or may not have gotten into an argument with Benjamin Voltaire, remember him? Fucking Montgomery *trash*."

Tyler spits the last name out like a curse, but it isn't surprising to me. He hates the Montgomerys on principle, and when it comes to Benjamin—the guy who's dating his sister—sometimes I swear his anger outweighs even my dad's.

"And he *hit* you?" I inspect his black eye. "For what?"

"Because he's a piece of shit, Juliette." He lets out another sigh, dragging a hand through his hair. "I tried to talk to Rosalie, and he...intervened."

"*What?*" My voice sharpens. "He wouldn't let you talk to your own sister? What did Rosalie do?"

He gives me a look. "Just sat there and stared at me with those big puppy dog eyes."

I frown. "That doesn't sound like her."

"Yeah." Tyler's jaw tenses. "I don't know what he's done to her, but it's like she's not even there anymore. She just smiles, and nods, and lets him pull her strings. It's pathetic."

He glances around and then lifts his shirt.

My eyes widen when I see the gun at his waist in a holster. "What the hell is that, Ty? Do you even know how to use a gun?"

He shrugs. "Protection."

"I can't believe you brought that here."

"Preston here yet?" he replies, peering around with his hand over his eyes.

He's clearly trying to change the subject, and it works.

I scowl. "How did you hear about that already?"

He smirks. "I know everything that goes on around here. Besides, Preston's got a big mouth; he's been spouting off for weeks that he's about to 'claim' you again."

"Yeah, I saw the *Rag*."

I glance around the courtyard.

Paxton's under the covered patio talking with a few people I've never seen, and Alex is leaning against the Roman-style column next to him, smiling like he hasn't got a care in the world.

Rude that they're here and yet they haven't even come by to say hi.

My mother flits around in another one-of-a-kind outfit, a gorgeous, emerald summer gown this time, laughing at something Mayor Penngrove is saying. I'm sure both her and my father are using this as an opportunity to blackmail people into donating to his campaign so they can keep him in power. He's been in my dad's pocket for years; no reason for that to change now.

"Where *is* Lance?" I ask.

I skim the area again like maybe I just missed him.

Tyler shrugs, but he avoids my eyes. "You know he doesn't like coming to these things."

"Yeah, but…"

It's me.

I don't say the last part out loud, but I guess I'm showing it on my face, because Tyler gives me a pitying look and says, "Lance is a dick."

Suddenly, he clicks his tongue and gestures toward the giant sliding doors leading to the veranda. "Speak of the devil…"

I follow where he's pointing, relief whipping through me when Lance appears in the crowd. He's not alone; his best friend Art is right there by his side, and as they get closer, I do a double take.

Art was always kind of scrawny and scrappy, but that's definitely changed. Now he's broad shouldered, his auburn hair perfectly styled, and his tailored suit fitted perfectly to his body.

He looks just like his dad, Mayor Penngrove.

"Art's…different," I note.

Tyler snorts. "Trying to be more like his dad every day."

I choke on my drink.

"Art?" I clarify. "Like his *father*?"

Art has always hated that his dad was in politics. Used to joke frequently about how he'd become an anarchist just to say "fuck you" to the system and ensure his father couldn't force him into following in his footsteps.

Tyler grimaces. "Unfortunately."

My mouth drops open when Art pats Lance on the back and then jogs over to stand next to his dad.

"You think Lance and Art are…?" Tyler continues.

"Are…what?" I reply.

"You know." He sticks his finger through the hole he's made with his other hand lewdly, wiggling his brows. "Lovahs."

I scoff. "God, who cares? *This* is why you get black eyes."

"Hey, I'm not judging. I'm just *asking*." He shrugs, lifting his hands in the air.

"You're being a prick."

I turn my sights back on Lance. I haven't technically seen much of my brothers since getting back, but the rest of them I talk to frequently enough where it doesn't feel like we've become complete strangers.

Lance is a different story.

It's like I don't know him at all anymore, which makes me sad because we used to be the closest.

I keep watching him and waiting for him to search the crowd to find me. Maybe give me a quick "I missed you."

But Lance doesn't even look in my direction.

All of my brothers treat me the same: like I'm furniture, decoration, good to be on display but not good enough for anything else.

Lance's frown is intense as he leans in and says something to Paxton and Alex, and then Alex nods and disappears inside.

"Why is everyone in our family so goddamn rude?" I mutter, trying to hide the hurt in my voice.

"What am I, chopped liver?" Tyler asks like I've offended him.

I grin, patting his cheek. "Never. Your loyalty is why you're my favorite cousin."

He smirks. "Exactly. I expect you to remember this moment when others try to tell you they love you more."

When Lance and Paxton disappear around the side of the house, Tyler's gaze follows them. "Stay put, okay?"

"I'm not a dog," I mutter into my champagne, even though the second Tyler gives me a sharp look, I cower like one.

"Fine," I relent.

He stalks off toward wherever my brothers just went, and I lean against the bar, taking another sip of my drink before setting it down.

"I'll just wait here!" I yell sarcastically to Tyler's back, irritation ringing in my ears.

This is ridiculous. In fact, the longer I stand by myself with not a single person coming over to say hello, the more pissed off I get.

Where did they all go?

When Preston makes an appearance, my mother's loud fake laugh ringing through the air, I panic, pushing through the partygoers and following the path Tyler just took to find my brothers.

My mother watches me closely, her lips tight and her eyes like daggers, but I just smile her way, give a little wave, and keep moving.

It's not like anyone will miss me back here, anyway, and what does she think I'm going to do? Make a scene?

Maybe she should have thought about that before forcing me back here on graduation day.

She can get over it. I'm not ready to face Preston, and I'm

too curious about where everyone disappeared to stand still and smile like a good little household pet.

I walk by the pool and cross underneath the veranda that's beneath the balcony of my room, until I'm on the side of the house. My heels sink into the grass, making it too difficult to walk, so I bend down and slip them off, holding them in my hand while the cold ground squishes beneath my feet.

There's a group of people standing together at the edge of the property, half of them on this side of the open gate and the other half on the opposite side.

My bare feet crunch on a loose piece of gravel and I wince, but I keep moving.

Paxton is next to Lance. And then there's Tyler, standing in front of all of them, his hands curled into fists at his sides, his posture rigid as he stares down the other group.

Anxiety punches me in the ribs, because Tyler has a *gun*, and he's not really known for his patience or even-keeled thinking.

Lance grips Tyler's shoulder and whispers something in his ear. Tyler jerks away, giving a withering look to Paxton and Lance before he throws up his hands and leaves toward the house.

What the hell is going on?

I take a few steps closer to get a better look at the faces of the people my brothers are facing off against.

Rosalie is the first one I notice. *Of course she is.*

Ever since she started dating Benjamin, she's been unreachable and causing enough mayhem that my parents have wiped their hands of her completely, refusing to even let her come to family dinners. She usually gets an invite to these bigger events still, although I'm surprised to see her show up to one.

My gaze flicks past her to the man at her right.

Merrick Carter.

Him, I know well. He attended Rosebrook Prep on the Montgomery Founder's scholarship, and we were in the same grade all the way from kindergarten to twelfth grade. Honestly, he was probably invited to this event. He's one of the most social people in all of Rosebrook Falls, and there's rarely a party he isn't attending.

Even if his best friend *is* Benjamin, who's standing at his left. He's a slimy, pasty guy with wavy blond hair and pinched features. Objectively, he's considered handsome enough, I guess, but he's always given me the creeps. He went to Rosebrook Prep also, but considering he's Marcus Montgomery's nephew and a Voltaire—a family that's always been *just* powerful enough to piss off my dad—I was told to stay away from him.

And then once he got his grubby hands on Rosalie, I didn't need any other reason to stay away.

Seeing him now sends a shiver down my spine.

I walk the rest of the way to my brothers and look at Paxton. "What's going on?"

"You shouldn't be here, Jules," he mutters, low enough that only I catch it.

Lance cuts a look my way, too. "Don't you have a debutante ball to plan or something?"

I glare at both of them. "Nice to see you guys, too. Do either of you assholes want to answer my question or are we just doing the whole 'me man, her woman, must protect' male posturing thing today?"

"We're taking out the trash," Paxton replies, his eyes fierce as he stares at the group. His voice carries, which I'm sure was his intention.

"You know, I've always thought you'd make a good garbage man," Benjamin says to Paxton with a smirk. "You've got the right people skills."

Lance crosses his arms. "Shut the fuck up, Benny."

My head snaps to Lance in shock. "*Benny?* I'm sorry, are we on a nickname basis now with the enemy?"

Lance side-eyes me with a grimace, and Benjamin flips him off. "Sure thing, Boss."

"Did you just flip him off at *our* home?" Paxton asks, his voice icy and direct.

I won't lie; he's intimidating. More so now than he was years ago. He reminds me *so* much of our dad.

Benjamin shrugs. "I've been known to be disrespectful."

Paxton tilts his head. "Are you being disrespectful to *us*?"

Benjamin's eyes flick to the security flanking our gates. "Will your security beat us back if I say yes?"

"No. But I might," Lance cuts in. "Merrick, you better get your boy."

"You know what, Lance, maybe it's *you* who should get your boy. You think you're God just because you can throw a punch?" Rosalie pipes up.

Lance smiles thinly. "We all know I hit harder when I'm angry."

"Okay," I chime in. "This is weird. You're all being weird. One of you needs to tell me what the hell is going on or I'll start loudly reciting embarrassing childhood stories."

Lance smirks, looking over at me. "Blackmail's not very ladylike, Jules."

My eyes widen. "Neither is threatening people in our driveway, yet here we are."

Paxton's mouth curls up. Barely, but it's there.

"Come on now, Lance," Benjamin interjects, throwing his arm over Rosalie and tugging her to his side like he owns her. "You were just fine when you were with us a few hours ago. Why so mad now? You didn't think we'd make the guest list?"

There's a collective intake of breath on our side, like all the oxygen has evaporated from the air.

Lance grows very still, and if looks could kill, Benjamin would be nothing more than a smear on the asphalt.

Nobody asks for clarification, but the accusation is there that Lance has been with the Montgomerys, and I can feel the trust between my brothers—the kind that was already thin and bruised—break apart and fall away.

My eyes narrow on the group of party crashers, slowly cataloguing every single one of them and committing them to memory.

I've never hated anyone the way that the rest of my family has, but them coming here and stirring up trouble like this? It's enough to put them on my permanent shit list.

At the end of the day, I'm loyal. And the Montgomerys have always gone out of their way to cause my family problems, both in business and in everyday life. Plus, Tyler swears it was Marcus Montgomery who killed his parents, *not* a boating accident.

My chest burns at the reminder of the loss.

There's movement to the side, next to the brick columns that house the entry gate, and it's only then I notice there's another person with them. He's wearing all black, hidden in the shadows of the setting sun as if he doesn't *want* to be seen. He's got what looks like an unlit joint in his mouth, and he's flipping a lighter on and off, the flame lighting up his face just enough to make out some of his features.

Icy blue eyes: ones currently fixed on me.

My heart stumbles, and my stomach flips.

Ryder.

I step in closer, because surely I'm seeing things, but Paxton grips my arm and holds me back.

"Ow," I complain, glaring at him. "What's your problem?"

Paxton shakes his head. "Nothing for you—"

"Little Rose."

The air stutters and mutates, like it bends for Ryder's voice alone.

He's off the brick pillar now, walking directly in front of Lance. I don't miss the way Rosalie's eyes follow him with a wistful glaze.

Ryder smirks, looking at me. "Having a party and didn't invite me? I'm hurt."

"Who the fuck are *you*?" Lance interjects, moving until he's shielding me better, his body taut.

Paxton's grip on my arm tightens. "Why is he calling you that?"

I don't answer him. I *can't*, because I'm too busy staring at Ryder.

What is he doing here? And with people like Benjamin Voltaire?

He's here, I think again. And he doesn't look surprised to see me.

Which means he knew who I was.

He knew.

And didn't tell me.

The realization is like ice sliding down my spine, chilling me from the inside out. Every touch, every flirtatious word, every moment of stolen intimacy feels like a trap now.

Ryder's eyes flash, and he doesn't so much as glance at Lance. "Welcome home."

A strange, weightless sensation hits my stomach, like when I miss a step on the stairs and think I'm about to fall.

His voice is calm and a touch flirty, like we're still *us*.

But we're not.

I guess, really, we never were.

Paxton leans down and whispers sharply, "Do you know him?"

Before I can reply, Lance's voice cuts in. "Don't talk to my sister. In fact, don't even *look* at her."

"Lance, we don't want any problems," Rosalie finally says, moving to stand next to Ryder. "You know as well as I do that I was invited here. They're just my guests."

"Bullshit," Lance snaps. "If you didn't want problems, you wouldn't be with them at all, Rosalie, let alone at our front gates. Let's not be willfully obtuse."

I rip myself from Paxton's hold, ignoring the way it makes my forearm burn, my focus still on Ryder.

"Juliette," Paxton hisses.

I shoot him a glare over my shoulder before stomping up to Ryder until I'm right in his face.

We're so close, I can hear his intake of breath, and electricity snaps between us the same way it always does. Only this time, it feels like it might burn me to a crisp.

"Jules," Lance tries.

"Shut up, Lance. I'll deal with you later," I snap, keeping my gaze on Ryder. "Who are you?"

His jaw tenses, and he licks his lips. "You already know."

I shake my head. "Don't play with me. What's your name? Your *full* name."

He grins, but it doesn't reach his eyes. "You first, Princess."

Someone next to him scoffs. Rosalie, probably. And I bristle, because even in just the few times we've hung out, he only calls me *Princess* when he's not being sincere.

"Uh-oh, kitten's got claws," Benjamin jokes.

Merrick lets out a low whistle. "Ten bucks says she'll hit him."

I lower my voice, dread dripping through my veins like a leaky faucet. "I need you to just…tell me I'm not the stupidest girl on the planet. Tell me who you are and why you're here with *them*."

His gaze breaks away and skims lazily over my brothers before landing back on me. "You're not stupid."

He doesn't answer my other question.

"Ryder," I whisper.

The tension radiates through me so strongly, it makes my voice shake.

Something that looks like remorse flashes on his face, but it's so quick, I can't be sure I've really seen it. That inkling from earlier breaks free and gallops through my chest like a stampede, and I back up a step.

I feel like I'm losing my mind. Like I'm staring at all the pieces of a puzzle but can't figure out how to slot them together.

Footsteps sound from behind us, and the air changes again to something harsher. Colder.

"What's all this?" The icy tone of my father breaks our stare-off, striding toward us with Tyler at his side.

"They're trying to—" Lance starts.

My father stops and puts his hand up. Lance presses his lips together and quiets, but I see the way it pains him to listen.

Then my dad turns toward Ryder, and shock covers his face for a brief second, so fast that if I blinked, I would have missed it. Every ounce of warmth drops away from him like a funnel siphoned it out, and hatred oozes from his veins like it was born and bred within him.

"*You*," he sneers.

Ryder doesn't flinch. Doesn't deny whatever was laced in my father's tone, but his jaw flexes and his expression hardens into stone. Like he knew this was coming. Like he's been waiting for the hammer to drop.

Which tells me one thing. He didn't just keep things from me.

He lied.

All the moments we shared. *Lie.* Every touch, every whisper, every smirk across a table. *Lie. Lie. Lie.*

"Roman Montgomery," my dad breathes. "You're alive."

And just like that, my world spins and my stomach bottoms out.

Chapter 19

Roman

FUCK.

The look on Juliette's face destroys me. Her lip trembles slightly and even though I keep trying to catch her eyes, to try and express...I don't know... *something*, she avoids my gaze.

But she's not my problem.

She *can't* be my problem.

I'm not here for her.

I bite down hard, my tongue pressed so tight to my molars I taste blood.

Placating Juliette isn't the marching order I've been given by my father.

It's about Craig Calloway.

And the way his face is void of color and he looks frozen, I think the message was well received.

I watch his reaction closely, trying to decipher if what my father told me is true. If it really *was* Craig trying to take me out all those years ago.

If so...

My mother grew dependent on pills because of that crash. Lost her job. Her passion. Her livelihood. In return, I lost her, and my sister lost stability.

Fresh anger burns through me, even though my heart speeds in my chest and my hands are clammy.

It's not really high on my list of things to do; being in the same area as a man who everyone implies wants to kill me.

"Surprise," I say to him, waving my fingers in the air. "You all right? You look like you've seen a ghost."

Juliette flinches at my words, like the venom in my tone is burning *her*. Her skin's gone pale, her jaw is slack, and her whole body is tight like a pinched wire.

I never wanted her to feel like this. Never wanted to *make* her feel like this.

My stomach twists violently.

I focus back on Craig. "Heard there was a celebration going on, so I figured I'd stop by and give you something worth celebrating."

Juliette visibly stumbles back, her hand rubbing her chest. One of her brothers, the same one who gripped her arm earlier, reaches for her again. This time, she doesn't fight it, allowing him to pull her away.

He turns and pushes her gently toward the blond man who came with their father. Without missing a beat, he wraps an arm around her shoulders and guides her away.

There's a flare of something *hot* inside me when he does, but I don't spend too much time focusing on it.

I *can't*.

Juliette Calloway isn't my problem.

Maybe if I repeat it a hundred times, it will sink into my

head, and this strange pull demanding I follow her will cease to exist.

"You're trespassing," Craig responds, his eyes like a knife. "I suggest you get off my property before I have you forcibly removed."

He nods toward the security guards manning the gate.

I suck on my teeth and tilt my head. "So interesting, your choice of words. *Forcibly removed.* People love doing that around here, huh?"

He lifts his chin, nostrils flaring the slightest amount.

Guilty.

Craig sniffs. "Get off my property and don't come back, or you won't like the consequences. Tell your father I don't appreciate surprises, and I don't appreciate being lied to."

I smirk.

His eyes narrow. "I hope you understand that your father has no real power here anymore. It's pathetic, really, how he clings onto that tiny little hill on the west side of town. Tell me, has he told you just how much he's given up to us over the years? How difficult we can make his life if he wants to keep playing these games?"

Benjamin scoffs beside me.

"Did he warn you how difficult I could make *your* life?"

My heart kicks against my ribs, my spine stiffening.

"Are you threatening him?" Benjamin spits, stepping forward.

Merrick slips between us, both of his hands raised. "Now, now, kids, let's all play nice."

"I have no reason to go after you, Roman," Craig continues. "If you want to come back from the dead and play like the

Montgomery name still means something in this town, then by all means. But a word of advice: stay away from my family, and don't get in my way."

He stares at me like I'm a bug that needs to be squashed, and then he turns on his heel and walks away, snapping at the others with him to follow.

They all do, dutifully, except for the tall and bulky one up front. Lance, I think his name is.

He tilts his head, staring at me with his arms crossed. "How do you know my sister?"

The question stings like a papercut. I force the smirk to stay on my face, but it isn't genuine.

"I don't."

He lifts his chin, jaw tensing. "Let's keep it that way."

I give a quick jerk of my chin.

And then he turns and walks away, too, until there's empty space where they all were standing. Quickly, the security guards who were off to the side during the entire exchange take their place.

I throw up my hands. "We're gone, boys. No need to get excited."

Spinning around, I give a look to Benjamin, and we move down the drive.

Merrick jogs until he's next to me, throwing his arm around my shoulder, laughing loud enough that it carries through the sky and over the trees. "God*damn*, you're about to make things more fun around here."

I give him a small grin, although I'm not really feeling anything close to happy on the inside.

He watches me, his dark eyes flickering.

We reach the car, and Benjamin pats me on the back, nodding his approval. "Villain looks good on you, my guy. Your dad's gonna eat it up."

I look at him, trying not to be offended at how easily he wraps an insult in a compliment. "How do you know that?"

Benjamin shrugs. "He's family. I know him as well as I know myself."

If he intended that to be a knife to the chest, he succeeded. I light the joint I've been holding, my anxiety crawling around my spine like spiders.

Merrick leans against the door of the passenger side of his car. "Nobody cares about how far up Marcus's asshole you are, Benny. I want to know the gossip." He watches me, curiosity brimming in his gaze. "How do you know Juliette Calloway?"

I blow out a cloud of smoke and smirk. "I don't kiss and tell, Merrick."

"Ah," he says, nodding like my non-answer gave him everything he needed to know. "Is it young love?"

Rosalie lets out a sardonic laugh. "Please, Juliette wouldn't know love if it hit her upside the head. She'd have to let people get close to her for that to happen, and she's always been a frigid bitch."

My gaze snaps to her, wondering how she knows Juliette and simultaneously wanting to throttle her for calling her a bitch. The intense reaction catches me off guard, because what the hell is my problem?

When I look back to Merrick, he's grinning at me like he can read my mind.

I shift uncomfortably.

He straightens, spinning around with his arms out at his

sides like they're wings. "If she's the girl you want, then we'll take Cupid's wings and we'll fly high. Rosebrook Falls is the place love goes to die, after all. Might as well tempt fate while you can."

A short laugh escapes me, and I shake my head. "What the fuck are you even talking about?"

Benjamin wraps his arms around the waist of Rosalie, smirking at his friend. "Merrick's always talking out of his ass; don't listen to anything he says."

Merrick stops spinning and points at him. "*You* should show me some respect, Benny. If it weren't for me, we wouldn't have even had an audience with the Calloways just now."

Rosalie huffs. "Uh, hello? I'm *right* here. It was my invitation."

Benjamin looks at her. "You didn't get us *in*, though, so your point's a little moot."

Rosalie peers up at him. "None of you said you wanted to sneak *into* the party. You should have just asked me how."

"Okay, how?" Benjamin asks.

"There's a spot on the east side of the gate that has a small hole under the brush. If you use it and keep to the perimeter of the property, it's a blind spot in their security, and it leads straight to Juliette's balcony."

I blow out a cloud of smoke. "How do you know that?"

She looks at me, her face brightening as she steps away from Benjamin's hold. "My brother used to brag about how they'd sneak out, him and Lance. They'd use Juliette's balcony because it faces the pool and has the most blind spots in their security."

"And who's your brother?" I ask.

She scowls. "Tyler. The one who brought out my uncle."

I blink at her.

"Tyler is Juliette's cousin. *Rosalie* is Juliette's cousin." Benjamin fills in the blanks.

My brows shoot up. "But you're hanging out with us?"

Her gaze shoots to the ground, and she shrugs. "I've picked my side."

Benjamin turns to her with an incredulous look. "You could have told us how to sneak in a little earlier, you know?"

"Like I said, you didn't ask."

I glance back at the mansion, a new kind of fire sparking inside of me. The need to explain my actions to Juliette snuffs out anything else that I was feeling. I don't know why it bothers me so much to think of her hating me or thinking I played her on purpose, but it does, and despite me repeating to myself like a mantra that I don't care about her…I do.

She's suddenly all I can think about.

I focus back on my group as Merrick walks around to the driver's side of the car and slips in.

"You coming?" he asks, leaning toward the rolled-down passenger window.

I shake my head, my hands in my pockets. "It's a nice night. I think I'll walk around for a bit."

Merrick's eyes flash, like he knows what I'm about to do, but he nods and then jerks his head at Rosalie and Benjamin, who slide into the car.

"Call me later if you want to kick it," Merrick says. "You'll need friends around here…ones you can trust."

I jerk my chin, and then they're off, and my heart starts pounding against my chest as I flip around to stare at the Calloway estate.

Keep to the perimeter…and it leads straight to Juliette's balcony.

Chapter 20
Juliette

ROMAN MONTGOMERY MAY NOT BE DEAD, BUT he's dead to me.

That's probably dramatic, but it's the only thought on my mind as I pace the length of the table in our formal dining hall.

Laughter floats in from the people tipsy off champagne and still schmoozing out back, but their joy doesn't come close to affecting me. My heels—the ones I've since put back on my feet—are the only other noise.

Although, my brother Alex's silent judgment *feels* loud.

Click-clack.
Click-clack.
Click-clack.

I don't even know what I'm so upset about. It's not like Ryder—no, *Roman*—and I really knew each other or owed one another anything.

But the second that thought crosses my mind, I know it's not entirely true. I was open with him in a way I'm not with other people. There was a freedom there, because he didn't know anything about me or who I was supposed to be.

But he knew the whole time.

Maybe he was using me.

But for what? To be cruel?

As a gotcha moment for my family? What could he possibly accomplish with that?

The more I think about it, the less it makes sense. I was the one who sought him out, at least after the first couple of times running into him. And it isn't like *he* sent the art tickets to Felicity.

Confusion spirals through me like I'm free-falling from a cliff, and I can't tell which way is up.

Alex is the only other person in here with me, after rushing after me when I stormed through the front door.

He doesn't have a clue what's going on, because he was the only one of us that wasn't out there.

"Why are you standing there like a creeper?" I snap, needing an outlet for my anger.

He frowns and then scoffs, moving to the chair at the end of the table, dramatically pulling it out and plopping down in it. "There. Happy?"

I give him a sarcastic smile. "Thrilled."

"Jesus, what the fuck is wrong with you?"

I stop pacing, giving him a look. "Why does there have to be something wrong?"

"Yeah." He puts his feet up on the table, crossing his ankles and leaning back in the chair. "You're really calm and put together right now. My mistake."

A grin pulls at my lips, and I shake my head, sighing. "I'm sorry."

He smiles, and it's so similar to our mother that it's physically painful to look at.

Alex is the only one of us who really favors her over our father. His brown hair is lighter, almost a golden brown instead of the black like the rest of us, and it has the perfect amount of wave that makes it look like it's styled even though he doesn't do a damn thing to it. His eyes are like honey mixed with green, and his looks are so movie star–esque, it's a miracle he hasn't up and left us for Hollywood.

He *is* an actor, after all, even if his degree is in philosophy.

"Do you want to talk about it?" he asks.

"About what?" I'm pacing again.

He waves his hand in the air. "Whatever's got you looking like you're about to huff and puff and blow this place down."

I stop and frown at him. "No."

Footsteps sound from down the hall, and Alex smirks. "Fine, you can talk about it with Dad instead, then."

"How do you know that's Dad?" I strain my ears trying to hear, but it could be anyone walking toward us for all I know.

"His steps sound different."

"That's such a weird thing to notice."

Alex shrugs.

Father rounds the corner into the dining room in the next second, and my mouth drops open, glancing back at Alex.

He winks, proud of himself.

My father stares at me, and I remain silent, every second making my skin itch from being under his gaze.

Does he know that I knew Roman? Is he mad at me? Did he hurt him?

The last question pisses me off, because why should I care?

Roman hurt *me*. Even if that's ridiculous after such a short amount of time knowing each other.

"Everything okay?" I finally ask to gauge the waters. "Who was that?"

His nostrils flare and then he clears his throat. "That was Roman Montgomery."

Damn, his poker face is good. I've never been able to get a read on him.

My mouth grows dry. "And who is that, exactly?"

Dad moves farther into the room, resting his hands on the back of a chair, his knuckles blanching from how tightly he grips it.

"Marcus Montgomery's son," he says.

Alex laughs.

I snap my attention to him. "What's so funny?"

"It's just impossible, is all. Marcus's son is dead, don't you remember it being all over the news? He's obviously joking, Jules." He waves his hand toward Dad, who is frowning over at Alex.

"I don't understand," I say.

"Well, sweetheart, that would make two of us." Dad gives me a tight smile.

"He's really Marcus's son?" Alex asks, the amusement dropping from his face.

"It would appear that way." He gives me a sharp look. "Why were you talking to him?"

I stutter, rearing back like he smacked me. "I...I don't know why—"

Alex laughs again in disbelief, his feet dropping to the ground as he leans in, eyes alight. "Holy shit, you're serious?"

Dad cuts him a glare, and I don't even know what the hell is going on.

"Dad," I say, taking a step toward him.

His gaze softens. "I'm sorry, honey, welcome home. This isn't how I wanted today to go." He opens his arms to offer a hug, and my chest warms, but before I take a step, my mother walks in, and right behind her is that dickhead Preston.

My father's eyes break away from mine, going to them instead, his arms dropping.

"There you are," my mother chirps.

Her eyes betray the playful lilt of her voice as they cut from my father to me, a hint of disapproval blazing in their depths.

I learned to play the game from watching how well she does it, actually, so it isn't difficult to wipe any look off my face and plaster on the practiced Calloway grin.

"We've been looking all over for you," she continues.

My father smooths out his features and walks to my mother, pressing a chaste kiss to her cheek and then reaching out to shake the man's hand. "Preston, glad you could make it."

I blink at them as they walk toward me.

To my side, Alex stiffens, a scowl marring his features.

Preston is conventionally attractive, and as much as I hate to admit it, that's only gotten better with his age. He's tall, although with my frame, when I wear high heels, we're close. He's lean but muscular, and he's in a perfectly fitted suit with sandy blond hair that's meticulously styled off his face. His smile is blinding and white, and his blue eyes sparkle when he takes my hand in his.

It's familiar, and just like it used to when he beamed at me in high school, my heart speeds, just a little.

But his palms are soft.

A memory of calloused fingers tangling with mine and a rough hand wrapped around my throat flashes in my mind.

I push it down, annoyed with myself, because honestly, fuck Roman Montgomery. Anything I thought I had with him can't exist.

It *doesn't* exist.

So, when my father tells Preston to take me back out to the party, I don't argue, and when Preston asks me on a date an hour later, I say yes, purely out of spite.

Chapter 21

Juliette

THE REST OF THE FUNDRAISER WAS...FINE.

As much as I wasn't into the idea of seeing Preston again, I'd be lying if I said he wasn't still as charming as he was the first time around. More so, now. But I've been disillusioned, because the charm doesn't negate how much he hurt me when he moved away and left me here with a single text.

All seeing him again showed me is that I'm no longer angry about the past. I can let go and move on, but my parents are out of their minds if they think I'm going to be with him. They're lucky I even agreed to date him at all, and I'm damn sure not going to let him take me to the VU Founders' Gala in a few weeks.

Part of me—the vindictive part—hopes Roman sees the tabloid headline that will inevitably run.

Stupid, really.

He obviously doesn't care.

Now that I'm back in my bedroom and the world around me is quiet, sleep is hard to come by. I throw the covers off and make my way to my balcony doors.

Why can't I just turn my brain off?

I debate calling Felicity to fill her in on the current state of my life but decide against it. She's either asleep or in Keagan's bed, and I don't have any desire to interrupt either way. Besides, once she hears Preston is being shoved into my orbit again, she might fly back just to be the go-between. I settle with sending her a text instead.

ME:

> Hope you had fun at graduation and did something in my honor like break up with Keagan!

> Also…maybe we should find a place together when you get back? I thought I could stay at home, but being here makes me feel like a kid again, and it's suffocating. DON'T say I told you so.

I purposely don't mention Ryder—*Roman*—because I feel like a big enough idiot already without her shoving my failures in my face.

Throwing the doors open, I move to the balcony outside and lean against the smooth railing.

It's quiet, every trace that there was a party earlier gone.

I've always loved having my room on this side of the house. It's separate from all the other bedrooms, and unless someone comes outside for an after-hours swim, it remains the most secluded part of the property once the sun sets.

It's a clear night, the stars winking at me, and I lean against the pillar that frames the balcony.

I hoped the silence would calm my mind, but it's having the opposite effect.

A breeze blows across my face, the noise making the ivy-wrapped lattice that runs up the house rustle in the wind.

For the first time since I saw Roman earlier—since I found out who he was—I allow the full breadth of my emotions to unfurl inside me.

My chest is tight, like my ribs are clenching in on themselves and my lungs can't expand. My jaw is sore from gritting my teeth so hard all evening, and worst of all, my heart falters and sputters every time I chastise myself for being such an idiot.

It's not like I was in love with the guy, but there was potential there. And I know it for sure now, because being with my ex tonight made me realize how much stronger my immediate connection with Roman was.

"Roman Montgomery," I murmur. "Why did it have to be *you*?"

"I'll be someone else, if it makes you forgive me."

I slap my hand over my mouth to keep from screaming, my pulse pounding as I jump back from the railing. There's a second's pause, and then I'm leaning over the balcony ledge and looking down, trying to find him.

"Roman?" I whisper-shout, then glance behind me to make sure nobody is coming.

My stomach drops like a lead weight at the thought of him being caught.

"Where are you?" I ask again, not finding him in the darkness. "Wait! Don't come out, they'll…they'll see you if you do."

I take a deep breath, trying to stay calm.

There's another noise, and then he appears over my balcony's ledge, a cocky grin on his face as he hangs onto the lattice.

"They won't see," he reassures, but then he pauses. "I don't think."

"What the hell are you doing here?" I hiss, wanting to smack the stupid smile from his features.

He frowns. "You're mad."

I cross my arms, releasing an agitated breath. "I'd have to care about you to be mad."

His lips purse, and then one of his hands lets go, his body swinging down, creating a large rattle when his back slams against the wall of the house.

My heart jumps into my throat.

"Be careful!" I demand. "What the hell is wrong with you?"

Roman looks at me pleadingly, the skin under his tattooed hand blanching white from how tightly he's holding onto the trellis. "Say you forgive me."

I glare at him. "No."

"You *are* mad."

I throw my hands into the air, annoyed by his antics and even more irritated at the spark of excitement that's blooming because he's here.

What kind of a person am I that even after knowing he's lied to my face and is the son of my family's biggest rival…I still react at the sight of him?

"If the fall doesn't kill you, my family might when they find you here. So, suit yourself…what do I care, anyway?"

"Juliette," he groans, his fingers slipping from the slats until his body drops another inch.

I lurch forward like I can save him.

"Would you cut it *out*?" I hiss, glancing behind me again.

Still, nobody comes.

"Say you forgive me," he demands again.

I frown at him, although I secretly like that he's here and trying to make amends. "You haven't apologized yet."

"You're right," he says. "I'm sorry."

I lean against the pillar of my balcony and look at him, part of me enjoying his suffering. "For?"

"Existing, I guess." The teasing lilt disappears from his voice. "And for not being honest, although there *is* a reason, if you'd let me explain."

I sigh.

His fingers slip more, and his body slides down. "*Shit*," he exclaims.

"Fine!" I half shout, and then repeat quieter, "Fine. I forgive you."

A beaming grin spreads across his face, and he easily pulls himself back up, throwing one leg over the railing and then the other until he's standing right in front of me on my balcony. "I knew you cared."

My mouth unhinges.

Anger thrums through me, and before I can stop myself, I'm shoving his chest. "Are you out of your mind? You could have killed yourself."

He grips my hands and holds them against his chest. "If you hate me, then I'm as good as dead, anyway."

"And now you're joking?" I shove at him again, and he chuckles, letting me go and falling against the pillar. "I do hate you," I bite out. "I *hate* you."

His smile fades, and a crease forms between his brows. "I came to explain."

I look to the side, my arms folding tight against my ribs. "Pretty sure I got the gist of it."

He shakes his head. "I didn't know who you were, Juliette. I swear."

I narrow my gaze. "Then why didn't you tell me your real name?"

"Because everyone in this town thought I was dead," he states. "And everyone who knew I was alive thinks *your* dad wants to kill me."

That makes me pause, but my hackles rise, wanting to defend a man who may not actually deserve a defense.

It's not like I don't *know* that he's capable of horrible things, I just… He wouldn't do anything that extreme.

Would he?

I cringe.

He definitely would.

"Why would he want to kill you?" I ask.

"Come on, Princess. You know why."

His jaw tics.

"Everything I said to you has been true," he rushes out. "I have a sister, and she depends on me. She's all I have in the world, and there are things I need to do to make sure she's taken care of."

My mind replays the moment I saw him tonight. How unsurprised he was that I was here. How he knew about the party beforehand. Still, for some reason, I don't think he's lying. The mention of his sister has my anger thawing, just a little.

I tilt my head. "When did you find out who I was?"

He grimaces, shoulders slumping. "My mother recognized you."

"You mean the mother who's supposed to be dead, too?" I snip. "No wonder she hated me on sight."

He cuts me a pleading look, like he's desperate for me to understand.

"So, it was before you saw me at the coffee shop again."

I'm not sure why that cuts worse than if he knew the whole time, but it does.

His jaw tenses again, and he gives a curt nod.

"Why do all that? Why continue letting me think this could be some—that we could be friends?"

"Because I wanted to know you," he replies simply. "I still want to know you."

My chest cramps, and I inhale a shaky breath.

"That's not very fair," I say.

He straightens and steps toward me. "I didn't plan for any of this."

"Like that matters." I move back until I hit the opposite side of the balcony. "You shouldn't be here."

"But I am."

Another step.

My hands press against the stone behind me like I can meld into the structure if I try hard enough.

"Why can't we be friends?" he murmurs, his eyes searching mine. "Why does this have to change anything?"

"Uh, I don't know, maybe because you think my dad is some mass murderer?" I say.

His eyes soften like he pities *me*.

"I don't give a fuck about that," he claims, his voice strong and sure. "I *only* give a fuck about you."

"Right." I huff. "That why you put on such a good show earlier for my family?"

Something dark flashes over his face like he hates what he's done.

"If you were anyone else," I murmur, looking at the ground.

"Well, I'm not," he retorts, his arms rising until his hands rest on the pillar on either side of my head. "Who cares?"

"*I* care!" I exclaim. "You have no idea how off-limits you just became."

His nostrils flare, his arms tensing. I ignore the heat sparking off his body, blanketing me, and honestly, it's the worst form of torture to have him be so close physically, yet the farthest away he's ever been.

"I *do* know," he whispers.

"Do you?" I stare at him. "You're a *Montgomery*, Trouble. If my dad saw you here with me, or worse, if my cousin Tyler did—"

"They'd what?" Roman cuts me off, moving in closer, his torso brushing against mine.

My mind flashes to Tyler's gun. "You know *what*."

"Whatever it is, it'd be worth it, as long as I got some time with you."

I grit my teeth, turning my head to the side and staring at the pool.

"I didn't choose my parents any more than you did, Juliette."

The way he says my name sends a shiver down my spine.

"And I didn't take you as the type to just bow down and do everything your family says, but maybe I was wrong," he continues.

Fire rages through me at his words, because as much as I want to rail against what he's saying, I can't.

It's true: I've never gone against my parents' wishes.

I've been slowly boiling in a pot of water, not even realizing I'm being burned alive.

I turn back to face him, hating the way my stomach flips and my chest cinches tight when our eyes meet. "Tell me why you were here tonight, then. Convince me it's nothing more than *our parents*."

His chin lifts, his Adam's apple bobbing on a swallow.

But he stays silent.

I nod, resignation filling me up like sand in an hourglass. "Then we're enemies."

He moves so suddenly I don't have time to avoid it. One of his hands grips my waist, and the other cups the back of my head.

His forehead presses against mine.

I gasp, my skin sizzling wherever he touches.

"You will *never* be my enemy." He states it as an absolute.

My lashes flutter, hope—as ridiculous as it is in this situation—flaring to life in my chest. "Even if we have to pretend we are?"

His expression shifts, flickering with something sharp.

A door slams in the distance, and my stomach folds in on itself.

I push against his hold, but he only grips me tighter. "You have to go."

"Meet me somewhere."

"Roman, *please*. Just leave. Before my family finds you here."

He shakes his head. "Not until you say yes."

Frustrated, I sink into his hold, my hands falling against the hard muscle of his chest. "Fine, meet me tomorrow at the cliff."

"You mean where I saved your life?" He smirks.

I swallow. "Yes, whatever, now *go*."

In the next second, he's gone.

The ROSEBROOK Rag

SPOTTED: Preston Ascott & Juliette Calloway...Back On?!

The exes were seen together at Mayor Penngrove's fundraiser, sparking major reunion rumors. Seems as though our sources were correct, and Preston Ascott is a man on a mission.

Love rekindled, or just nostalgia in a tux?

Either way, they look like Rosebrook Falls's golden couple.

#JulietteReturns #PrestonAscott #CallowayWatch
#HighSchoolSweethearts #RosebrookRag

Chapter 22

Roman

THIS SUIT IS ITCHY.

The material itself is perfect, like silk on the skin, each millimeter of fabric fitting my body like it was cut specifically for me. But I'm suffocating inside of it.

I don't know if that's from the clothing itself or because the thought of public speaking makes me want to die, but I'm about five minutes away from being at the podium that's perched in front of a dozen reporters with giant tripod cameras and microphones aimed directly at me.

We're at the foot of the gazebo in the middle of the town square.

It's busier today than it was when I arrived in town the other night, and definitely busier than when I snuck downtown at two in the morning to tag a building.

Businesses are open, the sun is shining, and people are out for their day. Everyone seems to know about this press conference my father's called, so beyond the reporters, there are rubber-necking citizens loitering around and filling out the rest of the grassy knolls.

There's a street busker a few yards away, sitting underneath a tree in the shade and strumming a love song on their guitar, and another sitting on a bench with a small flock of pigeons nibbling pieces of bread in front of them, but everyone else keeps stealing glances our way, like they're waiting for the real show to start.

I've always considered Rosebrook Falls to be a small town, but seeing it come alive with its residents gives me a new perspective.

My father's press secretary is at the microphone, answering questions from nosy reporters.

My dad is standing next to me, off to the right side, and he pats me on the shoulder. I tear my eyes away from the podium and glance at him. A giant grin spreads across his face like he's excited I'm here. Like he's *proud* to have me next to him.

It makes me feel…I don't know, weird.

I don't trust it.

And I hate that there's a part of me that revels in that smile from him, as if the kid inside me is bursting to lap up the approval like water.

Frederick's next to my father, stoic and silent.

The press secretary at the podium finishes, and the buzz in the audience draws my attention to the open grassy area surrounding the gazebo, my eyes searching for the girl I know I should force from my mind but for some reason can't.

Juliette.

I've thought of almost nothing else but her since coming here, and she's in every single inch of this town.

But she's not here. *Why would she be?*

My father nudges my shoulder. "You ready for this, son?"

The question makes my mouth go dry. Even being here in the first place feels like betraying my past, but a piece of me aches when he calls me *son*, like an old injury throbbing from the rain.

I look toward the reporters again, my stomach tensing. "Am I talking to them?"

He eyes me thoughtfully for a moment. "Maybe."

Frederick leans in close, his hand covering his mouth like he's coughing. I imagine he's covering his mouth so nobody can decipher what he's saying. "Marcus, you can't be serious. He hasn't had *any* media training. Who knows what he'll say?"

"You can stop them from running anything that would be detrimental, can't you?"

Frederick grits his teeth, his gaze sliding over the reporters. "There's no guarantee they'll listen."

My father hums, nodding along, and he slides his gaze back to me.

It's more than obvious that he takes Frederick's advice very seriously.

"Your lack of confidence is inspiring. I'm more than capable of fielding a few questions," I drawl, giving Frederick a lazy grin.

"Just don't mention any of the papers you signed," he snipes.

I shrug. "Sure, why would they care about the new stipulations on my inheritance, anyway?"

Frederick hums noncommittally.

I could give a fuck about what he thinks.

In fact, the only thing I care about is that I can't get my mind off that article I saw this morning on my way here.

Preston Ascott. Stupid name.

The thought of him with Juliette makes my head swim and my stomach turn.

The woman who was at the podium makes her way to us, her warm brown skin sheening from the heat of the day and her blue pantsuit crisp and straight. She nods at my father, who clears his throat, locks his eyes with me one last time, and then straightens his spine and waltzes to the microphone like the world bends in his favor with every step.

If I didn't despise him so much, it would almost be inspiring to watch.

"Good afternoon," he says. "Thank you to everyone for making the time to be here today. As you all are aware, the Montgomery Organization is built on a foundation of family. Trust. Longevity. In fact, it was my great-grandfather who built this town with his own hands. Crafted the very gazebo we're all standing in front of." He turns to wave his arm at the structure behind us, his eyes falling on the sign that says *This park made possible by Calloway Enterprises* in front of it. "Despite others trying to stake the claim."

His face drops so imperceptibly, I'm sure I'm the only one who notices.

"Some call it nepotism; others call it a foundation of legacy. The truth is, maybe it's a little of both."

This earns chuckles from the crowd, and I won't lie, I'm drawn in.

My father is a fantastic public speaker.

It makes me wonder why he's the one on the outskirts of town while the Calloways have dipped their hands into everything.

It seems like he's losing a game he should be a master at playing.

"I know a lot of you have been hoping for some front-page-worthy gossip from me for a long time." He looks pointedly to a person in the front, standing with a microphone labeled *The Rosebrook Rag*.

There's a shuffling of movement when he pauses and a few clicks of cameras.

My eyes follow the commotion and then lock on Paxton Calloway, who I know now is the oldest son and set to inherit everything that comes with the Calloway name. He's by himself in a black suit with an open collar, his shoulder leaned against a streetlamp with his hands in his pockets like he doesn't have a care in the world.

As if he's only here to observe along with everyone else.

He's wearing sunglasses, but I know he's looking at me.

Something dangerous flashes in my father's gaze. "I also know that *some* of you were hoping the Montgomery line would die with me. Well, I'm sorry to disappoint."

Now the gasps are audible.

"Twenty-three years ago, I made a mistake."

The word hits me like a battering ram, hollowing out my chest and scattering the pieces to my stomach.

"I'm not a perfect man," he continues. "And the truth is I fell in love despite being married. There were consequences to that mistake, ones that I regret."

More eyes flicker toward me, a few camera lenses turning my way.

Regret.

Consequences.

He's talking about me, of course. I'm the consequence of his actions, his biggest regret. He speaks as though he's still ashamed, as though he'd give anything to go back and make it so I didn't exist at all.

You'd think after all this time, I'd be numb to the sharp sting of his words.

"But out of our lowest points can come our greatest accomplishments, and after years of not being able to reach him—of being in the dark, thinking he was gone forever—I'm happy to say that sometimes the truth is stranger than fiction. Especially now that my only son is home. Roman Montgomery."

I don't have time to focus on the lies he spins, explaining the fake deaths, before I'm being ushered to the podium to stand next to him.

Something unsettling hits me heavy in the gut, but I stiffen my spine. If I don't do this, Brooklynn won't be taken care of.

And they need me, even if it means I have to become the spitting image of the devil.

Chapter 23

Roman

THERE'S NOT A LOT THAT TRULY SHAKES ME.

Not too many moments I can remember where I'm so nervous that I can't sit still.

This feeling: this can't-eat, can't-sleep, can't-breathe type of nervousness whipping its way through my system is entirely brand new, but it's all I've been feeling since the second I saw Juliette again in Rosebrook Falls. Since she agreed to meet me here at our spot.

Is it weird to think of something as *ours* when it's only the second time we've been here together?

I got to the secluded cliff in Verona County Park shortly after I was done with that farce of a show for the reporters, where I acted like I want to be there.

My mother texted immediately after it was over. No doubt she was watching the live stream.

MA:

You were great. I'm proud of you.

My stomach twists, because I think it might be the first time in years that she's said those words.

Juliette didn't tell me what time to meet her here, so I've been sitting at this picnic table like a pussy, hoping she actually shows.

The sun sank about an hour ago, slipping beneath the horizon and giving way to the moon. I've been sketching the entire time. Nothing specific, just random doodles to keep my hands moving and my mind occupied.

There's a scatter of vibrant stars, and a few dim trail lamps, one of them casting a soft glow behind the old picnic table where I'm sitting.

I sigh, crack my neck, and drop my pencil onto my black book. Then I stand, stretching out the stiffness in my back before walking to the rock—*the* rock—where I first saw Juliette.

Sitting on the edge, I call Brooklynn while I wait. Partly because I miss her, but mostly to distract myself from the dread seeping in, wondering if Juliette's going to show at all.

Brooklynn doesn't pick up, but she's probably just avoiding me, so I call her again.

And then again.

On the fourth time, there's a click. Her voice comes over the line, and the tightness in my chest eases.

"You know you're the *literal* definition of overbearing, right?" she says instead of hello.

My muscles ease. "I like to think of it as extravagant persistence."

She sighs. "What do you want, Bear? Or do you only go by Roman now?"

My heart thumps. "Call me whatever you want, as long as you're acknowledging my existence again."

She's quiet for a minute and then, "How is it there... You good?"

I glance out over the cliff, Rosebrook Falls stretched beneath me in the valley. "Depends on your definition of the word, I guess. I just told the world I'm not dead so, above average?"

"I watched it, you know...the press thing." She pauses. "You looked like him."

My jaw tics, stomach cramping. "Brooklynn—"

"It's whatever," she says quickly. "What are you doing now?"

"Hanging out at some park."

"Fascinating," she drawls.

I rub my neck and then glance up, my heart flipping.

Juliette's standing there, watching me.

"Hey, I gotta go. If I call you later, will you answer?"

"You bet." Her voice is sarcastic but I'll take what I can get.

"Love you, kid."

"Ditto."

Click.

"It's called Upside Down Rock," Juliette says immediately.

Her voice sends a shiver down my spine.

I can't help the grin that spreads. "You're here."

She quirks a brow. "I said I would be—what do you think I am, a liar?"

Shaking my head, I just stare at her because *damn*, she's pretty.

"You made me wait long enough," I say. "I was about to give up and go home."

Her head tilts. "And where exactly is *home*? Montgomery Manor?"

Standing up and stepping forward, I gaze down at her, my body tripping over itself like it wants to be near her more than I do.

"I don't want to talk about that," I reply. "I don't want to think about the fucked-up relationship our families have with each other. When we're here, I just want us to be...us."

Her throat bobs. "And what exactly does that entail?"

"Friendly things, I guess."

"Friendly things," she repeats, frowning.

"Yeah. I think you'll find I can be *very* friendly." I wag my brows.

She gives me a bemused look and then heads toward the picnic table, sliding onto the bench and placing her notebook down. "Well, come on then, *friend*, tell me something about you."

I follow her, slipping into the seat across from her and resting my hands on the table next to my own black book. I jerk my chin toward hers. "What's that?"

She gives me a chastising look. "I asked you a question first."

"Okay." I pick up my pencil and roll it between my fingers. "I spent years thinking my dad wished I was dead, and now that he wants me here, I don't know how to act like I'm his son. His wealth makes me uncomfortable, and if it weren't for my sister, I'd probably never touch a dime of my trust fund."

Her eyes widen.

"Shit, I'm sorry." I run a hand through my hair, my leg bouncing. "That was too heavy, right? You just asked, so I—"

"No," she cuts me off. "I just didn't expect you to be so honest."

I glance down at the table and then back at her, hoping my gaze conveys the words that I don't know how to say. "I'll always be honest with you."

She snorts.

"From now on," I amend.

Truthfully, I've never been open with anyone like this, and maybe I'm a dumbass for it, but it feels like I can share pieces of myself, and she'll hold them close and keep them safe.

I've never had that before, not since I was a little kid and my mom...

Well, I don't want to think about my mother. It's just been a while.

"And this is something you share with your friends?" she asks.

"I'd like to think of us as best friends, honestly. Now you go." I gesture toward her notebook. "Is that a diary?"

She drums her fingers on the table, and I want to grip them in mine. Instead, I aim for the journal. I'm only planning on tapping the front of it, but the way she rips it out of my reach has my interest piquing.

"Why are you so cagey about it?" My heart thumps faster, and I lean forward. "Is there something about *me* in there?"

She keeps her face carefully blank. "It's amazing that after all this time you still think I'm obsessed with you."

I throw my hands up in surrender. "Feels like something a stalker would do, is all. For all I know, you've doodled your first name and my last together a thousand times."

She scoffs. "You wish."

"Juliette Montgomery," I muse, smiling. "Has a nice ring to it, don't you think?"

It takes a second to realize what I've said, and when I do, my world tips upside down.

When did my subconscious start accepting that I'm a Montgomery again?

The corners of her lips flip up. "This isn't a diary, but it *is* where I write."

I smirk. "And what, I'm just supposed to believe you don't write dirty stories about me?"

She narrows her gaze. "Okay, first of all, sex isn't dirty."

The word *sex* on her lips makes my dick hard, and I will it to behave, because I'm not trying to embarrass myself out here.

"I assure you," I murmur, leaning just a little closer, "sex can be absolutely *filthy*. I'm more than happy to show you, if you'd like."

She cocks her head. "Wow. How selfless of you. Do you always offer personal demonstrations to your friends?"

I grin. "Only the *really* special ones."

"That's not even the kind of stuff I write."

"Oh no?" I tap the table, eyes locked on her mouth. "I'm not sure I believe you."

"I *don't*."

Her cheeks bloom that pink, and my pulse stutters.

I point at her. "You're blushing. That's proof of your guilt."

She glares at me.

"You know," I continue, lowering my voice. "I think you'd better let me read them—that way, I'd know for sure."

"Absolutely not."

"Come on," I tease, resting my hand on my chin. "It's only fair. I've just bared my soul to you. Not to mention my generous offer of lessons in smut, to further your literary prowess. I'm really putting myself on the line here."

"No," she repeats.

"Fine." I relent, watching her. "Should we have a secret handshake?"

She blinks. "What?"

I lift a shoulder. "Seems like something friends would do. You know, seeing as how we're *strictly platonic* and all."

She scrunches her nose. "We're not making up a handshake."

"Why not?" I smirk. "Scared it might be too intimate?"

Her eyes narrow. "Are you ever serious?"

I put my hand over my heart. "I'm seriously promising I won't be mad when I read about all the ways you want to take advantage of me."

"Oh my *God*," she groans and covers her mouth, but not before I catch the smile breaking through.

And *that* right there is why I'm doing what I am. There's nothing good in my life…except when I make Juliette Calloway smile.

Under the table, I nudge the tip of her shoe with mine. "Relax. I'm just fucking with you."

She lets the smile land fully now, and the breeze kicks up, catching a piece of her hair and sweeping it across her face. She brushes it behind her ear, and I think watching her is my new favorite pastime.

"I brought it with me because I didn't know if you'd show up, and I wanted to be able to write somewhere I wouldn't have to look over my shoulder." She fingers the pages of her notebook. "If I had known you'd be giving me such a hard time about it, I would have left it in my car."

"Why do you have to look over your shoulder?"

"My family doesn't—well, they don't really get the whole writing thing…so I thought if you didn't show, at least I could find some time to do it in private."

And just like that, I don't want to piss her off anymore. In fact, it pisses *me* off that the people who claim to love her don't let her do what she enjoys around them.

I nod and tap the top of my black book. "I brought mine, too.

You know, just in case. I'm fine with hanging out and spending time together so you can write."

"You are?" She looks at me from beneath her long lashes.

"Yeah. You'll probably write better, honestly, since now your muse is sitting right in front of you in the flesh." I put my arms out to each side.

She picks up her pen and launches it at me, and I laugh, ducking out of the way.

"You totally have main character syndrome," she says, pointing a finger at me.

"What the hell is main character syndrome?"

"Where you think everything's always about you."

My brows hike to my hairline, and I try to look serious. "Sounds terrible."

"Mmhm, truly. My best friend thinks the bigger your MCS, the smaller your dick size."

"Is that an official diagnosis?"

She shrugs. "It's held true so far."

I nod. "That's a bold statement. And I'm *extremely* well-endowed, so I think I'd like a second opinion."

She laughs, shaking her head. "Sorry. Your symptoms are too advanced. I'm afraid it's terminal."

"Damn." My smile drops, feigning disappointment. "Well, if being *under*-endowed means I get to be the center of *your* attention, then I'll take it."

Juliette quiets and bites the corner of her lip.

My eyes drop to the motion. I want to be the one biting it. Licking it. Sucking it into my mouth and having her taste on my tongue.

I spin the ring on my finger around so I don't launch over

the picnic table and grip her by the neck, demolishing these flimsy "friendship" boundaries we've put up.

"You really don't mind if I write?" she asks.

"Nah. Being around you is enough."

She beams at me and then pulls the notebook toward her and opens it up, crossing her legs on the bench and placing it in her lap. Immediately, she's lost in her own world. I pretend I'm doing the same with my drawings, but to be honest, I can't stop watching her.

She's…

Well, I think she's kind of everything.

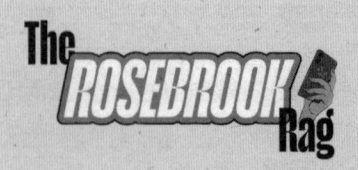

The ROSEBROOK Rag

Secret Son Shocker: Montgomery Heir Steps Into the Spotlight!

Marcus Montgomery's secret son is officially out of hiding and back from the dead. No ring, a sordid past, and now the heir to the Montgomery empire.

So where's he been all this time? And more importantly: Where is his mother?

We've got questions, and we won't stop until we get the answers.

#MontgomeryHeir #BackFromTheDead
#BachelorWatch #MontgomeryMoves
#RosebrookRag

Chapter 24

Roman

IRRITATION FLARES BENEATH MY SKIN, MAKING me overheat despite the crisp morning air. I toss my phone down, that *ridiculous* gossip rag article glaring up at me, and reach for my black book instead. I knew the headlines would be running rampant after yesterday's conference, but this is the first one I've seen personally, and it's also the most inflammatory.

Not that I should be surprised when something has the word "rag" in their title.

I'm on the front porch of my brand-new house, courtesy of my sperm donor. I've only been here for an afternoon, but already I can breathe easier not being under the same roof as my father. Montgomery Manor isn't a part of my history, and it feels weird pretending it is.

Between that and the shiny new black card weighing down my wallet, my conscience feels like it might break me apart.

I hesitate for a couple seconds before grabbing my phone again and opening up a new message.

This time to Juliette.

I've been trying to restrain myself ever since she gave me her number at Upside Down Rock, but denying myself is just making me want it even more.

ME:

> Rumor has it the hottest person to ever grace Rosebrook Falls is going to be drawing in an unknown location later today. You know, just in case anyone needs a muse for anything.

I toss my phone on the small table again.

Maybe she's busy. *Maybe she's with Preston.*

Groaning, I run a hand over my face. *Fuck*, I'm pathetic.

I focus back on my sketchbook, my hand flying over the piece I'm working on, the stress lifting from my shoulders one stroke at a time until nothing exists except pure emotion, one that bleeds through me and funnels onto the page.

Time drops away, and so does the outside stimulus, until I exist in a vacuum of focus.

A car comes rumbling up the drive, parking haphazardly, gravel flying from beneath its tires.

Merrick jumps out of the driver's side and closes the door behind him, walking around to the front and then leaning against the hood, crossing his arms and staring at me.

Despite not knowing him well, my gut tells me he's trustworthy. Someone who would have my back in a pit of vipers.

That's why I texted him earlier, asking if he'd come over to talk.

I set down my pencil and close the sketchbook on my lap.

Merrick breaks out into a blinding grin. "Nice digs."

"I'm surprised you came," I reply.

He mock bows, one hand going over his torso and the other out to his side. "When the prince of the dead calls, you answer."

I chuckle, shaking my head. "You make me sound like a bad guy."

He laughs as he walks toward me. "Depending on who you ask, I think you probably are."

When he gets up the three steps to the deck, he sits down in the wooden chair next to me.

My phone pings, and I snatch it up quickly, my heart jumping.

LITTLE ROSE:

> Pass. I like the characters of my raunchy stories to be generously equipped.

I smirk.

ME:

> Sounds like you're asking me to prove I qualify.

LITTLE ROSE:

> I'm asking you to leave me alone.

ME:

> Weird way to say "send me a dick pic" but if you insist…

LITTLE ROSE:

> I swear on everything that I will block you.

Amusement wrings my chest tight, and I don't even realize how big I'm cheesing until Merrick clears his throat.

"Sorry," I say, tossing the phone down on the table, and when I do the lock screen flashes that Rosebrook Rag article again.

His gaze homes in on it.

"Fucking vultures," he says. "They'd print literal shit on paper just so they get the readership."

"Seems that way," I reply, thinking about what they've already said about me and wondering what else they will.

He sucks in air through his teeth. "You know, you may not think of yourself as a prince, but I promise you, you're Rosebrook Falls royalty now, whether you want it or not. Be careful with them." He taps his finger on the headline.

"Reading it or being in it?" I ask.

He shrugs. "If you can't figure that out, then you're fucked either way."

I nod, his words settling against my skin like glue. "Noted."

He leans toward me, his dark brows drawing down. "Do you have any idea what the hell you're doing here?"

I blow out a breath, debating whether to trust him fully. But the truth is, even if I can't, I need to have someone on my side. Someone who seems down the middle, not tied down to one side or the other of this generational feud I've found myself in the middle of.

"Not a fucking clue," I admit, rubbing the back of my neck.

He whistles and shakes his head. "I had a feeling. You've got that freshly unboxed family trauma vibe."

I smirk. "Do I?"

He nods. "Tragic and broody. It's very Dickensian of you, actually. Almost romantic."

"Glad my unresolved trauma is giving you material."

Merrick grins. "Don't worry, sweetheart. Every tortured hero needs a sidekick. I'm here now, and I'll be that for you."

Even though anxiety is still gnawing at my insides, and I'm pretty sure he's being a smart ass, his words give me comfort. "Do you mean that?"

He lifts a shoulder. "Someone's gotta be in your corner who doesn't have skin in the game either way."

"So it's a pity friendship."

He smiles. "What, you don't want to be my friend?"

"Just trying to figure out who I can trust."

His brows draw in, creasing his forehead. "Well, I won't tell you to trust me, but I've got your back. Anything that shakes up these rich pricks in the area has my vote."

"Technically, I'm one of those rich pricks now."

He gives me a look. "Nah, you're not. You can wear the clothes and take the name, but you've known what it's like to go without. I can see it in your eyes. I'd trust you with my dollar before any of those motherfuckers."

Nodding, I lean back in the chair.

"So, who's got you smiling like that? You really testing out that 'love in Rosebrook Falls' theory?" he asks, looking pointedly at my phone again.

This time, there's a text on the lock screen.

LITTLE ROSE:

> Now you're leaving me on read? Guess I'll go find someone else who threatens me with dick pics then. 👻

The thought of *anyone* else sending her a picture of their dick makes anger lash at my chest.

Swallowing down the misplaced jealousy, I shake my head. "You know how it is."

He nods slowly. "Let me guess. It's complicated?"

"That's putting it mildly." I spin the ring on my finger. "You really want to be my friend?"

"Well, now I'm not sure. You're kind of making me feel like it's a bad idea." He nods to the phone again.

I laugh, running a hand through my hair. "I promise I won't send you a picture of my dick. Those are for *special* friends only."

I'm *itching* to tag somewhere public.

And while there is street art in Rosebrook Falls beyond the little bit that I've done, it's mainly kept to the HillPoint or to the campus on the other side of town, and I don't want to just come out to another artists' turf and paint over their buildings and walls. It's disrespectful.

I wasn't lying when I told Juliette that street artists are territorial.

But I can't ask anyone about it, because I don't want anyone to know that it's *me* doing the art.

I wear a mask, obviously, both to protect me from the fumes and to keep anyone from knowing my identity, but it's still risky.

Right now, I'm on the outskirts of the town where the train tracks sit unused near the base of the cliffs that line the county park. The train itself looks like it's been sitting on this track for at least a few years. There's rust on the metal and trash littering the ground from where others have come by.

There *is* some tagging on a few of the boxcars, but it isn't extreme, kept mainly to the edges.

The spot I pick is a little grimy from being abandoned for so long, but it's definitely usable. It's not like I'm trying to make a masterpiece here, and I don't have any stencils of my work to perfect the lines.

All I had time to do was hop on a bus to the city about forty minutes away and grab new paints.

Art is my expression, and in every other aspect of my life, I have to hold it inside, so the need feels amplified somehow right now to get it out.

They can tie my tongue, but they can't stay my hand.

Merrick didn't ask questions when I asked him to drop me off here; he just did it without any protest, loading up my supplies and smirking like he knew I was up to no good.

I grab the stepstool from beside me and lug the backpack of paints over my shoulder before heading to the train and dropping it all on the ground. I open the zipper and grab a few of the spray cans, black first and then a bright pink.

Next, I flip my baseball cap forward on my head, grab the bandanna I use as a mask to cover my nose and mouth, and tie it around my face. It's a simple black with the bottom half of a skeleton showing its jaw and teeth, and the second I have it affixed to my face, my muscles relax, familiarity blanketing me.

Lastly, I slip on thin black gloves and then cover my head with the hood of my sweatshirt, slipping it over my hat until I'm covered enough where I don't think I'd be recognized.

And then I get to work.

The sound of the can shaking and then the spray hitting steel sends satisfaction rippling down my spine, and I let myself get lost in the act, tension leaving my body with every stroke of the paint.

Two hours later, the sun has set too much for me to keep going—I forgot to pick up a light—so I grab the black paint and almost tag RMO in the corner of the piece, but I hesitate at the last second.

RMO feels too obvious now.

I paint a black rose instead with a simple R as the stem.

And then I pack it up and head to where I know I'll be able to see the piece from a good vantage point.

Upside Down Rock.

Chapter 25

Juliette

"FANCY MEETING YOU HERE, TROUBLE," I SAY TO Roman as I hike up to the cliffside.

I drink him in, heart stuttering because he looks like *him* again. There's a stark difference between the man in a pressed suit on all the news outlets standing next to his father and the mussed-up, tattooed guy standing in front of me now.

Oddly, I'm more comfortable in his presence this way than I would be if he were dressed up like a mini-Marcus.

He's in dark jeans and a zip-up hoodie, the fabric on his arms pushed up over his elbows so his sleeves of ink are on full display. He's got a backward baseball cap on, small tufts of his dark hair peeking out the sides like they can't be contained. He grins like seeing me is the best part of his day, and my stomach flips, pathetically hopeful that it is.

It's the best part of *my* day, and a little piece of me hates that, but clearly not enough to keep me from coming here.

He's perched against the trunk of a thick tree, and when I

plop down beside him, he nudges my shoulder with his. "We have to stop meeting like this, Little Rose."

"Well, I was promised a muse."

A genuine smile breaks across his face, and it lights up a place somewhere deep inside of me to see it. I don't know when it shifted from me disliking his presence to whatever *this* is between us, but I can't say I'm upset at the progression.

Wanting to make someone else feel good is…nice. It's the rest of the emotions when it comes to him that I wish I could will away.

He chuckles, his fingers tapping against his black book, and my eyes travel over the rim of the pages, desperate to peer into his world and see what his talented hands decide to draw.

"What are you working on?" I ask.

He pulls the book to his chest and clicks his tongue. "I'll show you mine if you show me yours."

There's a tone of innuendo in his words, and it sends heat flickering low in my stomach. I shift, clenching my thighs together. "That's hardly fair."

He shrugs and taps his temple. "Mutually assured destruction, Little Rose. You want access to my brain? I want access to yours."

My fingers tighten around my own notebook. The thought of him reading my words and laughing—or worse, thinking it's awful—makes my skin itch.

He nudges my shoulder with his again, tilting his head until our gazes lock. "What's the matter? Afraid I'll become even *more* attractive when you realize how incredibly deep I am?"

I lift a brow. "More like, afraid I'll have to pretend your stick figures are profound."

He barks out a laugh. "Rich coming from the girl who *definitely* writes love scenes and pretends they're not about me."

Scoffing, I roll my eyes. "You know wishing for it doesn't make it reality, right?"

He leans back, his gaze flickering to my mouth and back. "I do wish for it. Every night."

God, he's impossible.

I pivot. "I saw the *Rosebrook Rag* article on you."

"Ah." All hints of flirtation drop from his face.

Roman leans against the tree, his eyes skimming over the foliage, the picnic table, and then to the cliff, where the sun is starting to hit lower in the sky. His brows are drawn, and his blue eyes are piercing as he soaks in the view. He bends his legs, resting his arms on his knees, his thumb absentmindedly spinning the silver ring on his finger.

I squint, leaning forward to get a better look when I realize he has small specks of color on his wrist. Spray paint, if I had to guess.

He casts me a sideways glance. "What?"

"Nothing, you just look…" I gesture to his arms.

He brings his hands up to inspect them before giving me a wolfish grin. "I was painting."

"Graffiti?"

Nerves twist me into knots. I don't want him to get in trouble, because what if he does and then something happens to him? What if he leaves?

The back of his head thunks against the tree. "Why do you say it like that?"

My frown deepens. "Like what?"

"*Graffiti*," he repeats with a snobbish tone. "Like it's a dirty word."

"Okay, well, first of all, that's a terrible impersonation. I sound nothing like that."

He gives me a look.

"And secondly, I don't think that. I just... It's illegal, Roman. This isn't Cali. Don't you think you're playing with fire?"

He lifts a shoulder. "I'm not the only one tagging here."

"You're the only one making a statement with your art."

"Maybe you just haven't been looking hard enough."

"That's not the point," I argue.

"Then what is?"

"You know people will notice yours above the others," I say, softening my tone. "Whether you want to admit there's a difference or not."

Roman blows out a breath, and palms the back of his neck. "That *almost* sounded like a compliment."

My chest warms. "I think you might be the most talented person I've ever met, but things aren't as easy to get away with here, and I don't want something to happen to you."

He leans toward me, his eyes blazing. It's uncomfortable being so naked beneath his gaze, but he's pinned me in place, and I don't think I could move even if I tried.

Slowly, he reaches out, his large hand cupping my cheek, his thumb brushing against my bottom lip ever so slightly.

I suck in a breath, anticipation rolling through me like soft waves, and I press myself into the warmth of his touch.

"You gonna turn me in, Little Rose?" he asks.

I shake my head. "You know I'll keep your secrets."

"Good." Another brush of his thumb, only this time he lets it linger, applying the barest amount of pressure to my lip. "Thank you for caring, though."

I laugh, but it comes out breathy. "Yeah, well, despite you being an insufferable flirt and one of the most annoying friends I've ever had, I kind of like you."

"I kind of like you, too." His body leans toward mine until his mouth is so close, I can feel his breath on my lips. "You're my favorite secret, Juliette."

His gaze is like liquid fire, searing me from the inside out.

My heartbeat pounds in my ears. "Why are you looking at me like that?"

"You're just..." He swallows, his Adam's apple bobbing, and then he licks his lips and drops his hand.

"Just *what*?"

He blinks, his knee bouncing like he's shaking off whatever just had him suspended in place. "Nothing."

Disappointment hits me like a wrecking ball.

"You know, if we had a secret handshake, that would have been the perfect time to use it," he says, turning his voice into something light and teasing.

A smile crosses my face unbidden as he shifts the energy to something we both can handle. "You're never going to give that up, are you?"

"I just think it's bullshit. We're practically a best friends' club, meeting in the woods and trading confessions, but we don't have a handshake? Even the Boy Scouts have one."

I giggle. "They do not."

"What, so you're a Boy Scout expert now?"

His smile grows when I laugh.

"Come on," he says, standing up and brushing the dirt from his jeans. "I want to show you something before it gets too dark."

I scramble to my feet and follow him as he moves toward

the edge of the cliff, the sun spraying the sky with deep purples and pinks as it sets. "Cutting it kind of close, aren't you?"

He smirks, his dimples creasing his cheeks as he looks at me from his periphery. "Can you blame me? A pretty girl showed up and distracted me."

I bite my lip. "Now you're just flirting again."

He turns toward me, slips his hands in his pockets, and leans in until his breath ghosts across my ear. "Flirting with you is the best part of my day."

My heart flutters.

"What am I looking at?" I ask, trying to ignore how close he is and how I want him even *closer*.

His arm lifts, breezing by my shoulder as it does, and his body curls around mine from the motion like he's wrapping me up. He points in the direction of the old railroad, where a train that hasn't been in use in years sits on the unused tracks.

As soon as my attention goes there, I see it. The setting sun creates an almost halo-like effect around the artwork, and it's stunning, even if the sight of it causes fear to flood my veins. Fear for *him*.

The piece itself is a silhouette of a man on his knees, shackles around his arms, the word *Freedom* creating the chains that lock his limbs. Behind him is a road sign that says, *Welcome to Rosebrook Falls*.

The image is visceral, and tears spring to my eyes.

"You did all this today?" I ask.

I spin to face him and lose my balance from how quickly I move. His hands shoot out to grasp my hips, and my palms fly to his chest to regain my footing. The air pulls taut when we touch, and his fingers flex against me like he wants to grab me tighter but is resisting the urge.

I look up at him, heat flaring through my veins like embers catching flame.

"It's so strange," I admit.

"What is?"

"Seeing your art and feeling like you're painting pieces of my soul."

Our gazes lock, his fingers digging into my hips.

His jaw tics once. Twice. Three times.

But then he lets me go.

I shake off the feeling of rejection, my teeth sinking into my lower lip as he moves to the edge of the boulder and leans against it.

"What made you paint it?" I ask.

He watches me, his finger absentmindedly grazing the bottom of his chin, back and forth. "It was either that or *Eat the Rich*, but that felt a little too cannibal-adjacent, and considering *you* are rich, I didn't want to take any chances."

I huff out a small laugh. "You know you're technically rich now, too."

"The point remains."

There are a million different words on my tongue, prodding against the seam of my mouth, but I swallow them back down.

"Have you ever felt suffocated?" I ask instead.

"You'll need to be more specific."

It's hard to give the emotions life when I've spent so long ignoring they exist in the first place, but for some reason, being around Roman makes me want to experience everything that living has to offer. Even the painful parts.

"I've lived here my entire life, and I never realized just how many parameters were set for me until I stepped outside of them. And now that I'm back, it's just…"

His full attention is on me, his eyes searing through me like he can't see anything else. It's a heady sensation, and one that I remind myself I shouldn't like feeling.

"All of the time," he replies.

Sadness flashes across his face, and I ache to wipe away the look. I don't like it when he looks so lost.

"Felicity's been telling me for years to just grow a pair and break the rules." I smile thinking about her. I haven't talked to her much since I've been back, and I definitely haven't told her about Roman, but I know she'd approve of me coming up here to see a guy I wouldn't be allowed to see.

She'd probably throw me a party if she found out.

"Felicity's your friend?"

I grin. "Best friend."

He scoffs. "Do *you* guys have a handshake?"

"Maybe we do."

"You're not gonna tell me?"

Amusement wraps around me, and talking to him like this lifts all the weight of expectation off my shoulders. Where I expected him to feel dark and heavy and dangerous, he feels light and funny and…free.

"If I told you then that would negate the *secret* part," I say.

He sits against the edge of Upside Down Rock and crosses his arms.

"If it makes you feel any better," I add, "I've never had any scandalous rendezvous with her up in the hills."

He gives me a soft smile and then smacks his hands on his

thighs. "That's it. I'm tired of pretending like I'm not desperate for you to write about me."

I quirk a brow. "Yeah, you've been *really* subtle about it up until now."

"It's a gift."

"What's so story-worthy about us?"

He blinks. "You're incredibly hurtful today. You're lucky I have thick skin."

Laughing, I shake my head. "I've told you. I don't really write love stories."

Lie. I've written about us for years.

A slow smile blooms across his face, his eyes sparkling. "Who said anything about a love story?"

Heat floods my skin, but I don't drop his gaze. My heart thrums wildly in my chest, and my stomach is tight, but when he walks toward me with a slow and measured gait, I don't move from my spot.

"So, what *do* you write?" he asks.

I shift on my feet. "The world and all the people in it."

Another step, and he's close enough now that I can smell the citrus and sandalwood of his cologne. "And how would you write *me*?"

Like he's a light in the darkness, a northern star to my night.

"I think I'd write you as the sky," I say. "Big and vast and full of empty air."

He shakes his head like he's disappointed. "Your prose could use some work."

I bite my lip to keep from grinning.

Leaning in, he runs the back of his hand up my cheek, tucking a stray hair behind my ear. A shiver runs along the length of my spine.

"And what about me?" I reply.

He watches me, his jaw muscle tensing and his eyes burning. "I think I'd paint you into everything."

Suddenly, the air feels too thin. Like his words have sucked the oxygen from the atmosphere, and I'm left reeling.

"Oh yeah?" I somehow manage. "So that sketchbook of yours…that's all me?"

He lifts his hand, lets his palm trace a path from the side of my neck down to my collarbone, more of a suggestion than a touch.

"That sketchbook's the east," he whispers. "And you, Juliette, are the sun."

My breath whooshes from my lungs.

He dips his head down until I can count every single lash, and *God*, I need him to just *kiss* me.

His phone rings, the sound jarring against my eardrums and grating against my nerves.

Snapping upright, he drops his hand and takes three large strides back, running his fingers through his hair like he's trying to hold himself together. He tugs his phone from his pocket and frowns at it, tapping it against his palm like he can't decide if he wants to answer or stay here with me.

"Do you need to take that?" I ask, giving him the out if he wants it.

His brows furrow as he turns to me. "It's my mom."

My chest pulls thinking that he'd miss a call from her because of me. "I should go anyway."

His mouth parts like he wants to protest, but instead he just nods. "Okay."

I stand still, because my legs feel a little shaky from whatever *that* just was, and he doesn't move, either.

He just stares at me like if he does it long enough, one of us will disappear. Or maybe he's hoping our situations will change. That he'll be someone else, or I will, and this thing that exists between us won't feel so damn impossible.

Clearing my throat, I wrap my hand around the back of my neck.

He gives a small smile, and something hot and panicked starts to brew in my chest, so I turn and walk away.

The way it seems I'm always doing with him.

Chapter 26

Roman

"LET'S TALK ABOUT YOUR MOTHER."

I grit my teeth, eyes flicking toward my dad who's sitting on my front porch, sipping iced tea and watching the sunset.

"Let's not," I reply.

He gives me a disappointed look.

My thumb spins the ring on my finger so fast it blurs in my vision. The last thing I want to do is give him power by doing whatever he says, but at some point, I have to give up this weird need to stay in control and just trust this will work out.

If I don't, I might drive myself insane.

I may have already if it weren't for the fact that every night over the past week, I've snuck to Upside Down Rock and met with Juliette. Sometimes, we spend hours talking about everything and nothing and all the in between. Other times, we sit in silence and *create*. She writes her stories, and I draw *her*.

It's always her.

A sense of longing wraps around me.

Juliette would want me to face whatever my life has turned

into head-on. If we're relegated to dark corners and fake boundaries that don't come close to defining what we really are, the least I can do is make the sacrifices worth it.

"Fine," I admit. "But...I came here for Brooke. *She's* who I want to talk about. She needs health insurance and money for her meds. I didn't know what else to do."

He nods, grimacing. "You don't know what she's sick with?"

That familiar desolation rises in me.

Helplessness.

"No, it just came on a few years back. She has good days and bad. Lots of headaches, dizziness, vomiting. Seizures. But everything checks out in tests, so they don't know what's wrong."

My father looks sad. "Genetic testing?"

I shrug. "We only have Mom. No clue who her father is."

My dad frowns like the thought of my mom with someone else pains him. "If I had known you were struggling so much..."

A hit of gratitude smacks me in the face. I don't want to feel anything other than resentment toward him. The anger is comfortable. Familiar. This new sensation makes me itch. "Yeah, well, I needed a dad either way."

He swallows harshly, his gaze never straying from the backyard, but when he replies next, his voice is thick. "I should have done better to care for you. I didn't realize Heather—"

"That's right," I cut him off. "You didn't."

Who does he think he is, trying to have this heart to heart now? I've got news for him—he's about five years too late. Where was this man when I came to him the last time, when I was basically arms wide open, begging for him to care?

He wasn't sick then.

Dad leans forward, resting his elbows on his knees. "Have you spoken to Brooklynn about her trust?"

I clear my throat. *I would if she'd answer her phone.* "She won't be interested."

He sighs, then nods. "Well, in any case, I've got a health insurance plan with her name on it, Roman. She can't say no to that, can she?"

My lungs squeeze with hope, or fuck, I don't know what. But it's light and unbelievable, and like maybe being here *isn't* the worst thing in the world, even if it means giving up everything else that matters.

Even if it means I don't get Juliette.

I breathe in deep and rock back in the patio chair, gazing out at the sun. A million different thoughts swirl in my head, and a thousand different feelings spiral through me, mixing like a heavy sludge and slicking my insides.

But…I believe him. I think.

"Your mother needs to sign off on the papers for the health insurance, unless Brooklynn can afford to wait until she's eighteen and you think she'll accept it from me." He hikes his brows.

"I don't want her to wait."

I'm not sure he'll be around by then, anyway, so that's a risk.

"And your mother?"

My chest aches when I think about her. I've been avoiding her phone calls since I've been back, not even listening to her voicemails, because I'm angry with her. I'm *so* fucking angry, and getting this space from her just makes me more upset.

But then there's another part that recognizes it isn't really *her*, is it? Drugs don't make a person; they just hide them somewhere we can't find.

"She needs rehab. I want—" I choke on the words, and I try again. "I want her to get better, to be my *mom* again. But she won't go willingly."

"Son." He sighs. "Some people are beyond help."

My lips twist, emotion hitting me hard and heavy, and I refuse to accept that answer. I know I've thought about giving up on her, have tried a thousand times to get through to her with no success, but I can't just leave her out for the wolves to snatch up and carry off.

"I need you to try." The words are grit and grime as they cross my tongue. "I'm *asking* you to try."

My gaze is burning a hole through the ground, something thick sitting in the back of my throat and clogging my airways.

"Please," I rasp.

"So, call her, then."

"Who, Brooke?"

"No, your mother."

I unstick my tongue from the roof of my mouth. "Right now?"

"Right now."

I hate that he's here, hate that all of my playing cards are scattered in front of him and he's got me on strings like a puppeteer. I hate that he's about to see how I'm treated by the woman who's supposed to love me the most.

And more than anything, I hate that I care.

She answers on the first ring.

"I've been trying to get a hold of you." My mother's flat and void-of-any-human-emotion voice flows through the line.

"Sorry, things have been busy," I reply.

"Don't forget why you're there," she snaps.

I bristle. I'm annoyed that everyone in my life seems to have strings attached to me they can pull this way or that.

My father's lips twist in displeasure. "I assure you, Heather, our son is in no way lacking in his loyalty to why he's here," he pipes up.

My heart stutters because I didn't expect him to defend me, and the little boy inside of me who's dreamed of having him for things like that preens.

The line grows silent. Deathly so. And then a whisper that's so small and weak it's as if it's from another person entirely. "Marcus?"

It's a thousand knives carving through my chest when she has more of a visceral reaction to hearing her ex-lover's voice—who abandoned her—than her own child's.

I swallow harshly, cracking my neck and leaning forward, glancing up to my dad. His eyes are on me, not on the phone.

When he doesn't reply to her, I lick my lips and start talking again. "I haven't forgotten, Ma. How's Brooke?"

She scoffs, her voice hardening again. "She's fine, she's... Brooke. You know how she is, nose in a book, ignoring the world."

A smile quirks up my lips when I picture Brooklynn in her books. "But everything else is good?"

"She's taken care of." She sucks in a quick breath. "Marcus... are you still there?"

My throat swells and a burn radiates behind my eyes.

If she were still the mom I grew up with, she'd ask me how I was. And maybe when she did, I'd tell her about this girl I met. How she's so beautiful I can hardly breathe, and how doing this is costing me a chance with someone who I'm pretty sure I could love.

Huh.

"Is Brooke there right now?"

She clears her throat. "I'm not at home."

"Okay, well, she's being put on a health insurance plan."

"What?" Her tone flicks higher. "We're getting insurance? Oh, Marcus, thank you."

"It wasn't me, actually," he says, his gaze coming to rest on me again, a layer of understanding blanketing his view. "This is all Roman's doing."

Her tone changes again, until it's smooth as cream. "Of course it is. Roman's always been such a good boy."

Resentment bubbles up like acid, scorching through the cracks she's caused in my heart.

I lick my lips. "There are conditions, Ma."

"What do you mean, 'conditions'?"

My knee bounces faster. "You've gotta get some help. Rehab. Wherever we tell you to go."

I glance at my father because, well, we didn't exactly talk this out, but he nods, and more gratitude seeps into the moment.

"What did you tell him, Roman?" Her voice is low, a hiss that whips through the phone and latches onto my cheek, stinging like a slap. "Been running your mouth?"

"This is how it works now," I reply, my jaw tight. "We help you. You get clean."

"I can't," she whimpers.

Blowing out a sharp breath, my shoulders drop in defeat. That was my last card to play, and honestly, I hoped having my dad on the line with me would help the matter.

"Heather," my dad chimes in. "My lawyer Frederick will be sending a form for you to sign for Brooklynn's enrollment, and you *will* sign it, do you understand?"

A bit of my loyalty shifts and skews with every word my dad speaks.

"Frederick," she echoes. "Sure, of course."

"You'll sign it today," I push.

She pauses. "Hasn't taken you long to get that Montgomery bite in you, has it, Ry?"

I exhale slowly, my fingernails pressing crescent shaped moons into my palms.

"I want you to get help, sugar," my father adds.

The nickname he uses spears through me. It obviously affects my mother, too, because she sucks in a gasp. "Do I…" She pauses. "Do I get to see you?"

My chest twists that she didn't ask the same of me.

My dad looks like he's waiting on me to answer, and I let out a hollow chuckle. "She isn't talking to me."

"Heather." His voice is softer now, genuine remorse tempering the tone.

And for just a moment, I let myself wonder what my life would be like if he had been able to love her. If maybe he would have also loved me.

Would I have turned out any differently?

Would Juliette and I have met when I was a kid and been able to convince our families to put down their weapons and live in peace?

Would Brooklynn be dealing with the things she is now?

My father looks at me again, his face tightening. "If you get the help we offer, if you really *try*, then…maybe."

"Okay." Her voice is still small. Still quiet. So unlike the woman I've known, both before the accident and this shell of herself that she became after. "I'll sign the papers.

Brooklynn shouldn't have to suffer any more than what she already has."

Click.

Goodbye to you, too, I guess.

My father blows out a heavy breath. "Well, that went…"

"Better than expected," I finish for him.

He frowns and then looks out over the yard, rocking slightly in his chair.

"You did good the other day," he says. "Speaking to the reporters, I mean."

I glance at him and nod before sipping the iced tea one of his employees brought us.

"What now?" I ask.

My father shakes his head, placing down his drink and twisting in his chair to face me, a serious expression taking over his features. It hits me as I stare at him that we really do look alike. I take after him much more than my own mother, and I'm not sure whether that makes me angry or proud.

It's a weird mix of both, and the two sides warring for the spot makes me want to rip out of my skin.

"I know it was you," he says.

Confusion races through me, and I tilt my head, masking my reaction. "Know what was me?"

"The graffiti that popped up the other week on the train car."

My heart pounds against my ribcage. *Fuck.*

He picks up a manila folder, one that I hadn't even realized was there at his side, and then he hesitates, placing it in his lap.

"Remember our deal," he reminds me.

I huff, irritated he's questioning me. "I signed the papers, didn't I? There's no going back now."

"Good. Right."

He hands me the folder.

I lift a brow, looking down at it. "What's this?"

"A detailed explanation of the corruption by the Calloways."

"Okay…" I wait for him to clarify more, but he doesn't. He just stays still and silent like he's waiting on me to put things together for myself, which is difficult to do when I have zero moving pieces.

"I want you to paint it on the walls of this town." Something sparks to life in his gaze.

My face contorts in surprise. "You…*want* me to tag?"

"Sometimes the best message is delivered by a faceless ghost. And sometimes the best way to take down an empire is when you give people a sprinkle of doubt and let it fester." He pauses, licking his lips. "*Sometimes* to get rid of the rot, you have to rip everything out from the roots and start fresh."

I nod, even though I'm not sure I entirely believe him. "And what if I get caught?"

He shrugs. "You'll be protected."

"But you can't take care of this?" I lift the folder.

My father sniffs. "The Calloway ties are strong, son, and I've fought for years, but with me being sick and in treatment, I've let things get away from me. They own the politicians. The city council members. The board of trustees to Verona University. Every avenue I try, I get shut down. And every year, they dig their talons deeper into the town and push me out."

"What about the WayMont agreement?"

"All that agreement does is ensure the Montgomery Organization and Calloway Enterprises don't own above a certain percentage of the town. But shell companies aren't technically owned by Calloway Enterprises, and bribing political influence isn't, either."

"That's fucking bullshit."

He nods. "There are always loopholes. Craig has a business deal with people outside of this town. Influential people. They send in a group he says are land agents. They like to come to the HillPoint areas and coerce the neighborhoods into high-interest loans. I was too busy trying to survive to even realize what they were doing before it was too late. They've acquired ownership of land and businesses because of defaults on those loans."

"So, they basically own everything, despite an agreement saying they won't?"

"Almost."

I swallow. "Are you broke?"

He grimaces. "Not yet. But if things keep going the way they are…"

It does seem fucked up.

I finger through the documents. There aren't paper trails to what the Calloways have done, but my dad has collected enough information that I can cause suspicion.

My dad sniffs and then stands, adjusting his belt buckle and patting me on the back. "Knowledge topples kingdoms, son. All I'm asking is for you to enlighten the people."

"Conveniently leaving out *your* corruption, I'm assuming?"

He smirks. "I didn't ever say I was a saint. You've gotta lie with the dogs to get the bone."

My brows furrow, and I nod.

"Benny's around if you need any help with this. He's your go-to, but he and Frederick are the *only* ones you can trust with this. Understand me?"

"Yeah," I mumble, my focus still on the papers.

I pull out one of the pages, a glossy photo staring me in the face. One with three men huddled in the back alley of what looks like The Round Table Tavern on the edge of the HillPoint.

Moving down the page, my finger ghosts across the names. Tyler Bault. Art Penngrove. Lance Calloway.

Fuck my life.

I grit my teeth, reminding myself why I said yes to this.

For Brooklynn. For Ma.

But it doesn't stop the foreboding circulating in my chest, warning me that this is only going to push Juliette further away.

The ROSEBROOK Rag

Graffiti: Art With a Message? Or Vandalism Without a Cause?

A striking mural has surfaced on the wall of The Round Table Tavern in HillPoint, depicting giant hands tearing apart a map of Rosebrook Falls, with the land cracking under pressure. The phrase "Hands of Ruin" looms above, and a small black rose adorns the corner.

The bar, recently acquired by Mayor Penngrove's son, Art Penngrove, following a loan default, declined to comment on the artwork.

Is this an act of vandalism or a powerful piece of art?

#RosebrookRag #HandsOfRuin #SecretStreetArtist #GraffitiGate

Chapter 27

Juliette

TROUBLE:

What'd you write about today?

ME:

A girl who's concerned her friend will be hurt by her family because he's allergic to blank walls.

TROUBLE:

You worried about me, Little Rose? 😉

ME:

Yes.

I HIT *SEND*, AND IT FEELS A LITTLE BETTER ONCE I get it off my chest.

We've been texting back and forth the past few weeks, Roman and me, and every day, I get a text from him asking what I'm writing. Since the only time I actually *get* to write is when I'm with him, I've started using our messages as an outlet, and part of me thinks that's why he continues to text and ask.

But seeing his graffiti showing up more and more in the papers, watching my father get increasingly upset at very aggressive speculation being aimed in our direction…it makes everything uncomfortable for me.

I haven't forgotten Roman implying it was *my* dad who caused the car accident all those years ago, and I'm not naive enough to think he's wrong.

Still…I love my dad. And I hate that my brothers are caught in the fray of all this.

It makes me feel awful for continuing to meet with him. To talk to him. To enjoy his company. Like a betrayal to my family in the worst kind of way.

FELICITY:

> Why are you avoiding me? I've been back for over a week, and as penance for your betrayal, you're coming out with me anywhere I choose. I pick the outfit, the place, and the music.

I make a face as I read her text, but I guess fair is fair. I avoided her because I don't know what to say. I'm not sure how to talk to her without spilling everything about Roman and me, but I'm not sure I *should* tell her. Felicity isn't exactly discreet when she thinks that things should be a certain type of way, and the last thing I want is for her to dip her hand into something beyond her scope and ruffle feathers she has no business touching.

TROUBLE:

Maybe the guy in your story has no choice. Maybe it isn't about him at all.

ME:

Doesn't make it any better.

TROUBLE:

Does he grow up to be a famous artist with a gallery in Paris in the end?

ME:

Nope. He ends up in prison. Another cautionary tale, just like his much more intelligent friend warned him.

TROUBLE:

Tough crowd.

Conjugal visits?

I grin.

The couch cushion dips beside me, a heavy silence hitting the air.

"What's got you smiling like that?" Lance's voice cuts through my emotions, and my grin drops, my heart hammering as I slide my phone underneath my thigh.

I blink at him, shocked to see him home.

His hazel gaze takes in mine with concern. "What's wrong with you?"

His question snaps me out of my daze, and I roll my eyes with an audible huff. "Oh, now you care?"

He sits back and flinches like my words were a physical attack.

"Come on, Jules." He runs his hands over his face, and I don't miss that the knuckles are split open and scabbed. Worry lights up my middle, but I push it back down. "Don't be a bitch to me."

"You know, why is that always the default insult for women?"

"I don't—"

"*You...*" I point a finger at him, glaring. "Are an asshole. I'm mad at you."

His entire face drops, and he leans forward, resting his elbows on his knees, his wavy, black hair ghosting across his eye when he hangs his head. A muscle in his jaw tics.

"And you know what?" I continue. "Maybe you deserve for me to be a bitch to you. Has that thought ever crossed your mind, Lance? Or have you been too busy ignoring me to care?"

He clears his throat, his face drawn like I've pummeled him. Like *I'm* the bad guy here.

"California really did a number on you, huh?" he murmurs after a few quiet seconds.

Now, *that* pisses me off, and I shoot to a stand. I'm so mad it feels like I could spit fire. I'm not even sure *why* I'm so angry, other than the fact that nothing feels like it's been in my control since coming back.

"Did it ever occur to you that maybe it's this fucking family that's pissing me off?" I hiss. "Maybe it's only *you* I'm being a bitch to."

I shove a finger in his face, and he grits his teeth, his gaze growing dark. "Get your finger out of my face, Juliette, or I swear to God."

His voice is cold as ice, and so low I barely hear him say it. He's always had that dangerous quality to him, but he's never used it *against* me. It's always been to protect me. Having it flipped is jarring.

I drop my hand and let out a slow breath. "What happened to you?"

His jaw clenches, and he looks away from me, but there's something about him that screams of sadness, and it douses my anger, just a little.

Sighing, I plop back down on the couch and stare at him. "Do you know you used to be the only person I could say anything to? Now look at us."

"You still can," he claims, turning his head to face me again. The iciness in his gaze has disappeared entirely, leaving behind the soft warmth that I've known my whole life.

"I've been home for weeks now, Lance." I try to keep the hurt from my voice, but it cracks anyway. "Where have you been?"

His mouth opens and closes. He runs his fingers through his hair, making the silver chain around his neck rustle and gleam under the living room lights.

I put up my palm. "You know what? I don't even care at this point. But you don't get to waltz in here and act like we can chit-chat like old times. *You* don't deserve to know why I'm in a bad mood."

He swallows and nods, crossing his foot over the opposite knee, then resting his hand on top.

My gaze tracks along his cracked knuckles again, that

familiar worry surging through me. I want to ask him if he's all right, but again, I keep the words down.

He doesn't get to feel like I care.

Not when he doesn't seem to care about me.

Instead, I stiffen my chin. If he wants to call me a bitch and act like he hasn't been the biggest jerk on the face of the planet, then I'll just snub him. Sniffing, I lean forward to pick up the remote and turn on the TV, flipping through the channels.

"Jules," he murmurs, his voice coated with sadness.

I ignore him.

He shifts on the couch. "I'm sorry."

"For what?" I side-eye him. *Good job ignoring him, Jules. Real tough.*

He huffs, his head angling toward the ceiling before he looks back at me. "For a lot of things."

I lift a shoulder, swallowing down the emotion. "It's whatever."

"It isn't." He shakes his head and sighs. "I've obviously fucked up with you."

"Yeah, well." I flip the channel again, my finger hitting the remote harder than necessary.

"Art's dating this girl, and she's not really someone who has anyone on her side. His dad doesn't approve, and he's not willing to give her up, so he has me looking out for her."

"And that means you can't be around me, *why*?" I give him a look like he's lost his mind.

"It doesn't. There's just a lot going on."

"Mmhm, sure." I focus harder on the TV.

"Having you gone sucked, okay?" he finally blurts out. "You're the only family member I can stand to be around, and I—"

"So, you basically excommunicate me?" I scoff. "Real mature."

He grits his teeth, his angular jaw flexing. "I thought maybe you'd choose to stay away if we didn't talk."

I gape at him, my hand with the remote frozen in the air. "Well, that *sucks*."

He shakes his head again. "No, I—do you realize how fucked up our family is, Jules? And you're so good. The best. You're the only one worth a damn around here, and if you come back, if you get pulled into the family bullshit, they'll suck the light right out of you."

My brows draw down. "Lance, I don't need *saving* from our family. What's wrong with you?"

Even as I say it, I don't believe the words. Because maybe I do.

His nostrils flare as he stares at me, and then he exhales and grins at me, like whatever he was about to say, whatever has been weighing on him since he walked in, just disappeared. "You're right. I'm sorry."

I look at him like he's lost his mind. "I don't forgive you."

"Not even if I promise to never do it again?" he asks.

Tossing down the remote, I cross my arms and look at him. I want to stay mad, I really do. There's a huge part of me that's so hurt by his dismissal, and I'm not sure it will ever heal so that we can get back to where we were as kids. But then my gaze sweeps across his features again, and I really take him in.

His hazel eyes are more pronounced, but it's only because of the dark circles underneath, proving he isn't sleeping. His hands look like he's beat people half to death.

My chest squeezes.

No matter how angry I am with him, if I shut him out, am I any better than how he's been with me?

My shoulders drop, and I sigh. "Fine. But don't *ever* do it again."

Relief coasts across his eyes, and he beams at me, his smile pulling up higher on the right.

"Do you want to talk about it?" he asks.

I sniff. "Depends on what you're referencing, I guess."

He waves his arm at me. "Whatever it is that has you like this."

Another wave of irritation hits me, and I turn toward him, my anger recognizing him as a viable punching bag, regardless of whether it's truly him who deserves the ire or not.

"No, actually, I don't want to talk about it. Maybe when I first got home, and *no one* even blinked in my direction. Maybe when you came to that Penngrove fundraiser without a single, solitary 'I missed you, Jules.' But now? Now I'm *good*. No need to rehash how our parents are trying to marry me off to my ex like a Regency-era fever dream, or how I'm *allegedly* an adult but still sleeping in my childhood home."

I wave my fists in the air while I continue my tirade, and Lance's eyes grow wider with each spewed word. But I don't stop, because now I'm on a roll, and if he wants to hear things, then he'll hear them. "The leash is back on, let's all pretend like we're surprised."

After my rant, I exhale heavily, a little out of breath from how quickly the words left my brain and flew into the air, but I feel a little better.

Lighter, maybe.

"Jesus, I thought you said you forgive me," Lance says.

I purse my lips at him. "I do."

He nods slowly. "Yeah, okay."

"You know what I want to talk about?" I lean toward him. "I want to talk about *you*. About how you're never around, how you've made a career out of disappearing. Or why Benjamin Voltaire acted like you were besties the other night. And let's not forget the bruised knuckles, or how you suddenly don't give a damn that Ty has black eyes and is carrying a gun."

Lance arches a brow. "Ty has a gun?"

I give him a look. "*Had*, when I first got back into town. You didn't see it?"

He rubs the back of his neck.

My chest cramps. Him not paying attention to Tyler is new. They've always been inseparable: him, Tyler, and Art.

But maybe I need to give a little to get a little with him. Clearly, he's not going to be the one to open up first, and even if he hurt me, I still miss him.

He's still my person.

I watch him carefully, but his face is a blank mask. Impenetrable.

"Are you hanging out in the HillPoint?" I ask, point blank.

He flinches. "Don't ask questions you don't want the answer to, Jules."

I narrow my gaze. "If I didn't want the answer, I wouldn't have asked the question, *Lance*."

He scoffs and looks away. "Art owns property there now. It's not like I'm in danger."

"Right," I reply. "Because shady real-estate dealings are always *super* safe."

He cuts a look at me. "How do you know it was shady?"

I give him a thin smile. "I didn't. Not until you just confirmed it."

Lance sighs, leaning forward, resting his elbows on his knees, his head hanging. "I love you, Jules, but I can't tell you everything. Please just respect it."

My mouth sours. "Fine, then tell me why Benjamin acted like you two were friends the other night. Does it have to do with why Ty says you're never around anymore?"

"Ty's an idiot. And so is Benny, for that matter."

Benny? There's that nickname again.

My mouth drops. "Oh my God, you *are* hanging out with them."

Defiance ghosts over his face. The same look he used to get when Beverly would tell us we couldn't have dessert, or when Dad laid down an ironclad rule. The rest of us folded like lawn chairs, but not Lance. He'd get this glint in his eye like the rule was a dare; something for him to break.

"It's nothing," he says.

"You do realize saying that makes it feel like *something*."

His silence is answer enough.

I tilt my head. "Give me a crumb here, dude. Is it a cult? Some underground fight club? A super-secret sex scandal?"

He doesn't laugh. He doesn't even blink.

And *that* makes worry prickle along my spine more than anything else. "Lance, what the *fuck*? Dad will kill you if he finds out you've been hanging out in Montgomery territory."

"Rich, coming from you."

I frown, unease flickering inside me like a light switch. "What does that mean?"

He lifts his chin, his jaw stiffening. "How do you know Roman Montgomery?"

That question takes the wind out of my sails, and I press my lips together, suddenly not wanting to talk anymore. "Quit trying to change the subject."

"Stay away from him."

I scoff. "You sound like Dad."

He stiffens. "I am *not* our fucking father."

"No shit. Dad wouldn't be sneaking around with people like Benjamin Voltaire."

His face softens. "I didn't come here to argue. I came here to check in. I've missed you, and I worry about you. I don't trust anyone in this family to look out for you the way you deserve."

My eyes burn, emotion swelling in my chest. For as mad as I am at Lance, I can't help the fact that I love him so damn much. "I miss you, too."

"Where're Pax and Alex?" he asks, looking around.

I shrug. "I'm sure Paxton is around somewhere doing Dad's bidding, and Alex is probably at the theater."

Lance's phone chimes. He pulls it out, reads whatever is on the screen, and then his brows furrow, tension lining his face.

"Who's that?" I pry, leaning over his shoulder to try and get a good look.

I don't see much, mostly because his shoulder is the size of my head. "Jesus, Lance, when did you get so jacked? You're like a fucking boulder."

He smirks and flexes without shame. "I've always been the superior Calloway. I don't know why you're just now noticing."

I snort and smack him on the arm. "You're an idiot."

"And you're nosy." He moves his phone away from me, standing up and slipping it into his back pocket.

"I won't apologize for wanting to know who outranks me on your priority list."

Lance scoffs. "Don't be ridiculous. No one outranks you."

"What?" I look at him innocently. "I'm just saying, your phone goes off and suddenly you have to run. I'm drawing logical conclusions."

His nostrils flare like he's trying to rein in whatever he really wants to say.

"Is it Art's girlfriend?"

"It's not anyone you know." A hesitation, and then, "I do have to go, though."

I hide the annoyance, and I'm not surprised. It's not even worth fighting about anymore. "All right. See you whenever I see you, I guess."

"I love you, Jules. It's good to have you home."

My eyes burn, and I try to reply, but all I manage is a tight grin.

I unstick my phone from where it's stuck to the skin of my thigh and pull up my messages instead, getting lost in my own important person instead of thinking about all the ways my family hurts my heart.

Chapter 28

Roman

"JUST BECAUSE YOU'RE FILTHY RICH NOW DOESN'T mean *I* have to accept blood money."

Brooklynn's voice is defiant, but there's a tremble under it, just enough to make my chest ache. I don't correct her, even though after what Dad told me, I'm not sure how long the money will last if the Calloways have anything to say about it.

"Brooke…it's not that simple."

"So make it that simple," she retorts.

"He's getting Mom into rehab. She could come back to us."

Brooklynn makes a noise. "You're delusional, Bear. He's not some fairy godmother, he's a manipulative asshole in a fancy suit."

"He doesn't really wear suits."

I cringe as soon as I say it, knowing my ill-timed sarcasm won't land.

"He got health insurance," I continue, not sure why I'm defending him so much. "And if you'd just say yes to this trust, it will pay automatically every year for you. You'll never have to worry about it again. You'll have money at your fingertips, kid."

Say yes.

She makes a disgusted noise. "You sound like his little bitch boy."

I grit my teeth. "I'm *not*."

"What if he changes his mind?" she asks. "If he decides he doesn't *want* to help anymore? If he needs to use me to control you again?"

"He isn't—"

"Don't act like I'm naive to what's going on," she cuts me off. "I can put two and two together as easily as anyone else."

"I'm trying to take care of you."

"Well, *don't*. I can take care of myself. What do you think is gonna happen when Mom goes to rehab, anyway? That I'll come live there with you?"

The thought of her on her own freaks me out, but I know if I tell her that, she'll just force the issue even more.

"I know you can," I soothe. "You've always been the strongest one out of the two of us. I just don't want you looking back and regretting anything. I want you to let me make your life easier."

I'm not sure I'm doing a great job at selling it to her.

"I hate you for doing this," she whispers. "You just left me here. With *her*."

Her words cut through my chest. But if she needs to have me as a punching bag for her anger, then that's fine, I'll be that. I remember what it was like to be a seventeen-year-old kid with a ton of anger on my shoulders and nowhere to direct the pain.

I run a hand through my hair. "You know, once things settle down, you *could* come live with me. I know you hate me and all right now, but would it really be so bad?"

"My doctors are here."

"Connecticut has better ones."

I don't know if that's true, but now I have the means to get her the best care in the world, and I'll make sure she has it, whether she likes that or not. And it may not be safe for her right now in Rosebrook, but maybe one day...

"That all takes time." she says sharply.

"Not when you're a Montgomery it doesn't," I snap, my tone strong.

She scoffs. "Who *are* you?"

"Guess you'd better keep talking to me, so you can find out."

A blacked-out Rolls-Royce pulls into my driveway, and my spine straightens. That looks like my father's driver.

It pulls to a stop, and the door swings open, Benjamin appearing, followed by Merrick.

"Listen, I've gotta go. Just think about what I said, okay?"

Brooklynn sighs. "Yeah, all right."

"Love you, kid."

"Ditto."

Click.

I stare at the two guys standing in my driveway. "What are you two doing here?"

Benjamin lifts a brow and leans against the car, picking at his nails like he's bored, but Merrick puts his arms out and shimmies his chest. "Here to party, sweetheart."

I look behind me at my house and then back at them. "I think you're at the wrong place, then."

"Afraid not." Merrick jogs over to me and pats me on the back, his fingers digging into my shoulder blade. "We're taking you out."

My life is split into three parts.

Before the car accident, after the car accident, and then whatever this fresh hell is.

Before, I used to watch the life of my father like a kid looking at candy through a storefront window. So close but out of my price range.

Sitting here in the HillPoint at the Round Table with Merrick and Benjamin, things feel a little different.

Now, I have that life, and I wonder if there's a little kid standing outside a frosted window, gazing in and wishing he could be me. The thought makes me sick to my stomach. I'm playing a part now, emulating the way I envisioned my father when I was growing up.

I lean back in the booth, my ears tuning out the noise of the other bar patrons until it's a dull, soft murmur.

"How's life, sweetheart?" Merrick asks, tipping his beer.

"Would you quit calling me that?" I complain.

He grins, unfazed. "That good, huh?"

"It's fine." I shrug, my mind flicking to those stolen moments with the woman I can't get out of my head.

"Don't be so modest," Benjamin cuts in, looking at me before focusing on Merrick. "Him and Daddy are thick as thieves now. Practically sharing a toothbrush."

I want to get defensive, but I bite back the urge, knowing it will only make things worse. Instead, I smirk at him. "Jealous, Benny? You need a hug?"

He scoffs, lifting his chin.

Merrick slaps his shoulder. "Don't be so bitter, Benny. Roman can't help that he was born with a trust fund and perfect cheekbones any more than you can help that you're just the unfortunate cousin."

"I'm not fucking bitter." Benjamin shrugs him off.

Merrick cackles, slamming his hand on the table and picking up the other shot glass, raising it high in the air. "To Roman. May he be more than just another pretty face in a town full of assholes. And with any luck…" He winks. "A decent fuck, too. That way people will still like you even if you lose *Daddy's* money."

Benjamin cracks a grin and tilts his own glass. "We can only hope."

I down the shot, the burn of tequila scorching my throat and settling in my chest. I point a finger at Merrick. "I'm an excellent fuck."

"Is that right?" He leans in close, dark eyes sparkling. "I'm more than willing to test out the merchandise."

I click my tongue. "No can do, my friend. I'm too afraid you'd start writing me love letters on the back of bar napkins."

"Maybe I already am," he replies.

Benjamin groans. "God, get a room."

"Wasn't it you," I say, turning fully toward Merrick, "who said Rosebrook Falls is where love goes to die?"

He flops back in the booth, his arm lazily draped across the top. "Even ghosts have dreams."

"Speaking of dreams, I had one last night," Benjamin cuts in, swirling the rim of his glass with a finger.

"Oh?" Merrick perks up. "What was *your* dream?"

He leans in, lowering his voice to a whisper. "That dreamers lie."

Merrick looks at him, unimpressed. "Wow. Life-changing, Benny. Truly."

Benjamin shrugs. "I thought it was apt. This town's full of liars pretending their dreams will come true."

Merrick laughs. "Pretty philosophical there for someone who peaked in high school."

Benjamin flashes a grin. "Yet here you are, sitting at my table, drinking Tequila I paid for, and using the Montgomery name like you earned it."

"Jesus, Benny," I remark.

Merrick lifts his glass. "Shit, are we fighting or bonding? I can't tell."

A bartender walks over and sets fresh beers down on the table. She's pretty. I don't think she can be taller than five-three, and her copper-red hair is pulled back in a bun on top of her head.

"Thanks, beautiful Ginny," Merrick says as he takes his beer from her.

She gives him a smile and then turns her gaze on Benjamin, something colder taking its place, all nicety dropping from her heart-shaped face. "Where's Rosalie, Benny?"

He stretches out his arm over the back of the booth. "Do I look like Rosalie's keeper, Genevieve?"

Her eyes narrow. "I don't know, *Benjamin*, you seem to care enough when you're sticking your filthy pencil dick inside of her."

"She likes it when I'm filthy." He winks.

"You're a pig," she spits.

He shrugs. "She knows how it is."

"Well, if you see her, tell her I don't appreciate her not showing up for her shift tonight."

He nods, sucking on his teeth. "Will do."

"And you're tipping me sixty percent for being a prick. I'll add it to your tab."

"What?" He throws his hands up. "How is this *my* fault?"

She lifts a shoulder. "It's not. It's just because you're an asshole."

Something sparks in Benjamin's eyes, and I lean back, taking in the scene.

He laughs and shakes his head. "It's a wonder Art still walks around with a stick up his ass with how much *spirit* you have, Gin. Does that not translate to the bedroom?"

Art. That name sounds familiar.

She glares and spins around, stomping away, and he laughs. "Fuck, she's so hot. I don't know why she's sleeping with Art Penngrove of all people."

"Because he's the mayor's son, probably," Merrick says, swigging from his beer. "Women love power. Plus, it probably helps that he owns the place now. Bet she gets all the good shifts."

"She looked like she wanted to kill you," I chime in.

A dark look coasts across Benjamin's face. "One day, I'll ruin her. Mark my words."

"So, what's up with this place?" I ask, throwing my arm on the back of the booth and looking around.

"This is where it all happens, sweetheart." Merrick spreads his arms like he's unveiling a magic trick. "You want to know the *true* pulse of Rosebrook Falls? This is where you need to be."

I lift a brow. "At a bar in the HillPoint?"

Merrick grins wickedly. "It's more than just a bar. At least now that Art owns it. But it's good how well it hides it, don't you think?"

I squint. "What does that even mean?"

Benjamin says something else, but I'm not paying attention anymore, because like a beacon in a storm, my gaze snaps to the front door, laser focused on the women who just waltzed in.

One woman in particular.

Juliette.

My veins heat like every single molecule of my body is hardwired to react to her, and I track her as she walks through the space, moving through bodies and sitting down at the bar.

My heart slams against my chest, and my knee bounces beneath the table. I grab my beer and gulp down a mouthful just to give myself something to do.

But *fuck*, she's *here*.

And I'm a little drunk.

I break my gaze away, my eyes meeting Merrick's knowing look.

Clearing my throat, I take another sip of my beer, but my eyes trail back to her every few seconds, the urge to go to her so strong it takes everything in me to stay in my seat.

And I'm successful at it, too…until some douchebag walks up behind her and her friend, his arm a little too close to her exposed back and his eyes wandering a little too south.

Chapter 29

Juliette

"I CAN'T BELIEVE IT'S BEEN WEEKS SINCE WE'VE seen each other," Felicity says, bouncing in her chair at the bar.

Grinning, I set down my purse and glance around, hiding my discomfort. "And the first place you bring me is the HillPoint?"

She beams at me. "FAFO, bitch."

I scrunch my nose. "What the hell does *FAFO* mean?"

"Fuck around and find out, Jules. Disappearing on me has consequences."

"This is why my mother hates you."

She rolls her eyes and waves her hand in the air, clearly unbothered. "It's not my fault your parents are weird, uptight assholes."

"True." I press my lips together. "You should have asked, though. This is like…way out of my comfort zone."

I'm telling her the truth, but I don't really mind it. There's a thrill vibrating just beneath my skin because there's a chance Roman is here.

She frowns. "Well, yeah, but then you wouldn't have come. And anyway, doesn't Art own it now? That basically means it's Calloway-adjacent. You're practically on home turf."

Can't argue with her there.

Low lighting and deep-red booths line the perimeter, and the actual bar is long, extending the entire length of the wall on the right side just past the entrance. There are some tables scattered around in the center of the room, and a small stage at the front which I assume is for live music, although there's nobody on it at the moment.

My back is stiff, my shoulders squared, and I'm just waiting for someone to recognize me. To treat me like a kid and tell me that I don't belong here.

But after a few minutes, nobody does anything of the sort, and my tight muscles start to ease. I'm not naive enough to think that they don't recognize me, but no one seems to care.

"Relax, Jules," she says. "You look like somebody's about to walk up and pull a knife on you."

A pretty woman with pale skin, a *ton* of freckles, and gorgeous red hair pulled high on her head comes over and rests her elbows on the bar. "What'll it be?"

Her jade-green eyes meet mine and widen just a little, but she doesn't say anything.

She's *stunningly* gorgeous, and I think she's new in town. At least, I've never seen her before.

"Grey Goose martini, extra dirty."

"Oooh, fancy, I'll have the same," Felicity says. "Actually, no, you know what? I'll have a Long Island."

I make a face.

"*Don't* even get me started. Need I remind you of spring

break, freshman year? When I had to scrape you off the bathroom floor and hold your hair while you christened the hotel toilet and cried about letting down your parents?"

"God, please don't." My stomach rolls at the memory.

"Either of you want food?" the bartender asks.

Felicity tilts her head at the girl. "What's your name?"

"Ginny," she says with a wink. "Nice to meet you." Then she jerks her chin at me. "Your brother know you're here?"

I rear back, surprised at her line of questioning and more than a little put off by the fact she thinks she has the right to ask me that at all.

"Which one?"

Her eyes widen, and she drops the shaker onto the bar, pulling out a chilled martini glass, placing it in front of me, and then pouring. "Sorry, that was rude—it's not my business."

"Little bit, yeah." I frown at her. "How do you know my brothers again?"

"No offense, but I don't think it's possible to live in this town and *not* know your brothers." She gives a small smile, her eyes flickering between us. "Starting a tab?"

I nod, and then she grabs a towel and sprints away, busying herself at the other end of the bar.

Felicity sips her drinks and whispers, "Fifty bucks she had a thing with one of them."

I glance at the martini, and then Ginny. "Probably Lance. He'll fuck anything."

She cackles. "Definitely not Paxton, that's for sure."

"Well, yeah," I say. "He's married, dude."

Her eyes flick behind me and the smile drops from her face.

I spin around and immediately frown. "Ugh, I was hoping you weren't here."

Art Penngrove gives me a knowing look. "Little Juliette Calloway, slumming it in the HillPoint? What *would* Daddy Warbucks think?"

I roll my eyes at the comparison of a fictional character to my father.

"He'd ask why the rats talk now," Felicity jabs back.

His eyes flick briefly to Felicity and then slide past her like she's furniture.

She scoffs.

"You need to leave," he tells me.

Again, Felicity cuts in before I can. "I know your dad has a fancy title and all, but that's all it is, Arthur. A *title*."

"It's *my* bar." He glares at her.

"Maybe on paper." She shrugs. "We both know you can barely run your own bath, let alone a business."

His lips thin, and he refocuses on me. "Come on, Jules. I'll take you home."

"Hard pass, thanks." I grab my drink and smile wide as I take a sip.

He reaches for my arm, but before he can, a deep voice cuts in. "She said no."

My stomach flips.

Roman.

Art spins around, his gaze widening slightly when it lands on him. Art isn't small, but compared to how tall Roman is, he looks like a kid wearing his dad's suit.

I fidget in my seat, and Felicity gives me wide eyes and then wiggles her brows like she also finds him attractive.

"Roman Montgomery," Art says. "This isn't how I expected to meet for the first time, but this is family business." He throws a thumb toward me.

Roman's eyes flick to mine, then land back on him with a brow quirking. "And you're family?"

"Close enough."

"He's not, actually," I correct.

Art's head snaps toward me, his face dropping. "Jules, come on. You don't belong here. Your brother would—"

"Is Lance here?" I snap my head around, looking for him. "Is that why you're being so overbearing?"

His jaw tenses. "No, he's not."

"Then I'll stay, thanks."

Art sighs and attempts to grab me *again*, and now Roman physically slides in between us, his back resting against my arm. He's angled just enough where I can see him staring a hole through Art, his arms crossed as he leans against me.

Heat pours through my body at the close proximity.

Roman's voice is low, and he leans in, almost whispering to Art. "Try to touch her again, and I don't give a fuck who your dad is, or whether you own this place, you'll be leaving in an ambulance."

Art blanches.

Felicity practically swoons right out of her chair. "You heard him, Art. Get fucked."

"Felicity." He gives a tight grin to her. "Always the opposite of a pleasure to see you."

She smiles back and tips her drink toward him. "Choke and die, Arthur."

He gives me one more glance and then he mutters, "Fuck it," and storms off.

My gaze falls to Roman as he spins to face me, his features softening as he does.

My skin prickles, a dizzying heat working its way from my middle, up my chest and around my shoulders, the way it *always* does when he's around.

He's here.

Somehow, I knew he would be.

Gripping my chilled martini, I bring it to my lips, taking a sip and focusing on that burn instead of the way his eyes are searing into me.

"Well, I don't know who you are," Felicity starts, "but clearly my *best* friend does, and I won't lie, it's hurtful that I haven't heard about you."

Leave it to Felicity to break the intensity of the moment.

He looks at her, his lips curling up. "I'm Roman."

Her brows rise, and she sips from her straw before saying, "And I'm in love."

A laugh pours out of me, and I shake my head. "Felicity, this is Roman *Montgomery*. Roman, this is my best friend."

Felicity tilts her head. "You look familiar."

"I've got a common face, and it's been plastered all over the local news for weeks now."

"Well, thanks," I interrupt. "You didn't need to step in, but I won't lie and say I'm not happy you did. You can go now, though."

"Juliette," Felicity scolds. "Don't be so rude to our savior."

Roman smirks and crosses his arms. The movement makes the muscles on his inked-up forearms flex and highlights the veins that run beneath the sleeves of his shirt. "Finally, someone with manners. Juliette's been incredibly mean to me."

"Is that right?" Felicity's voice is amused.

He nods solemnly. "Completely unwarranted. Between you and me, I think it's because she has a crush."

I let out a dry chuckle. "*I'm* the one with the crush?"

He leans on the bar, looking at Felicity. "You know, I saved her life once."

Interest sparks in Felicity's gaze. "Did you?"

"Can we talk about literally anything else?" I chime in.

"No," they say in perfect unison.

"Wow." I blink. "You're like twins. This is a nightmare."

He ignores me and leans in closer to her. "Tell me something. Do you two have a secret handshake?"

"A what now?" Felicity asks.

"A handshake. I think that any good friendship deserves one. It's a sign of loyalty."

"Interesting." Felicity stirs her drink with her straw and then frowns at me. "Why *don't* we have one?"

I groan, slapping my palm over my eyes. "Great, now you've infected her."

"That doesn't answer her question, Juliette." Roman smirks. "Honestly, I'd like to know, too."

"Because we're adults."

"True." His eyes drag over me. "Adults usually use their hands for *other* things. I'm sure you can recall how easily I was able to make you com—"

My heart surges against my chest I slam my palm over his mouth. "Okay, that's enough!"

His eyes sparkle, and then there's a wet sensation on my skin. My mouth drops open. "Did you just *lick* me?"

Felicity cackles, her eyes bouncing between us like we're the best entertainment she's seen in years.

But along with her attention, I realize we've garnered other gazes, too. Ones that probably shouldn't see us interact. Ones that would *not* think twice about running and telling people that we were being friendly.

My face drops, and he must recognize the shift of my energy because he straightens from the bar and clears his throat.

Energy zaps between us, and I can't drop his stare.

"Roman!" a voice from across the room calls out, sharp and loud, like he's being reprimanded.

Roman stiffens, and when I meet Benjamin's glare, a sick and cold realization of just how public we really are douses me like an ice bucket.

"Your guard dogs are calling," I snip.

Roman's jaw clenches like he wants to say more, but then he snaps his mouth shut and looks to Felicity. "Ladies."

I don't move until he's all the way across the bar and sliding back into the booth next to his cousin and Merrick.

"You better start talking," Felicity demands. "Now."

Chapter 30

Juliette

TWO MARTINIS LATER, I'VE DIVULGED MY DARKEST secrets to Felicity. Maybe it's because I'm tired of holding the weight on my own, or maybe it's because I'm such a lightweight that the alcohol made the words stumble off my tongue. The only thing I didn't tell her was that Roman is the street artist responsible for the recent headlines.

"You've always been a cheap date," Felicity giggles when I tell the bartender, Ginny, that I want water.

"It's part of my charm." I lean against her. "I missed you."

"Did you?" She quirks a brow. "Seems like you were having fun without me *and* not filling me in. I feel like I should be mad."

I twist my lips. "You didn't tell me you broke up with Keagan, either, so let's just call it a truce."

She narrows her eyes and then nods. "Fair."

"*And* you're sworn to secrecy."

"Obviously." She sips her drink. "Although it's my duty to let you know that if you were going for incognito vibes, you both suck at it. I thought he was about to bend you over the bar."

I glare at her. "I'm serious, Felicity. This can't get out. You know what would happen if my family knew I was hanging out with a Montgomery."

She tilts her head, eyes wide. "No, actually, I don't. What would happen, Jules? They'd get mad at you?"

Is she mocking me? "It's not that simple."

She shakes her head. "You're so afraid of being disowned by your family that you're letting them dictate *everything* about your life. Aren't you tired of that? So what if you can't live in their gaudy mansion and you have to get a job? What's on your plate otherwise? Marrying that douche nozzle Preston and becoming your mother?"

I swallow around the barbs she's throwing. "I'm not marrying Preston. Be so for real right now."

She sighs and nudges me with her shoulder. "I'm sorry. I'm being a bitch."

I snort. We both know she's not sorry. "No, you're not."

Her mouth cocks up in a half grin. "True. Still, it's a downer. Let's talk about something else."

Something in the corner of my eye catches my attention.

It was just a flash, but I could have sworn it was Lance I just saw disappear into a dark hallway. My chest tightens, anticipation lighting me up and making my heart bang against my ribs. *Is he here right now? Did Art lie to me?*

"Hey, I've gotta use the restroom," I say. "I'll be right back."

"Sure." Felicity spins in her stool, leaning over the bar top to grab a napkin.

I'm off my own chair and pushing between the tables before I can think better of it, making my way to the small hallway next to the stage.

Goose bumps spring to life along my arms when I walk toward the back exit, like the air conditioning is turned on high. I continue around a corner, where I think I saw Lance, but stop short when it's a dead end.

And there's no one here.

I could have sworn. There's a door with no window at the end of the hall on the right.

Moving slowly, I make my way to it. I probably should hesitate before walking around in a bar I've never been to, in a part of town I know isn't the best, but the liquor pumping through my bloodstream is making my vision a little hazy and my mind a little numb and propelling me to take risks I normally wouldn't take.

I reach out and grasp the handle of the dark door, my heart suddenly pounding in my ears.

Why is everything back here so ominous?

I pull on it.

Immediately, it catches on a lock. I sigh and try again, like I can force it open through sheer will.

"I don't think you're strong enough to break it."

The voice is a deep rasp, and it sends shivers down my spine.

I spin around, a gasp stuck in my throat, my hands splaying flat against the door. My eyes lock on Roman's.

He's close to me, and *God damnit*, I hate the way my body flares to life just from knowing he's near. I shouldn't be back here with him. Not with the alcohol making me uninhibited. And especially not when we already forgot about the world and flirted *in front* of it.

I glance down the hall to see if anyone else is with him. They aren't. It's just the two of us. "Did you follow me?"

"And what if I did?"

"Now who's the stalker?"

He smirks and leans in. My stomach flips at his proximity.

"I learned from the best," he says.

Breathing deeply, I try to think logically here.

"What are you doing back here?" I ask.

He quirks a brow, stepping in closer. "I could ask you the same."

"I thought I saw..." I trail off, looking at the door and then back at him. "It doesn't matter."

"I miss you."

My hands leave the door and rise to push him away, but instead, my fingers dig into the material of his shirt, gripping it to pull him into me. "Don't say that."

"Why? It's the truth. You haven't come to our spot in *days*." His eyes are glossy, and there's tequila on his breath, but it mixes with that woodsy scent that's all him, and it's almost more intoxicating than the alcohol. Heat pools between my legs, and I suck in a breath, knowing I should back away but not strong enough to break the connection.

"Why can't I stay away from you?" I whisper.

He leans down, the tip of his nose skimming along the expanse of my neck and goose bumps sprout down my arms.

"If you figure out how, let me know."

Laughter flows down the hallway, and my heart shoots into my throat. My fingers grip his shirt tighter, accidentally pulling him in, and he stumbles, his arm flying to the door until it's resting next to my head, just a whisper of space between us.

His gaze darkens. "Come somewhere with me."

"We're in public, and...people have already seen us talking."

"So?"

I look at him incredulously. "So, I can't."

"Says who?"

I toss a hand in the direction of the bar. "Everyone."

He hums, reaching to tip my chin up until I'm locked in his gaze again. "Do you always do what everyone else wants?"

Ugh, he sounds like Felicity. And maybe it's the alcohol, or maybe it's the way that I've missed him, too, even though it hasn't been *that* long since I've seen him, but my resistance is growing weaker by the second.

His mouth ghosts against the shell of my ear, not touching, just teasing, and his voice is low and deep when he says, "Such a good little rich girl. Always playing the part. Come on, Juliette, live a little. I promise I won't tell."

My heart flips and free-falls, tension coiling deep in my abdomen. I hate that he knows me so well already; that he can take my insecurities about being who everyone expects me to be and use them to play me like a fiddle.

"I'm *not* a good girl," I say, but it sounds as fake as it feels. My mouth is dry, my fingers still bunched in his shirt.

"Prove it."

"Maybe I just don't trust you."

He lets go of my chin now, his right arm still next to my head, and his left hand covers mine on his chest. "What should I swear by?"

"Don't swear at all."

"If you'd just—"

I move forward suddenly, my front pressing against his. His words cut off, and he sucks in a sharp breath, his arm leaving the door and coming down to grip my hip *tightly*.

"I like you, okay?" I admit.

His eyes flare.

"But it doesn't matter. This thing with you, it's…reckless."

"So be a little reckless," he barbs back.

"It's too sudden, and you're actively trying to tarnish my family name, and, well, it makes me nervous. What if I do go with you, Roman? What if we break these boundaries we've set? Then what? We have this one night and then it's over like lightning, so fast you can barely speak the word before it's gone."

His fingers flex on my hip. "It doesn't have to be just one night."

"It shouldn't be anything at all."

I try to push him away so I can leave, but he tightens his hold on me, bringing me back, one of his hands sliding against my jaw and gripping the hair at the nape of my neck.

"But it is."

Chapter 31

Roman

I'VE WANTED TO PUT MY MOUTH ON JULIETTE'S again since the moment I climbed onto her balcony, and my heart is tripping over itself with the possibility of it happening right now.

But right before our lips touch, she stops me.

"Roman," she whispers.

My stomach sinks, but I grin anyway. "Say my name again, Little Rose."

Her eyes spark, and my hand that's threaded through the back of her hair grips tighter, positioning her head so her lips are angled up and her throat is exposed.

It would be *so* easy to dip down and taste her. *Mark* her.

The door behind us jolts, and it pushes her into me, throwing us both off-kilter and making our noses touch instead of our mouths.

"Ow, what the fuck?" someone mutters from the other side.

Alarm rips through me, and I grip Juliette's hip, pulling her away from the door. Her eyes widen, panic spreading over her features, and I can feel that she's about to run away from me. But I can't have that, not right now, not when I was so close to having her where I want her.

"It's locked, you absolute idiot." Another voice filters through the wall, muffled but close.

I move my hand from Juliette's hip, slipping it around her fingers instead. If we weren't rushed for time, I'd probably focus more on the way her palm fits in mine perfectly.

Instead, I pull her down the hallway and out the back exit until we're in the alley behind the bar. There's not much out here, just two blue dumpsters, a small shed, and a few chairs scattered in the left-hand corner like this is where the employees come out to smoke.

Juliette's gaze is scanning everything like she can't decide where to look: the line of cars, the wooden fencing along the left side of the building, the concrete wall to the right, or the puddles on the ground from yesterday's rain.

I grip her hand tighter, because I don't want her to run away. I know that we shouldn't be seen together. Not because I particularly care at this moment, although I probably should, but because *she* would care.

And that's a knife in my gut, knowing that no matter what I do, what I say, how worthy I become, I'll never be good enough for her.

Just like I wasn't good enough for my father.

The air is thick with humidity, and I feel it in my lungs. I pull her alongside me as we walk to the corner of the building and around the side of it until we're completely out of sight if someone comes out the back door. I glance around, making sure nobody else is loitering, but we're all alone.

Just us and an oddly high number of empty cars parked back here.

"That...was so dumb," she whispers, ripping her hand away from mine and smacking me in the chest.

She glares like she's mad at *me* for what just happened.

My eyes widen. "How was that *my* fault? I'm not the one running off at a random bar and pulling on locked doors." I step closer to her. "You should be thanking me."

She scoffs. "I didn't ask you to follow me."

I throw my hands out to the sides. "Yet, here we are."

She chews on her lip. "Clearly, being close to you in public isn't a good thing."

"You didn't seem to mind all that much a few seconds ago," I point out, grinning lewdly. Another step closer. "I know we have to lie to everyone else, but you don't need to lie to *me*, Juliette. I enjoy knowing you fantasize about me."

"Oh my *God*, you never give up, do you?" Her cheeks flush, and she groans, palming her face. And then she breaks out into laughter.

I smile, happy that I can make her do that. It feels personal, like its sound is meant just for me.

"I'm sorry," she says, straightening. "I'm mad that things are so complicated with us, and it's confusing, and I just... I don't want it to be."

My heart twists. "I get it."

Juliette glances around the back area, her brows furrowing. "Wonder why there are so many cars parked back here. Is this place really *that* busy?"

Shrugging, I follow her line of sight. She's not wrong. "Maybe they're here for something else."

She cocks a brow. "What else is on this street besides a few houses and shops that close at five?"

"You have a point." I purse my lips. After being in that back hallway with her and seeing people come up from a locked basement door, I'm starting to wonder if there isn't something else going on. Something that nobody is telling me.

It's not just a bar.

That's what Merrick said.

She runs a hand through her luscious, black hair, the curled ends falling over her shoulder and brushing against the top of her breasts. I fight like hell to keep my eyes gentlemanly.

"So, you want to tell me why you were snooping, Sherlock?" I ask.

"I wasn't snooping."

"Right."

She pouts. "If you're planning to argue with me the whole time we're back here, then you should just leave."

"We can kiss instead, if you want."

Her face blooms and she hits me that *be serious* look that she loves to give. "You're lucky I've even held your hand."

"You're right," I agree, holding my fingers up in front of my face and moving them side to side. "My hand isn't worthy enough to touch yours, if we're being honest. But it did, so now we have a problem."

"What's that?" she asks.

"I've realized that holding your hand isn't nearly enough."

Her cheeks flush again, and she glances at the ground, then peers up at me from beneath her lashes. "Some people would argue holding hands is more intimate than kissing. Hands are what saints use to show devotion."

She holds hers in front of her, palms toward the sky.

I quirk a brow. "Don't saints have lips, too?"

She nods, placing her hands together. "Ones they use to pray."

I move closer until the tips of my shoes touch hers, and my skin prickles from the proximity. "I'm *praying* to kiss you."

Her chest lifts with a heavy breath, and her mouth parts in invitation.

Heat floods through me, electricity snapping between us like little stabs of lightning.

"I'm no saint," she murmurs, her eyes dropping to my lips, then slowly rising again. "But if I were, saints don't move, even when they grant the prayers."

My stomach flips, nerves sizzling beneath my skin. I reach up, threading my fingers through the hair at the nape of her neck, just like before. "Then don't move while I act out my prayer."

I brush my mouth against hers: a gentle caress, barely enough to curb the insatiable ache to taste her.

She leans back, her shaky exhale painting itself across my lips.

"That tasted like a sin, not a prayer," she says, her tone breathy and inviting.

My stomach cinches tight, anticipation zinging through my nerves and heat coiling through my body, making me tense with *need*.

"Then give me my sin again," I rasp.

This time, she doesn't hesitate.

Her hands slide around my neck and tug me closer until every inch of her is pressed against me.

I groan, mouth parting as she pulls my bottom lip between hers, teasing me with the softest bite.

She's right—this *does* taste like sin—and when she moans, I nearly lose it.

My arm slips around her waist, my other hand angling her jaw as I kiss her deeper. Grip her tighter. Our tongues brush, and my cock jerks.

I skim my palm down her side, hitching one of her legs around my waist, anchoring her to me as I lean back against the exterior wall of the building, and enjoy the way her weight falls into me so perfectly.

She fits like she was made for me. Like this is always where she's belonged.

And all I can think about is how it would feel to bury myself inside of her.

To wake up next to her; her leg tangled over mine, and her arm flung across my chest like she's claiming me in her sleep.

To hear the quiet sigh she makes when the sun hits her face, or the way she hums without realizing it while she writes her stories.

To be *allowed* to know those tiny, ordinary moments like scripture.

To have all of her. Not just in the dark, but in the light—in front of everyone—soft and real and mine.

The sound of a door flying open rips us apart. She flies away from me, her back slamming against the concrete like she's terrified to be seen. Her eyes widen, chest heaving, her lips swollen and her hair a mess.

She's so gorgeous like this, it makes my chest ache.

Juliette's fingers reach up and brush against her puffy

mouth, like she can't believe what just happened. Or maybe she's remembering how good it felt.

A guy's muffled voice floats around the corner. "Come on, babe, just give me five minutes."

Then, a heady giggle that half turns into a moan. "I can't. I have to close tonight."

I stiffen, recognizing what it is that we're hearing. I turn to signal to Juliette that we should sneak away while we can, just loop around the other side of the building and back to the front, but she doesn't move.

Her head is tilted, her expression shifting like she recognizes the voices. Then she's moving past me, brushing so close her ass drags against my groin, and I swear under my breath because the universe clearly gets off on making me suffer when it comes to her.

There are loud smacks of two people making out, and then a grunt and a moan, and whoever is out there is *clearly* about to fuck, and honestly, it's not helping my situation.

Juliette leans forward even more, peering around a corner, and my eyes drop to her ass.

Jesus Christ.

"Art, cut it out." The girl's voice giggles. "I have to go back in."

Juliette straightens, and I jump back like I wasn't two seconds away from grabbing her and pushing into her like a caveman.

She spins toward me, grasping my forearm and dragging me away quickly until we're walking around the opposite side of the building.

I don't question her, because quite frankly, I'm pretty sure that I would follow her anywhere right now.

When we get far enough away, she stops. We aren't back

at the front, and we're still hidden from view, but now we're close enough where I can hear the people out front and the cars driving down the street.

Juliette's hands press into her eyes, her face scrunched up. "Oh, *God*. I want to bleach my brain."

A car door slams, and she stiffens again like she's realizing how close we are to the public eye, no longer secluded. She takes a giant step back.

I narrow my gaze at her. "Don't say it."

She shakes her head. "I didn't say anything."

Sighing, I slip my hands into my pockets and look at the stars before focusing back on her. "It's fine. You can't. I get it. Honestly, I can't do it, either."

"Because of your sister?" she asks.

The reminder is like an uppercut to my jaw. If she'd just sign the goddamn papers, I wouldn't have to worry about her anymore, and she'd be taken care of.

My mom, though…

"Among other things. Just…go before I do something stupid." I wave my arm toward the front of the bar.

"Okay." She pauses, her teeth sinking into her lower lip. "I don't *want* to go, though—you know that, don't you?"

Groaning, I grip the roots of my hair. "Don't say that to me right now."

I glance around, making sure nobody can see, and then I drift forward, lowering my voice. "I'm drunk. And you're…*so* fucking beautiful. And for some reason, every time I'm near you, it feels like I might die if I don't touch you."

She sucks in a breath, her cheeks flaming that deep pink I love.

"And I'm trying—really trying—to respect this invisible line we drew, but clearly, I suck at it."

"Why?" she asks, like she doesn't already know.

"Because every time you smile," I say, "every time you give me that little look like you can't decide if you want to throttle me or kiss me, I want to keep you forever."

Her mouth parts. "*Trouble...*"

I reach out, pressing my thumb to her lip. "Stop explaining yourself, and just...walk inside."

She hesitates, her eyes shining. "I wish we could be more, Roman."

"We *are* more, Juliette."

The Rosebrook Rag

Mystery Street Artist Strikes Again: The Calloway Puppet Master

A shadowy figure looms on the side of City Hall, puppets dancing off strings from his fingers. On one hand, the puppets are figures labeled: "Mayor," "City Council," "Judge," and on the other hand, the puppets are buildings.

"Fortune's Fool," which we all know is the local theater. "The Round Table," which is the tavern on Amesbury Road. "Old Main," which is Verona University's main building on campus.

But who is the shadowed figure? The title of the mural would have us believe it's none other than Craig Calloway.

Is our anonymous painter insinuating that the Calloways have everyone under their thumb in Rosebrook Falls?

Time for our reporters to dig up any secrets.

#RosebrookRag #GraffitiGate
#CallowayPuppetMaster #CityHallMural
#CallowayWatch #SecretStreetArtist

Chapter 32

Roman

THERE'S A PICTURE I'M STARING AT OF TYLER Bault shaking hands with someone I've never seen. The paper attached to the photo says his name is Brutus Myrddin, and they're passing something between them, although it isn't clear what. I Googled the name, but the only thing that comes up is Brutus's ties to some ragtag group of criminals called the Badon Hill Gang in Boston.

I want to ask my father, but that would involve me having to face him, and I'm still in the avoidance part of our relationship.

Someone knocks on my front door.

Who the hell is here?

Throwing it open, my arms crossed, I come face to face with Frederick.

"Can I help you?" I cross my arms.

"That depends on several factors, son." He presses his lips together and glances behind him before facing me again. "Can I come in? This is a delicate situation."

"Sure." I move to the side, and he gives me a grim smile, brushing by me and heading to the living room to sit down on the couch.

"Make yourself at home," I bite out.

He crosses his ankle at his opposite knee, blue and yellow argyle socks peeking from underneath his black pants.

There's an odd energy about him, one that feels tense and angry.

I don't sit.

Instead, I lean against the arched doorway, shoulder pressed to the edge. "What's up?"

He doesn't look at me. "Do you know how much influence and money it takes to kill a news story these days?"

"Can't say that I do, no," I reply.

He hums, nodding, and then he levels me with a look. "What are your intentions with Juliette Calloway?"

I stiffen immediately, my pulse shooting off like a speeding bullet.

"My intentions?" I arch a brow, keeping my tone light even though my body goes rigid. "Not sure I know what you mean."

"Bullshitter. Just like your father."

Now he's just pissing me off.

"Excuse me?" My hands curl into fists.

He stands up, gritting his teeth and smacking a photo down on the coffee table. Slowly, I step forward to grab it, and when I do, my stomach sinks.

Fuck.

It's a photo of Juliette and me on the side of the building at the Round Table. We aren't kissing, it's from when we moved around closer to the front, but still…it's intimate.

We're close together—too close—and I'm grinning down at her like she hangs every star in the sky. And she...

Well, she looks like she wants to get fucked, her gaze heated as she stares up at me.

My cock jerks.

Not the time, guy.

"Where did you get this?" I ask, my voice tight.

"I have a friend at *The Rosebrook Rag*. She gives me all the photos about my clients and their...*interests* before they run them." He sniffs, picking a piece of lint off his sleeve. "Answer the question."

I scoff. "You come into my house and slam down photos, asking *me* questions?"

He stands, brushing a hand down his suit and glaring at me. "That's exactly what I'm doing."

I grit my teeth and toss the photo back down. "This isn't what it looks like."

Frederick laughs. "You'll need to be better at lying when you say that to the press."

"And *you* don't know your place."

He rears back, his bushy brows rising on his head like he's surprised, but then his face drops into something dark and menacing. "You don't scare me, Roman. And I'm not here to threaten you, despite your *enthusiastic* anger."

"Then what's your point, Frederick? I don't have all day."

He smirks, glancing around the living space. "In a hurry to get back to all the things your father's having you do?" His gaze flicks to the manila folder on my table. "You're being foolish, thinking others won't catch on to the timing of the graffiti with your arrival in town."

Sighing, I run a hand through my hair. "I'm tired. And correct me if I'm wrong, but I'm fairly confident that as a Montgomery, I don't answer to you. In fact, isn't it the other way around?"

His mouth tightens.

He presses his finger on top of the picture until his nail blanches. "I'm giving you the benefit of the doubt, that you don't know any better. That you don't understand the volume of blood that runs in these streets. I'm also going to run on the assumption that you aren't trying to fuck Juliette Calloway for sport or some strange payback on your father's behalf."

My stomach twists again at his words, nausea working its way through me. "It isn't like that."

He nods, a heavy look drawing down his features. "I'll ask you again—what are your intentions with Juliette?"

I cock my head and blink at him, my face a blank canvas. But on the inside, my emotions are in turmoil. I have no idea whether he's using this to his advantage. If he's planning to take my words, use them against me, keep them in his back pocket as a power play.

"Why do you care?" I ask.

"I've known her since she was born."

And maybe I'm naive, but his words ring true. "How'd you pull that off, anyway? Being both a Calloway and a Montgomery attorney?"

Frederick chuckles quietly, but there's no real amusement behind it. "You'd be surprised how far you can get when you know how to shut your mouth and have people sign the right paperwork." He meets my gaze. "Loyalty's a currency in this town, Roman, and the smartest men are the ones who know how to write the fine print."

I study him, not sure if I admire his honesty or hate the way he says it; like morality is just a story people tell themselves to feel better.

My jaw tics. "So that's it, then? You don't pick a side, you just cash the checks?"

"Let me put it to you like this," he says. "The town is built on legacy, not law. On whispers, not verdicts. So the Calloways and Montgomerys might be on opposite sides, but they've both needed *me* to keep the game moving."

He leans back, lacing his fingers in his lap.

"They trust me. Not because I'm loyal, but because I'm useful. My job isn't to pick a side, it's to ensure the table stays steady while everyone plays their hand."

"And if both sides go to war?"

Frederick shrugs. "Then I win either way."

"I'm not trying to hurt her," I murmur, my chest feeling heavy. "She's…different. It's like the world shifts when I'm next to her."

"Virtue can easily turn into vice, my boy," Frederick says.

"Juliette isn't a *weakness*, she's…" I trail off because I don't know what to say.

She's everything.

Frederick sighs and lowers his voice, like he's telling me a secret. "Like I said, I've known Juliette since she was born. I've been to her birthdays, and I've seen her stumble and fall and pick herself back up more times that I can count. I've seen everyone in her life use her for their gain, while she takes nothing for herself. So speak plainly to me about the two of you, Roman, and maybe I can help you. Does she feel the same?"

"If you're so close, why don't you just ask her?" I eye him carefully.

"This feud between your two families brings nothing but destruction," he says instead of answering. "It decays the very foundation of the city itself. And above all, that's what I care about. *This town.* So believe me when I say that you need someone who understands how to navigate all of this. Especially if you're sloppy enough to leave trails like photos and spray paint."

I grit my teeth. "I told you already, that isn't what it looks like."

He smacks his hand on the table. "A jumbled confession can only receive a jumbled solution."

I snap, the words clawing out of my throat before I can stop them. "What do you want me to say, Frederick? That I saw her once and never forgot? How I think I fell for her before I even knew her name? You want me to spell out how we carve moments like they're stolen, and how she tells me things she probably doesn't say out loud to anyone else?"

His face softens with understanding.

"How it fucking *destroys* me knowing she's not mine, and she never can be, when I'd give up almost anything for the chance?"

My voice drops, my heart exposed and raw.

"What good would telling you that do me? Will you take my words and turn them into a 'solution'? I have news for you: I know Juliette and I can't be together. It's been made more than clear. So, we're not. Period."

Frederick swallows harshly and slowly nods. "Then look me in the eyes and promise me there's no story here."

"There's no story here," I say.

Lies. Lies. Lies.

"Very well." Frederick straightens his cuffs, running a hand down the front of his suit again. "For a moment, I thought you two might be…"

My chest spasms. "Might be what?"

"It doesn't matter." He gives me a sad grin. "If you're fickle, stay away from her. For both of your sakes. And if you aren't, promise you'll come to me first. I can help you, Roman. Both of you."

My brow furrows. "How?"

"Sometimes the only way to protect something as precious as love…is to take it far from where anyone can reach it."

Something twists low in my gut, like a screw turning into bone.

I don't answer him. I can't.

For all of his polished bullshit and monologues, there's a soft knowing in his words that cuts through me. Like he's reaching inside my chest and poking at something I've barely let myself name.

"Your father's asked me to help dissuade the public opinion that may arise thinking the vandalism is just one person. There'll be copycats of you cropping up over the next few days. *Do not* interfere if you see them tagging."

My brows rise. "Sure."

Frederick gives a sharp nod and leaves.

But I'm left with the ache his words left behind.

Sometimes the only way to protect something as precious as love is to take it far from where anyone can reach it.

Chapter 33

Juliette

"WHY IS LANCE HANGING OUT IN THE HILLPOINT?"

Tyler blinks like my question surprises him. He's sitting across from me at the local theater in the town square, Fortune's Fool, his feet propped on top of the auditorium seat in front of us.

We're both here waiting for the acting class Alex teaches to end so we can go out to lunch.

"How do you even know he's hanging out there?" Tyler replies instead of answering the question.

I shrug. "I know enough."

"Jules, you have no business going to the HillPoint," Alex pipes up from behind us, climbing over the seats and plopping into the one on my other side.

I glare at him. "You sound like Paxton."

Alex flashes a boyish grin. "Is that a compliment?"

"If you like being compared to an uptight asshole, then sure." I throw up my finger. "Also, I'll go where I want, thanks. Besides, I went with Felicity, so it's not like I was by myself."

Alex straightens from where he was leaning against the wall, his honey green eyes sparking with interest. "Felicity's back?"

"Yeah," I reply. "Put your tongue back up into your mouth."

He lifts a shoulder, pressing a hand over his heart. "She's the love of my life, not that I'd expect you to understand."

"*Christ*, here we go," Tyler exclaims, rolling his eyes.

My mouth drops open. "You can't just toss that word around, Alex."

"I'm not. I'm completely serious."

"Obsession and love are not the same thing," Tyler says like he's chastising a kid. "How many times do I have to tell you that?"

"A great love *is* obsession." He glares at Tyler like he's offended, but when he glances back at me, a soft smile lights up his face.

"That is an exceptionally creepy thing to say," I remark.

He gives me a look. "That's how we get sonnets, poems, tragic plays where people topple empires just to feel their lover's kiss. *Art*, you absolute ingrates."

"So love is art," Tyler muses, a deadpan look on his face. "Or art is obsession?"

"Art is life dressed up in prettier words," Alex hits back, stretching out one leg in front of him.

Tyler chuckles. "Someone put that on a shirt."

I force a smile, but Alex's words have me free-falling. Because if art is obsession and love is the kind of thing that fuels it...

Maybe that's why being around Roman is like standing too close to a fire, knowing how badly I could get burned, but reaching for it anyway.

"Hello?" Alex waves his hand in front of me, eyes wide, and then snaps his fingers in my face. "It's disturbing you can disassociate like that."

"I'm not disassociating, I'm thinking." I bat his hand out of the way. "You should try it sometime."

He scoffs. "I have a degree in *philosophy*. Thinking is literally my brand."

"Quoting Aristotle in Italian cashmere while flirting with theater majors doesn't count," Tyler points out, nodding toward the stage.

"I am who I am." Alex beams. "And besides, I'm incredible at monologues. You're just a hater."

Tyler leans forward, the auditorium chair squeaking. "Did we or did we not just watch you play a tree for the past hour while you called it teaching?"

"A tree with *gravitas*," Alex corrects, offended. "And anyway, I'm just using my degree the way Plato intended, by teaching through performance."

"You mean seducing impressionable freshman with bad lighting and soliloquies?" I tease.

"You only get away with it because you've got the Calloway genes," Tyler cuts in. "If you were ugly, none of this would be charming."

"That's probably true." I nod along. "But it works if you work it, so my advice is to stay the course."

"Thank you, Jules." Alex smiles at me.

"I'm not condoning your actions," I say, lifting a brow. "I'm just trying to let you down easy and give you a soft place to land because Felicity will *never* sleep with you. Keep your focus on the future Hollywood starlets, Casanova."

Tyler snorts. "He *does*. It's not like he's celibate, waiting for Felicity to lower her standards. Did you see that girl he was just coaching? She could barely walk out of here, she had so many hearts in her eyes."

Alex grins a movie-star-worthy smile. "I overheard someone say Felicity had a crush on a Calloway brother once."

I laugh. "You're delusional."

"And you're so sure she was talking about *you*?" Tyler adds.

Alex lets out a chuckle, running a hand down his black Henley. "I'm going to ignore your implication that I'm not the best brother."

Tyler points a finger at Alex. "You're lucky she hasn't put out a restraining order on you yet."

"If she didn't like me, she wouldn't text me all the time."

My hands fly up to my temples, a headache brewing. I squeeze my eyes shut. "Oh my *God*, please let me out of this conversation."

"Actually," Alex continues, whipping his head around. "You think she's at Second Circle Market right now?"

"I don't know, dude. If you two are so close, just text her and ask."

He nods, tapping his phone against his hand and shooting up from his seat. "I should go find her. You know…say hi."

"Hey!" I shout at his back. "I thought we were going to lunch."

He waves his arm at us. "I'll meet you there."

"Try not to get arrested!" Tyler calls out with a grin and then looks at me.

I quirk a brow and cross my arms. "Well? Answer my question."

He looks at his nails. "I can't remember it."

"What is Lance doing hanging out in the HillPoint?"

I watch his reaction carefully, but he's got a damn good poker face. I'm not one-hundred percent sure Lance was even there, but if anyone knows, it will be Tyler.

"How the hell should I know?" Tyler shrugs.

"Uh, because you two are best friends?"

He frowns. "Like I said, we don't hang out like we used to."

"Okay," I draw out the word. "Let me rephrase: What is *Art* doing owning the Round Table because of a debt collection? I thought you said he was his dad's shadow now."

"He is."

"And you think the mayor of Rosebrook wants Art being a loan shark and owning some run-down bar in the HillPoint of all places?"

"Guess so."

"And you're fine with it. You, the person who hates anything Montgomery more than anyone else in existence."

Tyler's eyes flash, his jaw tensing. "The Round Table has nothing to do with the Montgomerys now."

"I already know Art's fucking that bartender, Ginny, or whatever her name is. Is that why?"

Tell me that's all it is, I want to plead. But there's a sickening feeling taking root inside of me, like there're huge pieces of this town that I don't know anything about. Pieces that everyone else seems to.

Tyler looks at me like I've grown three heads. "No...it's because Art's got business there."

My face screws up. "Like he owns part of it?"

"No, Juliette." Tyler exhales a heavy breath like he's annoyed with me and then sits forward, dropping his head. "And stay away from Genevieve. There's nothing good about her."

"Then what is it?" I press. "You can try to avoid answering me all you want, Ty, but you know I'll just keep pushing until you can't stand the sight of me."

Tyler groans, palming the back of his neck, then lifts his eyes to meet mine. "Like, 'under the table, I'm in Montgomery territory for my dad because he's the mayor and needs to keep his hands clean' business."

Something foreboding whispers against the back of my neck, but I shrug off the unease.

"What does that even mean?" I ask. "Are you insinuating the mayor of Rosebrook Falls is doing illegal activity with Marcus Montgomery and using his son for it so it doesn't fall back on him?"

He blinks at me. "I did *not* say that."

"You implied it heavily."

"I just said it wasn't Montgomery's place anymore, actually. You're twisting my words."

My mind flashes with the mural Roman did on the side of city hall, the one depicting *my* dad controlling the mayor. That isn't surprising to me—I've known about our bribes and kickbacks to the town officials for years; it's just part of this world. But if the mayor is double-dipping and also fucking around with the Montgomerys, then...

He throws his hands up. "You know what? I shouldn't have said anything. Just...give Lance a break, all right? Your brother's loyal to the people he cares about, you know?"

I used to agree with that statement.

"It's not his fault your dad doesn't give a shit about him,"

Tyler continues. "*And* keeps a tight leash on his money. He's doing what he needs to do. It's not like he's working for Calloway Enterprises."

"Lance doesn't want anything to do with the family business."

"Not that one, anyway."

"Huh?"

"Nothing." He grins. "Lucky he doesn't, you know? More for the rest of us."

"Yeah, I already know how far up my dad's ass you are. Quit deflecting."

Ty chuckles. "Don't hate the player, baby, hate the game."

I laugh and shove his shoulder lightly. "That is *not* what that phrase means."

His brow quirks. "It is if we're talking about the deeply capitalist system we were born into."

My lips twist, something unsettling in my gut. "That's not a game, Ty. It's just the way it is."

He hums. "Maybe I'll see if my loving uncle will let me be your bodyguard or something."

I roll my eyes. "With your temper? You'd get me killed."

He shrugs. "I don't know, seems like you have a pretty cake gig doing nothing around here. How hard could it be?"

"That's not by choice." I cross my arms, insulted and a little embarrassed that it's noticeable even to him that there's no real direction in my life. "And please don't. I love you, but if I had to put up with you every day, I might actually kill myself."

Tyler presses a hand to his chest. "Quit pretending I'm not your favorite cousin."

"Not a hard title to claim when Rosalie's your only competition."

He purses his lips, sadness crossing his face for a fleeting moment. "Fair."

My stomach grumbles, and that's my cue. I stand up and put my hands on my hips. "Whatever, this entire family sucks. I'm hungry. Feed me."

Tyler smirks, but relief filters through his gaze, and I can't help but wonder if it's because I stopped questioning him about Lance.

He throws his arm over my shoulder, dragging me into his side. "As long as we can hunt down the lovesick puppy in time."

"Yeah, what's up with that?" I question. "Did… Are he and Felicity…?"

Ty looks down at me knowingly. "I think if there was any truth to what he was saying, you'd know about it."

His words give me a bit of reprieve.

"You know Alex loves things he can't have," Ty says as we make our way down the hall. "You reject him once and he's like a dog desperate for a bone. No pun intended."

"Gross." I screw up my face. "Can you not make sex jokes about my brother, please?"

"What?" he asks. "It's *natural*. We're all adults here."

I make a gagging noise, and Tyler laughs.

We're both so into our conversation that we don't realize when we round the corner and run almost smack dab into Frederick Lawrence.

My breath stalls in my throat, the amusement draining out of me like a wine that's been uncorked.

Tyler stiffens next to me. "Freddy, hi. Didn't realize you were back in town."

"Hello, Tyler. Juliette." Frederick's eyes are heavy as they land on me, something flashing in his gaze that makes my hair stand on end. But just as quickly as it came, it disappears.

"Hey, Freddy." I take him in.

He's been a fixture in my life for as long as I can remember, but it's been years since I've seen him. Once he started dipping his hands heavily into Marcus Montgomery's life, my family pulled away. I know my dad still uses him, when necessary, but it's not like he still comes to the family cookouts.

I snort to myself. *As if we've had family cookouts.*

He looks older. Worn out, maybe.

"It's good to see you," I say.

He gives me a soft smile. "Actually, I was looking for you, Juliette."

My brows hike up. "For what?"

He glances at Tyler and then back. "I need to talk to you about Roman Montgomery."

Chapter 34

Juliette

I'M NOT SURE WHEN IT HAPPENED, BUT I'VE stopped thinking about Upside Down Rock as a place I came when I was a kid and started thinking of it as *our* place. Mine and Roman's.

But now, for the first time in my life coming here, anxiety feels like it's choking the life out of me, and I don't know why.

It could be because I texted Roman to meet me here, and he didn't respond.

Or maybe it's because I had my tongue halfway down his throat and it's all I've been able to think about, even though I have a "date" with Preston coming up next week.

Or perhaps it's because Frederick told me—in front of Tyler, no less—that Roman and I had photos that were about to go live on *The Rosebrook Rag* until he stopped them. *And* that Roman already knows.

I thought Tyler was about to explode from how red his face got and how tightly his fists clenched. He stormed off and hasn't answered my phone calls since. I'm worried sick to death over the thought of him running to my dad and telling him, but I have to trust that he won't.

Still, I pull out my phone and shoot off another text to him while I wait for Roman to—hopefully—show up.

ME:

> Ty, PLEASE. Let me explain.

My stomach jolts when he replies, *finally*.

TYLER:

> I can't even fucking talk to you right now, how could you? A Montgomery, Jules? Really?

ME:

> Don't tell anyone. Please.

My heart is in my throat, hands shaking while I wait for him to reply.

TYLER:

> Fine. But you better have a damn good reason. I could kill you myself for being so reckless.

I blow out a sigh of relief, but anxiety has latched onto my edges already; there's no getting rid of it.

By the time Roman shows up, I'm so frazzled that I burst forward at the first crunch of his boots on the trail.

"How could you not tell me?" It comes out sharp, like an

accusation. My voice soars over the space, and I can almost *see* the illusion of hands shoving against his chest from my tone.

He stops, the gravel grinding beneath his shoe. "Tell you what?"

I take two large steps over to him. I'm not even sure why I'm so angry, but I am, and he's here, so he's getting my overload of emotion.

"That there were *pictures* of us," I snap. "That Freddy came to your house and warned you, and you didn't even have the decency to text me about them."

His mouth pops open, and I move forward, shoving his shoulders. "Are you trying to get us caught? It's like you don't even care."

He grips my wrists, and his eyes are serious as they bounce between mine, a crease forming in his brows like I'm a puzzle he's trying to work out. "Calm down."

That just enrages me further, and I'm about to explode out of my skin. I glare at him, my closed fists resting against his chest, his fingers warm and firm where he's holding me. "Don't you tell me to calm down. You think this is a game? I'm trying to *protect* you *and* your sister, mind you, and you just don't even—"

"I never asked you to do that," he cuts me off.

"You didn't have to," I reply.

"And just *what* are you protecting me from, Little Rose?" he asks, his fingers tightening around my wrists. "You act like I'm the bad guy, like my dad is the one who's the villain, and here you are with me, anyway."

He leans down, his nose brushing against my neck, his breath hot on my skin.

I shiver.

"Is it because deep down you know that your family is up to no good? That they aren't the heroes you pretend they are?"

His voice is a low rasp, but he might as well have shouted the words for how much they vibrate through me.

"That's not…"

I trail off, because I'm not sure why I feel this way.

"I don't know," I admit. "I just know that if something were to happen to you, I'd never forgive myself."

"And why's that?"

My heart pounds against my ribs. "Because you mean too much to me."

He groans, and then his mouth comes down on mine.

Immediately, I melt into him, my fists unclenching and my hands gripping the fabric of his shirt as I give into the feeling.

All I really wanted him to do was kiss me, anyway. Honestly, I can't even remember what I was so mad about in the first place.

A moan tears from my throat as we collide. It's almost brutal with intensity. He kisses me like he's desperate, like he's been on the edge of snapping for too long and I'm the only thing left to hold him together. His tongue slips across the seam of my lips, licking into me like he owns the space and is staking his claim, and I press into him, my body molding to his like it was made to fit there.

His hands find my waist, strong and rough and *firm*, and he lifts me like I weigh nothing.

My legs wrap around him and then the kiss breaks—his lips shiny and his breathing ragged—and his eyes are molten lava as they pour over me.

"You think I don't care?" Leaning down, he presses his mouth to mine again, his teeth sinking into my flesh and nipping just hard enough to sting. "You think I don't worry every single second that even *thinking* too much about you will take you away for good?"

His words slam into my chest and burrow deep.

"Stop thinking about me, then," I say breathlessly, before I put my hands around his neck and drag him down to me.

He grunts into my mouth, his hands sliding along the sides of my body and cupping underneath my ass, and I'm not sure who does what when, but somehow, we end up with my back against the trunk of a tree, his hips flush against mine.

"Impossible," he rasps. "You're *all* I think about."

I can feel him. Thick and hard and pressed right up against me. He thrusts once, his hips grinding into mine, and even through our clothes, his cock slides right where I need him. My body jolts, the bark of the tree scratching my skin.

The pain feels kind of good, and my head spins from lust.

He laves kisses down my neck, licks a stripe over my pulse point, and then bites, just enough to make me whimper.

His hands feel like they're everywhere, one holding me up against the tree and the other slipping beneath my shirt and tracing the curve of my waist before dipping lower.

He nips my lips again. "You taste like sugar."

I can only mewl, words having left me the second he started touching me.

This is all I've wanted. It's what I've thought about since I was lying on his couch in his apartment, and he was drawing me from across the room.

His fingers are under the waistband of my pants now, teasing, like he's asking me for permission. "Let me touch you," he begs.

"Touch me," I tell him.

His hand finds my clit immediately and starts a torturous rhythm, slow circles that do nothing but ramp up my absolute blinding need until my vision goes hazy and I'm gripping onto the back of his head, tufts of his hair clenched in my fists as I ride the wave that's *so* close to cresting.

"Fucking soaked," he grits out, dragging the pads of his fingers through the mess between my thighs and down to my entrance.

He doesn't push in, he just hovers.

"Your pretty pussy is *crying* for me, Juliette. You're about to make a mess all over my hands while you come against a tree, aren't you?"

A quick rush of fire licks at my spine as he continues to tease me, never touching me enough to give me the pressure that I need. I gasp, clutching at the back of his head, gripping tight while my body bucks helplessly into his palm.

"That's it," he encourages. "You get one stroke of my fingers in your tight little cunt and you're not even thinking anymore, are you? Tell me how bad you need it, baby."

This is *torture*.

"Use your words, Little Rose." His face is pressed against the side of mine, his breath hot against my ear. "Tell me that you want to be *handled*."

"Yes," I admit, although I'm sure I'll regret giving in so easily later. "*Please*."

He smirks, and then his fingers are *in* me, sinking deep and curling instantly, like he's known this whole time the exact angle my body needs. His mouth crashes back into mine, tongues tangling, and his other arm holds me tight, locking me in place against the tree like he's chained me there.

He works me relentlessly, with no hesitation. Just a devastating pressure and a controlled slide. In, out, curl them up and pet that spot inside that makes my vision go dark.

My mouth falls open and my hips jerk.

"God," I gasp out.

His teeth nip my jaw, and he corrects, "*Roman.*"

I start to answer his movements, rolling myself against his fingers, sinking down as much as I can, to feel him as deep inside me as possible.

"*Fuck*, you're so sexy," he says, the words sounding as if they've been scraped from the deepest part of him. "Ride it, baby. Get yourself off on me. Let me see your beautiful face as you fall apart on my hand."

His body is pressed so tight to mine that I can feel everything. His abs tightening. The flex of his forearm with every pump of his fingers. His palm grinds against my clit, rubbing in perfect circles, and he strokes me from the inside out like I'm a piano he's meant to play.

"Look at you," he groans. "Such a mess already and I've barely fucked you."

Heat coils around my spine and collects low in my stomach, my clit pulsing for him. *I'm so close.*

I cry out, my body vibrating in his arms, bowing toward him.

"Roman, I'm so… I think I'm—"

His nose brushes against mine, and his voice is low and commanding. "Come for me, Juliette."

And fuck him for being able to direct me so easily, but I do. I break apart into a thousand tiny pieces, and if he wasn't holding me to him, I think I'd scatter in the wind.

I ride that wave, my hips rolling into his palm and my pussy clenching around his fingers while I moan his name against a tree in the middle of the woods.

The tremors taper off slowly, but he stays in place, not moving. His hand is still buried inside me deep, his frame anchoring me like he knows I might float away if he doesn't.

My legs go lax, my breath hitches, and I drop down from where I'm sure my thighs bruised his hips. I feel almost boneless.

Our eyes lock, and his fingers leave me slowly, dragging them against my clit on the way out, and sending an aftershock zipping up my spine.

He never drops my gaze as he brings them up to his mouth and licks them clean.

Chapter 35

Roman

I CAN TASTE HER PUSSY ON MY TONGUE.

Well, almost.

It's been half an hour since I fingered her against the tree, her sweet little moans in my ear and her perfect body under my hands, and I can't stop staring at her.

She's sitting at our picnic bench, a cool breeze caressing her face and hair like it loves her just as much as I think I do.

The thought hits me like a smack to the face, and my mouth dries.

There's a blush permanently staining her cheeks, and every so often, she looks at me like she can't believe what we just did.

Neither can I, to be honest.

"You're staring," she murmurs, not looking up from her notebook.

"You're perfect," I reply, resting my chin in my hand. I gave up on trying to do anything other than watch her about twenty minutes ago.

I was worried she'd regret what happened as soon as it was

over, but I should know better than to think that about her. When Juliette Calloway decides something, she's in it for good. In fact, it was *me* who stopped us from doing anything else, insisting that we should take a second and just breathe. I don't need her to reciprocate; I just want to bask in this moment.

Up here. Just the two of us, where she feels like mine.

Frederick's words play in my head like a bad omen. About taking love away to protect it.

But I'm not concerned about *me*. I don't know her family dynamics well enough to trust that any of them would keep her safe if she made decisions they didn't agree with. Every day, it feels like combining our worlds is more and more impossible.

So, I just want to soak this up for as long as I can, before everything goes to shit, and I have to tell her maybe she's been right along. That we shouldn't even see each other anymore.

Her brows are furrowed, and whenever she blinks, her lashes dust across the very tops of her cheeks. Her lips are swollen, a bit of red marring the edges from where my teeth sunk into them and claimed them for my own.

A hit of satisfaction runs through me at the sight, knowing I marked her as mine, at least this once.

Unfortunately, I think she's marked my soul for good.

"My mother has a drug problem."

The words fly out of me suddenly, and even *I'm* a little surprised by them. I hadn't decided until this very moment to share that with her. But I want to give her something of me, something almost nobody else knows.

Her pen pauses on the page, and she glances up at me. And then realization crashes through her, her eyes widening and her hand covering her mouth. "Oh my God, Trouble. Those things I said when we first met… I didn't mean—"

"It's fine, baby." I shake my head to stop her. "I'm just telling you so you know me… My entire life has been about keeping her head above water and dragging my sister along for the ride."

She swallows heavily, laying down her pen and closing her notebook.

"Will you tell me about her?" she asks.

My chest cracks open, and that little box I keep deep inside—the one with the fortified locks—springs open, my trauma laying itself at her feet.

"Her favorite is oxy, but it's hard to come by so she settles for heroin. She's a mess. A manipulative shell of who she used to be, and I hate saying that because I want you to know that I love her. Despite what she does, the mistakes she makes… she was a good mom. And I *love* her." I force out the words again like maybe if I say them twice, it will be enough to bring her back.

My chest pulls so tight I can barely take a breath, but I lick my lips, spin my ring, and nod.

"She met my father at an art show. *Her* art show, in California. Similar to the one where you saw mine for the first time, actually."

She smirks. "I knew that was your art."

I grin softly, but it's coated in dejection that I can't shake.

"He was charming, and she was lovestruck, and she definitely didn't know—or maybe she didn't care—that he was married. They were together for two years before I was born."

Juliette's hand goes to her chest like she's trying to digest the information.

"I don't know why my father gave me his last name when

he never intended on letting me actually be *his*, but I'd see him every once in a while. And whenever he'd come into town, my mom would light up like the Fourth of fucking July, and I remember thinking, 'why can't I make her smile like that?'"

"Roman," Juliette whispers.

She stands up and moves to the bench I'm on, sitting down next to me and gripping my hand, tangling our fingers, holding them in her lap.

"It's stupid," I mutter.

Her thumb ghosts across the back of my hand. "It isn't."

"Then Brooklynn was born, and I don't know what happened. Maybe he was pissed that she wasn't his, or maybe his wife got fed up, but he stopped coming around. He stopped caring."

"He quit seeing your mom?"

I bite the inside of my cheek and stare down at our hands. "Nah, I think they still got together—she seemed happy then, still. At least, some of the time. But then something changed, and she took us on a trip when I was fifteen. Brought us here to Rosebrook Falls to visit and wrapped our car around a tree."

Juliette sucks in a breath. "And you think my father did it."

Slowly, I nod, gritting my teeth. "I don't really remember much of it, just waking up and not knowing what happened. Brooklynn and I were lucky. She had a broken arm and collarbone, and I had some gashes from the windows that shattered. But my mom, she broke her spine."

"I remember reading that you all were dead." Her voice cracks on the word, and she covers her mouth. "Sorry, I just… I don't like thinking about you that way. Or that my father is capable of something like that."

I bring her hand up to my mouth and press a kiss to the back, using her to ground me, because this is the first time I've really talked about it to anyone. It's hard for me to relive things, especially when the memories aren't what I thought they were. I'm still trying to piece everything together in a way that makes sense.

"My dad whisked us away, took us out of the hospital, sent us to a new spot in California…gave us new names. I never did know why. Never asked, I guess. I was too busy taking care of my mother while she relearned how to walk."

"That's a lot for a kid."

My eyes burn, and I push it back, not wanting to tear up over something that doesn't even matter anymore. Although, I guess that's not true. It matters a little; otherwise, it wouldn't hurt so goddamn bad when I think about it.

"It's a lot for anyone," I reply, my voice low. "She lived on oxycodone for a while. And the doctors, they let her… They did what they were supposed to do, you know? Pain meds work when they're used appropriately, and she *was* in pain, Juliette."

I say it with more force than necessary.

"But she grew dependent on them?" Juliette asks.

I nod, pursing my lips and breathing deep to keep the old wounds at bay. "Yeah. And then just like that, all her medical support disappeared." I snap my fingers. "I think my dad might have broken her spirit long before she broke her spine. She's never been the same since."

Clearing my throat, I spin my ring faster. "What nobody tells you is those pills help curb the emotional wounds, too, at least at first. And when that's the only kind of hurt left, and the doctors rip those meds away from you, well, some people spend the rest of their lives scraping at the hole they've unknowingly fallen into, just trying to numb the pain."

"I'm so sorry, Roman." Her voice is small and sad, like she doesn't quite know what to say. "She was an artist?"

A soft smile blooms at the memory, my chest lightening. "Yeah. A great one. She painted with bright, messy strokes; color everywhere. It was always under her nails, and all over the walls, and sometimes even in her hair."

Juliette smirks. "Sounds familiar."

My throat thickens.

"She'd play music too loud and dance barefoot in the kitchen, and I remember thinking that the whole world revolved around her laugh," I say, my voice ragged. "She wasn't perfect, but she was mine."

Juliette's eyes go glassy, her hand pressed against her chest like she's holding something in. "That's… I don't even—"

"And you know what the most fucked-up part is?" I cut her off, the words ripping out of me.

She shakes her head, swallowing.

"I haven't felt that way since. Not about anyone. Not until you."

She's quiet for a second, and then she's pressing her hand against my face, her eyes flickering between mine.

"I *am* yours. In all the ways that matter."

My palm covers her fingers, and I lean into her touch, closing my eyes and soaking her in.

"Even if we have to pretend we're enemies?" I mimic what she asked so many weeks ago, back when we were still acting like we didn't belong to each other.

A stuttered breath against my lips. A warm mouth. A simple kiss.

My eyes open, and I stare at this perfect, beautiful, impossible girl that fate keeps giving back to me.

"You will *never* be my enemy," she promises.

I nod against her, pressing our foreheads together and letting the quiet wrap around us like a blanket.

Eventually, I say, "My dad's offering to help her now."

"Well…that's a good thing, right?"

I just stare at her like my heart doesn't feel like it's being ripped from my chest. "Yeah, if she goes along with it then it is."

"You don't think she will?"

"I think my mom is lost in some kind of hurt I can't even fathom and has spent a majority of her life numbing that pain instead of facing it." I bite the inside of my cheek. "That's a hell of a habit to break."

She watches me for a moment, empathy shining in her gaze. "Do you think that's why the news hasn't found her yet?"

"What do you mean?"

She shrugs, and then says slowly, "I mean…it's unusual for *The Rosebrook Rag* to not find gossip and cling to it with every single part of them. When you came back, it opened up the question of whether your family was alive, too. But since then, there's been nothing."

My spine straightens, and a tic forms in my jaw. I hadn't even thought about that, but now that she's mentioned it…

"Maybe my dad is having Frederick keep her out."

Juliette's eyes widen. "Freddy?"

I shrug. "Makes sense, don't you think? He kept *us* from being in the papers, what's to stop him from doing the same with her? He said they show him all the pictures first. That he has a friend there."

The thought that my father may be protecting her, even with her being the way she is, makes me feel warm and...grateful.

"That could be it," she muses and then her eyes pin me in place. The tension snaps tight between us. She doesn't say it, but I can read between the lines, and I feel it, too.

This inevitability.

My father wants me here, to help bring down *her* family, and if I don't play my part, then it's *my* family who might pay the price. Her dad tried to kill me, and might still want me dead.

My chest squeezes tight, stomach bottoming out at the impossibility of it all.

Her fingers tangle on top of her notebook. "Do you think your mom and sister would still be protected...no matter what?"

My mouth is dry and I peel my tongue from the roof. "I think if I can convince my sister to sign some papers, she'll be taken care of regardless. But my mom..." I run a hand through my hair. "I don't know, Little Rose. I don't even know if there's anything left of her to save."

The words catch in the air and ricochet into my sternum. I press my lips together.

"Don't say that," she whispers. "She's still there, Roman."

I let out a hollow laugh. "I've said that a thousand times. *It's not her, it's the drugs.* But I don't know, sometimes life doesn't give us happy endings, you know? Sometimes the bad thing wins."

"Well." She lifts a shoulder and gives me a soft smile. "Then I'll have the faith for both of us."

And I know it right then, surer and steadier than I've ever known anything.

I love her.

"Will you come with me somewhere?" I ask suddenly, desperate to show her every piece of me.

She lifts a brow, looking around. "Are we not somewhere right now?"

I smirk. "Cute. But I mean somewhere else."

A softness enters her gaze and she bites on her lower lip. "Yeah, Trouble. I'll go anywhere with you."

Chapter 36

Juliette

WE'RE TWO TOWNS AWAY AND I'VE NEVER DONE anything like this.

When I agreed to let him take me somewhere, I never imagined it would be us sneaking out of Rosebrook Falls altogether and riding the train to get us *here*.

My heart is racing, adrenaline surging through my body as I let him lead me down a street in an industrial area. Our hands are tangled together, and it reminds me of back in Cali, before we knew who we were to each other...or before I knew who *he* was to *me*.

Things were simple then.

Now it all feels like an impossible mess. One that I'll only get out of if I decide to grow a backbone and stand up to my parents. The thought makes me want to puke.

"Where are we going?" I ask, my eyes flicking to where we're touching.

This is fine.

Actually, I'm totally cool with it.

It means nothing to me that his hand—the same one that was inside my vagina a couple of hours ago—is now entwined with mine perfectly.

"Hello?" I try again, my legs working hard to keep up with him. "Is anyone home?"

He still doesn't answer.

"Roman," I snap.

That gets his attention.

His gaze floats to mine, and he tightens his grip, bringing my knuckles up to brush a chaste kiss against them. "I still like the way you say my name, Little Rose."

My heart flips and I give him a soft smile. "Do you really plan on calling me that god-awful nickname the rest of your life?"

"That depends." His eyes darken. "Do you plan on being around for the rest of my life?"

I snap my mouth shut, something hot and sharp growing like a weed cracking through pavement. Because I can see it, our future together.

Mornings tangled in too-warm sheets. Him mumbling about my alarm going off and me pretending I didn't set three backups just to be sure. Coffee cups lined up on the counter and breakfast forgotten on the stove because when he laid me out on the kitchen table, he decided to eat *me* instead.

A dog we didn't plan to get but couldn't say no to.

A cat that roams the backyard and Roman pretends he hates because he knows I'm allergic, even though he secretly feeds it every morning.

He'd kiss my shoulder while I write, smudge charcoal across my cheeks without realizing, and I'd find little drawings of us in the margins of my notebook and in the drawers of his nightstand.

Soft.

Simple.

Terrifying.

Because none of it's real, and part of me wants to build it anyway, just to see if we could.

He stops us and turns to face me, his thumb brushing my cheek as he gazes into my eyes. "Where'd you go, Little Rose?"

I smile, ignoring the tangle in my heart. "Nowhere important," I lie.

He gives me a look but doesn't press.

"Where are we?" I ask, looking at a giant parking garage in the middle of a concrete jungle.

There's not much to see here other than a few buildings and warehouses mixed in with a parking garage every couple of blocks. It's quiet, not even a car going down the streets, and I don't know how he even *found* this place.

He pulls me into an elevator, the dings ringing in my ears as it slowly takes us higher. "You know, you're really living up to your serial killer lore, bringing me to an abandoned garage like this."

He smirks and then pushes off the side until he's crowding me against the wall.

My breath hitches, butterflies erupting in my stomach and heat pooling between my thighs.

"A murderer and a stalker," he muses. "A match made in heaven."

I laugh, shaking my head. It makes my cheek press into his palm, and I lean into the moment.

He tilts my chin up and then presses a kiss to my lips.

Chaste. Sweet, even.

"I promise not to kill you if you promise to follow me around for the rest of my life," he murmurs.

He smiles against my mouth and my heart clenches like it's trying to claw its way through me to get to him.

"That's a very dramatic way to ask me out, officially," I tease, trying to lighten the moment so I don't drown.

He doesn't pull back, just shifts his face up until he's looming over me, his arm resting above my head on the wall.

"Would you say yes?"

The elevator dings again and the doors slide open. I take the opportunity, slipping beneath his arm and heading out onto the open level of the top floor of the garage.

Roman doesn't move right away. He lingers in that breathless space between us, like he's trying to cement the moment in his memory.

Finally, he follows me out, an easy grin pasted to his perfect face. He reaches for my hand. "Come on."

He leads me down the length of the garage. It's just a rooftop really; flat concrete with a low ledge and the quiet hum of silence. But when he takes me to the very edge, my breath catches.

My stomach drops when I look out, realizing how high up we actually are.

"You're not seriously about to climb up there, are you?" I ask when he lets me go to step toward the ledge.

He flashes a boyish grin and moves beside me before jumping on top of the barrier and swinging one of his legs over until he's straddling the concrete.

"Be careful!" I snap, my arms flying out like he's about to fall.

He chuckles. "Funny, coming from someone who was lying upside down on a rock that hovered over open air when we first met."

"That was different." I cross my arms but realize that maybe I'm overreacting.

"I'm sure it was." He watches me, a question in his gaze. "What were you doing then, anyway?"

Sighing, I lean against the pillar and look out over the scenery. I wouldn't call it pretty, but it's peaceful in an odd way.

I ignore his question, looking at all the buildings. "Is this a ghost town?"

He shakes his head. "Just industrial. Not much pedestrian traffic."

I chew on my bottom lip while he waits for me to answer his first question.

"I was looking for Lance when we met," I finally say. "He wasn't there, obviously, but leaving meant I had to go back home, that I had to be…"

"The girl who plays piano and speaks four different languages?" he finishes smoothly.

I stare at the ground. "Yeah, something like that."

He pats the space next to him. I look at it and then back to him, my chest cramping, but I move forward and climb up the ledge to sit anyway. A small hit of adrenaline flows through me, and I break into a grin. "This is kind of fun. I feel like a kid."

He smiles and leans against the concrete wall at his back, one knee bent, his forearm resting over it like this is just any other conversation. I can practically see the tension rolling off him like steam, coiled under his skin.

And he's watching me like he wants to save me from something.

"Don't look at me like that," I snap, crossing my arms.

His brows rise. "Like what?"

"Like you're judging me for how I do what my family wants, even if they do terrible things."

He sighs, his head hitting the concrete wall at his back. "I'm not judging you. It just kills me."

That makes my facade of anger fall away. "*Kills* you?"

"Yeah," he says. "Watching you pretend to be what they want. Being on the sidelines and not able to do *anything* while you tuck yourself into a world where you're silent and on the arm of some fucking prick named Preston."

I open my mouth, but no words come out. My heart thuds loudly in my chest. "That's not fair," I finally say.

He chuckles, dark and deep.

"You think I don't get it?" he whispers. "I sold my dignity, my name, my freedom, all for a sister who hates me for the choice."

"Roman…"

He leans forward, his hand palming my cheek until he's pulling my face to his. Our foreheads brush, and his voice is so low I can barely hear him.

"I wake up *every* day and try to remind myself you're off-limits. That you're a Calloway, and I'm a Montgomery, and it's not possible for me to touch you, or want you, or imagine how good it would feel to wake up next to you."

My eyes burn and my fists clench at my sides. "So why say it, then? It just makes everything harder."

He exhales slowly. "Because I'm tired of pretending like I don't feel you in everything I do."

The words are soft, but they land like thunder, and a chill creeps up my spine, although I can't explain why. Maybe it's from how his face hardens like he's trying to steel himself against something.

I lick my lips, to say or do…I don't know what…but before I can, a noise breaks through the air, like a storm rolling over the horizon. At first, it's just a low, rhythmic hum. A vibration that you feel before you hear. But then it grows into a rumble, metal wheels clattering against rails in a cadence that echoes off the concrete buildings.

He moves his hand away, and I lick my lips like I'll be able to taste the remnants of him.

"Watch," he says, pointing toward the oncoming train.

Quirking a brow, I wonder what the point of all this is, but I listen and do what he says.

I watch.

Even though my body is hyperaware of every movement he makes.

A train comes racing along tracks on a hill in front of us, a high-pitched whine layered over the deep growl of the engine. The air whooshes like it's being pushed forward, and there's a faint hiss of brakes as it comes hurdling past.

And at first, I don't notice anything…but then I do.

A burst of colors, sprayed along the boxcars. Brilliant, bright, and intricate. It speeds along, and I soak it in, every sharp line, every blasted edge.

It blurs past in strokes of the rainbow, and then I see it: a mirage of pink and peach, with thorny edges jutting from the shadow. It's a rose, I realize. Twisting, and bleeding from the petals. Like it's wilting mid-bloom. Across the stem, in jagged letters, it says: "And with her kiss, I die."

My chest seizes and then my gaze snags on the corner.

RMO.

My breath lodges in my throat.

I try my best to tamp down my reaction, but the tears spring to my eyes anyway, because that felt like a love letter. One written in tragedy.

"Is that…" I cut myself off, not sure if I want the answer.

Roman's not even looking at the art. He's too busy watching me. And when he speaks, it sounds soft. Final, even.

"I told you, Juliette. I'm going to paint you into everything."

The ROSEBROOK Rag

BREAKING: Graffiti Bombshell Hits Mayor Penngrove's Office!

A jaw-dropping mural has surfaced overnight on the side of Mayor Penngrove's campaign HQ.

A towering image of who we suspect is Mayor Penngrove looming over the town, a leash around his neck that's held by a shadowed figure. The face of the figure? A logo.

Calloway Enterprises.

Is this a bold statement from our mystery artist about the mayor's reelection campaign?

The Calloway family is expected to address the rumors in the coming days.

#MayorPenngrove #GraffitiGate #CallowayWatch

#RosebrookRagExclusive

Chapter 37

Juliette

BEVERLY FLITS AROUND, HANGING UP A LOAD OF laundry in my closet, rambling about something or other, but my mind is stuck on Roman.

I've been nauseous ever since that night in the parking garage, his words ringing in my ears.

He hasn't reached out since, and it's been a week.

Years of being told that Marcus Montgomery and anyone with a hint of his blood is the enemy rings in my head, and my mind battles with what I've always believed and what I know I *feel*.

The truth is staring me in the face.

I think about how cagey Paxton has been on the phone with me and how ever since I got back, I've barely seen him at all. I think about how Lance has been lurking around bars in the HillPoint and implying I should stay out of town. I think about how my father claims to love me but is letting my mother use me as a tool by linking me up with Preston, simply because it puts another powerful player in their pocket. How he tried to *murder* innocent children to further his agenda; whatever the hell that even is.

My eyes track Beverly back and forth as she flits from spot to spot.

"Bevie," I call out.

My voice is sharper than I intended, but it makes her pause, peeking around the corner from my large walk-in closet and peering at me.

"What do you know about the Montgomerys?" I ask.

Her face grows serious, and she places down the clothes she was in the middle of hanging up on a nearby chair and moves to where I'm sitting, her face anything but calm. "The same as anyone else, I'd assume, child."

"I'm not a child," I snap. "Despite all of you constantly treating me like I am one."

Her face blanches, and she smooths down the nonexistent wrinkles in her shirt before staring at me for a few long moments.

"All I know is that after Marcus's wife died, he...well, he was grieving for a time, I guess. Your father took advantage."

My spine stiffens. "Took advantage how?"

"There were rumors he took over some of the dealings in the HillPoint, and that Marcus either doesn't know about it or doesn't care."

Surprised, I lean back. "Bevie, is my father the villain here? Is he really as bad as those spray paintings imply?"

Everyone knows they're about him. About *us*. There have been people protesting outside of Calloway Enterprises, demanding transparency. The number grows every time Roman paints something new.

Her cheeks pale. "Lord if I know, Juliette. Why does it matter? Would it make you love him any less?"

"It doesn't matter, I guess." I'm not sure if that's true.

"Everyone's a bad person to someone. You just have to figure out what *you're* willing to accept."

"What if the people I've been told to hate are the ones I want to love the most?"

Roman flashes in my mind again, and I choke on the thought of having to defend him to Tyler. To *anyone*, really. If they cared about me, wouldn't they just want me to be happy? If Felicity were here right now, she'd tell me to get my shit together and come to live with her. To say fuck you to the people who would put conditions on how I'm supposed to live.

And maybe she'd have a point.

Beverly watches me closely and then glances behind her at my closed bedroom door before sitting on the chaise next to me. "Did you know your balcony has cameras?"

"What?"

Panic infuses every nerve when she says it, my mind flipping through all the times over the years I've done things I shouldn't have. When I've snuck out with Lance and Tyler—or more recently, when Roman climbed over the railing.

"Beverly…"

She presses her lips together. "Unfortunately, shortly after you came back from college, they stopped working. Nobody has had the time to fix them yet." She hums, swiping her hands along one of my shirts that's in her lap, smoothing over the fabric. "Peculiar, don't you think?"

My tongue sticks to the roof of my mouth, and I speak even

though it suddenly feels like my vocal cords are scratching on sandpaper. "Thank you," I whisper.

She reaches out, pats my hand, and lowers her voice. "I'd watch out for your phone, too. Never know who might be able to tap in and see things."

I swallow and nod.

"Do you hate Marcus like my father does?" I ask.

"Seems silly to hate a dead man."

I rear back, all of my conversations over the past however many days coming to light. "Why do you say that? Is my dad trying to *kill* him?"

Beverly's mouth drops open, and her eyes widen. "*What*? No, because Marcus Montgomery is dying."

Shock hits me like a windstorm. "What do you mean, he's dying?"

"Never mind. I don't know much."

"Bevie, please. I want to hear it. Don't leave me in the dark the way everyone else does."

She licks her lips and then nods. "Marcus has stage-four cancer. He's… Well, he's not going to be around very much longer."

I try to slot together the new information, but it feels like square pieces being forced into round holes. "How do you know that?"

She shrugs, but she won't meet my gaze. "The help usually knows everything. People like to talk as though we don't have eyes to see or ears to hear."

Guilt hits me in the stomach. I hate that she's treated that way.

"Makes sense, don't you think?" she adds. "His son coming back just in time to take over his legacy."

"What if his son doesn't want his legacy?" I ask. "He just has no choice? Does Roman know?"

Beverly's chin lifts, a knowing glint coasting across her face. "These are questions better asked of someone else, I think."

I snap my mouth shut, my insides swirling like a maelstrom.

"Do you love him?" she asks.

"What?"

"It's a simple question." She picks a piece of lint off her shoulder. "Do you love him? Would you renounce your family for him? Do whatever needs to be done in order to keep him?"

My throat feels thick, my fingers wringing together. "Yes."

It's the first time I've admitted it. And it feels…lighter than I thought it would.

"Love doesn't survive in the dark, Juliette. It demands for you to step into the light." She looks at me, her eyes sharp.

I swallow. "What does that mean?"

"It means if you ever want to see the morning, you have to forsake the night."

I lift a brow, my chest heavy. "And the night in this scenario is my family?"

Beverly laughs. "Your family is *midnight*, Juliette."

"Have you ever loved anyone like that?" I ask. I don't know why the question pours out of me. Maybe because I'm desperate to have someone to relate to, or maybe I just want help making sense of how I feel inside.

She pauses, hesitating before she says, "I have."

Obviously, whoever it was is long gone now. Otherwise, why would she have been here all these years?

"I hope you know, Juliette, that I am *always* on your side. No matter where you go. My loyalty will always be to you."

I smile softly. "Even if I end up *forsaking midnight*?"

She pats my leg and stands up. "Especially then."

The Rosebrook Rag

BREAKING! Campus Protest Erupts Over Calloway Family Influence!

Verona University students are taking a stand against the powerful Calloway family, alleging undue influence over local governance and university affairs. The VU Quad transformed into a sea of signs and chants with messages like "Art is truth!" and "Not your puppets!"

The Calloway family has denied all claims, while rumors swirl that there's internal pressure for Craig Calloway to step down, which would leave his son Paxton in charge.

All eyes are on Rosebrook Falls, and whatever mystery artist (or artists) who is painting on the streets.

#GraffitiGate #CallowayWatch #StreetArtSpeaks #VUUprising

Chapter 38

Roman

"I HEARD AN INTERESTING RUMOR ABOUT YOU today," my dad says as he sits across from me at a restaurant called Dante's, located in the middle of the town square.

He doesn't look up when he speaks. Instead, he stares down as his knife slowly cuts into his steak, the blood oozing from the meat and onto the plate. His voice is calm, and he looks collected.

But his words send a spike of awareness trickling along my spine.

"Oh?"

My mind races, wondering what the rumor is, and why he asked me to come here tonight. He seems unhappy about something, and I think it might be the pace I'm painting at. I haven't had a chance to do too much more, but I've been procrastinating, because the urge to tag isn't there when it's being utilized as a weapon I have no control over.

The protest on VU campus, and the pictures that followed of Juliette having to shield herself from reporters made me sick.

"Benny says you've been...friendly with the Calloway girl," he says.

My stomach tightens, flashes of Juliette playing in my mind.

Her smile. Her laugh. The way she scrunches her nose when she's annoyed and bites on her lip when she's trying to keep from grinning.

A waiter stops by and picks up the wine bottle, pouring more into my dad's glass before leaving without a word. I wonder if he should be drinking that, but I guess I'm just happy that he's still able to drink and eat *anything*, even though for years I wished him dead.

Jesus, I'm a disaster.

"Benny's an idiot," I say, shrugging like it isn't a big deal. "She was at the Round Table and some guy was hassling her."

My father nods and then takes another sip of wine. "So, I don't need to worry about it?"

I reach forward, grabbing my own wine, and gulp it down.

Fucking Benny. Snitch-ass bitch.

My mask is carefully crafted, and I make sure it's impenetrable now as I reply. "What would there be to worry about? She's nobody."

She's everything.

He shrugs. "Benny says that the two of you seemed to know each other. That you were... I believe the word he used was 'intimate.'"

My mind races, figuring out what angle to play.

I set down my wine glass and lean back in my chair, sighing. "You don't have anything to worry about."

"Good," he says. "I don't mind who you fuck—that's none of my business. But I do care if the Calloways are tying you up in some sick mind game."

I scoff, and he cuts me a serious look.

"Do not underestimate them. I made that mistake once, and it almost cost me everything."

Emotion clogs my throat, because if I didn't know any better, I'd think he was talking about me.

"Juliette isn't like that."

The words come out slow, like a whisper. It's a risk to say it, but fuck it. I'm tired of sitting back while everyone has their own idea of who she is, too.

A look of understanding flows over my dad's face, and he shakes his head, but the anger I expected never comes. "So, there is something."

I clench my jaw, rolling the stem of the wine glass back and forth in my fingers, the red liquid sloshing around in the bottom of the glass. "Nah. Nothing that matters."

And fuck, does that hurt to admit.

"Some things are better left to die, son."

My chest squeezes tight, and I force a nod. "Is that what you did with Ma?"

"I loved your mother." His eyes grow sad. "But what I felt for her pales in comparison to the love I have for you."

My brows draw in, and an ache hits me right in the sternum, like something has clawed its way inside of me and ripped open old wounds. I let out a humorless laugh. "You have a funny way of showing it."

"I've made a lot of mistakes; I can admit that. But you're my legacy, Roman. The purest love I've ever felt was when you were born and I held you in my arms. You don't have to believe it, but it's the truth."

Another phantom pain spreads through my chest, and I reach up to rub it away.

My father takes a bite of his steak, his chin moving as he chews, his eyes locked on me like he's trying to convey a secret. "And I would have done what I did a thousand times over to protect you."

"Part of me still hates you," I admit. "I don't know that your soft words and pity acts can undo years of abandonment."

He grunts. "That's something I'll just have to make peace with when I die, then."

"Don't talk about yourself like that. I don't like it."

Shock filters over his face like a curtain.

"Who is Brutus Myrddin?" I ask, not wanting him to focus on what I just said.

He glances around like he's worried someone will hear. "He's the man the Calloways went into business with."

"Then why was his picture in the files you gave me?"

"Because he's a large part of why we've lost everything that we have."

"He partnered with the Calloways."

He dabs the corner of his mouth with a cloth napkin and places it back on his lap. "And was very upset that I wouldn't sign on the dotted line to dissolve the WayMont agreement. Doesn't matter. He's dead now."

"How did he die?"

My father takes a sip of his drink. "Shot in the back of the head and found on the bank of some river in Boston."

"Jesus."

"Enough of this talk," he says. "Things are getting back to how they should be, and that's why you're here. To make a statement. Craig's fumbling in his power now; people are waking up."

He coughs then, his napkin coming up to cover his mouth.

It's a vicious attack, and I'm reminded that he isn't well. Sometimes, it's hard for me to remember because he's so good at covering it up. "Enough shop talk. How's your sister?"

My mind is running a thousand miles a minute, trying to come to terms with the fact my father is giving me pieces to a puzzle and assuming I'm okay being left halfway in the dark while I expose people for secrets they'd rather have buried.

If it weren't for others who don't match my description being purposely caught on cameras around Rosebrook, people would surely know it was me already.

"She's barely speaking to me. How's Mom?" I reply.

She was supposed to be taken to the rehab facility in the hills of Monterey last week, and I've been vacillating between needing to know about her and wanting to let go so I'm not disappointed when her rehab fails.

"I haven't spoken to her," he says. "Nobody can for the first thirty days."

My stomach tightens. "But you know she's there, at least, right?"

"Of course." He looks offended. "Frederick checks in on her daily."

"Why Frederick?"

"Because I asked him to."

I nod along, but anxiety winds its way around me like a noose. "Will she be safe there?"

He leans forward, tapping his fingers on the table. "One thing about your mother is that she's very resourceful. I have no doubt that once the drugs clear from her system, she'll do everything in her power to come home to you. She may not show it, but she loves you more than life."

"Yeah." I pick at my napkin, not wanting to acknowledge the fact that I'm not sure I believe she'll actually get better. After all, someone has to want to better themself in order for it to stick, and she's never been willing before.

I assuage my thoughts by reminding myself that after her first thirty days I can check in.

"So, you're really not worried about Craig Calloway coming after me anymore?" I ask. "Or any of his children?"

"No. He controls much more of Rosebrook Falls than back then. Besides, you're very public here, and you're no longer a little kid. The only way he can get to you is if you let your guard down. Like, for example, with his daughter."

Too many emotions bleed together at his words, making the weight of knowing Juliette might never speak to me again hurt even worse. "I told you, she isn't like that."

"And I heard you. But let me ask you a question, and you think hard about the answer." He jerks his chin to a table behind me, and I twist around in my seat to look.

"If you and her are so close, then why is she here with the governor's son?"

Chapter 39

Juliette

PRESTON ASCOTT IS EVERYTHING I EXPECTED him to be.

Smart, polite, gentlemanly, and just as handsome as he was back in high school.

He opens car doors and pushes in my chair when we arrive at Dante's—the most renowned restaurant in our town, coincidentally owned by Paxton—and his eyes don't stray from mine for a single second that we're together.

It's nice.

In any other universe, I'd be having a good time. But I can't help the tinge of bitterness coating my tongue, knowing how he left me high and dry in the past, and that my parents still put us together like I'm cattle to be sold.

And that I'd rather be here with someone else.

But patience is a virtue, and if there's one thing all those etiquette lessons taught me, it's that waiting for the opportune time to make a move is paramount for success. For now, I'm playing the part.

I take a sip of my wine—the kind that Preston ordered for me when we sat down without asking what I'd like—and stare at him.

"Do you really want to date me again?" I interrupt whatever he's saying.

He stops, his blue eyes sparking with surprise before he clears his throat. "Are you not having a nice time?"

"No, I am," I reply. "Even though you've never apologized for the absolute prick way you broke up with me."

He grimaces. "I was a kid, Jules—"

I cut him off. "I just wonder if you're here because you want to be, or if it's because our family considers this political foreplay."

Understanding flashes over his face, and he gives a small smile before shaking his head. "*You* don't want to be here."

"Not really, no."

His lips purse, and he leans in, his hand covering mine on top of the table.

I look down at it, waiting to feel...*something*. But I don't.

Slowly, I move my hand back until he's not touching me at all.

"My parents didn't put me up to anything," he replies. "I'm a grown man who makes the decisions I want, when I want. And I *want* to take you out. I...I've missed you, Jules. Is that so bad?"

My shoulders relax. "No, that's not bad."

I do *not* want to date him again. In fact, thinking back, I'm not entirely sure if it was me who decided to pair up with him in the first place, or if it was something my mom whispered in my ear, even all those years ago. But I can't help thinking maybe he's stuck in this world, underneath his own family's thumb the same way I am, despite him saying the opposite.

"If you have a horrible time and hate me, I promise I won't push things. No matter how much your dad *does* scare me." He chuckles. "But I want you to want to be here, Jules. Remember all the fun we used to have?"

Not really.

But those aren't the words I latch onto. "Why does my dad scare you?"

He looks at me, confused. "What do you mean?"

"You just said, 'no matter how much your dad does scare me,' and I'm just wondering why that is? I mean, *your* dad is the governor. Why would mine be of any concern?" I rest my chin in my hand and flutter my lashes at him.

He takes a sip of his scotch and chuckles uncomfortably. "I mean, you have to know your dad is in bed with dangerous people."

"Mm. Please, keep telling me about what *I* know."

"You're still so feisty." He grins. "Give us a chance, sweetheart. If we happen to hit it off again and make our parents happy in the process…is that really such a bad thing?"

"Preston, don't call me *sweetheart*, or my six-inch heels will end up in your lap. And it won't be pleasant."

"Sorry, old habits." He puts his hands up like he's waving a white flag. "Tell me about wanting to move out. I hear you're wanting your own place?"

I tilt my head, keeping the smile on my face. "How did you…?"

He laughs. "Oh, I'm sorry. Are people not supposed to know about that? Your mom told me when we spoke the other day, and I just assumed it was public knowledge."

A sinking feeling hits me in the gut.

It makes me uneasy knowing everyone is talking behind my back.

Plus, the reminder of just how much my mother truly likes Preston, and how in her pocket he is even after all these years, hits me in the face like an open-palm slap.

"What?" he asks, his grin dropping. "What did I say?"

Shaking my head, I swallow and glance down at my lap before looking back up at him. "Nothing. It's just…you know how I feel about my mom."

He's no stranger to my tense relationship with her; he was often the in-between for us even back in high school and had to listen to me rant in the passenger seat of his car for hours after she did something that pissed me off.

"You're still giving her a hard time, huh?" He chuckles.

I bristle, setting down my wine glass a little too hard. "I don't know if that's what I'd call it."

"She just wants the best for you, Jules. One day you'll realize that. She loves you."

"My mother loves herself," I correct. "Everything else is an obligation."

Preston drums his fingers on the table, looking at me like I'm a child who's amusing him instead of listening to the gravity of my words. "She said you were still like this."

I grit my teeth, something hot and fiery unfurling in my chest. "Spoiler alert, this is who I am. Maybe you should go fuck her instead."

He frowns. "Watch your mouth. I'm just *saying*."

I breathe deeply through my nose, my fingernails pressing crescents into my palm.

"Mm," I hum, picking up my wine to take a sip. Mainly to

give my hands something to do so I don't reach across the table and throttle him to death. "Well, considering I've only seen her a grand total of three times since I've been back from college, *just saying* might not be a winning move on your part."

Preston grimaces, and then he leans forward, and here comes his damn hand again, reaching out to grasp the top of mine.

Why does he keep doing that?

He winks, and I imagine clawing his eyes from his face. "I'm on your side. Promise."

Pressing my fingertips to my temple, I shake my head again. "Right. Of course you are. Would you excuse me? I need the ladies' room."

He nods and takes his hand back, watching me closely. "I'll order us dessert."

"Great," I say flatly.

My stomach is reeling when I walk to the restrooms, trying to find the balance between being full of decorum, the way I'm supposed to be, and knowing that yet another person has taken what I say and shoved it into a box of "how cute, of course she's saying this," the same way that he always has.

I move into the single-stall restroom, walking to the sink and pressing the back of my hand to my mouth to hold in the scream.

My lungs feel like they're being squeezed by fists commandeered by my mother, and maybe it's because, deep down, I know this is the future they've always planned for me. Mapped out, airtight, and I've just been living in a carefully crafted delusion of my own making. Pretending that if I want what *they* want, if I perform well enough, it will start to feel like freedom.

I pull my phone from my purse and bypass Felicity's text asking if I've cut off Preston's dick yet, and bring up the group chat with my brothers.

The Calloway Kings (and Queen)

ME:

Can one of you come save me from this date?

ALEX:

You're on a date?

ME:

Yes. I'm at Dante's, and I just need to leave. Come get me, PLEASE.

PAXTON:

Just call the car.

Scoffing, I roll my eyes. Of course, Paxton would think it's that easy. I *can't* just call a car to take me away from the date that our parents put together. They pay the drivers.

ME:

Pax, what's it like to be permanently lodged up Mom and Dad's ass all the time? I can't call the driver. I'm trying to make a grand escape.

ALEX:

What's in it for me?

ME:

I'm not above begging.

ALEX:

And I'm not above bribing.

I chew on the corner of my lip.

ME:

...what do you want?

ALEX:

Haven't decided yet. Let's make it an IOU. Give me twenty.

Sighing in relief, I slip my phone back into my clutch and look in the mirror, running a hand down the front of my cocktail dress.

I'm just about to walk out the door when it pushes back against me, and I gasp, the apology on my lips for almost running into someone.

But before I can say anything, Roman's face fills my vision, his eyes stormy and his jaw set.

My jaw drops, and my stomach flips. "What are you—?"

"Shut up," he demands, walking into the restroom and flicking the lock back on the door behind him.

My heart thumps erratically in my chest as I gaze at him and then the door and then back again. "What are you doing here?"

He laughs humorlessly, his hands ripping through the roots of his hair. "Is he your man now? Are you with him, Juliette?"

"Is he my...?" My eyes widen, satisfaction curling like ribbons through me. "You're jealous."

He gives me a grin, but it doesn't reach his eyes. "Just wondering if you two were together when you were begging me to fuck you with my fingers."

I cross my arms, my eyes narrowing. I'm not going to sit here and tell him what he wants to hear just to soothe that giant ego of his. If he wants to believe the worst about me, some preconceived notion like everyone else seems to have, then who am I to stop him?

But it hurts he'd think that of me at all.

And maybe it's because I'm already on my last goddamn nerve, and maybe it's because everyone and their brother seems to know everything about me based on assumptions and what other people tell them, but I'm tired of defending myself against something I didn't even do.

I lift my chin. "Who I'm with is none of your business."

He chuckles darkly, but it's a humorless sound. He points at me. "Wrong answer, Little Rose. *You* are my fucking business. Do you want to know why?"

Swallowing harshly, I don't reply.

"Because no matter how many times we say that we're nothing to each other, I can't get you out of my goddamn head." He slams his hand against his chest. "Can't get you out of here, either, so fuck me, I guess, right?"

I throw my hands in the air. "I don't know what you want from me."

"I want you!" he exclaims, his arms dropping helplessly to his sides. "I just want *you*."

My heart free-falls at his words, and tears spring behind my eyes, the burn fierce as I try to keep them from falling.

"You've been the only genuine thing in my life since showing up to this fucked-up little town, the only thing that feels real, and now I don't know if even *that's* the truth."

He takes a step closer to me, and I step back.

"I want to stop craving you with every breath."

My stomach clenches.

Another step forward, and I take another one away, my back hitting the wall next to the hand dryer.

"I want you to tell me that he doesn't get to touch you," he murmurs, his blue eyes dark as they peruse my body, like he can burn away anything that isn't him from my skin. "That *nobody* else gets to feel you the way I did. The way I'm still desperate to."

My breathing becomes shallow, heat pooling between my legs, my heart pounding so fast in my chest I can't take a full breath in.

His hand reaches out, ghosting down the side of my face, across my collarbone, then back up until he's lightly cupping the front of my throat. "I want you to tell me to stop," he murmurs.

I lick my lips, but no words come out. Desire courses through me, like static electricity shocking everywhere it touches. The connection that was missing with Preston is now exploding at the seams, like the room itself can't contain it.

Roman leans down. "Every person in this town has warned

me away from you. My own father just sat across from me and accused you of playing games with me. But they don't know you, do they, Juliette?"

I let out a shaky breath. "No, they don't."

My hands tremble as I reach up and press them to his shoulders.

"*You* know me, Roman."

His fingers tighten around my neck, his other hand skimming up my thigh, over the tight fabric of my dress, until it's resting on my hip.

And then he pauses, like he's waiting for something.

"He doesn't get to touch me," I whisper. My hands glide over his shoulders and wrap around the back of his neck. "Only *you* get to touch me."

Before I can blink, he's on me, pushing me up against the wall and flipping my dress up to my thighs.

He groans when he shoves my panties to the side and sees me bare before him, and I can barely take a breath before his mouth covers my pussy, his tongue dragging through my folds and circling my clit.

I slap a hand over my lips and bite down to keep from screaming out because the sensation is so intense, but somehow, I muffle my moans.

"Fuck, you taste just as good as I imagined." He buries himself between my legs again, and the sight of him there on his knees while he licks me is enough to tighten my core and shoot me into the stratosphere.

My teeth dig so harshly into my hand I taste blood, but I can't risk anyone hearing me. Not when his father and Preston are both right outside this door.

The thought makes heat flash through me, knowing he's here fucking me with his tongue despite that.

"Is this pussy mine, Juliette?" he groans, his voice thick.

One of his fingers slips inside me and curls up, and my vision goes fuzzy.

"Tell me," he demands, sliding in a second digit. "Say it. Right now."

"Yes," I whimper, my free hand going to the back of his head and physically forcing him against me again. "All yo—yours."

His mouth closes around me while he starts gliding his fingers in and out, and he suctions his lips just enough to create a torturous pressure around my clit. It's rhythmic and overwhelming, and I'm *so* close.

"Fuck," I whisper, my gaze locked on how my fingers grip his hair and how his head is moving sensuously in between my thighs.

Tension coils around me like a snake and constricts.

"I want you to come on my face," he says, and with a final lick of his tongue and pump of his hand, I'm gone, blasting into outer space and falling apart in his arms.

My legs shake around him, and he *moans* out his pleasure like he's the one coming undone.

When I come back down, he's sitting back on his heels with a filthy grin, my arousal coating his lips and making them shiny.

He leans in and presses a kiss to my pussy, and I clench, still sensitive. But he doesn't back away.

Instead, he stands. His hands are already at his belt, his jaw tight, and his eyes wild.

My stomach flips and tightens, and then *I'm* reaching for

him, my fingers fumbling with the button of his pants, and he doesn't stop me. He just watches with that sharp, dark hunger that makes my insides feel like they're liquefying.

His breath stutters when I get him free, wrapping my hand around his length.

His dick pulses in my palm, already leaking at the tip, and the sound he makes when I stroke him shoots straight between my legs.

I drop to my knees, and his hand flies to the back of my head, his other hand tilting my chin up so I'm looking straight into his eyes. "*Goddamn.* Look at you."

My chest warms at his praise.

He releases my chin and fists the base of his shaft, dragging the tip across my lips. "Do you want my cock, baby?"

I nod, unable to actually speak the words, and then he jerks himself, tapping the head of himself against my mouth.

"Open those pretty little lips for me, Juliette."

I do, and he slides in slow, dragging over my tongue as he groans like he's losing his mind for me.

He's thick, my mouth stretching around him until my jaw aches, and I can feel every single inch as he starts to move; shallow thrusts that feed me more of him until I'm full. His cock hits the back of my throat and I moan.

His eyes roll back like the sound physically pains him.

And the sight of him losing control like this? It fuels my hunger.

I move, my hands braced on his thighs as I suck him down, my tongue swiping along the vein that pulses up the underside of his shaft.

"Fuck, Juliette." His hips roll, and when I tighten my throat, he throws his head back and moans, his fingers threading through the roots of my hair.

He jerks forward, and I take him even deeper, my mouth wet and messy, spit and pre-cum dripping down my chin, and when I swallow around him, he snaps, ripping away from me and surging up with a choked curse, grabbing me by the arms and hauling me up before spinning me around until his cock is hard and heavy between my thighs, and my hands are flat against the wall.

"I need to fuck you, baby."

I press my ass into him, forcing his cock to slip inside me, just a little.

"Are you on birth control?" he asks, jerking forward so his tip presses against my clit.

My thighs tense around him.

"Yes," I gasp out. "Please, just do it."

He lines himself up, the head of him nudging my entrance.

"Tell me it's mine," he demands.

My core clenches, that fire flaring up my spine.

"It's yours," I agree. "*Please—*"

He thrusts into me in one devastating stroke and buries himself to the hilt.

I cry out, my head falling back against his shoulder as my pussy clamps down around him, struggling from his girth. The stretch is intense, almost painful, but it's so good I can't think straight.

"You're so tight," he groans. "Don't fight it, baby. Let me in."

"I can take it," I manage, my body shuddering as I push back, trying to push him deeper.

"Of course you can take it," he replies, pulling all the

way out, until just the swollen head of him is pressing at my entrance. His arm wraps around my waist, holding me in place as he works back in. "You were *made* for me, Juliette. This body, this cunt, your fucking soul; every inch of you is a perfect fit."

He bottoms out on the last word, and I clench around him, my wetness dripping out of me and smearing down my thighs. He sets a relentless rhythm, his hips snapping against me repeatedly, his cock hitting every oversensitive nerve inside me.

One arm stays locked around my waist, pinning me to him, and his other hand finds my hair and fists it, yanking back just enough to make my spine arch and my mind go blank.

I gasp and he thrusts up into me.

"You feel that?" he rasps into my ear. "That's what being *mine* feels like."

I whimper, every part of me burning.

"You're mine too," I manage, my hips swirling back as I clench my pussy walls around him like a vise.

He chuckles, low and dark. "You don't get it, do you?" He pulls out just enough to torture me. "I've always been yours. The moment I met you, I was ruined."

The confession lands hard, cracking open the center of my chest.

He groans, his teeth sinking into the side of my throat.

I can't speak. Can't even breathe. All I can do is give in to the sensation, feel him stretch me open while his hand slides from my waist down to my clit, applying the perfect amount of pressure.

"Roman," I gasp.

"Give it to me, Little Rose," he murmurs, his voice sounding like it's scraped over gravel. "Make a mess all over me."

My orgasm crashes through me like lightning, my body locking up and my pussy spasming around him. I moan his name out like he's the only thing I know, and I grind into his jerky thrusts, riding every wave.

"Come inside me," I beg. "I want to walk back to him while you're leaking out of me."

He lets out a hoarse, broken groan, and then thrusts deep one last time, his dick jerking wildly as he spills.

We stay in place, the quiet feeling like cotton balls in my ears.

I'm trembling. Breathless. And his hands grip me like he never wants to let me go.

He slides out of me, thick and dripping, and I exhale heavily at the loss.

Roman doesn't say a word. He just spins me around, releases me and then kneels between my legs. His eyes drop to the mess we made, and before I can gather my thoughts, his mouth is on me again.

I jerk, overstimulated and out of my mind, and he pins my hips with both hands, his tongue dragging through the mix of us with a slow and deliberate type of pressure.

He moans, and then presses a soft kiss to my clit before placing my underwear over it.

Then he looks up at me with a satisfied smirk.

"What do I taste like?" I ask, my chest heaving from how hard I'm trying to control my breath.

His grin darkens, and he stands up and leans in until our noses brush.

"Mine."

A ragged whimper leaves me at his words and I rest my

forehead against his chest. "You're ridiculously possessive, you know?"

He hums.

Lifting up on my toes, I press my lips to his again, my heart flipping when I do.

This is right.

This is home.

This is everything.

He leans back and gives me a soft, sad smile, his thumb pressing into my bottom lip.

Heat spikes through my middle.

"I won't make a scene," he says. "But if he keeps touching you, I'll find him once he leaves and break every single one of his fingers."

I nod slowly, heat curling in my belly. "Damn you. I find that incredibly attractive."

He smirks, leans down, and presses his lips to mine one more time, and then he's gone.

Chapter 40

Juliette

"I THOUGHT ALEX WAS PICKING ME UP." I FROWN at Paxton, who's sitting behind the wheel of his Aston Martin.

Paxton quirks a dark brow. "If you wanted Alex to be the one to come, then you shouldn't have texted the group."

"Uh, no, I thought Alex was coming because he *said* he was coming. There's nothing wrong with you other than that stick wedged up your ass."

He smirks as he pulls away into the traffic, his watch gleaming as he steers. I don't know what kind it is, but I'm sure it's expensive. Paxton collects watches the way other people collect fine art.

"Don't be pissed because she likes me more," Alex cuts in, leaning forward from the back seat.

I yelp, my heart thundering as I press a hand to my chest. "Jesus, Alex, I had no idea you were back there."

"That's because you don't pay attention."

I scrunch my nose. "I don't even know what that means."

"Means you're not situationally aware," he says.

"Okay, well, not all of us are trained for deep-space survival scenarios. Sorry I'm not in Starfleet."

Paxton's eyes flick toward me. "Was that a *Star Trek* reference?"

I blink. "What? No."

He raises a brow. "Pretty sure it was."

Was it?

"Crap, maybe it was." I sigh.

He chuckles. "Don't sound so upset about it."

"I'm not upset, just irritated that Felicity is invading my subconscious."

"Felicity knows about *Star Trek*?"

I stare at him. "Why are you asking that like it's not *your* fault?"

"How the hell is it *my* fault?"

"Uh, I don't know, because you let her watch it with you?"

He makes an affronted face. "I absolutely did *not*."

"You did," I say. "It was storming outside, and she got freaked so you put on *Voyager* to distract her."

Alex hums. "I think I remember that too, actually."

"See?" I gesture. "Don't question me. I'm always right."

Paxton's mouth opens like he wants to argue, but then he closes it. And I could *swear* a hint of a smile passes over his face.

"Right," he says quietly, turning on the blinker. "I forgot about that."

I give him an odd look, and then put my feet up on the dash, wincing from how sore I am between my legs because Roman just fucked me silly.

My heart flips.

"Get your filthy feet off my dash, Juliette."

I give him a pointed look. "Stick up your ass."

He smacks at my shoes.

"Whatever," I mutter, dropping them to the floor and taking out my phone. "This just proves my theory that Felicity's words eat at my brain like a parasitic worm."

Alex groans. "Can we not talk about space worms while I'm trapped in this car? It's bad enough you both are talking about Felicity like either of you know her better than me."

I twist in my seat. "She's *my* best friend, you Neanderthal. Leave her alone."

Paxton looks at Alex in the rearview mirror. "You're an idiot."

"Technically, I'm the smartest one in the family," Alex corrects.

I scoff. "Says who?"

He smirks, leaning back. "They don't have to say it. Common knowledge, I fear."

"How'd you get away from your date, anyway? Does he know we came to get you?" Paxton asks, side-eyeing me as he flicks on the blinker and turns right.

My cheeks heat when I think about how I could feel Roman's cum dripping out of me while I made excuses to Preston. My body still hums with the feel of his hands, and the way he was trying to mold me into something that belonged to him.

"He thinks I'm not feeling well."

Alex laughs, and Paxton shakes his head.

My gaze whips back and forth between them. "What?"

"You couldn't have come up with something a bit more original?" The corner of Paxton's lips quirks up.

"It's a perfectly reasonable explanation."

"Every dude knows if a girl flees in the middle of a date, it's because she doesn't like him," Alex chimes in.

"That's not true," I reply.

But maybe it is. They'd know, wouldn't they?

I chew on my lip, wondering how convincing I was. "Preston didn't seem to mind."

"Your date was with Preston? Preston Ascott?" Paxton questions. "Your *ex*?"

"Yeah, and? What's the issue now?" I say sharply.

Paxton's always been a grumpy asshole, but ever since I came back from school, it's been on steroids.

"He's not good enough for you," he says.

"No shit," I agree. "Take it up with Mommy Dearest."

Paxton looks at me from the corner of his eye and harrumphs but doesn't say anything else.

Alex has also grown quiet.

"*Anyway*, I'm tired of talking about my failed date," I say. "Thanks for saving me, even if you're being a prick while doing it."

Paxton nods, a muscle in his jaw ticking.

"Tiffany didn't mind you coming to get me?" I press, because I feel like getting under his skin. Paxton *never* speaks about his wife.

He side-eyes me. "Tiffany doesn't get to tell me where to go or what to do."

Alex whistles from the back seat. "Trouble in paradise?"

"Things are fine."

I smirk. "Convincing, Pax."

Alex's phone goes off from the back, and the screen lights up his face almost as much as the giant grin I see when I turn around to look at him.

"Who's got you smiling like that?"

He wiggles his brows and looks at me. "Who do you think?"

"*No*. Felicity?"

He slips his phone back into his pocket and leans back with a lazy grin. "I don't kiss and tell, Jules."

Yeah, me neither.

"Felicity does, though, and she definitely would have told me if she was making out with you."

"I'll have you know, she's *this* close to agreeing to date me," he continues. "So, please go on with your theory about how she doesn't like me."

I'm not sure whether I believe him. If she decided to date my brother and not even tell me, I'll be pissed.

"Too bad you blew it with Preston," he jokes. "We could have had double dates."

"I didn't *blow* anything."

My face heats and I stumble over the words because technically, that's not true. I clear my throat and push Roman from my mind.

"Besides, you can double date with Pax and Tiffany." I give a wide grin to Paxton.

"Absolutely *not*," Paxton chimes in, his fingers tight on the steering wheel. "I don't want anything to do with that girl."

"Good God, Pax. Dial down the animosity, she didn't run over your puppy."

We pull into the front of the estate, and the quiet overwhelms the car as Paxton kills the engine.

"Well, kids, it's been fun, but I've got a *girl* to text." Alex smirks and waves his phone in the air before slipping out the back and disappearing inside.

"Thanks for the ride." I reach to open the car door but am stopped by Paxton's hand on my arm.

"Hey, I don't..." He sighs, shaking his head. "Do you really like Preston?"

Surprise filters through me, and I release the handle of the door and sink back into my seat, blinking at him. "What do you mean?"

He shrugs. "It's a simple question. Do you like him, or is this really another setup by Mom and Dad?"

I cringe. "I think you know the answer to that question."

Paxton's lips press together. "You know, I married Tiffany for them."

I knew that—of course I knew—anyone with a pulse can see how much he doesn't love her. But still, this is the first time he's ever admitted it out loud. At least to me. I don't know why the confirmation that my brother is stuck in a loveless marriage makes me so sad, but it does. Everywhere he goes and everything he does seems to be for someone else, and this is the first time I've realized that in that regard, we're alike.

My stomach rolls, because I love my brother, but I do *not* want to end up like him.

As the firstborn Calloway, he's been stuck to rules and rigidity in a way the rest of us never have, and if it feels like *I'm* in a cage, it's most likely just a fraction of what it feels like for Paxton.

"Yeah, I hate to be the bearer of bad news, but you're not very good at faking it," I tell him.

A sad smile spreads across his face, and his fingers tighten around the steering wheel like he needs something to hold on to. "I didn't do everything I've done just for you to suffer the same fate."

I tilt my head, his words pressing heavily on my chest. "What does that mean?"

Paxton is six years older than me, and maybe it's because of that age gap that this is the closest thing to a heart-to-heart that we've ever had.

His lips twist. "I want you to be happy, Jules. Out of anyone in our family, you deserve that. And if Preston makes you happy, then good. But if it's just some sense of loyalty to Mom and Dad, then...I want you to know I'll have your back."

"Thank you," I choke out, his admission making my throat swell and my eyes burn.

He smiles softly. "I know I'm not always the best brother."

"Don't—"

He shuts me up with a look. "But I'm here for you, even when it doesn't seem like I am. I'm on *your* side."

Swallowing, I nod. "Okay."

"Okay," he repeats, blowing out a breath like that took everything in him to say.

I'm frozen for a few moments, just blinking at him. "Are you worried about the accusations about our family?"

A giant part of me doesn't want to even bring them up, because every time I do, I'm hit with the feeling of being torn down the middle. Loyalty to Roman, or loyalty to them.

He shrugs and runs a hand through his hair. "Nah. Everything will blow over. There's nothing anyone can prove, and Dad seems to think he has it handled."

I nod, chewing on the inside of my lip. "Is it true what the news is saying? That you might have to take it over?"

He shrugs again. "Maybe, yeah."

"I'm sorry," I whisper.

He gives me a confused look. "What on earth do you have to be sorry for?"

"I don't know." I lift a shoulder. "I'm sorry you're not happy, I guess."

"I never said I wasn't."

"You didn't have to, Pax."

He glances down at his hands and gives a brief nod, and I slip out of the car, a heavy feeling weighing down my shoulders.

I walk inside and jump a mile high when Beverly's voice filters from around the corner. "How was your date?"

"Christ, Bevie, give me a heart attack." I press my hand to my chest. "It was with Preston, so it sucked."

It's on the tip of my tongue to tell her about Roman, but I don't get the chance before she changes the subject.

"Well, your father's home. So, I'd recommend you go up to your wing and stay there."

"Sure." I glance down the long hallway, wondering what my dad's getting up to. There's an overwhelming sense of dread whenever I think about him now.

But I listen, making my way up to my room, and pulling out my notebook, weaving my memories into fiction.

The girl let the wolf devour her. Not because she didn't know better, but because she did. Because she was desperate to know what it felt like to be undone by him. He sank into her like a curse whispered on the wind, and now she walks around like he's branded into her skin. Marked. Claimed.

She knows she'll dream of blood moons and velvet mouths, and of simpler times...when she still thought she could survive the ruin of him.

The ROSEBROOK Rag

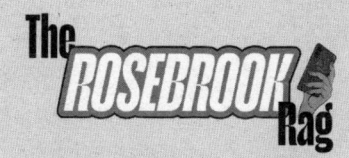

"We've done nothing wrong!"

The Calloway family hits back hard.

In a bold press moment, Craig Calloway slams corruption rumors as "outrageous" and "completely false," standing firm alongside his wife Martha and their eldest son, Paxton.

Facing protests and fresh graffiti, the Calloways claim it's all a smear campaign courtesy of Marcus Montgomery.

"We've built this town. We are this town," Craig said.

Paxton called for an independent investigation, adding, "We have nothing to hide."

Meanwhile, the Montgomery estate? Radio silence.

#CallowayWatch #GraffitiGate #RosebrookRag #FamilyFeud

Chapter 41

Roman

BROOKLYNN:

> I signed the thing.

RELIEF HITS ME SHARP AND HARD AT BROOKLYNN'S acknowledgment that she signed the trust. That means I don't have to worry. No matter *what* happens with me, she's taken care of. It's legally binding, and she has full access immediately to all the funds.

ME:

> Fuck, I can't tell you how happy that makes me. Thank you.

My thumb hovers over the screen.

BROOKLYNN:

> Do you know how Mom is, by the way?

The shift is subtle, but I feel the low hum of dread in my chest. The way it always is whenever my mother is brought up.

ME:

> We can't call her for another two weeks. When she comes out of isolation, we'll plan a visit, if you want? I'll fly in. How are you feeling?

BROOKLYNN:

> Okay. I feel great, actually. The past few weeks, I've had more energy and haven't had a bedridden day. I don't know what's changed, but I'm grateful for it.

ME:

> 🙏 Hope it lasts.

I let the words settle, rereading them once. And then again. My chest loosens just a little.

"Why the long face, sweetheart?" Merrick asks, sipping on a green bottle of beer, his eyes intense as they watch me from across our booth at the Round Table.

I give a grin back, not wanting to talk about it.

"Hello, Earth to Roman." Merrick laughs, snapping his fingers in front of my face. "You keep zoning out mid-brood and I'll have to start praying for divine intervention."

"Someone must be more important," Rosalie says as she sets down a fresh drink in front of Merrick with a smirk.

I glance down at my phone, my fingers gripping it so tightly my knuckles ache.

I texted Juliette.

Again.

But she hasn't replied.

Ever since I cornered her in the bathroom the other night, she's gone radio silent. It's driving me fucking crazy, wondering if she's done with me now.

She wouldn't.

At least, I don't think.

I deserve her silence.

The art's causing a bit more fallout than I expected. Or maybe it's going exactly as planned, and I just have my heart in the mix now, so it feels messier.

I'm starting to feel like my dad didn't tell me huge portions of the situation on purpose, like I'm painting blind and hoping for the best. And that makes me question things. Makes me feel like I'm not helping to dismantle a machine, but acting like just another cog.

Still, Brooklynn is feeling *healthy. Happy.* She's taken care of now, no matter what.

And my mom is getting help.

So, I'll do what I need to do.

I slide my phone in my pocket and sip from my drink.

Benjamin's late, not that I particularly miss his brand of company, and I'm about to ask where he is when he walks into the room from the back hallway, smirking at Genevieve behind the bar while Lance says something to her with a serious face.

There's something happening there with Lance and her.

He lightly grips her arm and she snips something with a sharp look. He grins at whatever it is, and my brows shoot to my hairline.

I've never seen him smile before.

Art Penngrove walks out from the back hallway next, and when he moves toward them, Lance's smile fades, and he drops Genevieve like she's burned him and turns his back.

Benjamin claps Lance on the shoulder like they're friends and laughs before making his way over to us.

My gaze stays on Juliette's brother, anger resonating deep, because why is it fine for him to mix company but impossible for Juliette and me?

I know Benjamin doesn't have the last name "Montgomery," but he's still on *our* side of things.

"There's the man of the hour. Where you been?" Merrick's loud enough to draw a few looks from nearby tables as Benjamin saunters over.

"What's up, Benny?" I give him a chin nod.

His eyes narrow in response.

What the fuck did I do?

There's a commotion at the front of our table, and then an older woman stands in front of us, a hat pulled low over her eyes like she's trying not to be seen.

"Hello, gentlemen."

"Hey, lady. You're blocking the view of the match." Merrick gestures to the UFC fight on the TV behind her.

She turns to look at the fighting and then back at Merrick. "What kind of a man are you? Barbaric, those fights. Disgusting."

Merrick laughs. "You're in the wrong place to be saying something like that."

That piques my interest. What's so wrong about saying that in a dusty bar that serves generic food and beer?

"Besides, I'm just a man like any other," Merrick continues.

"Just like the men in the fight. God made them, and he gave them the free will to ruin themselves if they want to."

I chuckle. "Don't worry about him, ma'am. He's always talking nonsense; nobody understands what he means half the time."

"He's not lying, though, is he?" Her eyes lock onto mine, a knowing look in their gaze. "We all have the free will to ruin ourselves…and sometimes others."

Nodding, my brows furrow, a heavy sensation hitting me with the seriousness of her gaze. "I guess you're right."

"Roman Montgomery?" she asks, her entire focus now on me.

I sit forward. "Depends on who's asking."

"I need to speak to you." Her eyes flick over the other men at the table. "In private."

Benjamin snorts and taps Merrick on the arm. "She's either here to confess her sins or beg for a good time."

"Oh, she's not here to beg." Merrick laughs. "And definitely not for him. No offense, honey, but Roman's not really known to go for the women who remember dial-up." He pauses, giving her a saucy look. "Me, on the other hand…"

Benjamin scoffs. "Jesus, Merrick, you'd flirt with a ghost if it had legs and liquor, wouldn't you?"

"And you wouldn't?" he fires back, grinning. "You've got that graveyard type of energy all over you."

"Merrick, you may know Benny, but you have no idea what *I'd* go for," I interrupt, then glance back at her. "What's your name?"

The woman glares at Merrick before looking at me with her chin raised. "I won't talk in front of rude men who think they can speak to me like I'm beneath them."

"He's harmless," I reiterate. "Just loves the sound of his own voice."

"In private." Her jaw clenches, and she lowers her voice. "I believe you'll want to hear what I have to say."

Benjamin's eyes narrow, recognition flaring through them. "Wait a minute; you look familiar. You a friend of Freddy's?"

She stiffens her spine. "I am, but I work for the Calloways, actually."

My head snaps to her, seeing her in a new light. "You work for the Calloways?"

"Roman, come on." Benjamin laughs like I'm being ridiculous. "You're not seriously going to talk to her in private, are you?"

I cut a glare at him. "Don't think because you're my father's bitch that I'll be yours, Benny."

Standing up, I jerk my chin at the woman, and she follows.

Merrick laughs, lifting his bottle and calling out, "Let me know how the old hag is, sweetheart! Maybe I'll take her for a ride!"

"Ignore them," I mutter, moving between the tables until we hit that back hallway I found Juliette in not too long ago.

Spinning around, I cross my arms and lean against the wall. "All right, let's try this again. What's your name?"

She looks behind her before finding me again. "Beverly. I'm here to give you a message."

My eyes flare, and I straighten. Worry for Juliette bubbles inside me. "What's the message?"

She eyes me. "I'm not sure if I should give it to you or not."

"Then you're wasting my time."

"The opposite. I care about Juliette, love her, even, and if you're just messing around to get in her head, just to leave her in it alone, then I need you to know something." She leans in. "I might not be strong enough to hurt you, but I know people who can. And I'll make sure you're hurting for the rest of your life."

My lips quirk, warmth filling up my chest. I worried that maybe Juliette didn't have anyone in her corner, not truly, anyway, and knowing that at least there's one person there with her beyond her family who she can trust makes me happy.

"I'm not playing games," I say. "I promise you that."

Her gaze softens. "She deserves someone who'll fight for her. Even if it's messy. Even if it seems impossible."

Impossible is the right word for it, unfortunately.

"She needs to see you," Beverly says.

My heart trips over itself. "Why didn't she just text me?"

Beverly cuts me a look. "She didn't suggest it, I'm just saying I can help make it happen."

I swallow harshly, my hands going in my pockets as I nod. *She's brutal.* Is this where Juliette learned it from?

"Did you truly save her life?"

"Kind of." Memories of a simpler time, when I was just a silly guy with bad ideas and flirty lines. Before I became the thing she isn't supposed to want. "Do you think she can meet me there tonight? Where I saved her?"

She blows out a breath and then nods. "I'll make sure of it. But Roman, don't just *show up* for her, and think she should continue to wait for you in the dark."

I frown.

"If you want her, *really* want her, then you must take her. *Choose* her. Don't look back. Do you understand what I'm saying to you?"

The silence is thick.

"I thought you worked for the Calloways," I reply eventually.

"I do," she confirms. "But that house will be the death of her. And I'll do anything to get her out."

My chest pulls tight, and I watch her closely.

Frederick's words flow through my mind, the same as they have ever since he said them.

Sometimes the only way to protect something as precious as love…is to take it far from where anyone can reach it.

Chapter 42

Roman

I'VE ALWAYS BEEN ABLE TO SNEAK AROUND without much issue. Ever since I was a little kid, for some reason, it's been natural to me. It's what makes it so easy to slink through the streets at night and paint on the sides of buildings, train cars, and the like.

But then again, back then, I was a nobody.

And I guess I'm still not entirely used to being somebody.

Ever since Paxton Calloway put my dad's name into the mix at their press conference the other day, insinuating that the paintings were a smear campaign, there have been reporters outside, waiting for me everywhere. Frederick told me to say, "no comment," and I have, but what I *want* to say is, "fuck everybody."

They're not wrong. It *is* a smear campaign, even if there's truth in it.

But the thing I've learned about reporters? They don't know how to *look*. They wait at the front door, or they're watching the windows. They don't realize how easy it is to scale a balcony or slip through the shadows from a back stairwell when you've been doing it since you were ten.

So, sneaking away tonight? It's as easy as breathing.

I'm in my painting gear: dark jeans, black baseball hat, and the skull mask low on my face.

It's late in the evening, the stars already blanketing the sky, when I get to our spot.

My heart trips and my stomach dips, and soon I see her, waiting at the edge of the cliff, the breeze blowing her black hair like it can't help but lace its airy fingers through the strands.

She's about twenty paces away and looks so goddamn beautiful it makes my chest ache.

"You came," I say.

She spins toward me, a smile blooming on her face. "You called, albeit very cryptically."

I take long, measured steps toward her. I want to savor this time, because I don't know when we'll get it again.

"It's good to see you," she murmurs softly, her eyes bouncing over my face, down my body, taking in the clothing I'm wearing. A grin lights up her face, like she's happy to see me dressed this way. "Coming from vandalizing our town or going?"

"Going." The corner of my mouth lifts, and I drop the backpack to my side, the rattle of cans hitting each other loud.

Her eyes track the movement, and she shifts from one foot to another before meeting my gaze. "I think I'd like to see it sometime. You in your element."

I tilt my head. "You've seen me draw a hundred times."

"Yeah, but...that's not really *you*, is it?"

I swallow harshly, because how the fuck is it possible that

this woman who I've known for a handful of days just seems to *get* me in a way nobody else does?

Stepping forward, I spin the ring on my finger, my stomach twisting with each move I make. I lick my lips and catch her gaze, holding strong. The air vibrates between us like it's a tightrope waiting to snap if we step the wrong way.

"I think," I murmur, "out of everyone in the world…you might know me best."

Her eyes flick to mine, and color rushes into her cheeks. Like usual, it slams me right in the chest. I love how soft she looks when she's not guarding herself, and the visceral *need* to keep her like this, is almost overwhelming in its intensity.

Her fingers twist in front of her and those teeth of hers bite into her lower lip. I move my touch, pulling it free.

"Don't do that," I say, my stomach tightening. "You'll bleed."

She nods, just barely. And then, "You know me best, too."

It hurts, hearing her say those words to me when everything feels so impossible. "But it doesn't matter, does it?"

She takes a shaky breath. Stares down at her hands, one thumb aggressively rubbing over the other like she's trying to erase herself.

"I've never *not* loved them," she says quietly. "Even when I hated what they did."

There's a weighted pause, but she doesn't look up.

"And then there's you." Her tone sounds frayed now, like the words are tearing up her throat.

I don't move. I'm afraid to breathe, worried that if I do, the pain in my chest might collapse my lungs.

"You're…" She swallows and tries again. "You're everything."

"Juliette—"

"Let me get this out." She throws her hand up.

My fists clench, heart pounding, gut fucking sick with nerves.

"You *feel* like everything," she amends. "But then I walk through town, and I see you there. On the brick. In the glass. On the campus."

She presses her palm to her lips, and her voice breaks. "Every time a new mural goes up, I feel like I'm standing in the middle of a war I didn't choose. And I can't tell which side I'm supposed to run from."

The space between us stretches tight, and I just stand like a stone statue, because what can I say?

What can I offer her? What can I do to tell her that I'm enough when I know that I'm not—when I *know* that if I leave, my mom will be left out in the dust.

"What are you telling me, Little Rose?" I finally force out, my jaw aching and my heart fucking bleeding onto the floor.

My fists are clenched, arms pinned to my sides because if I let them move, I'm afraid they'll reach for her.

"I can't stop loving them just to find a way to be with you."

And there it is.

The quietest knife with the sharpest blade, carving through my chest.

The burn climbs high and fast, spreading from behind my nose to my eyes. My lungs twist like they've forgotten how to work, and I press my knuckles to my mouth, swallowing over the sudden thickness in my throat.

Understanding flows through her perfect face like she's just figured out the answer to a problem she's been trying to solve, and she steps toward me, her head tilting.

"I love you," she says.

She takes a breath like she might take back what she said, and even though I'm frozen in place, I might die if she does.

If I move, I'll fall to my knees. If I speak, I'll probably beg. And I don't know if either of us will survive those things.

My chest feels like it's caving in, my throat's raw from the effort of staying silent, my eyes sting, and I *hate* this.

This isn't how it should be.

She should be able to love me, and I should be able to love *her* without limitation. Without this ridiculous feud between our families that has *nothing* to do with us.

And just like that, everything slots and re-slots into place, a physical click locking inside my body.

This whole time I've been torturing myself by having responsibilities, people that I can't walk away from. But Brooklynn signed the papers. There's money and solutions in her hands.

And when the hell has my mom ever done anything for me?

Juliette's lip trembles and she presses it flat like she's trying to swallow down her emotion before it kills her.

"You don't have to say it back," she continues, her voice barely above a whisper. "I didn't even realize until it was out there that it was how I felt, and I don't—"

God.

I blink, and then I'm moving. My hands find her face, rough and trembling, and I pull her to me like every second before her was a wasted moment.

Her breath catches on a strangled noise and then she's moving too, her fingers clutching at the front of my shirt as though she might fall if she lets go.

My mouth crashes against hers and I moan.

She tastes like something I've spent my whole life chasing.

She tastes like coming home.

"Don't you *ever* think you're alone in this," I grit out against her lips. "Don't you get it? Don't you know by now that you *consume* me?"

She whimpers, and I grip her cheeks in my hands like I'm afraid she'll disappear.

"I'm so in love with you, I've forgotten how to exist without you," I say. "I love you like I was *made* to love you. Like I came into this world just so you could carve out my heart and leave yourself inside it."

Her mouth parts, eyes glassy, but nothing comes out.

My hands slide to her jaw, thumbs tracing over her skin, like maybe if I hold her tight enough, the universe won't find a way to tear us apart.

"You're *it* for me, Juliette," I whisper. "You've always been it."

Neither of us move. Her fingers are still curled in the fabric of my shirt, but she's not pulling me closer anymore. She's just holding on, like letting go will break the moment. Like she knows we're at the precipice of something too big for us to keep.

I press my forehead to hers.

Her breath trembles against my lips.

And in the silence, I feel it. The shift. That invisible moment between where we've been pretending we are and where we *really* are.

The truth is simple: I love her. Desperately. Endlessly. Irrevocably.

But love doesn't erase blood, and the lines between our names are still drawn with a deep-red ink too dark to wash away.

As long as we both exist in Rosebrook Falls, it doesn't matter how much we want each other.

Our love burns so bright it's blinding.

But hate knows how to swallow up light.

Chapter 43

Juliette

"DO YOU HATE ME FOR BEING PART OF THEM?" I ask.

My voice is quiet, but it might as well be a scream in the stillness of the woods.

"Do you hate me for who *I* am?" he replies.

Somewhere between our confessions of love and the moments after, we sunk to the ground. I'm curled up in his lap and he's holding me tight, his fingers dancing along my spine like the boulder of truth isn't about to come crashing through our bodies and rip us both apart.

I press my face to the crook of his neck, my breath shaky as I bite back the feeling of dread that's curling through me with every second we stay out here, staring at the stars.

Eventually the night will end, and our weighted confessions will disappear along with it.

"Never."

"It's okay to care about people," he says after a long pause. "Even when they hurt us. Even when they turn into strangers."

His voice is love and threaded with a type of understanding that I'm not even sure *I* have when it comes to the way I'm feeling.

I hum, but my throat is too tight to speak.

"I'll stop," he continues. "The tagging. I won't do them about your family anymore."

That makes me look up, something rattling loose in my chest. "Thank you. Why were you doing them in the first place?"

"Because my father's dying...and he wants revenge before he goes." He kisses the top of my head.

Relief pours through me. I had been heavy with the weight of not telling him what I had learned. "You know?"

"*You* know?"

I swallow. "Yeah, Bevie told me."

He nods like he gets it. "Because she's friends with Frederick. Right."

I frown. "What? I don't think Bevie even knows Freddy like that. They never really talked when I was a kid."

Roman's eyes narrow, and he leans back slightly so he can look me in the eye. "Beverly. The woman who came to see me, right?"

"Short, a little mean, and a scowl on her face like she has a grudge against the world?"

"Yeah."

"That's her."

His brow furrows. "She definitely knows Frederick."

Rosebrook isn't exactly a sprawling city, it's just big enough to pretend we don't all live on top of each other, and Frederick's always been around in the background. Before he went halfway up Marcus Montgomery's ass, he was a regular fixture at my family's gatherings, and at one time in my life I had thought him and my dad were friends.

"Huh. Makes sense, I guess."

"I never wanted to hurt you," Roman says, his voice low.

His jaw's tight, eyes locked on me with that steady, weighted gaze of his that always makes me feel like he's staring into my soul.

He loves me.

"I know," I reply. Because I do.

"More than anyone else," he continues. "Your happiness is…" His throat bobs as he swallows. "It's all that matters."

"Don't say that," I whisper, even though my heart beats faster at his words. "I don't want to be put above your sister. Above your family."

His arms tighten around me, his chin dipping to rest against the top of my head. "Brooke's taken care of now, and my mom…" He exhales sharply. "My mom made her choices a long time ago."

My chest aches at his words, but I don't really have anything I can say to make it better. Truthfully, the idea of someone hurting *him* as much as she has makes it hard for me to find space in my heart to think of her fondly. But she still made him, so I hold on to that kernel of gratitude and hope she can find her way back.

"Do you trust Frederick?" he asks, his tone taking on a sharper cadence.

I chew on the inside of my cheek. "I guess so. Why?"

Roman's hand slides up my back, settling at the nape of my neck, and I relax into his lap, my head resting on his shoulder. His thumb rubs a slow, soothing circle, but his body is stiff, coiled tight beneath the otherwise steady touch.

He doesn't answer me right away.

"Roman," I say softly, pulling back just enough to look up at him.

He's gazing into the distance like he's not even here.

"Trouble," I try again. "Why?"

That gets his attention, and his gaze flickers across my face like he's memorizing it.

"All I can think about is what happens next," he admits. "After we leave this spot, and you go back to your corner and I'm forced into mine. What this looks like if we stay."

Something twists sharply behind my ribs.

He brushes his fingers along my cheek, his voice barely above a whisper now.

"What if we didn't?"

I blink. "Didn't what?"

"Didn't stay."

I stare at him, the weight of his words sinking in like I'm stuck in quicksand.

"Juliette..." He leans in, presses his forehead to mine. "Run away with me."

My heart stumbles and then surges, kicking against my bones in a violent rhythm. "What?"

His hands frame my face, pulling me in until he can press his lips to mine. Once. Twice. Sweet, chaste kisses, but they taste of desperation.

"Run away with me," he repeats.

The words strike like lightning this time, reverberating in the space between us like thunder.

"None of this matters without you," he says. "I don't give a fuck about *any* of it. Not the money. Not the name. I only want *you*."

I can barely breathe.

My brain's short-circuiting, flinging images at me of possible scenarios that are too fast to catch. Roman's hand in mine as we disappear into the night. An empty bedroom. My mother's stiff, stern silence. My brothers pacing the halls, sending me varying levels of angry and sarcastic messages. Felicity sitting next to Alex, or maybe even Paxton, waiting for a reply I'll never send.

I don't even realize I've gone still until Roman's thumb brushes across my cheek again.

Running away with him would mean ripping out the roots I've spent my whole life pretending were planted by me.

But maybe they've never been roots at all. Maybe they've been chains disguised as comfort.

"Say something," he whispers.

"I'd lose everyone," I reply. "If we do this… If we run. I'd lose everyone."

He blows out a steady breath, warm against my skin.

"Maybe not forever," he says. "Frederick said something to me once, about how he could help us if we asked. And Beverly…I think she'd help too, don't you?"

"I hope you know, Juliette, that I am always on your side."

Hope, dangerous and sharp, hits me in my sternum.

"We don't have to disappear for good. Maybe it's just for now. Just long enough for things to quiet down. If I leave, I lose the empire."

I suck in a breath, my eyes widening.

"That could be the answer. Once there's no Montgomery fortune to my name, and Frederick's dispersed the inheritance back into the town, who cares if I come back? Would your dad?"

My throat tightens, forehead creasing as I think about what he says. "I don't know... Maybe?"

"You'd still be you. Still Juliette. You'd just be her... somewhere else for a little bit. Somewhere we get to choose. *Free*."

He cups my cheek and I lean into his touch like it's the only thing keeping me steady.

Somewhere we get to choose. Free.

How long have I ached for that?

"Could we really come back someday?" I whisper.

His jaw tenses. "I can't promise that. But I promise I won't stop trying. And we'd be different. Stronger."

A pregnant pause.

"Together."

The light dims after he says it, reality creeping in like it always does. "But your father..."

"I don't care about him." His voice is adamant. His tone is sure. But I don't believe it for a second.

I shake my head. "What if you lose him? What if I take you from time you'll never get back?"

He presses a finger to my lips.

"I'm choosing you," he says. "*Please*. Let me choose you."

I want to. God, I want to. But fear clutches at my ribs.

"Don't let the what-ifs ruin our happy ending, Juliette." He smooths the crease between my brows, his touch like a promise. "Don't let the bad thing win."

And that does it. There's a steady ache in my chest, spreading outward and wrapping me in its heady claws. It's heartbreak mixed with hope, and that's a devastating cocktail.

"You're sure Freddy will help?" I ask.

He nods.

I twist in his arms until he's cradling me, and I lift my hand up, pressing it to his cheek. His gaze is open, and full, and *everything*. I see our future in his eyes.

"My only love sprung from my only hate," I murmur, caressing his face.

His gaze flickers, and I let my thumb trail down to his jaw. His stubble scrapes against my skin.

"Okay, Trouble," I whisper. "Let's climb the walls they built for us, and get our happy ending."

Chapter 44

Roman

"WHY ARE YOU WILLING TO HELP JULIETTE AND me?"

I don't waste time mincing words, because I need to know that Frederick will help us. There's a charity gala tonight, one that the entire town is going to be at, and one that my father has requested I attend.

It will be my last hurrah. And Juliette's. After she agreed to my reckless plan, we worked on logistics.

"When will we go?"

"The VU Founders' Gala is this weekend. Let's play our parts until then. Give time for you to talk to Freddy. And then we'll slip away."

Frederick rubs his chin. "Because I believe you two are the key. The match that will light the flame and burn down the feud, or perhaps...the balm to finally end it."

I scoff, slouching deeper in the chair across from him. "I don't care about the feud. Let them fucking kill each other and bleed out in the streets as long as they leave Juliette and me the hell alone."

It sounds crass, but I mean every word. Juliette might feel differently, but that's because she loves deeply, even those who don't deserve it. Not that she'd admit that fact, because the guard she holds around herself is ten thousand feet tall and made of stone.

Frederick looks battle worn and weary. "When I first came to this town twenty-five years ago, I thought I'd stumbled into an old money type of elegance." He laughs. "But what I walked into was a war masquerading as civility."

He leans forward, elbows braced on the edge of his desk. "Every day since, I've had to play diplomat. Remember I told you that being a master of the game meant you controlled it, and that's true, but it's goddamn tiring. It's never-ending. Bribes. Council seats. Land grabs. Calloway and Montgomery both using people as currency."

"So, you're tired," I deduce. "That doesn't mean anything to me."

"This isn't *tired*, this is bigger than that. I've prayed for something to end it. Maybe not with fire, or blood, or a handshake. But if it comes because of love…" He smiles faintly. "Who am I to stand in the way?"

I cross my arms, grinding my teeth. "So you're saying my father is just as corrupt as Craig Calloway, and yet somehow, you think Juliette and me are the answer?"

His eyes narrow. "Don't insult either of us by pretending you didn't already know that."

I don't answer, because he's right.

"Both of your families have built empires on exploitation," Frederick says. "You think that money grows from honest soil? Wake up, Roman."

I rake a hand through my hair. "None of this shit matters to me, Frederick. I'm not asking about morality, I'm asking if you can help me and Juliette disappear."

Frederick nods, and there's something almost too smooth about the motion. "It's what I've wanted since I've seen that picture of the two of you together. The son of a Montgomery and the daughter of a Calloway. Two houses alike in dignity, bound by legacy, divided by greed. What better way to end a blood feud than with the two children they *need* vanishing from the board entirely?"

"You make it sound so tragic." My chest tightens.

He pauses, eyes gleaming. "Sometimes, the world needs a little tragedy to move forward."

My brow furrows.

"Besides," he continues. "You'll be safer if you're away from here. I don't know what Marcus was thinking allowing you to stir up public outrage for the Calloways when they're tied together with the Badon Hill Gang."

My heart falters and I lean forward. "It was just me painting some conspiracies on the wall."

Frederick looks at me like I've grown three heads. "He really didn't tell you much, did he? Every painting you put up is a slap in their faces, and the Badon Hill crew? Those men don't care who holds the brush."

My stomach drops like a lead weight. "He told me that was done. That Brutus guy is dead."

His face pinches. "He lied."

A hollow ache blooms in my chest.

I had thought we were making progress, that in the end, my father had started to see me as something more than what he's made me feel my entire life. But this? This is proof that even the good moments were built on bad intentions. He's been using me, pulling strings behind my back like I'm a puppet in motion.

My thumb spins the ring on my finger like I can unscrew the past from my skin, but it still clings on.

Somewhere deep inside, that kid staring outside of a window looking in breaks all over again.

Because how could I have been so stupid to think that this time would be different.

I blow out a breath, beating down the hurt. "If I leave… what happens to my mother?"

Frederick's face softens. "She'll be safe. Taken care of. Your departure doesn't change what's already in motion for her."

I study his face. There's no hesitation. No flicker of doubt. Just a polished calm, almost as if he expected me to ask.

The words should comfort me, but they don't.

Still…I'm done sacrificing everything for a woman who *expects* me to always be there to pick up the pieces.

I love her, and I'm hopeful that one day I'll get to feel that returned in a way that doesn't hurt. But I won't give up my *greatest* love for a woman who's never been willing to give up hers. And my mother's greatest love has always been the high.

"She understands more than you think," he adds, his voice quieter now. "She would understand."

Something about the way he says it…

I shake off the feeling and give a short nod.

Frederick clears his throat. "I feel like I should remind you that by leaving, you'll be forfeiting your inheritance."

"You can have it. I only want Juliette."

A fire lights up in Frederick's eyes, and it looks a lot like hope.

"Good."

Staring at my father is different when I know he might be dead soon.

Does it really matter when he's using you for his gain?

He took it upon himself to not be in my life for the first twenty-three years of it, and now that I'm here, now that he's helped my sister and our mother, does that mean I have to rearrange all of my feelings to fit his narrative? I don't think it does. In fact, I think it might make me hate him more. It's selfish on his part to force me to feel something other than resentment and then rip it away when I've finally had a taste.

I showed up to Montgomery Manor like the dutiful son I'm pretending to be, and found him in the sitting area, hooked up to an IV with a hospice nurse in the room across the hall. I stand in the doorway for a minute, my eyes drinking him in, trying to find the evil on his skin.

He's flipping through a paperback, his eyes half lidded from whatever cocktail they're giving him to keep the pain at bay, and he's propped up in one of those stiff, pretentious chairs he seems to love, like even when he's dying, he needs to feel like he's holding court.

But he isn't dressed for the gala.

And he looks the same as he always does, a little pale and a little frail. Still the man I've watched from a distance my entire life through lenses and newspaper clippings.

My polished shoes clack on the hardwood, and I swipe a hand down the stiff tuxedo as I make my way toward him.

I know he can hear me, but he doesn't look my way. Just stares vacantly in the distance, like he's watching ghosts walk the corridor.

"You ready?" he asks. "For the gala tonight."

"More than you seem to be," I reply.

He looks at me now, his brow furrowed like the secrets of the world are being whispered into his ear. "The papers are already calling it the event of the season."

I glance at the fireplace. "They would, I guess."

A beat of silence passes between us.

He shifts slightly, grimacing. He's obviously in pain, and my middle pulls tight, aching somewhere deep. I hate that after everything I know now, I still feel it.

"You're not coming," I say in a monotonous tone.

He shakes his head. "No point in putting on a suit just to bleed through it."

"You could've told me." Anger pulses through my veins. "I wouldn't have wasted the trip out here."

"I didn't know I needed permission to stay in my own house." He goes back to staring vacantly into the hall. "I figured Freddy would've told you."

"What's he got to do with this?"

"Freddy said the press would eat it up, me being too weak to stand and arriving in a wheelchair. That it would overshadow the event."

Of course he did.

"Since when do you care about being overshadowed?" I ask.

"I don't, but Freddy knows what's best."

"You trust him a lot," I murmur, guilt hitting me. If he knew Frederick was helping me leave everything, he may not feel the same way.

He looks at me with tired eyes. "He's never given me a reason not to."

My gut twists, but I push it down.

I exhale, forcing a calm tone into my voice. "I just thought you'd want to be there with me. To see me at the biggest gala of the year, representing our name."

He watches me closely, and for just a second, I think I see something. Remorse, maybe. But it's gone before I can catch it.

"I've seen you plenty, Roman."

"You haven't," I argue. "I don't think you've ever really seen me. You've only always seen what I can do for you with the Calloways."

He lets out a dry laugh. "It was never about them, son. It was about ensuring there'd be something left when I was gone."

"But you never let me *be* part of that," I snap.

His eyes flick up. "I didn't want to lose you to it."

"And now here we are."

The silence stretches.

"I've been angry at you for a long time, you know? And I had thought that *finally* maybe I'd be able to stop carrying it."

He frowns. "But that's changed."

"I know the truth," I spit out. "About the Badon Hill Gang. About that guy Brutus not really being dead."

He doesn't react.

"You *used* me."

He nods once, like he's accepting all of the accusations I'm hurling his way.

"I've never known how to be a father," he says after a while.

"Barely know how to really be a man. This empire that I inherited...it's all I've ever known how to control."

There's a melancholy hint to his tone, and I want to hold on to the anger, but I'm just...*tired*.

"I'm leaving," I say.

I move closer, stop at the edge of the rug.

"For good. I won't be back."

His fingers twitch slightly on the armrest. "Is that supposed to pain me?"

"No," I say, quieter now. "I think I stopped trying to hurt you a long time ago. The only thing I care about is figuring out how to have *you* stop hurting *me*."

Finally, he glances at me. His eyes are sunken, rimmed in shadow.

We sit in the silence for a moment, and then he says, "You think walking away makes you better than me?"

"No," I say. "I think it makes me free of you."

His eyes narrow slightly. "And what will you do without all of this?"

"Live," I say. "Love someone without lying to her. Be someone my sister can look up to."

He leans back slowly, like the weight of his bones has finally caught up to him. "There's no redemption in this world, Roman."

"Maybe not for you," I say. "But I'm done carrying your sins on my back."

"Freddy thought you'd stay. That this would be enough."

My brows shoot to my hairline, confusion racing through me like a river breaking a dam. "What do you mean, Frederick thought I'd *stay*?"

He shrugs. "This whole thing, me letting you come back, he's the one who pushed for it. I thought it was too risky and was willing to just die and have everything in your name, hoping that one day, you'd be safe enough to come home and claim it."

That doesn't make any sense.

His words circle in my head and then drop to my feet, and I step closer to him, my voice low. "Are you telling me that Frederick Lawrence convinced you to have me come home, and then had me sign a piece of paper the moment I arrived saying if I left, it all would go to him?"

My father's face shows a hint of recognition. Of wariness. Of betrayal.

The weight of it hits me in slow, suffocating waves. My chest pulls taut and my throat dries.

Every step I thought I was taking toward *us*, toward Juliette and me, is steeped in someone else's agenda.

The realization is a punch to my gut.

"He said he'd help us leave," I murmur, more to myself than him. "Juliette and me."

I swallow the burn raging through me, my hands falling limp at my sides. My body's still, but inside, something breaks.

"Who made sure Brooklynn's trust went through?" I ask, my lungs seizing tight.

My father says nothing, but his eyes harden, suddenly alert and sharp as glass.

Fuck.

"She has it already," I plead, half telling him and half asking. "She has a house, insurance, the money in her bank."

My father swallows harshly.

"Tell me you looked over the papers. Tell me that there's

not a loophole, something that would be triggered if I disappeared."

"I can't tell you that, son. I'm not the man who writes the fine print."

My heart shatters, blood pounding in my ears.

Chapter 45

Roman

I'M IN THE BALLROOM OF OLD MAIN, THE FRONT-and-center building of Verona University.

My eyes flick over the room, people in overpriced outfits and million-dollar jewelry blinding against the crystal chandeliers overhead. There are round tables with black cloths interspersed throughout the area, a makeshift stage at the front, a clear podium at the center, and a row of chairs behind it.

The Calloway Enterprises logo is emblazoned onto almost every single thing in the space, and there are stock photos of smiling faces handing out food to those in need plastered like movie posters on the wall.

I don't find Frederick in the crowd, but I do find Juliette, and my heart shoots into my throat, my stomach drops out, and every single inch of my being aches to go to her. To take her hand in mine and walk out of this place. To disappear into a world we can make ours, the way we whispered about up on that cliff.

My chest feels hollow knowing that's not possible now.

I can't leave. Not yet, at least. Not until I know my sister is taken care of.

So, I don't go to her. I just stand here, in a room full of people who wouldn't give a shit if I fell to pieces right in front of them, watching the only thing I've ever wanted move through a world that won't ever let me love her freely.

Will she resent me?

The thought tangles in my chest like barbed wire, so I push it aside, closing my eyes for a moment to breathe through the pain. When I open them, I focus on why I'm here, and the conversation I had with my father after we learned that Frederick was playing us both.

"Go to the gala, Roman," my father demands. "Smile for the cameras. Let him think nothing's changed. I just need some time, give me some time to make this right."

I hesitate, searching his face for the truth, because honestly, I don't trust him.

"Why do you even care, after everything?" I ask.

His look strips away any power, any pride, any anger. And suddenly he just seems like a man with a failing body and a son he never really knew how to love.

"Because I love you."

I scoff.

"It's the truth," he says. "I've done a lot of things I'll have to burn for after death, and that's my penance. That's on me. But you... you're the type of man I always wished I was."

His eyes grow watery, and I force my face to stay blank.

He doesn't get a reaction after all this time.

"I'm sorry, son." His voice is strained. "For everything."

A smack on the back of my shoulder brings me out of my reverie, and I turn to look at Benjamin, who gives me a grin. "There you are."

I raise my brows, because why is he looking for me?

Benjamin laughs. "Don't give me that face. I'm bored to death schmoozing with all these people." He leans in. "We've certainly caused some tension in this town, huh? It's fucking *vibrating*."

I grimace. "Don't sound so happy about it."

Rosalie saunters over and links her arm through his, her face angled down, half hidden by the fall of her hair, and she doesn't make eye contact with either of us.

"Hey Rosalie," I greet.

She flashes me a look, and a smile, but then looks at the ground again, as if she's trying to hide something away. I'm about to ask if everything's all right, but Merrick walks up and beats me to it.

"You look like you've just trudged through a thunderstorm," he says, tilting his head. "Everything good, baby girl?"

Rosalie stiffens. "Just tired."

Benjamin doesn't even glance at her. Just sips his drink and scans the crowd.

Merrick catches my eye, his smirk fading.

Juliette moves into my line of vision behind him, and my breath catches in my throat.

She's always beautiful, but she looks the part of Rosebrook

Falls royalty tonight in a sleek black dress with a high neck and no sleeves. She spins around, and her back is entirely exposed, a line of crystals draping from the nape of her neck down her spine and ending just above the hemline, which rests at her hips.

Blood rushes through me, arousal pinning me in place. *Jesus Christ.* How the hell am I supposed to stay away from her all night when she looks like that? There are a hundred different people here, and I don't give a single damn about any of them, my eyes stuck on her like glue.

She's talking to a group of people but twists around, glancing over her shoulder, her gaze locking on mine. It's only a moment, but it hits me like a gut punch.

For a heartbeat, I let myself believe that maybe this could still work.

That she's still mine, and I'm still hers, and our entire lives aren't commandeered by people whose greed for money and power overshadow empathy and love.

"Sweetheart." Merrick nudges me with his shoulder. "You've got that tortured, broody look on your face again."

I break out of my trance and blink at him. Shit, how long have I been staring at her?

Merrick has a knowing glint in his eyes. And I consider telling him everything, because I want to have somebody on my side I can trust.

But can I trust him?

Sighing, I run a hand through my hair. "Just don't like being in these stiff-ass penguin suits." I pull at my cuff link to get my point across.

"Well, whatever ails you, I don't think you'll be able to solve it here."

My chest aches, knowing he's right. He steps in closer, slinging his arm lazily around my shoulder, and moves me farther away from our group. "Then again, if it's love you're looking for, it seems you may already think you've found it."

My heart stops in my chest. *How the fuck does he know that?*

I quirk a brow. "Merrick, I'm not in the mood for your riddles."

He chuckles. "Just be careful, Roman. I told you I'd always have your back here, and I mean it, so when I tell you that throwing away whatever it is you're about to gain, all for a girl you lust after... It's not worth it."

This feels like an important moment. My eyes flick to Juliette's again, like I can't help but seek her out, and my stomach flips just from the sight of her.

"Why do you think I'd be throwing anything away?" I ask, suspicion rattling through my bones.

He shrugs. "Just a guess."

"What if it isn't lust?" I ask him.

He chuckles. "So, you're a lover, Roman? You fall to the whims of it as easily as others?"

I quirk a brow. "You don't believe in love?"

He shrugs. "I believe in a chemical dependency that our brains create, and I believe in hurt feelings and missed opportunities once it wears off."

He waves his arm toward the Calloways. Toward Craig and Martha, who both look stiff and polished on the other side of the WayMont Ballroom, but do *not* look like they enjoy each other's company, and then toward Paxton Calloway and the strawberry-blond woman on his arm. Polished. Perfect.

But none of them look at each other the way I look at Juliette.

"Agree to disagree," I say to Merrick.

Merrick leans against the edge of the bar and dips his chin. "There's a lot of love here in Rosebrook Falls. Love of money. Love of notoriety. Love of…greed. But love of another person over everything else? I think you'll only find disappointment."

Chapter 46

Juliette

THE VU FOUNDERS' GALA IS THE EVENT OF THE year—*every* year—in Rosebrook Falls.

The who's who from all over Connecticut and beyond make an appearance, spending ungodly amounts of money for a table and then even more money on the silent auction. I'd love to think they do it for the charity portion, and I *used* to be naive enough to think so when I was younger and still believed in everything Calloway, but now I know it's mainly to show off their wealth and get a nice tax write-off. A proverbial pat on the back so everyone can go home and sleep at night with no guilt over the wealth disparity that lines the streets of this country.

It's also one of the only times I can guarantee that my entire family will be all at the same place, at least for a few hours.

I feel a presence at my side and glance over to Felicity sliding into the chair next to me, her gown glittering like a blood-red chandelier. She looks both stunning and annoyed, which is par for the course when it comes to her and events like this.

"Please tell me I'm allowed to openly mock the people here," she mutters.

"Haven't you been doing that since we walked in?"

"Well, you know me, I hate to break character." She leans closer, lowering her voice to a whisper. "Paxton's little wife looks like she bought out the entire bridal section of a department store and rolled herself in glitter just for fun."

I snort, my eyes flicking to where Tiffany sits next to Paxton right across from us. "She can probably hear you."

"Good," she says, taking a sip of champagne.

Paxton's glaring at us, his jaw tight and his fingers tapping an irregular beat against his napkin on the table. His gaze flicks to Felicity, then immediately away.

Alex plops down next to Paxton with a dramatic sigh. "God, these things are the worst. Who do I have to fake charm to get out of here?"

"Let me know when you figure it out," Felicity replies.

Alex glances across the room, to where Lance is standing with Tyler and Art. "If Lance would actually pretend he likes us, maybe he could help."

I scoff. "Tough luck. He hasn't even said hi tonight."

"Want me to go kick his ass?" Felicity offers.

"Actually, since you're both here," I pipe in, pointing to Alex and her. "Are you dating Alex, Felicity?"

She widens her eyes and then kicks my foot under the table.

"What? I deserve to know if you're sneaking behind my back."

"We've been over this a thousand times. I'm *not* dating him."

"Yet," he interjects.

"Ever," she snaps back with narrowed eyes.

And then come my parents, my mother looking like the

belle of the ball, my father stiff and polished on her arm. They glide effortlessly into their seats, which lets me know dinner is about to be served.

"Isn't tonight just magical?" my mother croons in a sickly-sweet voice.

"Nothing says magic like tax evasion for a good cause," Felicity says with a raise of her glass.

Paxton chuckles under his breath, and Felicity's eyes cut to him before turning back to her champagne.

My mother tenses at her comment, but recovers fast, which is not surprising. She's always had a gift for pretending not to hear things she doesn't like.

My father clears his throat, and Paxton straightens before looking at Felicity. "Let's try to be gracious tonight."

"Oh, I'm incredibly gracious. Just not delusional."

I smirk and hide it behind my hand.

Tiffany shoots Felicity a look like she wants to stab her with a fork, but Paxton doesn't miss a beat.

He lifts his drink. "You know, for someone who wasn't even invited, you sure have a lot of opinions."

"I was invited," she says, sweet as syrup. "By someone who likes having me around. I'm not surprised you have no experience with what that feels like."

Paxton quirks a brow. "Tell me, Flick, you practice being such a bitch in the mirror, or does it come naturally?"

Flick. I haven't heard him use that nickname for her in years. He started calling her that back when she was a kid, because she'd always flick *everything*. Her hair, his forehead.

From the way Felicity startles when he says it, she hasn't heard it in a while, either.

She grins. "I don't need to practice making you feel small. That part's effortless."

Paxton's gaze narrows but he doesn't reply. He just starts tapping his napkin again with that same jittery rhythm, like his bones are trying to crawl out of his skin.

Tiffany leans into him, running her hand down his arm, and he rips his eyes away and turns to his wife.

Dinner is served on silver platters by servers in crisp black vests, and everyone falls into their polite, empty chatter. The kind we've rehearsed since we were kids. Compliments. Fundraising buzzwords. Laughter at jokes no one actually thinks are funny.

I chew my steak slowly, thinking of how quiet Roman had looked standing in the back of the ballroom. How haunted. How distant.

Anxiety wrings my stomach tight. *Has something changed? Is he just playing the part?*

My mother's voice cuts through the fog. "Juliette, have you spoken to Preston tonight?"

My fork stills against the edge of the plate. "Unfortunately."

"Maybe you can take a walk with him in the promenade later after the meal," she replies, dabbing at the corner of her mouth with a napkin.

I stare at her.

And something inside of me breaks. I'm tired of being told where to stand, what to wear, who to smile at. Tired of being a passive part in whatever world she's carved out for me.

"I'm not going on a walk with Preston," I say, setting down my fork.

She quirks a brow, fire flashing in her gaze. "And why not?"

"Because I don't want to."

Alex chokes on his drink.

Paxton stops mid-chew.

"Don't be childish, Juliette." My mother laughs like this is all a joke. "You've known each other forever. It would do you good to be seen together again. People talk."

"I don't care if people talk," I say through gritted teeth. "I'm not interested in being part of some curated fairy tale for them to gossip about over dessert."

Across the table, my father clears his throat again. A warning.

But I'm already past the edge. And honestly, *fuck* him, too. He's not a good man, and he's never cared enough about me to actually be an active participant in my life.

"I'm not marrying Preston," I continue, my voice growing sharper. "I'm not going to help you with your little fundraising events. And I'm not going to keep pretending I want a life I never asked for."

The silence is instant. All that polite chatter at our table dies at once.

My mother looks at me like I've slapped her.

"So what, then, *do* you plan to do?" she hisses out.

I swallow around the panic climbing in my throat and I fist my hands, pretending they don't tremble.

"I'm going to write."

My mother blinks. "Write what?"

I shrug, the urge to curl in on myself under her gaze strong. But then I look over to Paxton, and he gives me a small smile and a nod. My spine straightens.

"Books. Stories. Things that make people feel something real."

She laughs, like she thinks I'm joking.

"I've spent my whole life being loyal to this family," I continue, my voice rising. "I've done everything you asked of me. Smiled when I wanted to scream. Performed like it was second nature. But I'm done twisting myself into whatever shape you need to be proud of me."

My father doesn't say a word. My mother opens her mouth, but nothing comes out.

Paxton sets his silverware down carefully. "She's right."

My mother stiffens. "Pardon?"

He leans back in his chair, arms folded across his chest in that calm, calculated way that makes him the perfect protégé for my father. "You can control a lot of things, Mother, but I won't let you control her anymore."

"Paxton," Dad cuts in.

"No," Paxton says. "She's done performing. I won't have her life, her *light*, stolen because you two can't put your family over your bottom line."

The silence drops like a stone.

And I stare at him with my heart stalled out. He's never stood up to them for me. Not once. And now he's doing it like it costs him nothing, even though I know that's not the case.

My mother recovers, but just barely. "You're defending her throwing away her future? Her name?"

"I'm defending her choosing something that actually belongs to her," he replies.

His voice isn't loud. But it's firm. Unshakable.

"And if either of you have a problem with that, then you can deal with me." His gaze cuts between them. "We all know what it would mean if I decided to stop sitting back and started taking charge."

My mother's lips turn white as she presses them together. My father's cheeks turn red.

But no one argues.

Even Felicity is silent, her mouth open as she stares across the table at Paxton, who's eating like he didn't just threaten to push dad off the throne and take the crown.

It hits me then: the guilt.

Knowing I'm about to leave everything, even when he just put himself on the line.

I wonder if they'll think of me once I'm gone, or if they'll write me off like I was a bad habit they couldn't wait to kick.

The thought spears through my body, causing a deep, throbbing ache.

I do my best not to look back at Roman, because the last thing I want to do is draw any more unnecessary attention when we're about to do something as crazy as skip town. But it's hard, knowing he's only a few feet away. I give into the urge.

He's talking to Merrick and Benjamin, but his eyes drop to mine the second I look at him, like he was waiting for them. It makes my fingertips tingle and my stomach flip with nerves, and it's so stupid how both of our families are here playing nice, but the two of us are cursed to be forever apart because fate decided to make us who we are.

Except we're about to take fate and tell it to fuck off.

I force my stare away, trying to not be suspicious, and as soon as I do, my gaze snags on another person.

Tyler is glaring at me like he knows all my secrets and wants to flay me alive for them. It makes dread trickle down my spine, and my fingers twist in my lap as I clear my throat and force myself to look away. With everything that's been going on, I had forgotten that Frederick had shared my secret.

"Excuse me," I say, pushing back from the table and catching Tyler's eye. I haven't spoken to him since Frederick stopped us and sloppily said Roman's name in front of him, and I know it's overdue. I can't leave here without smoothing things over.

He's always been one of my closest friends, and I can't stand the thought of him thinking the worst of me. Even if I know he'll hate me when he finds out I'm gone.

I walk out front until I'm in the night air and sit down at a bench in the VU courtyard. The red and brown bricks are what I choose to focus on until Tyler slips into the space next to me. His arm goes around the back of the bench, his legs sprawling out in front of him, a frown on his face and his eyes alert.

"Roman Montgomery won't stop staring at you, you know? You two are fucking obvious, and it's disgusting."

My stomach twists, and I shrug, hoping it comes across as nonchalant. "I fail to see how that's my problem."

He gives me a knowing look. "Do you think I'm stupid?"

I shrug again. "A lot of people stare at me."

He nods, gazing out over the space again. "Maybe I'll tell Lance, then. He'd fuck him up so he couldn't stare at *anything* again."

"Even he's not *that* overprotective." I watch Tyler carefully and then ask, "Why do you hate him so much? You don't even know him."

"He's a *Montgomery*."

"He can't help that any more than you can," I say.

Tyler's lips twist, and he crosses his arms with a grunt. "You don't know what you're talking about."

"And whose fault is that?" I snap. "Maybe if all of you dropped the brutish 'I'm strong man, she's weak woman' act, you'd realize letting me know things is better than keeping me in the dark."

He grunts, his jaw tensing.

I lean in, hopeful that maybe I'm getting through to him, just a little. Because if I can get through to Tyler, then maybe I can get through to everyone else, and I really *will* be able to come back here one day. "Tyler. It's *me*. Be honest. Do you only hate them because my father tells you to?"

He slams his hand on the bench, the metal rattling beneath us. "I hate them because they're responsible for *my* parents' deaths."

"Roman didn't do that."

He lets out a humorless laugh. "He's the whole fucking reason it happened, Juliette. Take off those rose-colored glasses and look around. You want to know who the bad guys are? We're it. Killing my parents was retaliation for your father trying to kill Roman and his sister."

I rear back like he slapped me. "What are you talking about?"

He tilts his head, a pained smile crossing his face. "Don't act surprised. I thought you wanted to know."

"I don't—"

"I'm on the city council because your father gives us all kickbacks to vote accordingly. He *funded* Art's father's campaign because Mayor Penngrove makes sure the Calloways come out on top with building codes and property taxes. The judges have their wallets lined so they'll look the other way when our land agents suddenly threaten a business owner within an inch of their life to give up their property."

My brows furrow. "I know they do things that aren't necessarily aboveboard, but Art's dad wouldn't…"

He laughs under his breath. "He's *in* on it, Jules. All of them are. The police. The mayor. The governor. The criminal organizations you don't even know exist because they don't have to step foot in town to make people do their bidding." He throws his hand out toward the building. "There are things going on underground, underneath these very buildings, that would make your skin crawl."

My mind whirls. *How could I not have known?*

"Okay, fine." I try to make my voice sound strong. "That doesn't explain why you hate Roman; it sounds like we should hate ourselves. Hate his dad, hate everyone who has lived here. But he's a victim of circumstance, Ty. Surely you can see that."

Tyler lets out a sardonic laugh. "Roman Montgomery should have stayed dead."

There's fire in his gaze, and I know that no matter what I say, it won't change a thing.

Tyler has had serious anger issues ever since he lost his family, and I grew up ignorant to the truth.

Civil blood stains civil hands.

I'm sick.

"My parents didn't deserve to die. And for a long time, the only peace I had was knowing once Marcus was in the ground, it was over. I was *this* close to breathing again, Juliette. But now that piece of shit is here, and he's got you twisted around his finger."

I swallow, feeling ten inches tall from his glare. Tyler's never looked at me like this before, like he's seconds away from snapping and I'm seconds away from being dead to him.

"He's taking another family member from me, and he doesn't even have to try. It's not *fair*."

"It's not like that." I force the words out.

"Bullshit. He's manipulating you the same way our families have played the game for generations. You're just too innocent to see it."

I shake my head, but his condescension is wearing thin, and I can feel the drip of anger bleeding through. "I'm *not* innocent, Tyler. I just want to make my own choices; I don't want to be chained to a certain life because of my last name."

He leans in to whisper in my ear. "Too bad, Jules. You're caged just like Lance, only you're too naive to see it."

"No," I say, my nostrils flaring.

He laughs, throwing up his hands. "Fine. Think whatever you want, but it is what it is. Don't preach to me like you're some minister of peace just because you've let Montgomery dick poison your vision."

I swallow the hurtful words like sharp knives cutting through my insides. "Ty, I love him."

He looks at me like I've stabbed him, betrayal shining in his gaze.

"You *love* him?" he says. "You're playing right into their hands, Juliette."

My chest spasms. "You don't understand."

But maybe he does, and that makes nausea surge through me like a tidal wave.

"I don't need to." He laughs and rubs a hand over his face like he can't believe what's happening. "I'm smart enough to recognize that not everything is black and white. That there's nuance in every situation. But I promise you, Juliette. If you choose Roman Montgomery, then you're dead to me."

"Don't say that." I reach out and try to grip his arm, but he rips it away, scoffing, his eyes watering like even looking at me makes him sad.

"I'm telling your brothers. They need to know. He's playing a mind game with you, Juliette. There are no innocents in Rosebrook Falls. You're getting involved in something you don't even know you're about to be in the middle of."

"What's that mean?"

He shakes his head. "You're fucking everything up, that's what it means."

"Ty." My voice breaks.

He ignores me, standing up and walking away.

"Tyler!" I half yell.

A few random college students are hanging outside of the *Sic et Non* dormitory, and they turn toward me at the noise.

My chest aches, and I reach up to try and soothe the burn, but it's no use.

I knew that choosing Roman would mean letting go of everyone else. I just hoped they'd understand *why* I was doing it.

Chapter 47

Roman

I DON'T SEE JULIETTE FOR THE REST OF THE NIGHT.

It makes my skin crawl and my nerves skitter like fire ants, because I need to talk to her; to tell her everything that's happened. Explain why I can't just pick up and leave even though I promised her the world.

Before I second guess myself, I'm weaving through the ballroom, and scanning every corner trying to find her.

Something doesn't feel right.

And my dad isn't answering his phone.

There's a weight in the pit of my stomach, heavy and solid, like dread poured concrete in my gut.

When I come up empty inside, I slip through the side doors and make my way out of the building, into the space between the main structure and the university's courtyard. The wind bites at my cheeks, but I barely feel it.

Where the fuck could she be?

A low throb starts behind my eyes, the kind that comes with too many loose ends and nowhere to put them.

"What are you doing out here?"

I spin, my heartbeat kicking against my chest like a loaded gun. "Jesus, Frederick. Don't sneak up on people like that."

He doesn't smile, doesn't even so much as smirk. Instead, he cocks his head to the side, taking me in like he's seeing me for the first time. "What are you doing out here, Roman?"

My mouth is dry, my tongue sticking to the roof like glue. "Needed some air," I say, keeping my tone even. "Why? Is that not allowed?"

"Your father was asking for you back at the manor," he replies. "Said he wasn't feeling well."

My stomach twists. "Is he okay?"

"He's resting."

I nod slowly, my throat spasming as I swallow. "Thanks for letting me know."

"You seem on edge, everything all right?" he questions.

I shift my weight, trying not to let him see my jaw tighten. "Just nervous about what we're planning to do."

Voices filter from around the corner of the building, footsteps and half-drunk catcalls echoing off the edges of the campus's brick, and then Merrick, Benjamin, and Rosalie show up. Merrick is drunk; it's more than obvious. His bow tie is untied and lazily strung around his neck, and his hair is mussed up, his arm thrown around Rosalie's shoulders as she drags him over to us.

Relief flows through me at them being here. Now I'm not alone with Frederick.

"Benny, come and get your friend, *please*," she complains. "He's deadweight and doesn't know his limits."

"I know my limits," Merrick slurs. He rips his arm back

from her and then stumbles toward us, almost tripping over his shoes.

"Fucking hell, Merrick, I told you not to drink so much," Benjamin snaps at him, running a hand through his hair and stopping a few paces from us.

Merrick throws his hands out to his sides, spinning in a circle. "It's a party, is it not?"

He stumbles and rights himself, running a hand over his face and *giggling*. He looks at me and grins. "I'm drunk."

I lift a brow, amused. "No shit."

Frederick cuts Benjamin a harsh glare.

Benjamin swallows and breaks their stare. "Come on. With our luck, we'll run into a goddamn Calloway out here, and it'll turn into a fight."

Merrick closes one eye like he's trying to aim down the barrel of a gun and points at Benjamin. "*You* are one of those guys who pretends he doesn't want to fight but is always ready to have one."

Benjamin scoffs, picking at invisible lint on his sleeve. "I am not."

Rosalie laughs, and Benjamin tosses her a cutting look. "What?"

"You totally are," she says. "Someone does the smallest thing and then you're pissed, and if you're mad, then you're always the first one looking for a fight."

He scowls but then shrugs like he's accepting his flaws. "All the more reason for us to leave here and go back to our turf before something bad happens. I'm too valuable to stick around and get hurt. Right, Freddy?"

Frederick tilts his head, slipping his hands into his pockets. "You should leave."

Merrick guffaws. "You're an idiot."

Benjamin quirks his brow. "Yet out of the two of us, I'm the only one standing straight and talking sense."

More voices echo in the distance, and a group of people walks around the same corner in varying states of disarray.

Frederick sighs.

"Great," Benjamin complains. "Here they come."

Merrick squints and sways. "Wow. Look at that. I still don't care."

I follow their line of sight and see Tyler at the front of the group, talking to Juliette's brother Lance.

"Leave it alone, Ty," Lance mumbles when they get close.

Tyler looks like he's ready to murder someone.

"Nah," he says, flicking a glare our way. "You leave it alone. I'll talk to them."

He stomps over before the others can stop him and halts right in front of us. He flicks his gaze to Frederick, and his lips thin.

Benjamin crosses his arms, and Merrick just smiles. Rosalie shrinks in on herself, and I wonder what the story between them is. She's Tyler's sister, yet she doesn't seem to want anything to do with him.

What kind of a brother just abandons his sister and pretends like she doesn't exist?

I imagine doing that to Brooklynn, and it makes my chest ache.

"Hey, Roman. I want to have a word with you," Tyler says.

Merrick cackles. "Just one word? Put it with something else, Ty, like a fist. Benny here wants to fight."

Tyler's eyes narrow, and he cracks his knuckles. "I'll fuck *Benny* up any day, just give me a reason."

Merrick sways, his arm propping on my shoulder to keep him steady. I let him, because he's already escalating this situation, and the last thing we need is for him to fall over.

"You can't find a reason without me giving you one?" Merrick taunts. "That's lazy, Ty."

Tyler sneers, his gaze landing on me before going to his sister. "I can't believe you're hanging out with a Montgomery, Rosalie. I know you've always stooped low, but he's gutter trash."

Merrick laughs, and I bristle. "*Hanging* out? You make us sound like we're a band of groupies. If you wanted to hear us make some noise, that's all you had to say."

He straightens, something sinister flashing through his gaze now, suddenly seeming a lot more sober than he has for the past few minutes.

Frederick steps forward, shielding Merrick from view. "You want to talk to Roman, then you go to a private place, Tyler. This is public. It's a bad look for everyone, and reporters are always lurking in the shadows just waiting for one of us to show our hand."

It hits me then, fully, what's happening. Tyler wants to talk to *me*, and Merrick has been protecting me, even through his drunken slurs.

Gratitude fills my chest, but it mixes with dread, because I don't know why Tyler would have anything to say to me unless it involved Juliette, and *that* I don't like at all.

Besides, I don't need Merrick to fight my battles.

Merrick gives Frederick an incredulous look. "What do I care if they see? Let them watch."

This is getting ridiculous. I maneuver around them. "You want to talk, Tyler, then let's talk."

Tyler smirks at Merrick and Frederick and then gives a mock bow, and we move over to a different part of the sidewalk, far enough away that they can't overhear us but close enough that everyone's eyes stay stuck on us.

Juliette's brother Lance hasn't said a single word. He just stands off to the side with his arms crossed and his lips twisted into a frown as he watches us. Almost like he's waiting for something, although what, I can't be sure.

"Leave Juliette alone," Tyler states, crossing his arms and pinning me with narrowed eyes.

"I don't know what you're talking about."

My heart beats faster, nerves making my insides jump. *Something isn't right.*

"She told me," he spits.

"Told you what?"

He smirks. "Everything. She's my cousin. Did you think I wouldn't know?"

My lungs cramp. *Everything?* I don't believe that she would.

"Tyler." I sigh, running a hand through my hair. "You're not my enemy. If you would just—"

"I don't care," he cuts me off. "Nothing you say will excuse the harm that your family has caused me. I bleed out every day, *alone*. No father. No mother. No goddamn sister. And now you want to take Juliette, too?"

He moves his gaze to Rosalie, something sad flickering in his gaze, and then he hardens again. Takes a step forward, his head tilting as he looks at her.

His nostrils flare. "Rosalie. Is that a bruise on your face?"

The air whooshes out of me, and my brows hike, as I spin to face her and Benjamin. "What?"

Is that why she's been hiding her face all night?

Tyler reaches into his waistband, and before I can blink, he brings out a gun.

Immediately, I throw up my hands, my heart pounding in my ears. *Jesus Christ.*

"*Tyler.*" Lance's voice echoes like a boom, and then everyone is close again, trying to regain control of the situation.

"What the *fuck*, Ty?" Rosalie screams. "Where did you get a gun? What the hell is wrong with you?"

Frederick stands on the side, his hands still in his pockets.

"Shut up, Rosalie," Tyler says. "I'm doing this for *you*."

"Tyler," I say, making sure to keep my voice even-keeled.

His eyes are watery, like he's trying to hold back tears.

Merrick moves to stand next to me and Benjamin. "Ty, if you want to fight someone, fight *me*. With your fists, you coward. At least then it would be fair."

I can't believe this is happening right now. All I want to do is go be with Juliette, but instead, I'm here with people trying to fight my battles and one of her cousins holding us at gunpoint because Benjamin's a piece of shit. I knew that this town was messed up, but this is another level.

Lance steps forward again, his brow furrowed and his gaze locked on Tyler. He moves slow and steady, almost as if he's trained to, and Tyler doesn't even realize how close Lance has gotten, because he hasn't taken his own eyes off Benjamin or me.

His hand is trembling so badly, the gun shakes. "Uncle Craig would kiss the ground I walked on if I got rid of you both." His eyes flash. "Everyone would be better off."

"I'll leave," I say with my hands up.

"I don't care!" he spits. "I want *her* to be free."

I frown. "Who, Juliette?"

Tyler's grip grows stronger on his gun, and he re-aims, his hand steadying.

The night is so quiet around us, it's like even it can feel that moving would be perilous.

And then Merrick—drunk as shit—sways.

Pop.

For a second, there's no movement. I question if I even heard the gun go off; there must be a silencer on it, because the noise was muffled. It didn't crack against the sky. But then, a flurry happens.

Lance grips Tyler's hand and disarms him like it's as easy for him as breathing, and he tosses the gun to the side so he can restrain him by the arms.

But Tyler's not fighting them; he's staring next to me with wide eyes like he can't believe what he's just done. His mouth opens and closes. "I didn't, I don't—"

Merrick stumbles and falls, his hand gripping his side and blood pouring through his fingers.

"*Jesus.*" I jump forward, my hands replacing his, trying to stanch the bleeding. I drop to my knees as he falls to the ground.

Fuck. Fuck. Fuck.

From my periphery, I see Frederick walk forward, bend over, and pick up the discarded weapon. He stares at it in his hands and then says something to Tyler, making Lance's eyes grow wide. But I don't know what. All I can hear is the panic whooshing in my ears, and all I can feel is Merrick's blood soaking my fingers.

Benjamin is shell-shocked. He looks down, sees Merrick,

and a calm fury replaces everything else on his face. Lance is talking to Tyler and trying to calm him down, and Rosalie is sobbing.

But all I can pay attention to is Merrick.

"*Fuck*," he mutters, and then coughs.

"Merrick." I don't know what to do, how to stop the wound, or who to call. I want to reach for my phone to dial 911, but I don't want to move my hands in case it makes him bleed out faster, or—I don't know, but I need to do something.

"You're okay, you're okay, *shit*," I manage.

"Just a scratch, sweetheart," he forces out, silent tears tracking down his cheeks.

"Tyler, you absolute idiot." Benjamin's voice rings out sharp and sure, and my gaze snaps up to everyone, seeing Frederick step into the middle of the courtyard and face Tyler, the gun flat in his palms.

Lance is now comforting Rosalie, Tyler standing frozen still.

"Ro-Roman."

I snap my gaze back down to Merrick.

"No—nothing good can come from you being here. The people…the people you think you can trust are not what they seem. So, if you love…" He pauses again, gritting his teeth. "Love her. Choose *her*. These families are cursed." He cries out in clear pain, and then his eyes focus on everyone else, and he tries to sit up. Somehow, he makes his voice strong. "Do you hear me? A *plague* on both your houses!"

He drops back to the ground, gasping, and then his body goes limp, and he slips from my grasp.

"Somebody *do* something!" I yell out. "Get over whatever bullshit this is and call for help."

Benjamin unfreezes from where he's staring at Merrick, his face ghostly white, and then he nods and spins around, running back inside the building.

If I wasn't so focused on Merrick, maybe I could stop what happens next, but I don't.

"Freddy, listen, you gotta understand." Tyler's voice is panicked.

"You had *one* job, Tyler. One thing I ask of you, and I'd let Benjamin give her back."

What the fuck?

Frederick looks down at the gun and then back up to him. "But you're always causing problems."

Lance stiffens, and he bursts into movement, but it's too late.

Frederick moves the gun. Aims it.

And shoots Tyler right in the chest.

The world freezes again.

And then Rosalie lets out a guttural scream.

The next few minutes are complete chaos.

"Ty," Lance yells out, his voice rough and deep, like he's trying to hold it together. He grasps Tyler's body in his arms, and he's shaking so violently I can see it from where I'm still holding onto Merrick.

I'm frozen in my spot, because Merrick is still breathing, and I'm afraid if I move, if I let go, then he'll die.

The gun hangs loose at Frederick's side, and Tyler is on the sidewalk with blood pooling beneath him and a hole in his chest.

Bile rises up my throat, and I glance away, nostrils flaring as I keep it down.

This is not the time to freak out.

"You are so *fucked*!" Rosalie screams, pointing at Frederick. "I hate you. I *hate* you, do you hear me? Uncle Craig won't let you get away with this!"

Frederick laughs and walks forward, brushing the barrel of the gun down Rosalie's face. "I'm fucked?" He swings around, giving me a side glance, and then looking back at them. "I'm the *boss* here."

What?

Rosalie drops down next to Lance and Tyler, big fat black mascara tears running down her face and streaking on her cheeks.

"Tyler!" she screams instead, her voice broken. "Ty…*please*."

"Shut her up, Lance, or I'll do it for you." Frederick points to Rosalie.

Lance glares at him. "You were supposed to end all of this, not make things worse. We trusted you."

My heart twists, confusion making my head throb and my stomach drop.

Frederick cracks his neck and then turns on his heel, walking toward me with slow, deliberate steps. "Lesson number one. Never trust anyone."

It takes me a moment to realize that he's talking to me.

"Fuck *you*, Frederick," I snap.

He crouches down next to me, and then before I can even process it, he reaches for my hand, pressing something cold into it.

The gun.

My fingers wrap instinctively around it, and then I panic, dropping it to the ground. It's too late, though. It's right there. My grip, smudged with Merrick's blood.

My prints are all over that weapon.

"You're out of your mind," I whisper, my voice cracking.

Frederick smiles. "Can't believe you'd do all this just to help your father seek his revenge."

My eyes widen.

"There are witnesses," I say, my chest feeling like it might explode from the pressure. "You can't spin this."

"Yet everyone here knows what they saw." He looks back to Rosalie and Lance, who both have looks of grief but resignation on their faces.

Tyler twitches on the ground.

Frederick stands and straightens his tux. "Tyler's always been a loose cannon. Everyone knows it. He snapped and shot Merrick, and you jumped in, got caught in the chaos."

I shake my head.

"I got here just in time." He grimaces. "Unfortunately, I wasn't quick enough to save you from ending your own life."

He picks up the gun and aims it at my head, and it's only then I realize he's wearing gloves. Like he was prepared for this moment.

My breath leaves me in a whoosh.

I stare up at him, my heart racing, my fingers still halfway inside of Merrick's bullet wound, and my mind trying to claw its way out of this nightmare. "Who *are* you?"

He leans in close, shoving me from Merrick's body and pressing the barrel against my head. "I'm the one who's about to inherit everything your family's built. You signed on the dotted line, after all."

Jesus Christ. It's all about money. That's all any of these people care about.

My eyes flick to Rosalie, who has quieted now, soft sobs coming from her, and she looks broken.

She meets my gaze, but only for a second before she drops her face back down.

I let out a disbelieving laugh, but I don't have time to think things through right now. Shock wraps its icy tendrils around me. I swallow, looking at everyone one final time, because how is this real life?

My fingers are soaked in a deep, musky red, and nausea churns in my gut when I focus on them, so instead, I stare down at the blood-stained sidewalk, and then to my clothes, where spatters are streaked across the white of my tuxedo like paint.

My hands tremble.

"My father won't let you get away this."

Frederick smiles. "Marcus made this town bleed for decades. He was about to go *broke* right at the end, like a dog. The world is better off without him. Your family was never supposed to be the one in power."

A sledgehammer to the stomach would shock me less. I stumble back, slipping on the ground as I stand. "You killed him."

He shrugs. "I put the poor man out of his misery. It's amazing what a few zeros and an underpaid nurse will agree to. Especially if you frame it as a mercy."

The world tilts.

The blood on my hands is sticky now, tacky and dark. My tux is ruined. My fingers won't stop shaking.

Lance's eyes meet mine, and then a noise comes from the side of the building.

Loud yelling and a door slamming closed.

Frederick curses under his breath, standing tall. His grip on the gun tightens.

And I don't think.

I stand up, and I run.

Chapter 48

Roman

THERE'S STILL BLOOD ON MY HANDS.

Not physically—I spent the past twenty minutes scrubbing them in the bathroom of the gas station at the edge of campus—but mentally, all I can see on my fingers is red and the memory of a gun I was never meant to hold.

My mind is running a thousand miles a minute.

Merrick's body.

Tyler twitching on the ground.

Frederick's smile as he told me my father was dead.

I don't know how to tell Juliette what happened, not sure if I *can* tell her.

And the game has changed completely. Frederick tried to *kill* me.

I can't even focus on that right now, on the fact that technically, if my father is dead, I'm the new Montgomery patriarch.

My stomach lurches violently, bile teasing the back of my throat.

Frederick's going to need me dead for his plan to work.

What the fuck am I going to do?

And he knows everything. *Everything.*

My sister. My mother. He's been my father's closest confidant for years.

My hand trembles as I pull out my phone and call Brooklynn, praying to God she answers.

"Roman?"

Her voice hits me everywhere and I close my eyes. "Hey, kid."

"You okay? You sound weird."

I drag a hand down my face. "I'm fine, are you home?"

"Yeah, why?" She hesitates. "Is something wrong?"

I shake my head, swallowing around the knot in my throat. "Just needed to hear your voice."

There's a pause on her end, and I can picture her frowning, arms crossed, like she knows I'm full of shit.

I grip the edge of the gas station sink, knuckles going white. "You're safe? Doors locked?"

"Dude, I'm not twelve."

"I know," I murmur. "Just…humor me."

Another second passes, and her voice softens. "I'm safe. I promise."

I exhale, some of the weight loosening in my chest. "Good."

"Hey, speaking of, is Mom with you?"

I freeze. "What do you mean?"

"I know you said not to try and contact her at that fancy rehab, but I called anyway, you know? I was worried…and they said she never checked in."

I turn away from the mirror, ripping the bow tie until it's hanging loosely around my neck. "I'm sure she's fine."

Lie.

Her voice cracks. "Do you think she's okay?"

"I think she's smart enough to lay low when needed. I'll find her."

"You always say that like you can fix everything."

A small smile breaks through the panic swirling like a hurricane in my chest. "And have I been wrong yet?"

She exhales. "Be careful, Bear."

I stare at the wall, my throat thick. "Love you, kid."

"Ditto."

We hang up, and for a second, the world stills.

Then I slide the phone back in my pocket, and everything starts moving again.

Juliette. Frederick. My father's legacy. My mother, missing.

And me, somehow still standing in the middle of it all.

My fingers curl around the holes of the trellis as I climb up the side of the house until I can swing my legs over the railing of Juliette's balcony.

It's late.

And quiet.

Part of me is worried that her doors will be locked and I'll have done all of this for nothing, but it's a risk I'm willing to take. I have to know that she's okay.

She wasn't at the gala, she wasn't at Upside Down Rock… This is me hoping she's here.

I know I should stay away. Should focus on what the hell I'm going to do next, but there's a high chance I might end up dead before morning, and I can't *not* see her one last time. And

I'm a little on edge, worried that Frederick might do something insane like use her to get to me.

Slowly, and as quietly as possible, I walk across her balcony until I'm facing the double French doors, my reflection gleaming in the windows. Swallowing, my hands tremble as I reach out and try the handle.

The door clicks open immediately, and I blow out a large sigh of relief, my nerves quieting as I open the door and walk inside, my eyes immediately searching for her.

Her room is large, a four-poster king bed in the very center and detailed crown molding around the edges of the walls.

At least two of my entire studio apartments could fit in here with space to spare, and it hits me fully, maybe for the first time, that she's grown up in this atmosphere, and I'm just now learning how to embrace it.

How, if I somehow make it out of this alive, I'm going to have an empire to take over, and a legacy to fix.

"Juliette," I whisper into the dark.

Nobody answers.

My breath catches from the type of fear that creeps in with cold fingers and grips your spine. Each step is slower than the last, my pulse a staccato rhythm beating in my ears.

The shadows seem to bend around me as I move deeper into her room, my gaze scanning the area until I land on the shape of her on the bed.

She's not moving.

I step closer and her outline sharpens. An arm is draped over her blanket, her hair spilling like ink across the cream pillow.

She lets out a tiny snore, and my legs nearly collapse.

I press a hand to the nightstand just to stay standing, the sudden rush of relief blurring my vision.

Juliette's here. She's safe.

The pale light of the moon streams in through the windows, kissing her skin, and I swear I'll spend every moment for the rest of forever thanking God that she's all right.

She looks so innocent when she's this way, and my heart physically cracks in my chest knowing that when she wakes up in the morning, her world is going to break in two. And I can't take her away from mourning her cousin. From her family.

Not like this.

How fucking naive were we to think that running away would solve *anything*?

My fingers dust along the side of her face and across her cheekbones, lightly, like she might dissolve into nothing if I touch her too hard.

She's so beautiful it hurts.

She's the only thing that feels *good*, and I don't want to give that up. I want to foster it instead, water it like a seed and watch it grow, and maybe in another life, we'll be able to.

Her lashes flutter, and my fingers stall.

She blinks up at me, hands tucked beneath her chin, lips curved in a lazy smile.

It undoes me. Completely. Something inside me cracks, splintering right down the middle like a bone breaking.

"Hi," she murmurs.

"Hi," I whisper back, my voice hitching on the word.

She studies my face, and slowly awareness creeps in, and she jerks upright in the bed.

"Are you *crazy?*" she hisses. "You're sneaking into my room now?"

"I had to see you," I admit. There's a knot in my throat, and it's hard to form the words.

Her eyes dart to the window. "What if someone saw *you?*"

"They didn't."

"Are you sure?"

Sighing, I run a hand through my hair, praying she doesn't see it shake. "I need to tell you something."

Her eyes darken, and she slaps a hand over my mouth. "No."

Her palm is warm. Familiar. And it's shaking, like even if *she* doesn't know, her body does; something has changed irrevocably between us forever.

I run my fingers over her face again, drinking her in like fine wine, desperate to touch her, to catalogue every single inch of her so that I can draw her a thousand times and keep her with me always.

She chews on her bottom lip, and the spaghetti strap of her pink silk tank top drops off her shoulder and rests on her upper arm.

My eyes follow its trajectory.

"I need to tell you something," I say again, although it's barely audible. Just a raw rasp lodged somewhere between my ribs and my throat.

Her pouty lips part, and her tongue swipes across the bottom one. I keep myself from leaning in and repeating the motion with my own like muscle memory.

But I can't force myself to move.

"What is it?" she asks.

The words stick on my tongue like smoke.

I open my mouth.

Try to speak.

Fail.

And I'm a fucking coward, but I can't be the one to tell her. Not when she's looking at me like I'm giving her the world, and I know how much worse things are going to get when I walk away.

Images of her cousin, twitching on the ground, flash in my brain and I grit my teeth, my eyes closing as I try to force it away.

"I love you," I breathe.

She stares at me for what feel like the longest seconds of my life, her bottom lip getting chewed half to death, and then the most beautiful smile graces her face, and I think it might kill me.

"I love you, too," she whispers back.

My heart gallops, stutters, rages against my ribs like it's trying to tear me apart to stay by her side…but I ignore it. Because I know that tomorrow, she might think of me differently.

She moves to her knees and scoots close, wrapping her arms around my neck, her perfect fingers threading in my hair. "What's wrong?" she whispers.

I grit my teeth. "I can't—" My voice breaks, and I choke back a sob.

"Roman," she murmurs, leaning in and pressing kisses to my face. To my eyes, my cheeks, my nose, my lips. "It's okay, Trouble."

It's not.

I lean in, gripping her face in both of my palms like she's the only thing tethering me to Earth, and I force her gaze to mine.

"I need you to hear me," I tell her, my voice thick. "No matter what happens, I will love you for the rest of this life, and every one that comes after. *You* are my reason, Juliette. I'll spend every moment sketching you into the corners of this world." I pause, swallowing hard. "And when I'm gone, I'll paint you in the sky."

She sucks in a breath. "You're scaring me."

"And you've *wrecked* me."

In this moment, there is nothing else that matters. There is only Juliette.

I press my forehead to hers, trying to memorize her smell, her breath, the warmth of her skin beneath my palms. Maybe if I can burn my touch deep enough, it'll stay with her after I'm gone.

She's mine. I'm hers. That's an irrevocable truth of the universe.

But if this is all we get in this life, then let this be the moment I carry into the next.

My breath falters, chest squeezing like the fist of death is closing around it.

And then I kiss her.

Our mouths crash together, messy and urgent. It's not pretty, our teeth bump and our breaths tangle, but it's real.

It's *us*.

She moans into me like she's starving, and I grip her tightly, terrified she'll vanish if I let go.

She pulls away, her lips brushing mine as she whispers, "Promise me something."

I groan, my body thrumming with fire. "Anything," I say, my voice hoarse.

"Promise me that no matter what happens with us, even if

we have to stay away from here for years, you'll try to mend the rift between our families."

A lump forms in my throat. I want to tell her the truth. That the damage runs too deep now, and that some wounds never heal.

But for her, I'll die trying to reach peace, anyway. "I promise."

She nods, slipping her arms around the back of my neck, pressing her forehead to mine. "I know something's wrong, and I won't make you tell me right now. But I do want you to tell me."

"Juliette." My voice cracks.

"Shh," she soothes, her fingers running through my hair.

We stay like this, suspended in a fragile moment where nothing else exists other than her breath against my skin, and her heartbeat echoing mine.

Her eyes lock onto mine, and her fingers tighten around my neck. "I want you to make love to me, Roman. Whatever it is, just let it go. Be with me. We can worry about the rest in the morning."

There's a choice here. And maybe a better man would choose differently, but I'm not that man.

I'm desperate for her.

My hands snap to her waist and drag her into me, my lips fusing to hers.

I groan at the taste of her and then I'm pushing her back on the bed, and she's spinning us until she's on top and can clamber into my lap.

Her thighs bracket my hips, her sleep shorts riding up as she rocks forward, grinding herself down until I feel her heat pressed flush against me.

One of my hands tangles in the thick waves of her hair, tugging her back just enough to bare her throat, and the other grips the small of her back like I'm trying to tie us together.

I harden beneath her.

"Fuck," I breathe against her mouth.

She smiles, wicked and soft all at once, and nips at my bottom lip like she knows exactly what she's doing. Then she rolls her hips again.

It breaks something open in me.

I buck up to meet her, matching her rhythm, my cock straining against the thin barrier of my boxers, and these ridiculous fucking pants, and *Christ*, has anything ever felt this good? I grip her tighter, dragging her down harder against me, thrusting up as she rides the friction between us, our bodies moving like they've been waiting for this, aching for it. My fingers twist in the hem of her sleep tank, and then slip down the front of her stomach, feeling it tense and release. And then I'm dipping beneath the waistband of her tiny little sleep shorts, and I'm where I want to be most, pressing the pads of my fingers against her center.

She moans when I apply pressure, and I swallow the sound with my tongue.

I flip us around, her back hitting the mattress, and I'm on top of her in the next instant, a raging inferno of carnal need, unable to focus on anything else besides how badly I want to claim her.

She's mine. Even if the world says otherwise. Even if the clock's already ticking down on this moment.

The next few seconds are a blur of hands twisting in clothes: me tearing off her shirt and tossing it to the floor. I pause to drink in the sight of her; those bare breasts rising with her shallow breaths, and her skin flush and glowing in the moonlight.

"Perfect," I mutter, cupping them in my hands, thumbing her nipples until she gasps, wiggling her body beneath mine and pressing her hot little cunt into my dick.

Her fingers twist in my hair. "Roman."

I trail kisses down her stomach, my palm slipping back to her slick pussy. I find her clit and circle it. She writhes, her hips chasing the pressure.

"Always so soaked for me, dirty girl," I rasp. "Is this what you want? Me between your legs and making you squirm?"

She whimpers, and my cock throbs behind my dress pants.

I move back up to press my mouth to hers, fingers slipping inside her until I'm stretching her open.

She breaks away, fumbling at my shirt, frantic and clumsy, tugging at the buttons until they pop free.

A sharp gasp and her eyes narrow as she leans in, staring at my clothes.

The blood.

She glares at the crimson stains like she's trying to will them away. "Roman...what is that?"

"It's what I need to talk to you about, I just—"

"Never mind," she says, cutting me off. "I don't care. I don't... I know something's wrong, but I just... I don't care."

I watch her for a moment. And then two.

But I'm a selfish man, and if she's willing to overlook my sins and let them stay in the dark for a while longer, I won't be the one who stops her.

I shrug it off and crush my mouth to hers before she can ask again. Before she changes her mind.

My pants drop next, and then I'm slotting myself between her thighs, the heat of her pussy dragging a groan from the deepest part of my chest.

"Tell me you're sure," I beg.

"I'm sure."

Everything after that is a haze, and I'm lost to her.

She guides me, fingers wrapping around my cock with a possessive grip, and then presses my tip to her entrance, but she doesn't let me in.

Instead, she flattens her palm, holding me there as her hips begin to roll back and forth. Slow. Torturous.

I glide between her folds, my length glistening from her wetness and how badly she's making me leak.

"Jesus, Juliette," I choke, bucking into her on instinct.

Her thumb swipes over the swollen head, spreading my pre-cum down my length as she strokes me with a singular purpose.

"You're close already," she whispers, her mouth at my ear. "You want inside me so bad, don't you, Trouble?"

I moan into her shoulder, putty beneath her hands.

"Let me take my time with you, baby," I plead.

She shakes her head, her hand tightening against me as she physically *pulls* me into her until the head of my cock is poised at her entrance, teasing her center.

"Goddamn," I rasp, my arms about to give out from how stiffly I'm holding myself above her.

Her hand moves again, trying to guide me in, and I smack it lightly away with a grunt, grabbing both her wrists and pinning them above her head in one hand.

"No," I force out. "Not yet."

I lean back just enough to look at her—*really* look at her. Her skin glows with a sheen of sweat, her arms trembling from where I've locked them in place, her breasts rising with every quick, broken breath. She sees me watching, and her gaze lights up like a wildfire.

Her thighs fall open, glistening with arousal.

My heart falters and cracks.

I'm going to lose her.

Maybe to tomorrow.

Maybe to my death.

Maybe because I'm too much of a coward to take her with me.

But right now, she's mine, and I'm going to make sure she feels me long after I'm gone.

"You want me to fuck you, Little Rose?"

I drag the thick head of my cock along her soaked slit, her wetness coating me. I press the tip to her clit, teasing us both mercilessly, and then slide it back down, skimming her entrance without pushing in.

Not yet.

She mewls, her body arching against me as I keep her wrists pinned above her head. "Roman, *please*."

I grin. "Please, what, Princess?"

That nickname does her in, and she glares at me, even as she trembles beneath me. "Please put that big mouth to better use," she bites, lifting her hips to grind her hot cunt against my dick. "Unless all that talk has always been just *talk*."

A groan tears itself straight from my chest.

Her breath stutters.

"You're the one spread open and begging, baby. You think you're in charge here?"

She smirks, rising as far she can and licking my neck. I hiss, tightening my grip on her arms, and thrusting forward just enough to nudge into her.

"You look like you needed the win," she replies.

"Jesus," I mutter, letting out a quiet laugh, even though my chest pulls so tight it makes the sound catch in my throat. "You're so goddamn mouthy."

I push my length in another inch.

She gasps, hips rocking up into me, and I hold myself steady above her, arms trembling from the effort it takes to not just sink into her and lose myself completely.

"Give it to me, Trouble," she demands. "Stop torturing us both."

I slide in to the hilt, her pussy clenching around me the second I'm bottomed out inside her.

Heat rushes through me; up my thighs, along my spine, bursting behind my eyes. She's wet and tight and perfect, and I'm already fighting the edge.

"You feel that?" I whisper, pulling back out and then slamming back in. "The way you open up for me so fucking good?"

"Yes," she moans.

"That's all *mine*." I bite down on her shoulder, my palm keeping her wrists pressed to the mattress. "This pussy. That sound you make when you come. The beats of your heart and the thoughts in your head. All of it. *Mine*."

I release her arms now, and her legs lock around my waist, her hands shooting to the back of my neck and pulling me down until we're chest to chest.

Heart to heart.

Her thighs tremble.

"You're mine, too," she replies, the way she always does when I get possessive like this.

I love it—the way she has to make sure we're equals in every way, even in this. Because she's right. I'm hers. Only hers. Forever.

"Of course I'm yours." I press the words into her mouth. "I feel you everywhere, Juliette. You're in my goddamn bones."

I start up a faster rhythm, fucking her harder, and her heels dig into my lower back, urging me deeper. Every thrust is brutal and full of need, our slick skin slapping, her body rising to meet me over and over.

And right now, nothing exists outside of this.

No danger.

No death.

No blood feud.

Just *us*.

The way it's supposed to be.

"Come for me, baby," I demand. "Let go. I want to *feel* it."

She breaks.

Her whole body bows beneath me, her pussy clenching hard around my cock as she comes with a cry that rips through the room. Her nails scratch down my back, and my pace stutters, hips jerking as I press deeper. I let go with a groan that's more pain than pleasure, my cock twitching inside her as I spill deep, her walls still fluttering around me. My vision goes white. My body locks. And then everything shatters.

I collapse on top of her, and we stay like that, breathing hard, and our hearts pounding.

Her fingers trace slow circles along my spine. I press a kiss to her shoulder, noticing a bite mark I don't even remember leaving.

It flares something primal and possessive inside me, though, and I wish I could ink it permanently into her skin. A mark that proves she was mine, even if the future may be unclear.

"Holy *fuck*," I murmur, panting against her neck.

She hums again, her hands stroking my hair, my neck, my back, fingernails teasing my skin and sending shivers. That, mixed with the aftershock of my orgasm, and I'm practically melted against her, unable to move.

And yet, my chest is still heavy. My throat is still tight.

I manage to pull back just enough to see her face. Her sweat-damp hair clings to her skin, and I brush it away gently, my knuckles skimming along her cheek. Her eyes flutter closed under my touch.

Everything inside me stills.

I could spend forever right here. Just *watching* her. Breathing her in.

But eventually, I give in, sleep claiming me.

The room is dark when I wake a few hours later; gray light bleeds around the edges of her curtains, soft enough where I could still pretend the morning hasn't started. And for a second, I allow myself to pretend. I let myself believe I could stay.

That this could be our morning, *every* morning.

But even now, I hear the tinkling of Juliette's house coming alive, and I know that's not reality. It slips under my skin like the cold edge of a blade.

There's a weight in the pit of my stomach.

I stare at the ceiling, unmoving. My arm is numb from where she's tucked into me, warm and soft and breathing slow, her fingers curled loosely at my ribs like she's meant to be there. I don't want to go.

Still…I ease her arm off my chest, pressing a kiss to her fingers before laying them on the bed.

I don't breathe as I re-dress in my clothes, and after they're on, the white shirt unbuttoned, and the reminder of what happened last night spattered on my sleeves, I sit at the edge of her bed with my elbows on my knees, digging my hands into my hair until my knuckles ache.

Behind me, she murmurs something in her sleep.

I close my eyes, swallowing at the way my heart's shattering into a million icy splinters.

My skin is still sticky with her sweat. My senses still drowning in everything *her*.

I don't want to go, I repeat to myself.

But I know that I can't stay.

Chapter 49

Juliette

I WAKE UP TO MY MOTHER SCREAMING.

It's an odd noise, and it takes me a few seconds to recognize it for what it is. I'm not sure I've ever heard her expel so much emotion before, so having it as an alarm clock is a jolt to my system.

Jerking upright out of bed, I glance around, my first thought being that maybe she knows Roman was here last night. Maybe he's still here.

My hand immediately reaches next to me, but the bed is cold, like he's been gone for hours.

There's a piece of paper on my pillow that looks like it was torn from my notebook, and I grab it, smiling because he left me a note.

I love you. I'm sorry.
  I'll sketch you into every corner of the world and paint you across the sky.

—RMO

P.S. Don't trust Frederick.

My smile falters.

My brows pull together, and I read the note again, slower this time.

The "I'm sorry" sits heavy in the center, like it's bleeding through the page.

I think back to how he was last night.

The way he touched me like he'd never again get the chance.

The way he stared at me like I was the most beautiful piece of art.

The way he kept confessing his love and begging me to remember.

My stomach turns. He was saying goodbye. And he was *apologizing* for it.

The paper trembles in my hand, and I crumple it up, throwing it to the side as my heart rips from my chest like his words have claws.

And now he's *not here*. Like everything he promised means nothing.

Another wail from my mother brings me back to the present, my mind narrowing like tunnel vision, and I throw back the covers and slip out of bed.

I'm just at the door to my room, about to go investigate and see what the hell is going on, when it swings open, Beverly storming in with wild eyes, rimmed red around the edges.

"Bevie," I gasp, throwing a hand to my chest. "What is it? What's happened?"

She looks behind her, and my mother's sobs come up the curved staircase, as though she's in the foyer.

Beverly shuts the door behind her and rushes to me, fingers gripping me tightly as she drags me across the room and into the closet. She doesn't speak, and when we get there, her lips press together, all the color drained from her face as she rummages through my clothes, pulling odds and ends out for me to wear.

"Bevie," I try again.

And again, she ignores me.

"Beverly!" I snap, rushing forward and physically stopping her from moving any more. My hands cover hers, and I expect her to be trembling from how panicked she seems.

But she's not.

Foreboding trickles down my spine, and I have a terrible feeling that whatever it is has to do with Roman.

He came here last night to say goodbye.

I bat the thought away, my heart feeling like it might disintegrate into dust if I think about it for too long.

"What's happened?" My eyes spring back and forth between hers, trying to see some truth in her tear-stricken face.

She opens her mouth, and her head shakes slightly. "It's Ty—Tyler, child."

My chest squeezes. *Did he tell everyone about Roman and me?* My face heats, and my heart pounds out an anxious rhythm.

"What about him?" I can barely get out the words.

Beverly stares at me for one second.

Two.

"He's dead."

My brows furrow as I try to process her words.

"No," I say. "That's impossible."

Beverly gives me a pitying look and wipes a tear away from her own cheek before she goes back to ripping my clothes apart, like she's trying to pack a bag for me.

"What are you doing?" I ask.

I should be feeling some emotion, but I can't believe her words. They don't feel real, and she has to be mistaken.

My mother's scream reverberates in my memory, and my stomach cramps.

"No," I say again. And then I'm moving, bounding forward and jerking Beverly's hands roughly from where they're in my dresser drawers. "No," I repeat. "You tell me what's really happening right now."

Her lips roll together.

"Where is Tyler?"

Her gaze widens like she can't believe I'm about to make her say it again.

"Where is he!" I half yell.

Beverly jerks back from the noise and then moves in closer. "He's dead, Juliette."

I stumble back from her, my hand pressing against the deep throb in my chest.

It isn't possible. Not Tyler. He was fine last night…a little unhinged, maybe, and a lot mad, but nothing that would lead to his *death*.

"Child," Beverly starts, moving toward me and pressing her hand to my cheek, forcing my gaze to hers.

I hadn't even realized I was staring at the ground.

Shaking my head, I grip her fingers in mine and hold them against my face. "Don't call me that. I'm not a child."

Sorrow flashes in her gaze, and maybe I should be crying. Half of me expects the tears to form any second, but whether it's from shock or disbelief, I'm just…numb.

"Tell me how it happened," I say. "How long has everyone known?"

"I assume your parents knew last night; they never came home," she whispers, and her hand drops, picking up the discarded clothing and shoving it into my hands. "But we have to get you out of here."

My brows furrow, and I shake my head again. "I'm not leaving, Bevie. Not if Tyler's gone, I can't—" The words lodge in my throat, and my hand flies to cover my mouth so I don't scream or sob or...*something*.

"He told everyone about you and that Montgomery boy," she says slowly. "Lance knows. Your mother knows. *Everyone* knows."

I grit my teeth, wrapping my head around what she's telling me, but it just doesn't make any sense. "He wouldn't."

But I know even as I say it that he would.

A sick sense of dread trickles down my spine. "How did he die?"

Beverly looks at me with pity, and it makes nausea rise in my throat. "It was Roman, Juliette."

My world stops. "You're...you're sure?"

Now tears do well. For Tyler. For Roman. For all that could have been, being smashed to pieces in front of my eyes.

My breathing grows rapid, and my vision narrows until the corners darken, and *it hurts* to take in air.

"No, it couldn't have been him. He wouldn't—he wouldn't do this."

But I remember the blood on his shirt. The apology in his eyes. The goodbye in his touch.

He wouldn't.

Beverly sits me down on my bed, and I blink.

Funny. I hadn't even realized we had moved from the closet.

"It wasn't him," I repeat like a mantra. "Are we even sure Ty is gone? What if… What if…"

"Shh." Beverly grabs me and pulls me to her chest, and I break apart in her arms, finally crying for Tyler, for Roman, for this mess that seems to be getting worse instead of better.

"He wouldn't do this," I say again. "He—he loves me, Bevie."

She pats my arm and pulls back, staring me dead in the eye. "All men lie, Juliette. All men cheat. They're all wicked."

"Not him." I shake my head vigorously.

I may not know much, but I know my heart. And I know his. Maybe he's a Montgomery, but he wouldn't hurt me this way.

But he knew, my mind whispers.

When he came to me last night, a sense of urgency in his touch, maybe he knew that Tyler was gone. And he didn't tell me.

"I have to talk to him." I shoot to a stand, and Beverly rears back.

She scoffs. "You will *not* talk to the man who killed your cousin."

"You don't know he did that," I say through gritted teeth, anger infusing every piece of me. "And it isn't as though Tyler would have been welcoming him with open arms. If there was a fight, I'm sure Roman wasn't the instigator. He wouldn't."

But Tyler would.

My heart pitches in my chest, diving into my stomach and bleeding out at my feet. I feel like I'm betraying Tyler for even thinking the words, but in the same breath, I'm betraying Roman if I *don't*.

"Juliette."

"I need to speak to him, to… Is he in jail? Have they arrested him?"

She shakes her head and breaks her gaze from me, like she can't stand to look at me anymore. "They can't find him, Juliette. We have to get you out of here, do you understand? Your mother, she… Well, she's angry. Devastated. I won't stand by while they decide what to do to you just to get to him."

"I don't understand anything about this. Why do I need to leave?"

She leans forward and grips my arm tighter. Sounds from downstairs filter through the hall and into my room, and her gaze goes to my closed door, and when she focuses on me again, she seems frantic.

"Do you trust me, Juliette? I need you to trust me."

"Of course I do."

She takes a flask out of her back pocket, and my eyes widen when she hands it to me. "Drink up. It will help with the nerves."

I open it and sniff it, grimacing. "Ugh, what is it?"

"Stop asking questions and do it."

Her words feel like a slap against my face, but I listen to her and swallow the bitter liquid.

She sighs in relief after I drink it all down. "I'm sorry, I just…your mother is volatile. Grief makes people lash out in strange ways."

Realization at what she's saying hits hard. "You think my own family will hurt me."

I don't phrase it as a question.

"I'm not willing to allow you to stick around and find out." She nods toward my balcony. "I assume you know how to sneak out and climb down the lattice still?"

I swallow again, my mind jumbled and my heart sore. I nod.

"Good. Then you have to go." She shoves the clothes into my hand. "Change and go *now*. Someone is waiting down the street for you. She'll help you get away, just until things calm down."

"Who?" Confusion runs rampant now, and every nerve ending in my body is on edge, because what she's saying doesn't make sense.

But I guess nothing really makes sense right now.

"Someone you can trust." She moves toward me and presses her hand to my cheek. "I'll come and find you when it's safe, and we'll clear everything up. Together. I won't let anything happen to you, Juliette."

"And Roman?" My breath hitches on his name, a pulsing ache spreading from my center through every part of me. "He'll come looking for me," I say, stumbling over the words, not knowing if they're true. "I need to see him. I…I know he didn't do this, Bevie. I *know* it."

Beverly's jaw tenses, and she nods. "I'll do my best to find him."

My arm snags on the shirt as I pull it over my head, throwing it on hastily. "He didn't do this, Bevie. Trust me, please."

"I'll distract them." She jerks her head toward the door and then reaches out and cups my cheek. "Be safe, Juliette."

And then I'm gone, out the door, not stopping to think about what I might be leaving behind.

The ROSEBROOK Rag

BREAKING: DEATH, INJURY, AND A MISSING HEIR—ROSEBROOK FALLS IN CRISIS

The Montgomery legacy may have just cracked beyond repair.

Last night, Marcus Montgomery—reclusive patriarch of the Montgomery family—was found dead inside his estate. Officials are quietly calling it a suicide, citing a long-term illness "few were aware of." But those close to the situation say the details feel off...and the silence? Deafening.

Adding fuel to the fire, a shooting erupted just hours later, leaving two individuals hospitalized. The names are being withheld "out of respect for the families and the ongoing investigation," but what we do know is this:

Roman Montgomery is missing.

And the police? They're not just looking for him to deliver the news about his father—they're also calling him a person of interest.

#MontgomeryMystery #MissingRoman
#RIPMarcus #RosebrookRag

Chapter 50

Roman

FREDERICK LAWRENCE.

Frederick Lawrence.

Frederick Lawrence.

His name repeats on a loop in my head, and the more I replay what happened the night before, and previous days of him meddling in the center of everything, the more off-kilter I become.

He knows everything. He's had his hands in *everything*. He's played both sides for years, and he's never made a secret of being a lawyer for both families.

My body is stiff, my neck is sore, and if I hadn't taken the risk to sneak back into my place and get new clothes, I'd be disgusting.

Right now, I'm hiding behind a parked car in the alley behind the Round Table, waiting to see Benjamin.

He texted late last night, before I got rid of my phone, and begged me to meet him here.

It's probably a trap, and I'm most likely the stupidest fucking guy in the world, but what other choice do I have?

The moment he gets to the back entrance, I have him shoved up against the brick, a pocketknife at his throat.

He throws his hands up, but he doesn't fight me.

His eyes seem hollow, dark circles underneath them.

"Roman," he breathes, like he's *thankful* to see me.

"Tell me what's going on, Benny," I demand. "No more half truths. No more bullshit."

"Merrick's alive."

Relief coasts through me, and I blow out a deep breath, my eyes flicking to my hands without thought and then back up. I got his blood off me after scrubbing for what felt like hours, but knowing he's still breathing makes the vise grip on my chest ease, just a little.

I drop Benjamin from the wall and back up a few steps, keeping a healthy distance between us. "And Tyler?"

Benjamin swallows and runs a hand through his hair, his fingers shaky and his skin sallow like he's trying not to puke. "I'm not sure about him. I don't know."

"You'll forgive me for not believing a word you say."

Benjamin nods, his tongue pressing against his cheek, and then he exhales like he's steeling himself for something. "I didn't mean for this to happen."

My chin lifts and my jaw tenses. "For *what* to happen?"

He swallows, his Adam's apple bobbing.

"Spit it out, Benny," I snap.

His brows draw in, and his face contorts like he's trying to hold back tears. "It wasn't supposed to get so out of control. Merrick was never supposed to be involved. To get hurt. I didn't—" He chokes on a sob, and he's pacing now, his fingers tearing at the roots of his dirty blond hair.

"Benjamin," I say, my voice loud and direct. "You're rambling. Tell me what's going on."

He stops. "Frederick Lawrence isn't who he says he is."

"No shit," I reply. "Neither are you, it would seem. How could you, Benny? How could you betray the family this way?"

"For *my* family!" he snaps and then tugs on his hair again. "Uncle M lied. He covered things up. Made *her* out to be the problem when all she ever tried to do was survive."

My heart trips. "Who?"

He meets my gaze, his eyes hollowed out by grief. "My aunt Eleanor. Marcus's wife."

The name lands like a sucker punch to the ribs, and I stumble back a half step.

"That's…" I shake my head. "What do you mean? She's dead, she died, my mom always said…"

"That she was unstable? Dangerous?" Benjamin's voice cuts deep. "That she made Uncle M fucking miserable?"

"No, she always said Eleanor was the reason why I couldn't come back."

Benjamin lets out a short, humorless laugh. "She did hate you, Roman. You were the proof of everything that was taken from her. Uncle M humiliated her. He had a child with his mistress and then gave *you* his last name. And when she planned to run away with Craig Calloway, he had the fucking gall to kill her for it."

I stare at him, but the world is tilting again, everything I thought I knew being rearranged. "That's not…"

"It is," he replies.

"You're lying."

"I wish I was."

I shake my head. "He wouldn't have—"

"He *did*," Benjamin snaps.

My jaw clenches. "What does this have to do with Frederick?"

He hesitates, glancing around like he's concerned someone might overhear. "Because Frederick is her half brother."

My brows lift. "Frederick's a *Voltaire*?"

"Not officially. Unlike *some* people, he didn't get the name when he was born to an affair. But he came searching and found Eleanor. They kept it secret so that nobody else would know, so that he would be safe from the Calloways *and* your dad. They've never liked us Voltaires getting too much power in the town."

I run a hand over my face. "So, you betrayed my dad."

If it wasn't coming directly from Benjamin's mouth, I wouldn't have trusted it to be true. I always assumed Benjamin was loyal to the end, the very definition of "ride or die."

He doesn't flinch, and he doesn't argue. He simply says, "I stayed loyal to *my* family."

"And staying loyal means framing me for murder? Getting Merrick shot?" I lash out.

His jaw tics, nostrils flaring. "That wasn't supposed to happen, man. It's all too fucked up now. I came here to talk with you, and to…to make it right."

My brows rise. "I'm getting really tired of riddles, Benny."

He presses a hand to his mouth, his face losing color.

"Are you about to puke?" I ask.

He breathes deeply.

"Why now?"

Benjamin's face shifts. "It was always supposed to be now."

He leans against the wall.

"Uncle M is dead. And you're the last piece left. You're the only thing standing between Freddy and what he's been setting up for years."

I scoff. "You give the guy too much credit."

"You don't give him enough." He pins me with a deadly stare. "They've been waiting for you to break."

I meet his eyes. "I don't break."

He lifts a slow, mocking brow. "You don't think you already have?"

I lunge forward, grabbing the collar of his shirt and shoving him against the brick. "You think this is what broken looks like?"

He doesn't flinch. "I think this is what it looks like when someone realizes everyone around them was playing a different game."

My heart's slamming against my ribs, but my voice comes out cold. "What are you talking about?"

"Freddy's been building this for *years*. Ever since Eleanor died and he saw you, pathetic and begging and *alive*, on your daddy's doorstep."

I slam him harder into the brick. "Say that again."

He smirks but there's no fire behind it. Just something sad and dark and already bleeding.

"You think I'm wrong?" He laughs. "You think your blitzed out mother didn't show up a week later, all wide eyed and itchy, spinning her version of the story to anyone who'd listen?"

I let go of him like he burned me.

My brain whirls so fast I feel motion sickness.

Benjamin shakes his head as I back up another step.

"Why would my mom..." I don't finish the thought, because I already know.

Money. Maybe even my dad. It's not hard to manipulate a person who's a shell of themselves and willing to do anything for their next fix.

"Frederick got to her."

I know it like I know anything.

"Ah, see?" He clicks his tongue. "Now you're starting to get it."

My chest hollows out and my stomach surges.

"Your mother handed you over, Roman, wrapped in a bow. She worked on your psyche, and Freddy whispered in Uncle M's ear. The perfect storm."

I wish I could argue, but it all rings true. It all makes so much sense that it kills me.

"Why are you telling me this now?" I rasp. "Why did you beg me to come here?"

He grits his teeth, water lining his lower eyelids. "They fucked with my best friend. He's lying in a goddamn hospital bed, and this was never supposed to be…" He shakes his head. "I'm trying to atone."

"Bit late."

"Well then, you can ignore me when I tell you this next part." He spits the words at my feet. "They're taking Juliette because they know it will bring them *you*."

Chapter 51

Juliette

THE SECOND I GET DOWN MY LATTICE, SOMETHING feels off. But Beverly wouldn't lead me astray, so I trust in her words, and even though everything is confusing right now, I follow her directions and make my way to the edge of the property, my mind whirling with who I should be looking for.

She never gave me their name.

There wasn't time, I remind myself.

Even if what she was saying doesn't make much sense to me, there's not a lot that *does* make sense right now, and all I know is that if Roman is suspected of murdering Ty, then my family will *never* let me get to him.

And I have to get to him.

Maybe when my mind isn't going a hundred miles a minute and my heart doesn't feel like it's about to beat right out of my chest, I'll be able to sit in the grief of Tyler being gone, but every time it tries to surface now, I push it back, compartmentalizing it as best as I can so that I can focus on getting to Roman and figuring out the truth.

What if he did it?

My inner thoughts are traitors, whispering the what-ifs like an eerie lullaby to my subconscious. Would it really change anything if he did, though? I'd still love him, even if he did something I'm not sure I can forgive. I feel sick at the possibility but push it to the side, too, and I cut that thought into a thousand different pieces so it won't surface again.

I may not have known Roman for years, but I know his heart. He wouldn't have done this. Not to me. Not for anything. I hold on to that truth, knowing it's what will get me through this until I can find him.

It's still early enough for the morning sun to be behind clouds, dew on the grass and an odd mist that clings to my skin, making it tacky. When I get to the edge of the property, there's a car idling.

Just like Beverly said, someone's waiting for me. Anxiety squeezes my middle tightly, but I ignore it and quicken my steps to get there.

I approach slowly, my heart thudding in my ears. The woman standing by the passenger door straightens when she sees me. She looks familiar, but I can't place where I know her from. Maybe if my brain was working better, but for some reason, it's not.

Probably the shock of everything.

She's a bit older, her face having deep lines like she's lived a hard life. Her brown-black hair is pinned back, and she's wearing a soft gray cardigan. And she's just so…damn…familiar.

She gives me a small smile. "Juliette?"

I swallow, unease flickering deep in my gut as I nod at her.

"I'm here to take you to Roman."

I hesitate, my brows pulling in and my footsteps stuttering. "That's not…Bevie said I couldn't see him."

She grins wider, her fingers absentmindedly scratching at her opposite arm. "Change of plans."

Her voice is calm. Reassuring, even.

I tilt my head, my vision going fuzzy before snapping back into place. "How do you know Roman?"

She eyes me carefully before opening the passenger side door. "I never said I did. Hurry up, if we don't want to be seen then we need to go."

My stomach churns but I slide into the car and she's there in the next second, slamming her door closed and driving away.

The interior smells faintly like leather and alcohol remover, and the silence coats my skin like razors.

"I'm sorry about your cousin," she says after a few minutes. "And about Roman. I can't imagine what that feels like."

The words make my throat ache. I don't want to talk about Tyler. I don't want to *think* about Roman.

"Yeah, thanks," I mutter, resting my head against the window. The cold feels good against my overheated cheek.

My eyes close and then I shake my head. *Why am I so tired?*

The woman nods, eyes still on the road, and I drift off, unable to stop myself.

"Hey," I mumble, trying to get my head on straight and force my lids open.

They slide shut again.

A familiar woman is standing over me and shaking me awake.

I'm not really all here, my brain feeling like egg yolks that got scrambled. I squint up at her.

"You're…Roman's mom?"

She freezes, her hand gripping me tightly on the shoulder.

Suddenly, my memory filters in, and I realize where I am. How I didn't recognize her…and now she's here.

I press my hand to my forehead, banging it a few times, trying to unmuffle the memories.

"Yeah, sweetie, I told you that."

"You did?" I scrunch up my face, trying to recall.

I look around, realizing we're at the entrance to the trail that leads to Upside Down Rock.

"Why are we here?" My tongue trips on the words.

"This is where he said to meet," she replies smoothly. "Where you two first saw each other, isn't it?"

My stomach twists, but I nod. "Yeah."

"You're sure you're okay to walk? It's a little rocky."

"I'm fine."

But I'm not. My legs feel strange when I climb out. Like they've been replaced with something heavy and loose. I wobble, and she's there, steadying me with a hand under my elbow.

"Careful," she murmurs. "Let me help you."

I nod, too tired to argue. I let her guide me up the trail, let the trees blur around the edges. Everything feels sticky. Slow.

"What was in that drink Bevie gave me?" I ask, my tongue thick.

She doesn't answer.

We walk.

Or…she walks. I stumble.

My knees drag. My arms tingle. I blink slowly, once. Twice.

Something isn't right.

Something's *wrong*.

"Where's Roman?" I ask.

Or maybe I don't ask it. Maybe I just think it.

We reach the cliff, and I search for him, but he's not here. He's not...

And then the world tilts, and the sky smears sideways, and I'm falling.

Darkness rushes in.

Chapter 52

Roman

I'VE NEVER BEEN A VIOLENT PERSON, BUT RIGHT now I could burn down this entire town.

"I swear to God, Benny, if they touch her, I will make sure *everyone* pays for it. Where are they taking her?" I ask, standing over him.

He shakes his head and rasps out, "I overheard Freddy telling someone to get her to him. That he'd take her to the spot where you saved her. They know it will draw you out."

My brows furrow. *Upside Down Rock.* "How do they know where that is?"

Benny gives me an incredulous look. "Freddy knows everything, Roman. Haven't you figured that out? There's a reason he's able to kill news stories and bend them the way he wants. You and Juliette were photographed years ago, and he got the pictures."

Maybe if my mind wasn't so singularly focused on finding her, I'd be able to focus on what the hell he just said.

I scoff. "How do I know I can trust you?"

He gives me a look. "You don't really have a choice, do you, cousin?"

I've never driven faster than when I get behind the wheel of Benjamin's car, and before I can blink, we're at the base of Verona County Park.

"What happens when I go up there?" I ask Benjamin as the car idles.

"Juliette will be there, but listen, he's expecting you."

I grit my teeth and nod. If something happens to Juliette...

"I don't care," I say. "He can have me as long as he lets her go."

He nods once, and I reach out to grab his arm.

"I'm going to find Lance, okay?" he reassures me.

My heart pounds against my ribs. "Lance was *there*. Isn't he in on this?"

"Lance is a prisoner just like everybody else. Freddy promised him a way out, and he's desperate for it. But there's no fucking way he'd let them hurt Juliette."

I blow out a deep breath and nod again, throwing open the car door and trekking up the hill. Fury lines my blood, and my focus is singular.

Get to Juliette.

If it's me Frederick wants, then fine. He can have me.

When I get to the open space at the top of the cliff, I don't see Frederick anywhere.

My eyes skim over the area, and on top of the picnic bench where I fell in love, there she is.

She's knocked out cold, laid out on her side, and her hands

and legs are bound with what looks like rope. My vision narrows, and I race to her, picking her up from the table and dragging her onto the ground and into my lap, my hand brushing her cheek. "Juliette."

Her head lolls to the side, and I lean forward and press my trembling lips to hers, my stomach filling with dread. "Little Rose, wake up, *please*."

My fingers grip her neck, trying to find a pulse, and a breath of relief hits me when I do.

Not dead.

No blood, either. Thank God.

Juliette whimpers, and my gaze moves back to her, my hand on her cheek. Her eyes flutter open, and she groans again, shifting like she's trying to move her hands.

Fuck. I should have started to untie those right away. I move to try and untangle the knots, but before I get anywhere, footsteps sound behind me, and then Frederick walks into the space, a smile on his face.

"Roman, you made it," he says.

Juliette's eyes close again, and she's back out, another small whimper leaving her.

"What did you do to her?" I spit at him.

Gingerly, I put her on the ground and move to stand in front of her, like I can keep him from even looking at her too closely.

I still have the pocketknife on me from earlier, and I've never been a murderer, but if he tries to get close to her, I will kill him. Even if it gives me nightmares for the rest of my life.

He looks around. "Just us?"

"Isn't that what you wanted?" I ask.

"I wasn't sure Benny would follow through. He's a little fickle, runs on emotions, you know?"

Did Benjamin trick me here? Am I all alone in this?

"That's funny," I say. "I was thinking the same thing about you."

Juliette whimpers yet again, and even though I was just trying to wake her up, now I want her to stay asleep. I don't want her to have any memory of this; maybe then, she can wake up later and it will just feel like a bad dream.

"Me?" Frederick laughs. "I'm the opposite."

"So, you planned to shoot Tyler last night?"

He grimaces. "An unfortunate hiccup. However, Tyler shouldn't have gotten in the way of things. He had a part to play, and he did *not* play it well."

"What part?"

I'm hoping that if I can keep him talking, then maybe it will give Benjamin time to get to Lance. Assuming he meant what he said.

His grin widens. "Doesn't really matter now, does it?"

"What is all this, Frederick? Why go through all this just to get me?"

His smile drops. "You Montgomerys are all the same. Always with an overinflated self-worth. This has been years in the making." He throws out his arms and glances around him like I should be impressed by the large empty space. "And finally we've done what we've needed, and you're here. I'll admit, a little messier than usual, but still…" He leans in, his eyes gleaming. "We're about to finish the job."

We.

The word slams into me and I resist the urge to look around.

"Who is *we*, Frederick?"

He doesn't answer. But he doesn't need to.

There's a slow, measured click of shoes on gravel behind him, and then she appears, and all of the air leaves my lungs like she's personally reached into my chest and ripped it out.

"Ma," I croak out.

She smiles. "Hey, Ry."

Anger, blinding and fast, rushes through me. "Do *not* call me that."

She smiles, coming to a stop next to Frederick, her eyes wild and her skin sallow.

"I never meant to hurt you," she says, like this is just a misunderstanding.

My eyes flicker behind me to Juliette. She's not moving, and her face is too still. Her pallor too white.

"What did you do to her?" I grind out.

"No idea," Frederick says, and my mother cackles.

He looks at her. "Did Beverly tell you what she was planning to use?"

My mother shrugs like the girl lying crumpled against the rock doesn't matter.

And another knife stabs its way into my back. No, worse, into *Juliette's* back.

"You drugged her," I whisper.

Ma's lips purse and she picks at her cuticles. "Don't be so dramatic."

I take a step forward, ignoring the way everything inside of me wants to reach out and throttle this woman who's hurt me so badly while all I've *ever* wanted to do was be her son. "Tell me she'll wake up."

"She'll be fine," Frederick confirms. "Eventually. She's just... resting."

"Because you fucking *drugged* her!" I snap.

"Because we needed to ensure she'd cooperate," he replies calmly.

My breathing is ragged as my eyes shoot wildly back to my mother. "Just how involved in this *are* you, Ma? Jesus." My voice breaks. "Why would you do this?"

"Because he didn't pick me," she sneers. "Because no matter how many nights I gave him, no matter how many years I waited, I was never enough."

I stare at her. At the hollow shell of the woman who raised me.

"I loved Marcus," she whispers. "I thought if I stayed close—if I stayed loyal—he'd give me something back. But he just kept me in the dark. And then Eleanor died, and everything started to fall apart, and Freddy found me and promised it could be different."

My throat burns.

"What'd he promise you?" I ask, then hold up a hand. "No, wait, let me guess. Drugs? Money?"

She doesn't deny it.

"He made it easier," she says. "And all I had to do was follow his rules. Get you desperate enough to go back home, while he convinced Marcus to let you back in. It wasn't supposed to be this way, you know? You were supposed to have a reason to come back, and then a reason to run away, leaving the money to *us*."

The words hit like a gunshot to my brain, filtering like sludge down through my body.

"What did you say?" I tilt my head, my body vibrating with untapped rage. "What did you just fucking say?" I step forward. "Repeat those words exactly to me."

Her mouth opens and closes like a fish.

"You said, 'get me desperate.'" I curl my hands into fists to stop the shaking. "Just how did you do that, *Ma*? Did you…" I lick my lips, breathing deep. *There's no way.* "Did you do something to Brooklynn to make me go running to my father?"

Guilt flashes through her eyes, and she gulps, staring down at the ground.

Oh my God. Nausea surges through me, my body revolting from the implication that she was messing with Brooklynn in order to get to me.

I bite down so hard on my tongue, I taste the blood, and I stem the burning in my eyes by pressing my palms into the sockets. "Did you know what was wrong with her?"

Frederick scoffs. "I'm done wasting this time. She knew. She poisoned her just the way I asked. Enough to get her sick and enough to keep you pathetic and *desperate*, just like she said."

My eyes fly back up to my mom, the remnants of my heart breaking into a million pieces and lodging in my throat, my eyes, my fucking teeth.

"I should kill you," I hiss at her.

She stumbles back like I've struck her. And I want to. I want to hit her. Want to wrap my hands around her neck and scream *why* while I watch her suffer the same way she's made Brooke and me suffer.

Frederick steps in again, smoothing his suit like this is just business.

"Your mother's choices are tragic, yes," he says. "But let's not forget who put the gun in her hand. Marcus. The Montgomery name. The town that rewards cruelty and punishes honesty."

"And that's what this is?" I snap. "You punishing the town?"

"No," he says. "This is me cleansing it. Eleanor was my sister. And Marcus killed her."

"You couldn't save her, so now you're what? Playing God?"

"I'm *rewriting history*," he says, reaching into his pocket and pulling out the gun from last night.

My blood runs cold, and I step to my right, trying to make sure I'm as far away from Juliette as possible while still shielding her.

It's me he's after. He wouldn't be stupid enough to kill a Calloway child, *would he*?

"Spare me the theatrics," he snaps. "You've already lost."

I shake my head. "I'm not my father. I don't play your game."

"You already did," he says, smiling faintly. "The moment you showed up at that gallery in California. The moment Juliette smiled at you, and you smiled back. The second you called your father, and he asked you to come home."

My chest heaves. *The art show?* I look at my mother.

Of course. It was her who got me that show. And hadn't I thought it was strange Juliette was there, of all places?

Jesus Christ. Is anything about my life real?

Juliette stirs behind me with a soft groan. My breath stutters at the sound.

Frederick clocks it instantly. "Oh, she's waking up? That's inconvenient."

He raises the gun.

My heart stops, and my vision goes red.

I lunge.

We hit the ground hard. My elbow connects with his ribs and the gun skitters across the dirt, landing just inches from the cliff's edge. We both scramble, blood and dirt marring our skin, and I hear Juliette's voice behind me, weak and disoriented.

"Roman?"

I grab the gun first.

And I don't hesitate.

I aim it at Frederick's head.

He freezes beneath me, chest rising and falling with short, shallow breaths. There's a scratch down the side of his face and blood in the corner of his mouth.

My mother screams, but she doesn't come to his aide. Instead, I hear her turn and run. I don't look to see where she's gone, all I know is that she's not near Juliette, and she's not next to me.

I don't take my eyes off of Frederick.

My hand shakes as I press my finger to the trigger.

"You won't shoot me," he laughs, his hands raised in mock surrender.

Something catches my gaze behind him, and hope surges through me like a wildfire.

My arm *hurts*, bits of rock and twigs embedding themselves in the flesh, but I ignore it.

I flip the safety, the click loud in the air.

Frederick's eyes widen, and then I lift the gun from where it's aimed at him, and lay it in the outstretched hand of Lance.

I stumble back as soon as Lance takes my place, and I run over to Juliette, who's barely conscious and still laid out on the ground.

"You're really the biggest piece of shit, aren't you, Freddy?" Lance says.

I expect him to raise the gun, and he does, but instead of

shooting him, he pistol-whips him, and Frederick's face flies to the side.

"You're making a mistake," Frederick spits. "We both know that if you kill me, there's no escape for you."

What is he talking about?

"You thought you could take my *sister*?" Lance's voice is a dangerous rumble, and I rip the rope from Juliette's arms and drag her body into my lap just as he swings again, his fist meeting Frederick's cheek.

I think I see a tooth fly from Frederick's mouth, but I can't be sure.

Lance immediately kicks him in the gut. Over and over, like he's lost all reason.

"Are you out of your goddamn mind? I will stay in those underground cages for the rest of my life before I'd *ever* let you touch her." Lance aims the gun.

Underground cages?

"Lance," Benny says, appearing from the trees.

Lance's teeth grit. "*You* shut the fuck up, Benny."

Frederick laughs from the ground and then groans, curling in on himself. "He'll kill you if you stay down there."

Lance shrugs. "Then I guess I'll see you in hell."

He shoots.

Again.

And again.

And again.

The birds fly from the trees like they can sense the death in the air.

Benjamin rips the gun from Lance's hand, wiping it down with his shirt and then pressing his own fingers to it tightly.

"Why the fuck did you do that?" Lance asks.

"It couldn't be you," he says, turning toward him. He looks like he might puke or pass out. "You know it couldn't be you. She needs you."

Lance nods, and then his eyes flicker over to us and widen when he realizes that Juliette is lying in my lap, breathing but still knocked out.

He walks over and looks at me with a grim expression. "Is she—"

"She's alive," I cut him off. "But we need to get her to the hospital."

He nods again and then meets my gaze. "Take her. And Roman, *thank* you. For loving her enough to save her."

The ROSEBROOK Rag

County's Top Lawyer Exposed as Criminal Mastermind in High-Stakes Power Plot!

Hold on to your pearls, Rosebrook Falls, because *everything* just exploded.

In a scandal that's rocked Rosebrook Falls to its core, high-power attorney Frederick Lawrence has been revealed as the man behind a years-long scheme involving murder, manipulation, and a twisted attempt to seize control of the Montgomery estate.

The real shock? He wasn't working alone.

Earlier today, Paxton Calloway held a press conference confirming all of the rumors were true.

Heather Argent (yes, *that* Heather Argent: Roman Montgomery's once-thought-dead mother) was keeping Roman under her thumb, while Lawrence pulled strings from behind the scenes.

His motive?

Revenge.

Turns out, Lawrence had a lot of secrets and they went beyond his clients. He was the secret half brother of Eleanor Voltaire, Marcus Montgomery's late wife, who tragically died five years ago.

The conspiracy came crashing down when Roman Montgomery stepped in to save Juliette Calloway from a planned abduction, unraveling the entire plot in a single night.

Frederick Lawrence framed Roman for the shooting on VU Campus just two nights ago, and when he had no way out…he turned the gun on himself.

And if that wasn't enough to whet your drama-loving appetites? That graffiti painting the Calloways as the villains?

You'll never believe it…

Frederick Lawrence.

Heather Argent has vanished and is currently wanted for questioning. But perhaps even more shocking: Beverly, the Calloway family's longtime house manager and nanny, wasn't Beverly at all.

Her real name?

Cassandra Troy.

She's currently at large.

Rosebrook, your secrets are showing. Is there anything else left to uncover?

#ScandalInTheFalls #JusticeForJuliette

#RomanMontgomeryRises #FamilyFeudWho

#HeatherExposed #FrederickFraud

#EleanorDeservedBetter #RosebrookRag

Chapter 53

Juliette

THERE'S A BEEPING NOISE THAT WON'T SHUT UP, and it's making my head pulse in time to its rhythm.

My mouth is dry. I try to swallow, and it feels like sharp razorblades cut through my throat.

There's literally nothing that feels good on my entire body, except for the warmth that's encasing my left hand.

I force my eyelids open, and they come undone like they were stuck together with glue. I blink a few times to clear the haze from my vision.

My brow furrows. I'm in my bedroom at home, but there's a beeping monitor, and it's hooked up to my arm. The noise grows faster as I come to, my heart pounding against my chest, and I'm trying like hell to piece together my memories.

Roman's mom, and then feeling out of it, and now…I'm here.

I look down and let out a short gasp, my heart ratcheting up even more when I see Roman at my side, his hand encasing mine and his slow, controlled breaths puffing against my arm.

He looks concerned even in sleep, his head resting on my shoulder, and he's gripping me tightly.

The door to my room flies open, Felicity popping her head in. "Everything okay?"

I blink.

"She's awake!" she yells into the hallway before bouncing around the corner.

I stare at her and she lets out a choked laugh. "Holy shit, Jules. When you decide to let loose and live, you really take that literally."

There's a warm hand on my cheek, and I twist to look into the cerulean-blue eyes of Roman.

My heart flutters.

"Juliette." His voice comes out as a pained croak.

I lift my arm and stroke down his jaw, and he practically rips the glass of water from Felicity's hand when she reaches the side of my bed, wordlessly holding it out for me.

She scoffs. "Can I not be reduced to the beverage girl in my own best friend's resurrection arc?"

I laugh, but it makes my head throb.

Roman gives her a look and then holds the straw to my lips, and I drink greedily. The water is cold and perfect, soothing my parched throat.

"You're here," I say to him.

"I'm here," he repeats, bringing my hand up and pressing tiny kisses to the back of it. "Never leaving you again."

"How did—"

"Shh." He reaches forward with his free hand and brushes it down my hair, petting me like he needs the feel of me under his hands to know that I'm real.

"Miss Calloway," Felicity interrupts, her fingers gripping my ankle. "As your self-appointed and completely untrained nurse, I'm supposed to get your vitals. But also, your entire house is full of large, angry men who keep pacing, so…"

"Give us a minute," Roman snaps. "Go tell everyone waiting that she's awake."

Felicity cocks a brow. "Did you not hear me scream it at them?"

"So tell them again."

"Fine, but only because I'm a sucker for a good love story." She squeezes my ankle again before letting go. "But *no* making out until we're sure she's okay."

Roman doesn't even dignify her with a look.

Felicity tosses a wink and then disappears into the hallway, shouting loudly again, "She's awake, you idiots, did nobody hear me?"

"We heard you. Goddamn, you're like a gnat," Paxton replies, his voice distant like he's yelling back at her from the bottom of the stairs.

I raise a brow. "Snippy."

Roman smiles, pressing another kiss to my hand.

"I was so worried." He leans in and brushes his mouth against mine. "You are never allowed to get kidnapped again."

"What, like I did it on purpose?" I narrow my eyes. "It was *your* mom who took me, in case you forgot."

"I didn't forget," he says, voice quiet. "I will *never* forget."

There's something haunted in his gaze, and it twists something deep inside me. "It's okay, you know? And it's not her, Trouble. Remember? It's the drugs. Not her."

He grunts. "It *was*, Juliette."

I shake my head, then wince at the ache it produces. "No, baby. It wasn't. Drugs change a person, right?"

His jaw tenses. "You don't know everything she's done, you—"

"Doesn't matter," I say. "I mean, it does, but…for your own heart? It doesn't matter."

He sniffs but doesn't give me an answer. And I don't push because honestly, I'm out of my depth with it, and grief takes time to process.

My chest pulls, and the fog clears just enough for me to remember small pieces. "What happened?"

"The short version? Frederick Lawrence was a piece of shit who has manipulated everyone for years, alongside my mother, and now he's dead, my father's also dead, and you're safe. That's all I care about."

"What? Oh my God, *Roman*," I blurt out, my heart aching for him.

He shakes his head. "I don't want to think about it right now. I'm fine. You're here. Brooklynn's safe. And I'm *fine*."

I swallow. "Okay."

My stomach drops as more of reality seeps back in through the haze. "Ty," I choke out. "Is he…?"

Roman's jaw clenches, something dark passing through his gaze, but he shakes his head. "He's in the hospital, but for now, at least…he's alive."

"It wasn't you? I know it wasn't you, but Bevie said he died and—"

"Beverly lied to you, Juliette. For years, actually."

My heart pounds, and as much as I want to rage against

what he's saying, as much as I want to pretend like that isn't the case, I know that it is.

"That's not even her real name. It's Cassandra Troy."

Honestly, it doesn't hurt as viscerally as I expect. Maybe so much has just happened, that I'm numb.

"Are you sure she wasn't tricked?" I ask. "Bevie was *everything* to me growing up."

He strokes my hair again. "If they find her, then I promise I'll make sure you can ask her yourself."

She's gone. Of course she is.

He smiles softly, leaning in and brushing a kiss against my lips. "Do you think Felicity will kill me if I let you ride my dick real quick?"

My mouth drops open. "Roman!"

He shrugs, looking anything but sorry. "You're alive. I'm alive. The last forty-eight hours of my life have been a huge wake-up call. I think we both deserve a little pleasure."

"I'm hooked up to a heart monitor," I deadpan.

"Exactly." He nods. "Now you can't hide how easily I make your pulse race."

"You are so *annoying*."

He grins, catching my wrist when I reach out to smack his shoulder. "And you love me."

"Kiss me, Trouble."

Grinning, he leans down and presses his lips to mine. I tilt my head, but before either of us can fall too far into it, the door creaks again and familiar voices come barreling through.

"Well, is she alive or what?"

That sounds like Alex.

"Thank the lord," Felicity banters back. "I swear, if I had to listen to Paxton pace one more time…"

"She was almost *murdered*, Flick."

Paxton, obviously.

"Oh my God," she complains. "Don't make it sound like *I'm* the villain. Out of all of us, I'm the one who will end up hand-feeding her ice chips and defending her honor."

They all stumble into the room mid-argument, followed by Lance, who doesn't say anything.

He just stops and his eyes lock on mine.

And for a second, all of the noise dulls.

His posture's tense, and his expression is as broody and tortured as ever, but I see the crack in his mask.

"She's clearly alive," Lance mutters, his voice breaking slightly over the words. "You can tell by the sarcasm already leaking out of her pores."

My heart falters and my stomach tangles.

"Good to see you, too," I say, trying to sound as dry as he makes me seem.

Roman tenses beside me, but I nudge his side. "Relax. He's been making fun of me since we were kids. This is affection."

Lance's mouth lifts in the faintest almost-smile. "He knows how much I love you."

I lift a brow. "Does he now?"

He shrugs. "What, you think he was the one who saved you? All alone?"

Roman smirks. "I could've done it alone."

Alex groans, dramatically dropping onto the chaise. "Can we not do the whole masculine martyr monologues right now? She just regained consciousness, not upped her tolerance for testosterone."

Paxton sighs, frowning at me. "We tracked you with Benjamin Voltaire, who for the first time in his life was helpful. Lance got to you before the rest of us."

"I heard Roman punched a tree," Felicity pipes in. "Did you punch a tree?"

Lance chuckles. "He totally punched a tree."

Roman scoffs. "It was symbolic."

My eyes fling back and forth between all of them. Roman is…joking? With my brothers.

What the hell happened while I was drugged and knocked out?

"You know what else is symbolic?" Alex waves his hands. "The fact Jules survived. Poisoned, betrayed, dragged up a cliff like the last act of a Greek tragedy, and still, she rises."

Felicity snorts. "You're so dramatic."

"I'm just saying," he continues, completely unbothered. "If this were a play, we'd be in the final act. The masks are off. The villains are dead. The lovers are reunited. All that's left is the curtain call."

"Jesus," Lance groans. "You teach a couple acting classes and now you think you're the narrator of *Hamlet*."

"I'm a *philosopher* at heart, Lance. You know this. It's not my fault I'm good at everything." Alex grins.

"I give it five minutes before he starts quoting Nietzsche," Paxton mutters, flopping onto the end of my bed like it's his own personal chair.

"Well that just shows how much you don't know me," Alex says. "I'm in my Sophocles era now. Chaos, fate, tragic women with killer one-liners…"

He waggles his brows at Felicity.

I tune them all out, focusing on Roman.

"Thank you," I whisper, squeezing his hand. "For coming back. For saving me. For not letting us end." My throat tightens, tears pricking my eyes. "I thought I had lost you."

"You will *never* lose me." He leans in, resting his forehead on mine, ignoring the bickering of my family. "Fate always brings us back together."

I close the space and kiss him, soft and slow, full of every word I don't know how to say.

"You still gonna paint me in everything?" I ask, a brow raised.

His lips twitch. "On my hands, in the sky, in the space between one breath and the next."

"You can't paint *breath*," I remark.

"That sounds like a challenge."

I shrug. "Maybe it is."

Someone clears their throat.

"Okay," Alex says. "This was a cute moment and all, but if they start dry humping in front of me, I'm leaving."

Felicity throws a pillow at him. "You'd cry if they broke up. Don't pretend."

"I'd cry," Lance pipes in.

Everyone turns to look at him, and my mouth pops open.

He shrugs, eyes still on Roman and me. "What? I can be emotional."

"Wow. Vulnerability? In *this* house?" Felicity jokes.

Lance smirks. "Don't get used to it."

"I think it's sweet," I say. "I need the vulnerability, especially since our parents aren't here, apparently." My voice pitches up. "Where *are* they?"

Felicity snorts and cuts a look to Paxton. "This guy wouldn't let them come in with us."

Paxton shrugs. "I promised you I wouldn't let them fuck with you anymore, and I meant it."

I choke on my gratitude, pressing my lips together and giving a sharp nod. If I try to talk, I think I'll cry.

I'm not sure what the future holds, but I'm positive I'm done with the two people who barely raised me and forgot that love should lead above all.

Lance straightens and my heart sinks as he gets ready to leave. "I've gotta go."

"And do what?" Paxton quirks a brow.

Lance lifts a shoulder. "There's some people I have to look out for."

Felicity says something smart back, but I tune them out, watching Lance as he heads for the door. There's something heavy in the way he carries himself, and I have more questions for him that I'm dying to get the answers to.

"Lance," I call out.

He stops, turning just enough to meet my eyes.

"Thank you," I say. "For everything. For being the one who got there."

His jaw works like he's trying to find the right words. But in the end, all he does is nod.

Roman kicks everyone else out seconds later, and then he saunters to me with a wicked grin, and I exhale, reaching for him as he climbs into the bed and draws me into his arms.

His thumb brushes along my cheekbone, eyes tracing me with reverence.

"I'll paint you in the sky, Little Rose," he promises.

"Then I'll write you in the stars, Trouble," I whisper back. "That way we'll always be together."

He grins, a playful look in his eye. "That's *exactly* what a stalker would say."

I roll my eyes.

"You love me."

"I do," I admit.

And I kiss him to prove it.

They weren't perfect. They were mess, and complication, and arguments that ended with apologies whispered between silk-laden sheets.

But when it mattered, he showed up, and she let him in. Not because it was easy, but because it was real.

And maybe their story wasn't built for glass slippers. Maybe they never fit the mold.

But it was theirs. And it was art.

If she was the sun, then he was every constellation in the sky.

For never was a bond the stars could show,
As boundless as Juliette...and her Romeo.

Epilogue

Juliette

THIS ISN'T THE FIRST FUNERAL I'VE EVER BEEN TO, but it is the one with the most people.

My hand grips Roman's as we sit in the front row, listening to the minister talk about legacy and friendship, about the founding family and all that it means. About passing the torch and never forgetting who came before.

I've cried a few times, but I've held it together pretty good other than that.

Everyone who is anyone is here, and it's crazy to me how out of control things can be one second, and then, with a little bit of money and influence, glossed over and pushed under the rug. Molded to fit the narrative instead of the truth.

Frederick Lawrence died as a disgrace.

I look to my right, my chest growing warm when I see Tyler—still recovering from his wound—his arm draped across the back of Rosalie's chair. He must sense my gaze, because he looks at me and winks.

There's not a day that goes by where I don't thank God

that he made it, that he survived. There's still a lot of bad blood between him and Roman, but time heals all wounds. At least, that's what I'm telling myself.

If my dad can bury the hatchet enough to be here attending Marcus's funeral, then I have hope that the rest of my family and Roman can one day mend the rift and forgive each other for being manipulated by the people who were supposed to love them.

I'm not holding my breath, but at least everyone is alive.

And now the feud between Montgomerys and Calloways is being buried with Marcus. I guess when a man throws himself into danger to save your daughter's life, it becomes clear that some grudges shouldn't be held on to simply because of the blood that runs through your veins.

Roman is the Montgomery empire now. And Paxton's set to take over for my dad, although I'm not convinced it was entirely voluntary on either of their parts.

They're going to work together—Roman and him—even though Roman is in over his head. Paxton said he'd help him navigate the business waters. It's not like *I* have any idea of what the hell everyone does.

My mother is another story, but she doesn't really get a say in my life anymore. Not since I moved out and took up residence with Roman at Montgomery Manor in the HillPoint.

Besides, now that my father is retiring (being pushed out), the two of them have decided to go on a perma-vacation. Sail around the world or something.

I wouldn't know, because I haven't spoken to them.

I wish I could say that everything is better, but I still have so many questions about that night and about the people involved.

Beverly—Cassandra—is still missing. And so is Roman's mom.

My heart cramps when I think about her and the trauma that she's left him with. He hasn't told Brooklynn about any of it yet, and honestly, I don't blame him. How do you tell someone that their mother allowed you to be an unwitting pawn in a fucked-up person's scheme?

Benjamin is next to Merrick, both of whom are sitting on Roman's other side, and while I don't relish the idea of any of them being close to Roman, he seems to want them there, and I trust in his choices.

And then there's Lance, sitting next to Alex and Art, that bartender girl Ginny—who I know for sure now is Art's girlfriend—from the Round Table on Art's other side.

Again, I have a lot of questions, especially after Roman filled me in on everything that I missed while I was passed out on the ground at Upside Down Rock.

But there's time for that later.

My gaze lands on my father, something unsettling rolling around in my gut.

There's still something sinister happening in this town, and my dad is far from innocent.

I can't help but think about the fables that Beverly used to tell us when we were kids. About how the foundation of this town was built on broken hearts and buried secrets.

Civil blood stains civil hands.

Who was she, really?

My spine prickles with anxiety when I think about how effortlessly she embedded herself into our lives, and I wonder if she was planted there on purpose, or if she was manipulated like everybody else.

Hopefully, she stays wherever she ran off to, and I never have to find out.

Roman's hand slides over my thigh and rests possessively on top, squeezing. I lean into him, giving him the support he needs. He said he isn't sad about his father's passing, that he expected it, but I know it still has to hurt. Especially since he didn't get much closure, in the end.

Whether he admits it or not, he was thrust into this life without a choice, and knowing your father won't be around to guide you would be a heavy weight on anyone's shoulders.

But it's like he said: sometimes we don't get our happy endings. Sometimes the bad things win.

And life is life, you have to work through the shit that doesn't go your way and figure out how to heal through it.

The minister finishes his speech, and there's a somber feeling in the air. I look around one more time, and my eyes snag on someone standing off to the corner.

It's a man. He's tall, tan, and lanky. Sunglasses hide his face, and black hair that can be tucked behind his ears whips in the breeze. There are two others behind him. All three of them dressed in suits. Like they're here for Marcus's funeral, too.

I squint, trying to get a better look, but I don't think I've ever seen them before. The man in front gives a short dip of his chin, and then he spins around and walks away, the other two following him like guards.

When I move my gaze to where his face was angled, it lands on Lance.

He's staring after them, a frown on his face. Ginny is worrying her bottom lip as her gaze bounces between them.

I don't miss how their eyes meet behind Art's head.

My heart pinches tight, and the hair on my arms raises, but I shelve the feeling for now.

Today is a day of mourning.

Tomorrow, I'll worry about the rest.

And I know I won't have to do it alone.

Roman has half the reins to Rosebrook Falls now, after all. And secrets can only stay buried for so long.

Roman

Two Months Later

We're at the Round Table, Juliette tucked perfectly under my arm, her body relaxed and her cheeks flushed from the alcohol she's been sipping.

Felicity's perched across the booth, swirling a glass of wine while she listens to Alex rant beside her, flinging dramatic hand gestures.

"I'm just telling you," Alex says, his voice rising above the guitar player crooning in the corner. "I need something with roots."

Juliette scoffs. "You've literally lived here your entire life, Alex."

"And?" He glares at her. "Maybe I'm getting tired of pretending to be someone else all the time. I want to *be* someone. Me. Alex Calloway."

He drums his fingers on the table.

"Maybe I'll start a theater company. Or a coffee shop. Or…a theater company *inside* a coffee shop."

Felicity snorts into her wine. "You could call it *Bard & Beans*."

"Yes!" Alex snaps his fingers, eyes lighting up.

He grabs her face, pressing a quick kiss to her lips.

They both freeze, Felicity's eyes going wide.

Juliette stiffens underneath me.

I smirk, leaning back, enjoying that for once, the drama isn't concerning us.

Before anyone can adjust to the very clear shift in the air, a shadow falls over the table.

Lance.

He's been making more of an effort lately, especially since Juliette is around the HillPoint now, living with me, but their relationship is still tense. He's cagey, and disappears for days, and then shows back up and acts like nothing's wrong.

He's wearing all black, rain from outside speckled across his shoulders, and his expression is unreadable and calm in that unnerving way only Lance can manage.

Still, when his eyes meet mine, he gives a jerk of his chin. There's an unspoken bond between the two of us, ever since we saved Juliette.

Merrick glides around him with a fresh round of drinks, and slips in the booth next to Juliette, raising a brow toward Lance. "Well, well, look what the dark and broody wind blew in."

"You just missed Alex's midlife crisis," Juliette chimes.

"Tragic," Lance mutters, plopping down next to Alex, squishing him closer to Felicity. "Was he crying again?"

"Almost," I say.

Alex huffs and points his glass at no one in particular. "Epictetus would say true strength is mastering your emotions, not being ruled by them." He pauses and then adds, "Which is why I'm only crying on the inside."

Felicity rolls her eyes. "Would he also say you're a drag?"

He frowns at her. "That's hurtful."

"Philosophy is *boring*. I prefer it when you're acting out lines from something fun."

Across the bar, someone laughs. It's warm and melodic, and Lance's eyes flick toward the source like a moth to a light.

Genevieve.

He doesn't say a word, and when I glance around the table, nobody else is paying him any mind.

But I see it. Because I've *felt* it.

The twitch in his jaw.

The way his fingers curl like he's holding himself back.

The way his gaze lingers too long before he forces himself to turn away like it didn't mean anything.

He looks at me now, maybe recognizing I'm the only one who noticed whatever the hell *that* was.

I raise a brow, and he frowns before he looks away from me, too.

And just like that, whatever tension was pressing at the edges of the room dissipates, folded back into the warm haze of clinking glasses and laughter.

Merrick's trying to convince Alex that opening a theater-coffee hybrid would make him hemorrhage money.

Felicity's scrolling through a menu, even though the only food they have here is already half eaten on the table.

And Juliette's leaned against my side, her head resting just below my shoulder, a soft smile tugging at her lips like the world's finally righted itself enough to let her breathe.

For the first time in a long time, I'm not thinking about what's coming next.

I'm just here.

With *her*. With family.

The only person I'm missing now is Brooke. She's still in Cali, doing her own thing, although she said she's looking into VU as a potential college. Something about their Comparative Literature program being one of the top in the nation.

I close my eyes, wrap my arms tighter around Juliette, and breathe her in like she's the only thing I've ever known.

Somewhere across the room, a glass drops. Someone shouts too loud. The guitar player singing on the stage fumbles over a chord.

The world keeps turning.

But this feeling?

This is *ours*.

And I'll spend forever painting it across the sky.

Extended Epilogue

Roman

"ROMAN," SHE WHIMPERS, HER FINGERS THREADing through the strands of my hair, her soft curves molding to me. "Someone could see us."

I glance around the office—my new office at the Montgomery Organization—and tighten my grip on her thighs.

"Who?" I murmur against her throat, kissing the pulse pounding beneath her skin.

She shakes her head. "I don't know, doesn't this place have custodial workers or something?"

I shrug. "Fuck if I know. I don't even know anything *about* this business."

She giggles, her arms wrapping around my neck and resting on my shoulders, her fingers still in my hair. "Well, Paxton said he'd help get you acclimated, right?"

I frown. "Don't talk about other men when I'm trying to fuck you."

She snorts. "Ew, it's my brother."

"Even worse."

She grins, her teeth sinking into her bottom lip like she's trying not to laugh. "You're ridiculous."

I lift her onto the edge of the desk, pushing her dress higher up her thighs. "And you're still overdressed."

Her breath hitches. "Roman—"

"Don't say no." I reach beneath the fabric and find the edge of her panties. Lace. Always lace these days, like she's trying to tempt me at every turn. "Not after you kissed me like that in front of half the town earlier."

"I *kissed* you. You're the one who glared at Art like he tried to lick my neck."

"He looked at you like he wanted to." I tug her panties down her legs, slow, deliberate. "And, you were wearing *this* dress. I should've carried you out of the town square, press conference be damned."

"You practically did," she breathes, her hands moving to unbutton my pants. "We probably shouldn't fuck on a desk on your first day."

"I'm the boss now," I whisper, my lips brushing hers. "And it's not my first day until tomorrow."

She grins. "That's a good point."

That's all the encouragement I need. My hand slides between her thighs, fingers gliding over her already slick heat.

She gasps, hips jerking into my palm, her legs spreading just a little wider for me.

"Fuck, baby," I murmur against her mouth. "You're soaked."

Her fingers tug my belt free, her voice a breathy whisper. "Maybe I've been thinking about this desk all night."

"Don't tell me that," I groan. "I'll cancel the rest of the week's meetings and keep you on it."

Her dress bunches around her waist, and my fingers dip

lower, parting her folds, teasing the entrance. She's pulsing beneath my hand, sweet and wet and *so fucking ready* for me.

"Have I told you how hot you are when you talk all business-like? Who knew you had it in you?"

A bit of trepidation seeps into the moment. I'm about to take over as CEO of the Montgomery Organization. Officially. And I have no goddamn idea what I'm doing. I don't even know what the organization does; not fully anyway.

"I'm not sure I do."

She bites her lip, watching me like I'm the only thing in the world worth seeing. "Roman. I'm trying to keep it sexy, and you're ruining the roleplay fantasy."

"What?" I ask, sliding two fingers inside her and curling them just right. "You started this."

She lets out a soft cry, grabbing my shirt with both hands, eyes fluttering shut. "You're such a problem."

I pump my fingers in and out slowly, deliberately, watching the way her mouth falls open, her thighs tremble, her chest rises. "You knew what I was when you climbed on top of me the first time."

She opens her eyes, glaring at me. "I did *not* climb on top of you."

"Oh, that's right." I lean down, nipping her neck. "You just conveniently followed me around until you couldn't resist begging me to touch you."

She moans, grabbing a fistful of my hair and tugging my face up to hers. "God, I hate you."

I grin against her lips. "You love me."

"I *do*," she agrees, the words spilling out. "Now quit ruining the moment. I came here for one reason only, and that's to be fucked like I'm a naughty secretary."

Her legs fall open wider.

"I've been a very bad girl, Boss Man. Are you gonna punish me?"

"Bad girl?" I echo, my fingers still moving inside her, slow and deep. "You're past bad, Little Rose. You've been fucking *insubordinate*."

She shudders, her walls fluttering around my fingers, and her grip in my hair tightens.

"You seduced the CEO," I murmur, withdrawing my fingers and bringing them to my mouth, licking them clean just to watch her eyes darken. "You broke about six company policies in ten minutes."

"Allegedly."

I grab her hips, spin her around, and press her chest to the desk, her ass high in the air, her heels still on. "You interrupted a meeting."

"There *was* no meeting," she gasps, laughing breathlessly as I shove her dress up around her waist.

"You don't know that." I grip the backs of her thighs, spreading them, baring her completely. "You didn't check the calendar. Another mark against you being good at your job."

"Maybe I *wanted* to get caught," she says over her shoulder, voice syrupy and taunting. "Maybe I wanted everyone to know who I belong to."

That sends a rush of possession racing through me.

"Keep talking like that and I'll bend you over this desk harder and remind you exactly what my name means."

She moans, arching into me. "Then stop teasing me and *do it*, Roman."

I shove my pants down just enough to free myself, then line

up and press the head of my cock to her dripping center, sliding it through her pussy lips.

"You want your punishment, baby?" I ask, dragging the tip over her clit before dipping just inside her and pulling back again. "Or do you want to beg for it?"

"Fuck *you*," she spits, breathless. "I'm not begging—"

I slam into her in one brutal thrust, and her words cut off in a cry that echoes off the walls.

Her body clamps around me, hot and tight and fucking *perfect*.

I don't give her any time to adjust. I just grip her hips and pound into her with a wild, relentless rhythm, her moans turning into incoherent pleas as I fuck her against the desk, every thrust a claim, every slap of skin a promise.

"You feel that?" I growl, slamming deep. "That's what happens when you misbehave at work."

She gasps, her hands scrambling for purchase on the slick surface of the desk. "Roman—*fuck*—"

"That's it," I breathe, leaning over her, one hand pressing between her shoulder blades, the other snaking down to rub circles on her clit. "Come for me, baby. Be a good girl now."

And she does.

With a cry that's half my name and half broken sound, her body seizes around me, her orgasm crashing through her like a wave, and I follow with a growl, thrusting deep as I spill inside her, hips jerking as every drop empties into the girl who stole my heart.

I lean down, brushing a kiss to her spine.

"You were made for me," I tell her, matter of fact.

She hums, drowsy and soft, turning just enough to meet my eyes with a smile on her lips.

"You say that like you're surprised."

I shake my head. "Not surprised, just certain."

Later that night, we're lying in bed together, her asleep and me staring up at the ceiling and overthinking.

The rhythm of her breathing settles something restless inside me, and when her fingers curl around mine in her sleep, pulling my hand to her chest like she's anchoring me to her heart, I *know*.

The next time I tell her she's mine…I plan to be on my knee, with a ring in my hand, telling her we're forever.

**WANT MORE EMILY MCINTIRE?
DISCOVER THE FIRST BOOK
IN HER SUGARLAKE SERIES**

Chapter 1

Alina

Eleven Years Old

I LOVE DANCING.

Always have and always will. Been in classes since I was four years old. Daddy likes to joke and say I'll dance my way into the worst kind of trouble, but I think that's a load of bull. Why would I want to get in trouble? I'm eleven now, way too big to be sitting in a time-out chair. It's just my favorite thing to do in the whole world and it's the only time I really feel *free*.

My older brother, Eli, will tell you I've got two left feet, but don't believe him. He just gets annoyed Mama lets me pick the music when she sends us outside to play.

I pick a new station on the radio and smile big, tapping my foot against the sidewalk.

"Lame," my brother huffs, shooting his basketball into the hoop. "Change it, Lee. You know I can't stand country."

My honey-blond hair tangles behind me as I spin to face Eli. I stick my tongue out at him and tell him to shove it where the sun don't shine before I turn to face our house. It's nothing fancy, but it's all I've ever known as home. A three-bed, two-bath, one-story right smack in the middle of Sugarlake, Tennessee, with white siding, blue shutters, and the prettiest tulips you'll ever see. I love picking them when they bloom in the spring, but Mama gets mad when I do because tulips are "a labor of love," so instead I just come out front and stare at them every chance I get.

Eli bounces the ball between his legs and groans, bringing my attention back to him. "Seriously. I can't practice my free throws to this shit."

I roll my eyes at his potty mouth. He thinks he's so big and bad because he's fourteen now, and he loves to curse every chance he gets.

"Don't let Mama hear you talk like that or she'll wash your mouth out with soap again." I stick my finger between my lips, making a loud gagging noise.

I've never had it done to me, but watching Eli go through it is enough to make me never want to speak a bad word *ever*.

He stops dribbling and runs his hand through his honey-blond hair, shaking his head. "Yeah, Miss Alina May, never doing a bad thing in her life. Why don't you leave me alone and go introduce yourself to the new neighbors?" He gestures to the house three doors down where there's a big moving truck in the driveway and a girl playing on the front lawn.

I put my hands on my hips and strain my eyes trying to see better. It's not the worst idea Eli's ever had.

The girl's smaller than me and hula-hooping away without a care in the world, her blackish hair swishing against her porcelain shoulders with every swing of her hips. She looks friendly enough, and since my best friend, Becca, is out of town for the summer at church camp, I really have nothing better to do than make a new friend.

"Okay, I will." I make my way across the lawn before spinning around and pointing my finger at him. "But *not* 'cause you told me to, Eli. I'm doin' it 'cause she looks nice."

He smirks and tosses the basket into the hoop again.

I'm almost to her house when a boy walks out of the front door and slams it behind him. I stop in my tracks and watch with wide eyes as he turns and flips off the closed door with both middle fingers, and then sits on the front steps and lights up a cigarette.

My brows shoot to my hairline.

He doesn't look that much older than me, definitely not old enough to buy cigarettes, but the way he's puffing on that smoke so well I imagine he has no trouble getting them whenever he wants. He leans his elbows on his knees when he inhales, and I'm mesmerized as it swirls into the air.

Is he the new girl's brother?

He has brown-black hair, although his is cut so short I can almost see his scalp, and he isn't as small, but he is kind of gangly looking.

It's only when he turns his head and stares straight at me that I realize I'm standing in the middle of our street gawking like a weirdo. My cheeks heat, so I quickly look down and start walking again.

No sense in turning back now, that would be even weirder.

The girl sees me as I get to the edge of their front yard, the Hula-Hoop falling down her body and a huge smile splitting across her face. She bounds over like a fairy flittering from tree to tree.

Dang, this girl is bouncy.

"Hi!" she squeals. "I'm Lily, what's your name?"

I open my mouth to answer but she keeps talking, so it's hard to get a word out.

"I've been so worried about not making any friends, but then here *you* are, and oh!" She pops up on her tiptoes, her nose almost brushing mine. "Your eyes must be the bluest things I've ever seen."

I stuff my hands in the pockets of my jean shorts and stare back at this girl who I think might be a little wacky.

I'm fixing to kill Eli for suggesting I come over here.

"Thanks," I reply.

I look behind her to where the boy is watching us, stone-faced.

Eli calls expressions like that "resting asshole face." I don't know if this kid is an asshole, but he sure doesn't seem happy to see me. I shift my focus back to Lily.

"How do you talk like that?" I ask. "Just goin' and goin' for so long without havin' to breathe?"

Immediately, I want to take my words back. Daddy says I have no filter, but I've always thought saying what's on my mind is the most honest thing I can do, and if I'm nothing else, I always want to be honest. I hate liars.

Guilt hits my chest when her smile drops, and I'm worried I hurt her feelings, but then she throws back her head and laughs, and I'm so relieved I join her.

She links her arm with mine and pulls me farther into the yard.

For such a small thing, she's awful strong.

"Just have a lot of energy, I guess." She pats my arm with her sparkly pink fingernails. "My mom used to tell me I had enough energy to light up all of Chicago."

"I think I believe her." My eyes are wide as I grin. "I'm Alina May Carson, by the way, but my friends call me Lee. I live three houses down that way."

Lily brings her hand up to cover her eyes from the sun while she looks toward where I point. "That your brother?"

"Yep, that's Eli." I glance at the boy on the steps again. "Does he like basketball? Eli never lets me play, he says basketball's not meant for girls, but he'd probably let another boy practice with him."

Lily scrunches her nose, twisting to look at the kid on the steps. "Oh, that's my brother, Chase. He doesn't like much of anything really unless it involves making our foster parents mad."

"Oh."

I'm not sure what a foster parent is, but I don't want to seem stupid, so I nod like I get it.

"Chase!" she yells. "Come here and meet Lee."

My stomach buzzes like a hive of bees as Chase crushes his cigarette beneath his worn black boot and stands, walking over to us. He doesn't stop until he's right in front of me, my eyes level with his chin.

When he's this close, I can see the scar running through his left eyebrow, and for some reason, there's an urge to reach up and trace it. My fingers curl into the palms of my hands to keep myself from actually doing it because *that* would be really weird.

There's something about this boy.

He hasn't said a word yet, and I'm already dying to know him.

AUTHOR'S NOTE

This story is told through a first-person limited, emotional lens, and characters often speak from pain rather than perspective.

The way addiction is shown here reflects how one character, shaped by deep hurt and loss, sees the world around him and the people in it. His understanding is incomplete, and his view of those who've harmed him may not tell the full story.

Please know this depiction is not meant to define addiction or the people who experience it.

Addiction is complex, and it impacts people and families in many different ways. If you or someone you love is struggling, you are worthy, you are not less than, and you are not alone.

Below are some resources:

SAMHSA's National Helpline—1-800-662- HELP (4357)

National Institute on Drug Abuse—drugabuse.gov

Alcoholics Anonymous—aa.org

SMART Recovery—smartrecovery.org

CHARACTER PROFILES

Juliette

Name: Juliette Calloway
Age: 21
Place of Birth: Rosebrook Falls, Connecticut
Current Location: Rosebrook Falls, Connecticut
Education: Bachelor's Degree in Psychology
Occupation: Writer
Income: Heiress
Eye Color: Brown
Hair Style: Long, straight, and black
Body Build: 5'9" and skinny
Preferred style of outfit: She loves pink but wears comfortable clothes as much as possible
Glasses?: No
Any accessories they always have?: No
Level of Grooming: High level of grooming
Health: Healthy

Handwriting style: Pretty cursive, regimented and perfect
How do they walk: Head held high and good posture
How do they speak: Sarcastic
Do they gesture?: Yes, especially when annoyed
Eye Contact: Almost always
Catchphrase?: "I'll write you in the stars"
What do they find funny: Dry humor
Describe smile: Bright and big
How emotive: Not very unless provoked; she keeps things under lock and key
Type of Childhood: Wealthy, very regimented, always doing what her parents want
Involved in School?: Yes
Named most likely to: Marry someone important in the yearbook
Jobs: Never had one
Dream job as a child: Writer
Hobbies growing up: Writing and sneaking out with Lance
Favorite place as a child: The little alcove underneath the main staircase, and Upside Down Rock
Any skeletons in the closet?: No
If they could change one thing from their past, what would it be?: Allowing her parents to dictate her life
Describe major turning points in their childhood: Lance disappearing more and more, her brother Paxton getting married, her aunt and uncle dying
Three adjectives to describe personality: Guarded, Witty, Loyal
What advice would they give to their younger self?: To stand up for herself and fight for the people she loves
Criminal Record?: No

Father:
> **Name: Craig Calloway**
> **Occupation:** Owner and CEO of Calloway Enterprises
> **What's their relationship with character like:** Strained. She wants him to be proud, but he's very removed from her life because all he cares about is his company and their name.

Mother:
> **Name: Martha Calloway**
> **Occupation:** Being Craig Calloway's wife; running charities
> **What's their relationship with character like:** Awful. She doesn't like her, has a lot of resentment, and isn't very present.

Any Siblings?: Three brothers: Lance, Alex, and Paxton

Closest Friends: Felicity Rimini

Enemies: The Montgomerys, and her cousin Rosalie

How are they perceived by strangers?: Composed, aloof, and untouchable

Any social media?: Yes, but it's very heavily guarded and filtered because of who she is

Role in group dynamic: The grumpy one who wants to just stay home

Who do they depend on: Felicity, her brothers, Beverly

What do they do on rainy days?: Hide away and write

Book-smart or street-smart?: Book-smart

Optimist, pessimist, realist: Realist with a slight edge toward pessimist

Introvert or Extrovert: Introvert at heart but knows how to play extroverted

Favorite Sound: The sound of someone saying her name like they mean it

What do they want most: Freedom and happiness

Biggest Flaw: Pleasing her parents no matter the cost

Biggest Strength: Her ability to keep going even if her heart is shattered. She doesn't crumble, just tucks the pain away and is able to walk into a room full of people who've already decided who she's supposed to be

Biggest Accomplishment: Surviving and keeping her *true* self alive through everything

What's their idea of perfect happiness?: A quiet life that doesn't require pretending

Do they want to be remembered?: No

Possession they would rescue from burning home: Her journal

How is their moral compass and what would it take to break it?: It's pretty good but she will break it in a heartbeat for people she loves

Pet Peeves: Forced small talk and being told to smile more

What would they have written on their tombstone: "Probably stalking Roman in the afterlife."

Their Story Goal: To stop playing the part everyone has cast her in and live on her own terms. At first, it's about escape, and then it becomes about truth. She wants to figure out who she is when no one's watching and be able to love whomever she wants freely and without constraint.

Roman

Name: Roman Montgomery
Age: 23
Place of Birth: Monterey, California
Current Location: Rosebrook Falls, Connecticut
Education: Partial college education (left before completing to take care of family)
Occupation: Unofficial heir to the Montgomery fortune, and street artist
Income: Old money with strings attached
Eye Color: Icy blue
Hair Style: Short but messy on top, brown: so dark that in some lighting it looks black
Body Build: 6'2", muscular and lean
Preferred style of outfit: Dark jeans, white shirt, black hoodie, baseball cap backward
Glasses?: No
Any accessories they always have?: A silver ring and sometimes a chain on his neck
Level of Grooming: Medium, looks good but never looks polished
Health: Strong
Handwriting style: Slanted and a little chaotic like he never learned cursive properly but still makes it look good
How do they walk: Like he owns the room but doesn't want you to know it
How do they speak: Smooth and low
Do they gesture?: Sometimes
Eye Contact: Always

Catchphrase?: "I'll paint you across the sky"

What do they find funny: Dark, sarcastic humor and making people blush

Describe smile: Crooked and knowing

How emotive: Controlled until he's pushed

Type of Childhood: Broke, struggling, and faced with realities children shouldn't have to face

Involved in School?: No

Named most likely to: Wind up in jail in the yearbook

Jobs: Artist

Dream job as a child: Artist

Hobbies growing up: Always drawing

Favorite place as a child: Anywhere he could be alone

Any skeletons in the closet?: Yes

If they could change one thing from their past, what would it be?: Not being able to help his mom

Describe major turning points in their childhood: His fake death, his father not being around, his mother becoming addicted to drugs

Three adjectives to describe personality: Charming, Flirty, Mysterious

What advice would they give to their younger self?: Don't trust anyone

Criminal Record?: Not officially

Father:

  Name: Marcus Montgomery

  Occupation: Public figure and owner/CEO of the Montgomery Organization

  What's their relationship with character like: Nonexistent, then filled with bitterness. Cold and performative. No trust.

Mother:
> **Name:** Heather Argent
> **Occupation:** Artist
> **What's their relationship with character like:** Complicated and toxic.

Any Siblings?: One sister: Brooklynn (Harper)
Closest Friends: None that he'd admit to
Enemies: Craig Calloway
How are they perceived by strangers?: Handsome, charming, and mysterious
Any social media? No, he hates being perceived
Role in group dynamic: The quiet leader
Who do they depend on: Nobody but himself
What do they do on rainy days?: Watches the storm. Smokes. Thinks too hard
Book-smart or street-smart?: Both but definitely street-smart
Optimist, pessimist, realist: Optimist
Introvert or Extrovert: Extrovert
Favorite Sound: Used to be his mom's laugh. Now it's Juliette's
What do they want most: To protect the people he loves
Biggest Flaw: Taking care of everyone else at the cost of himself
Biggest Strength: His unwavering loyalty
Biggest Accomplishment: Let him know if you figure it out
What's their idea of perfect happiness?: A life with Juliette and his sister taken care of
Do they want to be remembered?: Only by Juliette
Possession they would rescue from burning home: His black book

How is their moral compass and what would it take to break it: Skewed, he's done bad things for good reasons, and it would break entirely for Juliette or his sister

Pet Peeves: Hypocrisy, wealth disparity, his father

What would they have written on their tombstone: "Here lies Roman. He's annoying even in death, but we love him the most anyway." (Written by Juliette)

Their Story Goal: At first, Roman's goal is simple: take care of his family. But along the way, he has to come to terms with the way he shows up for others—often at the expense of his own happiness. He learns that sometimes, you have to take responsibility for things you never asked for and find a way to make them work in your favor. He also has to accept that not everything can be fixed. Some things stay broken. Some people will disappoint you. And life doesn't always hand you a happy ending. What matters is learning how to be happy anyway.

ACKNOWLEDGMENTS

Keeping this short and sweet.

To *you*—my readers, my McCulties: Thank you for always showing up and reminding me how magical this world can be. Thank you for letting me tell these love stories and for experiencing every ounce of joy, heartbreak, and messy, beautiful in-between right alongside me.

To my editor, Christa, and her entire team: You make me a better writer every time. Even when I'm blushing as you correct the logistics of my sex scenes, or you ask "What's this?" and I quietly delete instead of figuring out what I was trying to say.

To my agent, Kimberly, and everyone at Park, Fine & Brower: Thank you for believing in me, fighting for me, and always propping me up with grace and grit.

To the entire Bloom and Piatkus teams: Thank you for taking the chance on my books and helping me bring these characters and stories to life.

To team Emily: You are my brain, my organizers, and my

sanity. Thank you for carrying things when I couldn't and for always pushing me forward.

To my cover artist, Apryl: You're so disgustingly talented, it makes me SICK. In the best way.

To my publicist, Katie: Thank you for being my road mom and letting me dream up the wildest marketing ideas—and then somehow making them happen.

To my best friend, Sav: Thank you for being my rock. I don't know who I'd be without you and I'm still waiting on that place in the Smokies.

To my husband, Mike: Thank you for showing me what real, soul-deep love looks like. You are home.

And last but never least, to my daughter, Melody.

You are now and always, the reason for everything.

I love you forever.

Do you love contemporary romance?

Want the chance to hear news about your favourite authors (and the chance to win free books)?

Kristen Ashley
Ashley Herring Blake
Meg Cabot
Olivia Dade
Rosie Danan
J. Daniels
Farah Heron
Talia Hibbert
Sarah Hogle
Helena Hunting
Abby Jimenez
Elle Kennedy
Christina Lauren
Alisha Rai
Sally Thorne
Lacie Waldon
Denise Williams
Meryl Wilsner
Samantha Young

Then visit the Piatkus website
www.yourswithlove.co.uk

And follow us on Facebook and Instagram
www.facebook.com/yourswithlovex | @yourswithlovex

PIATKUS